IT WAS A MATC

Thorne studied the flush o...
clinging to her face, her g...
seen a more beautiful woman, nor one more ~~~~~~ s
peace of mind.

"That was a perilous jump you just took, Miss Carstairs. Excellent, but perilous," he pointed out, his voice curt to mask his rising desire.

The laughter vanished from Alexandria's face. She spun on booted heels to face the man who was her unwanted fiancé. "You mean perilous for a woman?"

"For anyone," Thorne corrected her. "Although only a woman would be so foolhardy as to risk her life on such an unpredictable horse."

"You've seen Lexington before?"

Thorne never took his eyes from Alexandria. "My horse beat him in his last race. I never forget a horse."

"Too bad you can't say that about the women you meet," she said sweetly, her eyes glittering like shattered glass.

"Some women are forgettable," Thorne said, without missing a beat.

Alexandria folded her arms across her chest. "What a pity for those you find who aren't."

Thorne appeared undisturbed. "Don't ride that horse again."

"You can't tell me what to do!"

"According to your father, I have every right to do just that," he reminded her, though he had no intention of actually marrying this hoyden.

Turquoise eyes rounded. Alexandria took a step backward. "You can't mean you might still offer for. . . ." She swallowed loudly.

Her obvious dismay annoyed him. He was considered an excellent catch. She was the one who was scandalous. "Your jump ended the discussion between your father and me."

She groaned. "Why didn't I wait a little longer?" she muttered, though not quietly enough.

"You planned this to make me back out of the contract, didn't you?" Thorne guessed, his irritation growing.

"Yes," she admitted. She favored Thorne with a condescending look. "I shall marry no man. Ever."

It was a challenge he could near refuse!

The BARGAIN

FRANCIS RAY

ZEBRA BOOKS
Kensington Publishing Corp.
http://www.zebrabooks.com

*To Ann Maxwell, who always believed in me
and who always listens.*

ZEBRA BOOKS are published by

Kensington Publishing Corp.
850 Third Avenue
New York, NY 10022

First Pinnacle Printing: November, 1995
First Zebra Printing: June, 2000

10 9 8 7 6 5 4 3 2

Printed in the United States of America

One

BIRMINGHAM, ENGLAND, 1859

I may be the next one to die.

That persistent and unsettling thought weighed heavily on the once-broad shoulders of Squire Oliver Carstairs as he paced the length of his study. That he was fifty-nine years old and, according to his physician, in good health, did nothing to alleviate his anxiety. For in the past six months he had cast dirt upon the graves of three close friends who also thought they were in good health.

Hands clamped behind his back, Oliver paused to gaze out the velvet-draped open double doors leading to the formal landscaped gardens and the park beyond. Ten thousand acres stretched around him, and it was all his. In the past that knowledge had always brought a sense of pride to a man whose great-grandfather had sold rags in the street. Now it brought a problem he had thought he'd need not encounter for many years. He had to proceed with all haste for the betrothal announcement and marriage of his only child and heir, Alexandria.

For the first time in over an hour the squire's pursed lips relaxed into a smile. Thinking of Allie, as everyone fondly called his daughter, always made him smile. Oliver chuckled to himself. Well, almost always.

There had been times since the death of her mother that he honestly hadn't known how to handle a young child who'd tested at least twice, no matter the consequences, every rule he'd ever laid down. But she was also everything he could have hoped for in an heir.

Even at her most rebellious, she remained loving and fair. Her nimble mind enabled her to read at three and to do sums at four. Oliver taught her not only about the estate and his business interests, but also to be self-reliant. She was bright, talented, and an able administrator. She was also a woman. His smile faded. He had taught her wrong.

Queen Victoria sat on the throne. She, like so many others, thought a woman should have no rights, that she should be meek and obedient to her husband. Allie gave orders; she didn't obey them unless it suited her. How could she ever defer to a man's guidance? How was she going to handle being thought of as brainless and subservient, as some men were apt to think of their wives?

Badly, he thought, without a moment's hesitation.

"Have you told her yet?"

Oliver glanced around to see the housekeeper, Tillie, with his afternoon tea. He distinctly remembered telling the butler he didn't wish to be disturbed. Tillie had probably brought the tea in just to annoy him and to show him that she, not he, was in charge of the household.

"No, I haven't," Oliver answered, then turned back to stare out the door.

Tillie set the silver tray on the Chippendale table. "I didn't think so. I haven't heard her talking to herself."

Oliver whirled. "The marriage will be for Allie's own good."

"I'm not the one you have to convince," Tillie pointed out, as she poured tea. "Allie has enjoyed too much freedom to accept willingly the restrictions placed on a married woman."

"I blame myself for that." Oliver crossed the room, then lowered his considerable bulk into an overstuffed brocade chair.

Tillie smiled as she added three lumps of sugar and a dollop of cream to the tea. "I'm not sure Allie gave you any choice."

"Probably not, but I should have tried harder," Oliver said, picking up the delicate cup only to set it down without drinking.

"For her own sake she has to marry a man of wealth and power within the next few months."

"What . . . what if you're wrong about your . . . er . . ." Her voice trailed off.

"My imminent death," Oliver finished for her. "I hope I'm wrong, but I can't take a chance of leaving her unprotected."

A frown crossed Tillie's angular face. "Allie will never be happy being the wife of a lord. She'll fight you on this."

"I know." Sadness touched Oliver's rounded features. "Allie and I have had our differences, but we've always been able to talk things out."

"There's always a first time," Tillie pronounced, and left the room.

Oliver had a feeling in his gut that Tillie was right. But Allie's outrage on learning of her betrothal would be infinitesimal in comparison to that of her intended.

Thorne Graham Blakemore, the Fifth Earl of Grayson, was a rakehell of the first water who at thirty-two showed no signs of settling down. Dark and compellingly handsome, he had been known to send mothers scurrying from the room with their innocent daughters faster than if someone had yelled "Fire." Those less virtuous stayed and helped him earn the nickname "the Devil's Angel."

A moment of unease swept through Oliver before he forced himself to recall a younger, gentler Thorne. Praying he had made the right choice for his daughter, Oliver rose and went in search of Allie.

Outside, as he neared the stables, he heard the nicker of horses and the faint yelp of a dog. Rounding the corner of the large red-brick building, he saw a group of men watching a rider trying to coax a big bay stallion over a four-foot wood railing. The prancing animal snorted, twisted his long, elegant neck, and balked, refusing to acknowledge the knees pressing behind his shoulders, or the bit in his mouth. Admitting defeat for the moment, the rider guided the horse away from the obstacle.

Nodding briefly to the men, Oliver continued until he was

within fifty feet of the dueling horse and rider. As Oliver watched their progress, another movement caught his attention. His gaze narrowed as the shadow beneath an oak tree became substance.

A gray wolf stood silently on the perimeter of the training field. Lean and powerful, the animal looked at the slim figure atop the bay, then back at Oliver. He took a step closer.

"On guard duty, are you?" Oliver said softly, and turned his attention back to the unfolding battle of wills. Nearing the wood railing, the bay refused the jump for a second attempt and then a third.

After each failure the rider leaned down, patted the animal on his sleek, damp neck, and whispered encouragement. On the fourth attempt, the stallion increased his speed instead of slowing. He cleared the railing by mere inches and didn't stop until he'd jumped the two remaining obstacles positioned a hundred feet apart.

Dismounting, the jubilant rider offered the bay a carrot. He chose the rider's hat. As the mischievous horse pulled at his rider's headgear, a thick, tawny braid tumbled to a small waist. Laughter, deep and musical, erupted from Alexandria as she grabbed for her hat.

Fatherly pride curved Oliver's lips into a smile as he started forward. Allie had done with that horse what he and everyone else on the estate had doubted could be done. Oliver stopped in mid-stride.

Not because the wolf had matched him step for step; he had expected that. Nor was it the sight of his daughter's slender frame in a loose-fitting white shirt, a hip-length leather jerkin, and scandalous breeches encasing her long legs. He was used to her unorthodox manner of dress. It was because the horse reminded him that once Allie had made up her mind, there was almost no way to get her to change it.

"I thought I told you to let Kent train that horse."

Alexandria jerked around. As she saw her father, a smile began at the corners of her sensual lips, then spread upward, past the high cheekbones to turquoise eyes beneath delicately arched brows. Rescuing her teeth-marked hat, she slapped it back on her head. "Lexington doesn't like men. Do you, fellow?" she asked, stroking the horse's blaze-marked forehead.

"That may be, but if you think I'm going to allow you to jump that unpredictable horse over a five-foot fence, you're mistaken," Oliver warned, and closed the distance between them. "He has always balked at anything over three feet."

All playfulness left Alexandria. "The month Lord Talton gave us to train Lexington to take the fence is up in three days. He'll put him down if I fail." Her gloved hand fisted on the bridle. "I won't let that happen."

"You should never have gotten involved and offered the services of our trainers when you knew the horse had balked at taking the fence at two other races," Oliver said. "I blame myself for taking you to that race."

"I'm glad you did; otherwise, Lord Talton would have destroyed Lexington after he lost to Cross Currents," Alexandria reminded her father. "But I know he can make the jump."

"If he does, you won't be the one to take him over. I won't have you risking your life to save that of a horse."

"He'll take the jump only for me."

"That may be, Allie, but the fact remains that you're a lady, not a jockey. If you can't remember, perhaps I should consider banning you from the stables." Oliver ignored Allie's incredulous gasp and held up his hand to forestall further arguments. "My word is final. Now, give Lexington to Peters. I need to talk with you."

Only for a fraction of a second did Alexandria consider defying her father. Over the years she had learned when she could push him and when she couldn't. This was one of the latter. He had a definite reddish cast to his whiskered jaws that signaled he was past reasoning and nearing anger.

Alexandria started toward the groom, but the man backed up and pointed behind her. Without looking, she struck the open palm of her right hand against her thigh and ordered, "Stay,

Wolf." She had spoken for Peter's benefit. Although her hand signals were simple, the staff remained uneasy if she used them without a verbal command. After four years, her father was the only one besides her who was unafraid of Wolf.

Relinquishing the horse, Alexandria looped her arm through her father's. "You really wouldn't carry out your threat and banish me from the stables, would you?" she asked. She loved her father, but she was not going to let a horse be destroyed because he was afraid she might get a few bumps and bruises.

Oliver glanced down at his daughter's legs, frowned, then shook his head and started toward the house. "I want you to start wearing your riding habit."

Alexandria groaned. "I did try, but all that flapping material scared Lexington and the other horses."

"It wouldn't if you rode sidesaddle, as ladies should, and not astride," Oliver reasoned.

"I can't control Lexington or several of the other horses when I ride sidesaddle," Alexandria told him. "Jeremy is posted at the gatehouse to warn me if we have any visitors. You know our people won't say anything about how I dress. Besides, with my memory, I'd forget which side I rode on the day before and I'd be lopsided."

The answering smile at her jest didn't come. Instead, her father opened the black iron gate to the gardens behind their house and gave a long-suffering sigh. "Lopsided or no, you're going to have to take your place in society one day, and that means a sidesaddle. I can't trace my ancestors further back than my great-grandfather, but your mother's family dates back to a knight who rode with William the Conqueror. Ladies don't ride astride."

Barely managing to keep from groaning, Alexandria plopped down on a stone bench in front of a row of red rosebushes in full bloom. Only faintly did her mind register their sweet fragrance or the shadowy bulk of the wolf who lay at her feet. It was going to be one of those talks.

Each time her father brought up her mother's ancestors, it

meant he thought he'd failed in her upbringing. To correct matters, he'd insist she act as befit the daughter of a titled lady. That meant a crinoline and a corset.

Only a man who hated women could have invented such torturous attire. Just thinking about cinching her waist to eighteen inches caused her stomach and back to ache. And, in a crinoline, with her skirts swinging and swaying with each tiny movement, she felt as awkward and gangling as a newborn colt.

Glancing down at her breeches, she thought again of how fortunate men were. They could do as they pleased, and damn the consequences. Already feeling the corset biting into her skin, she said, "If the knight was anything like Mother's family today, he probably spent more time in the dungeon than serving William." Stretching her legs, she crossed her booted ankles. "I'd like to think Mother was a foundling, but no one in her family would have taken her in."

"The greed of your aunts is what I want to talk with you about. You're only twenty, and if something were to happen to me before you reached twenty-one, you'd have no caring relative to counsel you." Oliver paced the length of the stone bench. "Lord Holden's untimely death made me realize how vulnerable women are."

Alexandria looked askance at her father. "Lady Holden and her two stuffy daughters are as vulnerable as foxes in a henhouse. The estate manager is already threatening to quit because of their meddling, and Lord Holden's younger brother escaped back to London three days after the funeral."

As if her father didn't hear her, he continued. "Then there was Curtiss's death, only three weeks ago. Before that, it was Hempstead. All my friends are dying."

Alexandria had nothing to say this time. Lord Holden's stupidity had caused his death when he'd had the misfortune to pass out drunk in front of his pond and fall in. He'd drowned while insensible. Curtiss and Hempstead had each taken ill suddenly and died within a week. Uneasy, she stood. "Father, can we talk about something else?"

"I know how upsetting this is to you, and it's not a subject I favor, either." Oliver tried to produce a smile, but it never materialized. "Without the protection of a husband, you'd find your aunts trying everything within their power to take from you all I've tried so hard to provide you." He took a deep breath. "For your own sake you *must* marry as soon as possible."

"No!" As Wolf surged to his feet and went to Alexandria, she for once ignored the warm nose nudging her hand. "Nothing is going to happen to you." Seeing the determination in her father's face, she rushed on, "If you're still worried, I can go with you when you travel to London in three weeks. I will show you that I can run your iron and steel foundries as easily as I run the estate."

"Allie, you're an intelligent woman. I want you to think now with your mind instead of with your heart." Gripping her tense shoulders, he stared into her frightened eyes.

"The men here follow your orders because they've known you all your life. More important, they love and respect you. My business associates and the workers in London and in Liverpool will look upon you as something of a curiosity at first; then, once you fail to go along with what they want, they'll look down upon you and considered you meddlesome. Others will dislike you on sight simply because you're richer and smarter than they are."

Her chin lifted. "I'll take that chance. If other women can make a success of their businesses, then I can do the same."

Oliver momentarily lifted his eyes heavenward, as if praying for patience. "You can't compare a millinery shop or a modiste shop to a business with over five hundred employees, Alexandria. For myself, I know you could manage the foundries and my other business interest as well as I, but you won't be given a fair chance. Besides, your mother's sisters have important friends. They might use your work as an excuse to have you declared unbalanced so they can gain guardianship of you and thus your money. No woman of consequence will ever allow herself to be directly involved in trade. The only way I can protect you is to make sure the man I choose for your husband is more powerful than they are and can manage your business interests."

"Since you obviously have given this a great deal of thought, I assume you have already picked out my jailer." Oliver winced, but Alexandria had not finished. "Am I allowed to ask who he is, or will I simply meet him at the altar?" Alexandria didn't try to keep the hurt and accusation from her voice.

"The Fifth Earl of Grayson."

Alexandria's eyes widened. She gasped aloud in horror, "You can't do that to me. Grayson is a scoundrel."

Oliver's gaze never wavered. "Allie, you've been reading those half-penny papers again. The earl is considered a fine catch. Not only is he a wealthy man in his own right, but he is also the Duke of Ashton's grandson and heir."

Alexandria pulled away, her eyes dark with anger. "I don't care if he's heir to the throne of England. I won't marry a lecher and be subjected to his debauchery," she said heatedly.

"Yes, you will!"

Her body jerked as if she'd been slapped. Never before had her father used that tone of voice with her.

"I've already sent a message to Lord Grayson, asking him to meet me."

"He won't come," Alexandria predicted, praying she was right.

"Perhaps not this time, but his father signed a betrothal contract that assures me eventually he will come."

"A betrothal contract?" Disbelief shimmered in Alexandria's eyes. "You have a betrothal contract and you never told me?"

"I intended to tell you when you were old enough, but when you were, it didn't seem to matter. Try to understand that I wanted you to have a fine future, with a man of your class," Oliver explained. "Your mother was gone and I did what I thought was best."

As Alexandria looked at her father's worried face, she tried to control her spiraling anger, but it was impossible. "A good match depends on the man, not on his title. You've always taught me to judge a person by what he does and not by what he has," Alexandria reminded him. "Lord Grayson has accumulated and discarded women with total disregard for their feelings. You can't consider a marriage to him a good match."

Oliver cleared his throat. "I'm sure he'll act more circumspectly once he learns of the betrothal."

"He doesn't know?" Alexandria asked in dismay.

Oliver glanced away from the condemning expression in his daughter's face. "I did not feel a need to press the matter until lately."

"Father, you can't do this. It isn't fair to either of us, and I won't be shoved off on a man who doesn't want me."

"He'll want you. I've made sure of that."

"What are you talking about?"

Her father smiled. "A wedding, Allie. Weren't you listening?"

Alexandria watched her father walk away and gritted her teeth. "Apparently you weren't the one listening. I will never be any man's chattel. I'm going to make sure Grayson refuses to accept the betrothal contract if I have to shoot him."

Two

The Honorable Earl of Grayson,
   It is of the utmost importance that I see you at your
earliest convenience. I await your instructions.
                              Your Humble Servant,
                              Esq. Oliver Alexander Carstairs

Thorne Graham Blakemore, Fifth Earl of Grayson, crossed his muscular arms over his wide chest, then leaned broad shoulders against the red velvet carriage upholstery. He needed to think about the message that had been delivered to him the day before. The request puzzled him.

To Thorne's knowledge there was not a single reason why Carstairs would have a need to see him. Although their estates shared a common border, they had seen each other socially only rarely. In his younger years he had visited the squire once to inquire about purchasing one of his prized thoroughbreds, but that afternoon his father had informed Thorne that they could not afford to feed the animal. He had not gone back.

The last time he'd seen Carstairs had been shortly after Thorne's father's death, seven years ago. The squire was one of the few men who'd come to pay his respects to the entire family instead of to the widow in the privacy of her chambers.

Thorne shifted as the well-sprung coach hit a rut, his anger no longer racing through him with the swiftness of liquid fire. He'd spent the first part of his life trying to make the woman who bore him love him, the second half trying to forget she existed. His mother Marianne corrupted everything she touched. It was well worth the extra ten thousand pounds he'd sent her yearly for the past five years to have her sign over to him the guardianship papers on his sister, Judith.

Judith was as loving and sweet as Marianne was vain and selfish. He certainly hoped the countess decided to stay in Paris the rest of the Season. Judith was having a difficult enough time in her debut without having to live down gossip about Marianne. Their Aunt Margaret was enough of a bother.

Since they'd arrived at Grayson Hall two days ago, Aunt Margaret had been nagging him to return to London. He had no intention of explaining the reason for their hasty departure to anyone. To Aunt Margaret, refusing to tell her something was like waving a red flag before an enraged bull. At each opportunity she charged.

Just then the crested coach passed through a black iron gate flanked by a six-foot brick wall of the Carstairs' estate. Thorne absently glanced at the cottage house and beyond to the immaculate grounds. Carstairs had continued to do well for himself. A winding two miles later the coach halted in front of an imposing three-story Georgian mansion.

Without waiting for his footman, Thorne stepped down from the carriage. Straightening his beige-colored frock coat, he started for the ornate entryway. Just as his highly polished Hessian touched the second stone step, an old memory pricked him. Ignoring the stiff-backed butler patiently waiting beside the open door, Thorne surreptitiously glanced around.

No clump of mud wrapped in white paper to resemble a snowball came flying through the air to hit him in the chest, as it had done the last time he was here. Lord, what a hoyden Carstairs' daughter had been at the age of nine!

Faced with apologizing or going to bed without supper, she'd gone to bed, mumbling under her breath that Thorne had called her a brat and should have to apologize to her. Ten minutes later Carstairs had excused himself to oversee a worker freeing his daughter from a tree branch. She had tried to climb down a tree next to her bedroom window and her dress had gotten caught. To give her credit, she hadn't been scared, just angry she hadn't made good her escape. Fervently hoping the squire's ill-mannered daughter was in another country, Thorne continued up the steps.

"Good afternoon, Lord Grayson. Squire Carstairs is in his study. Please follow me," the butler requested, and started down the hall.

The double mahogany doors opened before they reached their destination. A tall, robust man appeared, a smile on his whiskered face. "Thor . . . I mean, Lord Grayson, thank you for coming. Please come in and have a seat."

Thorne accepted the hand offered. "Thank you, Squire Carstairs."

"Would you like something to drink?" Oliver inquired, heading to the sideboard. "A brandy, perhaps?"

Thorne took a seat, but not before noticing that the squire's hands were shaking as he lifted the crystal decanter. "A little early for me, but please help yourself."

"A little early for me as well." Setting the square bottle aside, Oliver took a seat in the wingbacked chair across from the earl's. "I was surprised to discover you at Grayson Hall with the Season on."

Thorne's midnight black eyes flicked to Oliver's fingers, which were marching nervously back and forth across the arm of his chair. "Were you?"

Oliver twisted in his seat. "Yes. I . . . are you planning to stay long?"

Carstairs is up to something. Thorne felt a vague sense of disappointment. He had respected Carstairs and thought him a forthright man. "That all depends."

Oliver nodded. "I heard you might be interested in buying stock in the Pemberton Railroad Company."

"From whom?"

"I don't remember," Oliver said, and watched Thorne's eyes narrow. The earl knew Oliver was being evasive. He obviously didn't like discussing his business affairs. This wasn't going at all as Oliver had planned.

"Why did you invite me here?" Thorne asked quietly, yet there was no denying the impatience or the suspicion in his commanding voice.

Oliver took a deep breath that strained the gold buttons on his waistcoat and answered, "You have to marry my daughter."

Thorne didn't blink, didn't move. Indeed, he'd heard the same six words often since his eighteenth birthday. The last time was three years ago, and the distasteful occasion had taught him that fathers were as greedy for his title and money as were their daughters. "Am I to understand that you think I have acted improperly toward your daughter?"

"Heavens, no," the squire hastened to assure him. "My Allie would have laid a shiner on you if you had."

Thorne frowned at the man's obvious pleasure. Apparently the hoyden was still a hoyden, and her father was demented. "Then why must I marry her?"

"Forgive me for putting it so poorly." Oliver leaned forward in his seat. "Since I have already made a botch of things, I may as well just say it. Before his death, your father and I signed a betrothal contract for you and my daughter."

A dark brow climbed toward wavy black hair. Thorne thought he'd heard every conceivable scheme to get him to the altar, but apparently he was wrong. "My father has been dead seven years. Why are you just now bringing this information to light?"

Oliver glanced out the French doors, then back at Thorne's imposing figure. He certainly was taking it better than expected. However, telling a man who'd commanded several daring encounters in the Crimean War that you thought you were marked for death and therefore wanted to see to your daughter's welfare didn't seem the thing. Since lying was distasteful, Oliver gave a half-truth. "Your reputation hasn't been the kind a man relishes in a son-in-law."

"I wasn't aware that my reputation had taken a turn for the better," Thorne pointed out.

"It hasn't," the squire said, his expression disapproving.

Thorne took the reprimand stoically. He answered to no man. "My time is very valuable, Squire. Unless you wish to produce some evidence, this interview will come to a quick end."

"You've changed greatly from the young man I used to know."

Thorne stood. "Good day."

Oliver followed suit, his face as stern and unyielding as Thorne's. "Unless you want to pay me a quarter of a million pounds, I suggest you reconsider walking out the door."

"This is no longer amusing."

"I assure you, my daughter's future is of the utmost importance to me. If you want proof, then you shall have it." Walking behind his desk, Oliver withdrew a document from the drawer and handed it to Thorne. "You will see that your father borrowed two hundred thousand pounds without any collateral. The money was my daughter's dowry to you."

Cold black eyes briefly scanned the contract. "Why did he come to you?"

"No one else would lend him the money," Oliver explained. "Grayson Hall and his three smaller estates were already mortgaged, and your grandfather refused to lend your father another pound. I wanted my daughter to marry well. It seemed a good exchange at the time."

Thorne heard what Oliver hadn't said. Apparently his daughter would make the witches in Shakespeare's *Macbeth* look like fairy princesses. Having foreseen this, Oliver had sought to buy her a titled husband.

Thorne's father, with creditors snapping at his heels and a vain, spoiled wife to please, had been selfish and desperate enough to sell him one . . . his son. But both had underestimated Thorne. He would sell everything he owned before he married some ill-bred woman. There was enough debauchery and scandal in the Grayson line. "You will have the money within the week."

Oliver met the contemptuous glare without flinching. "I think you had better read on."

Thorne read the contract more closely. He couldn't believe it. His gloved fist tightened. Paper crinkled. "Damn!"

"I wanted to make sure you wouldn't find a reason to refuse." Oliver looked pleased for the first time since Thorne had walked into the room.

"You made sure of that! A quarter of a million pounds a year sure," Thorne said through stiff lips.

"I wanted half a million."

"I can pay it," Thorne countered.

"I know you can, but for how long?" Oliver planted both hands on top of his mahogany desk. "Your grandfather believes that a man should spend only what he makes. He'll lend you no more than he did your father. You've done well paying off your father's debts and restoring all the properties he mortgaged. I know it was very costly."

"Apparently I missed one of his debts," Thorne said sarcastically.

"Knowing your father, he probably tore up his copy as soon as he left this house," Oliver said, then straightened.

Thorne didn't take offense at the slur against his father's honor. He, of all people, knew that his father had been a weak man made weaker by a wife who took every opportunity to throw his shortcomings in his face. When he could take it no longer, he'd killed himself.

"I'll have to check on the validity of these papers," Thorne said, his mustache a slash of black over his tightly compressed lips.

"I expected as much." The squire nodded. "What you hold is a copy. My solicitor is expect—"

"Father." The door swung open and Alexandria rushed into the room. Her face was flushed and beautiful. The end of her tawny braid brushed the rounded curves of her hips with each impatient step. "Kent says I have to ask you before I can ride Lexington."

"A-Allie," Squire Carstairs choked out. Grimacing, he sent a skirting glance toward Thorne. "We have—"

"You know I'm an excellent rider. I am always careful."

"I know, but—"

"Anyone can make a mistake. I only sprained my wrist when I fell off Montclair," Alexandria explained, flexing her slim wrist as if to prove that she was now healthy.

"What about the time you were tossed off Arroba?" Oliver questioned, his bushy eyebrows bunched.

Alexandria sighed. "The fall merely winded me."

"Allie, I—"

"This is your daughter?" Thorne asked, incredulous.

She was in . . . breeches!

Stunned, the earl let his gaze travel in disbelief up the girl's close-fitting pants, which clearly outlined her long legs and soft curves. He blinked when he saw how the tweed material cupped her woman's softness. Jerking his gaze up higher, his eyes lingered on the leather jerkin draped over her full, beautiful breasts.

"Sir, I believe you have me at a disadvantage."

The sensual huskiness of her voice forced his gaze up to her face. He blinked again. Her eyes, direct and challenging, were a vivid shade of turquoise. For the first time in Thorne's memory, a woman returned his bold appraisal, then dismissed him. Her delicate nose lifted, giving the impression that she was looking down at him, although she was in fact several inches shorter than he was.

Oliver cleared his throat. "Lord Grayson, may I present my daughter, Alexandria Elizabeth Carstairs."

Gracefully crossing the Persian carpet to Thorne, Alexandria executed a perfect curtsy. Her hands were dainty, her wrists delicate. She looked up through her thick lashes and smiled at him. It was like sunshine streaming through a waterfall, unexpected and breathtaking. *She is exquisite.* She came upright.

"Sir."

Thorne finally dragged his gaze from her mouth and encountered a pair of stormy blue-green eyes. He frowned because the lovely vision before him continued to smile.

"Please forgive the interruption," she said.

Alexandria was gone before Thorne realized he'd not spoken. He felt as if he'd been picked up by a whirlwind and set down in another place. She'd dismissed him at a glance, but her beauty and her sensuality pricked him to the core. His frown deepened. For a moment she had made him forget that desire made fools of men, and that women used that desire to fulfil their own selfish greed.

Squire Carstairs cleared his throat. "I know it doesn't speak well of Alexandria to wear breeches, but she does like to ride. . . . my God! Did I tell her no?" His eyes rounded. "Grayson, answer me."

Thorne slowly turned from the door, his mind elsewhere. "I'm sorry, what did you say?"

For a moment the squire looked as if he might like to throttle his guest. "I asked you if I told Alexandria no about riding Lexington, of course."

Thorne tried to think, but he hadn't had a coherent thought since Alexandria had sailed into the room. It was obvious from the way Carstairs was staring at him that the other man thought Thorne had a weak mind.

"I—" Thorne broke off as his host ran to the door, only to grasp the knob and look back at the earl.

"You'll get there faster. Run to the training area and stop Alexandria," Oliver ordered. "You know where it is."

"Squire, what is the matter with you?" Thorne idly wondered if the squire were the one with the weak mind.

Oliver, his face desperate, took two steps toward the earl. "Do it, man! She's going to try and put that damn stallion Lexington over a five-foot wall!"

Thorne needed no further urging; he ran. If the squire had spoken of another woman, Thorne would have called the idea preposterous, but he'd seen the laughter and the challenge in

Alexandria's eyes. He also remembered another young girl who'd tried a similar jump and failed.

Thorne reached the edge of the training field as a groom booted Alexandria into the saddle. "Stop her!"

The young man turned to him as Alexandria dug her heels into the horse's sides.

The groom stared at Thorne, then beyond at the squire, who was waving his arms and yelling. Upon hearing the squire's frantic cries, other workers stopped what they were doing and came running.

Thorne shouted again. Finally the groom understood. Whirling, he ran toward the horse and rider.

It was too late.

Alexandria and Lexington were racing toward the makeshift wall, and there was nothing anyone could do to stop them.

Three

"We can do it, Lexington," Alexandria said, leaning low in the saddle. "Take me over that wall like the gentleman you are and I'll give you a extra bag of oats *and* my hat. Dump me in front of that snobbish earl and you've got as much to lose as I."

Her hands tightened on the reins as she remembered Lord Grayson's snub in the study. He hadn't even addressed her. His disapproval had been obvious, and that was the way she had planned it, yet it still angered her. The jump meant more to her now than ever. Thrusting the earl from her mind, she concentrated on the wall.

Lexington ran, gathering speed with each pounding hoofbeat. Nearing the jump, Alexandria sat deeper in the saddle, urging the stallion on and fighting to keep his head up. The big bay gathered himself beneath her; his powerful muscles bunched. They were in the air. He seemed to hang over the stone wall, then they landed on the other side with a bone-jarring jolt.

Stretched all out, the thoroughbred took the next two obstacles with a foot to spare. All was quiet for several seconds in the field, then joyous shouts broke out.

"She did it! She did it!" the squire cried, pounding Thorne on the back.

Alexandria rode directly to her father and was in his arms before the relieved groom could take Lexington's reins. "We did it!"

The squire crushed her slim body to his. "If you ever again do anything so dangerous, I'll—"

"You'll take a currying comb to my backside," Alexandria finished for her father, her radiant smile testifying that she was not worried about the threat.

Thorne studied the flush of Alexandria's cheeks, the thick, lustrous braid hanging down her back, the wisps of tawny hair clinging to her sweat-dampened face, her glowing turquoise eyes. He had never seen a more beautiful and alluring woman . . . nor one more dangerous to his peace of mind.

"An excellent jump, Miss Carstairs, but perilous," he pointed out, his voice curt to mask his rising desire.

The laughter vanished from Alexandria's face. She spun on booted heels toward Thorne. "You mean for a woman?"

"For anyone," Thorne corrected her, then added, "Although only a woman would be so foolhardy as to risk her life on an unpredictable horse like Lexington."

Irritation swept through her. First he snubbed her, then he called her a fool. For a moment she was too stunned to speak.

Oliver saw his daughter's face and quickly spoke into the charged silence. "You've seen Lexington before?"

Thorne never took his eyes from Alexandria. "It was my horse who beat him in his last race. Besides, I never forget a horse."

"Too bad you can't say the same thing about the women you meet," Alexandria said sweetly, her face angelic, her eyes glittering like shattered glass.

"Some women are forgettable," Thorne said, without missing a beat.

Alexandria folded her arms across her chest. "What a pity for those you find who aren't."

"Alexandria!" her father gasped.

Thorne appeared undisturbed. "Don't ride that horse again."

Alexandria snatched her arms to her sides. "You can't tell me what to do."

"According to your father, I have every right to do just that," Thorne reminded her, although he had no intention of honoring the contract.

Turquoise eyes rounded. Alexandria took a step backward. "You can't mean you might still offer for . . ." She swallowed loudly.

Her obvious dismay annoyed him. He was considered an excellent catch. She was the one who was scandalous. "Your jump interrupted your father's and my discussion."

Alexandria groaned. "Why didn't I wait a little longer?" she mumbled to herself, but not quietly enough.

"You planned the jump to make me back out of the contract, didn't you?" Thorne guessed, his irritation growing.

Oliver turned to his daughter. "Allie, is this true?"

She had never lied to her father and she wasn't about to start. "Yes," she admitted, hating the disappointed look on her father's face. It was all the earl's fault. "I'm sorry, Father, but I told you how I feel about being married."

"Suppose you tell me," Thorne requested tightly.

Alexandria favored him with another condescending look. "I shall marry no man," she said, and gave the earl a chilling perusal from the top of his ruffled black hair to the tips of his dusty black boots, then whirled to leave.

Annoyed, Thorne lifted his hand to stop her. Woman or not, no one insulted and dismissed him in one breath. Before he could touch her arm, a menacing growl gave him pause. Out of the corner of his eye he saw . . . a wolf.

"Don't move, if you want to keep your hand." Alexandria smiled despite her words.

Thorne's gaze lanced upward and clung to Alexandria's. "I think it is you who should tell that animal not to move. You must know that most men believe in swift retribution if harmed. Think long and hard before you set your pet on me."

The emotionless voice of the earl caused Alexandria to reevaluate the man before her. Instead of retreating, as others did on seeing Wolf, the earl waited with an unnatural stillness. His casual stance was gone. She could sense his coiled alertness, power leashed and waiting for her decision. If crossed, he would make a relentless and merciless enemy. Now more than ever she had to break the betrothal contract.

"Wolf." The growl stopped and the animal nudged against her leg. Slim fingers plowed through gray fur in reassurance to both of them. "You would hurt Wolf because he was trying to protect me?"

"There was no need."

"He didn't know that. You shouldn't have reached out toward me. You saw the others moving away."

Thorne looked around. She was right. Everyone had left except the three of them. But Alexandria had held his sole attention since she'd raced away on Lexington. For the first time in memory, a woman had made him reckless. However, he'd be damned if he'd admit it. "Let's just say I don't frighten easily."

"Perhaps you have yet to meet the right person? Goodbye, Lord Grayson."

Thorne watched her walk away and realized that he had just been issued a challenge. Alexandria would bow before no man, but he'd never considered himself just any man.

"You've done it now."

Startled, Thorne turned toward the squire. "What?"

"Threatened one of her animals, and Wolf, her favorite, at that."

"He really is a wolf?"

Oliver nodded. "She found him as a cub. It was a week before anyone discovered that she was sneaking out to feed him or that she was sleeping with him in her playhouse cottage. He's better than ten men guarding her. Believe it or not, he has never even scratched her," Oliver said, watching the hundred-and-twenty-pound Wolf walk docilely beside Alexandria.

"Someone needs to take her in hand," the earl mumbled.

"Too bad it won't be you."

"What?" Thorne snatched his attention from the tantalizing motion of Alexandria's leather jerkin swinging back and forth over her hips like a beckoning pendulum.

"Weren't you listening?" the squire asked, as if he were

speaking to a weak-minded person. "You threatened Wolf. She will never forgive you for that."

"Was I supposed to politely offer him my hand?" Thorne asked, knowing his voice was getting louder, yet for once unable to control his temper.

The squire shook his head. "I did want my daughter to be a countess. And with our estates bordering each other, it would have been perfect to see my grandchildren." He offered a bewildered Thorne his hand, shook it, walked off, then turned. "Is it true that Lord Wilson lets his wolfhounds have the run of his fifty-seven room castle? Never mind, I'll send him a note this afternoon."

"Am I to believe that his father signed a marital agreement as well?" Thorne inquired, not even trying to keep the sarcasm from his voice.

"Good heavens, no." The squire laughed. "But if you will look at the contract again, it says that I have to agree to the marriage. Otherwise, you still have to pay the quarter of a million pounds a year to me until Alexandria marries. I couldn't hand my little angel over to just anyone. Now, if you'll excuse me, your lordship, I have some correspondence to attend to." Whistling, Oliver continued toward the manor.

Thorne couldn't believe it. He had been snubbed by a hoyden and dismissed by her demented father. He looked back in time to see Alexandria entering the stable. Wolf turned and bared his fangs in front of the door as if guarding Alexandria. Thorne felt like baring his own teeth. What kind of crazy family was this, anyway? He might be bored, but he was no fool.

He was leaving and he was going to make sure that he never saw another Carstairs as long as he lived. He could take on a challenge, but not if it meant ending up at the altar with a turquoise-eyed spitfire who smiled when she was angry and who kept a wolf as a pet. He was returning to Grayson Hall to some peace and quiet.

* * *

"Thorne, we simply must return to London."

Thorne closed his eyes as if that would make his aunt disappear from the entranceway of Grayson Hall. Opening them, he saw her still blocking his path. The dull ache in his temple accelerated. Aunt Margaret could nag with the best of them.

Just under five feet, she somehow always managed to appear closer to a full six feet when she set her mind to something and you stood in the way. Perhaps it had something to do with the vibrant colors she always wore. Today she wore a shocking shade of purple that hurt his eyes.

"Please, Aunt Margaret, not now," Thorne said, trying to reach the sanctuary of his study.

"The Season was just beginning. We have to return," Aunt Margaret continued, trying to keep up with Thorne's long strides. "How do you expect Judith to make a decent match, stuck out here? You don't want her to be a spinster like me, do you?"

"Aunt Margaret, please."

Somehow she reached the study first and placed herself squarely in front of the door. "Thorne, I am not without feeling. I know how all those mothers paraded their daughters before you like a butcher showing his best cut of meat, but you will simply have to suffer for your sister's sake. After all, you're thirty-two years old. You should be used to women throwing themselves at your feet."

A pair of angry blue-green eyes flashed before him. "Not all of them."

"All that I've seen," Lady Margaret stated matter-of-factly. "But we're digressing. If we must stay for a few more days, please find out who is at their estates near here. Perhaps some nice bachelor became bored with the Season and you can invite him to tea."

"Lord Wilson, perhaps?"

Lady Margaret sent her favorite nephew her sternest look. "Do be serious, Thorne. Even in London there is talk about the man's sanity. I'm all for being kind to animals, but giving twenty hounds each a room in one's home is going a bit far."

Thorne rubbed the bridge between his eyes. "I was only making an observation."

"Not a very good one. You'll do better if you put your mind to thinking of acceptable young men for Judith." In a swirl of taffeta, Lady Margaret stepped around Thorne and headed for the spiral staircase.

Feeling properly chastised, Thorne reached for the brass doorknob. His aunt was right: he should have been thinking of Judith, not of a turquoise-eyed witch. Judith had suffered enough because of him. The pounding in his head increased. He opened the door to his study.

"Is Aunt Margaret after you again?"

Thorne turned at the sound of Judith's soft voice. If his aunt was a peacock, then Judith was a wren. Small in stature, she somehow tended to blend into the surroundings, making people forget she was there. Few noticed her delicate beauty and lustrous black hair.

"You're frowning, Thorne. You'll get wrinkles." Judith sent her brother a teasing smile as she closed the small book of poetry she had been reading.

"Why do you always wear such dark colors?" he asked, his gaze sweeping the brown silk tea gown.

"I like dark colors," Judith answered, her smile slipping.

"Wouldn't you like something in a shimmering turquoise?"

"Shimmering turquoise? What made you think of such a color?"

Thorne ignored her question. "I seem to remember seeing brighter colors on the other young ladies making their debuts."

Judith's lips tightened. She opened her book again. "I prefer not to be so obvious."

Thorne knew the reason . . . the same reason they'd left London. "Aunt Margaret thinks we should return for the rest of the Season. I was selfish to drag you back here with me because I became bored. How about returning in the morning?"

Judith smiled, but somehow it never took the shadows from her black eyes. "Still trying to protect me, aren't you?" Placing the red and gold leatherbound book on the small table by her, she stood. Her bell-shaped skirt rustled softly while she slowly seesawed from one foot to the other as she crossed the Aubusson carpet to her brother.

"You took the blame when I was chasing you and fell off my horse, and now you have Aunt Margaret thinking you left because of the women after you. You should have told her the truth. You knew how it was tearing me up inside to be paraded out each night, hearing the other women talk about the crippl—"

"Don't say that word!"

A small, shaky hand touched the hard line of his jaw. "No matter if I say the word or not, the truth remains. One leg is shorter than the other, and the only person brave enough to risk embarrassing himself on the dance floor during the nine parties I attended in two weeks was you."

"Judith—"

"I know what you're going to say." The hint of a smile touched her tightly compressed lips. "If my Prince Charming is out there, I sincerely hope he hurries before he's too old to carry me off."

Some of the tension left Thorne. "He'd better ask my permission first."

"Whoever said rakes make the worst guardians was right." Judith smiled, and this time it wasn't forced. "I guess it's knowing how women throw themselves at your feet."

Thorne looked thoughtful. "Not all of them."

"The woman doesn't exist who can resist you," Judith teased.

"Not only did one resist, she set her pet wolf on me."

Judith's eyes widened. "What?"

"As you can see, I am unharmed." Thorne squeezed her hand in reassurance.

"Who is she? Do I know her? How did it happen?" Judith demanded, one question tumbling out after the other. "Please sit down and tell me every word."

Noting the interest in Judith's voice and face, Thorne allowed himself to be pulled onto the brocade couch beside her. Lord knew, during the eleven years since her accident, there'd been little enough to interest her.

Fifteen minutes later, Judith sat staring at her brother. "She must be very beautiful."

Thorne pushed to his feet. "I didn't say she was beautiful."

"No, you said she sailed into the room like a whirlwind. Her turquoise eyes sparkled. Her hair shone like—"

"Don't you usually sketch in the morning?" Thorne interrupted, his mustache a slash of black above his mouth.

Judith bit back a smile. "I've already finished, but I think I'll write a few letters." She rose. "I'll see you at dinner." At the doors she paused. "Do you think you'll be seeing Alexandria again?"

"Not if I have anything to say about it."

"Good." Judith continued out the door, unconcerned about her brother's puzzled frown.

"Allie, the footman from Lady Judith is here with another letter for you," Tillie informed her.

Alexandria glanced up from the account books to the housekeeper's expectant face. "Tell him the same thing I told him the other two times: my schedule does not permit any more engagements."

Tillie shook her mobcap-covered head in disapproval. "It's not like you to lie, Allie."

Allie felt the same way, but she wasn't going to admit it. "That arrogant man won't get to me through his sister."

"How do you know he's trying?" Tillie persisted. "I heard he and his sister only recently came back from London. Seems she didn't do so well with her debut because—"

"Tillie, I don't like to hear servants' gossip," Alexandria said, making a notation on the page. "Now, please give the man my answer."

The housekeeper didn't move. "A tea would be nice. It would be your chance to meet another nice lady."

"She would probably view me as oddly as the other women in the area do because I don't want to sit around and press flowers in a book or paint." Alexandria rubbed the nagging ache in her temple, an ache that had been there ever since she met Thorne Blakemore. "Just give the messenger my answer. I want to get through with these accounts before Father returns from the village."

"If your conscience wasn't guilty, you could have finished them hours ago."

Alexandria glanced up sharply, but Tillie was already closing the door behind her. Tillie was famous for having the last word. Usually Alexandria dismissed Tillie's predictions without a second thought, but this time her words wouldn't leave.

"I am right; he would use his sister." Hearing the words aloud, she glanced to the floor beside her. She always talked to herself when she was really worried or upset. Usually Wolf was around to look at her in understanding; today he was gone.

Wolf had slipped through the French doors over an hour ago. He was leaving more and more frequently and staying away longer each week. She was losing him. Knowing the day would come when he wouldn't return hadn't prepared her for his going. No one was ever prepared to lose something or someone they loved.

She hadn't understood her mother's words about going to heaven until they were standing over the mouth of her grave. It was then that Alexandria understood why her mother had made her promise to take care of her father. At the age of five she had left her childhood behind and never looked back.

She had lost her mother; she couldn't lose her father now . . . or his respect.

He'd been angry with her before, but this time it was different. Somehow they were growing apart and she had no idea how to make things the way they used to be. She had tried so hard after her mother's death to keep her promise.

Knowing how a man valued a male heir, she'd become the son her father'd never had. She'd grown up loving the freedom men took for granted and hating that women were subservient to them. She vowed that it would never happen to her. Now everything had changed. Her father was determined that she marry soon. Today, he had chosen another prospective bridegroom.

Lord Wilson was coming to dinner tomorrow night. The man was three times her age, fat, and balding. She knew her father wouldn't let her marry such a man, but he was giving her warning that he would not be put off from his goal. Why couldn't he understand that she didn't want to marry anyone, not even if he were as handsome as Lord Grayson?

Alexandria straightened in her seat. Where had that thought come from? Wheresoever, she was sending it straight back. She detested the man, and his sister was probably just as snobbish.

"I'm sorry, Lady Judith, but Miss Carstairs sent word that her schedule does not permit any more engagements," the footman said.

"Thank you, John," Judith said softly.

"I'm sorry, dear," Lady Margaret said consolingly as the servant liveried in blue and gold bowed and left the drawing room. "Despite the fact that her mother was the daughter of an earl, it seems the Carstairs girl has no manners."

"It's all right. It isn't her fault she's busy and I hunt for things to do." Judith stood unsteadily. "If you'll excuse me, I think I'll go to my room and finish the drawings I began this morning." The door closed softly behind her.

Thorne came down the hall and saw Judith brush across her cheek quickly with the back of her hand, then start for the stairs. "Judith?" he called. She didn't answer. Deciding against going after her, he entered the drawing room.

"What's wrong with Judith?" he demanded of his aunt.

Lady Margaret jabbed her needle through the pattern of a

rose she was stitching before she spoke. "That selfish little daughter of Squire Carstairs turned down three of her invitations to tea within six days."

Thorne frowned. "Judith doesn't know Miss Carstairs."

"She wanted to." Another stitch in red. "Judith has it in her head that people tolerate her only because of you. Since I gather that you and the young lady in question took an instant dislike to each other, and because of the lady's rather independent nature, Judith wanted to meet her."

"How do you know about my meeting Miss Carstairs?" From childhood, he and Judith had kept each other's confidences.

"Deduction." Lady Margaret pushed her wire-rimmed spectacles back on her nose. "Judith sent her an invitation which any other woman in her social position would have fallen over herself to accept. Yet she's declined three times. You visited Squire Carstairs and have yet to mention his daughter. I've heard she's very beautiful."

"I've met beautiful women before," Thorne said tartly, annoyed that a turquoise-eyed spitfire haunted his dreams and mocked his self-control.

"Yes, you have, but when I mentioned the squire's daughter in passing to test you yesterday, your mouth became tight . . . the way it is now."

"Aunt Margaret."

"Yes, dear?" Lady Margaret inquired sweetly, her eyes innocent.

"Please tell Judith her guest will be here within the hour." He headed for the door.

"Oh, my," Lady Margaret said, then smiled. "How I wish I could be a mouse and witness that encounter."

Four

"Miss Allie, Lord Grayson is here to see you."

Alexandria's grip on the ivory handle of her quill pen tightened, but she did not look up from the ledger. Grayson's visit was almost a certainty when she refused his sister's invitation. "Please tell him that I am busy."

Tillie lifted one thin eyebrow. "Somehow, I don't think getting rid of him will be that easy."

"Please relay my message."

"I hope you know what you're doing."

Alexandria glanced up to see the door close. "What can he do, drag me off?" The last words had barely crossed her lips when the door swung open again. Lord Grayson's imposing figure filled the entrance.

"You'll find me harder to dismiss than a footman," he rasped tightly.

Intense astonishment widened her eyes. Lord Grayson's action was totally unexpected and quite inexcusable. Her father would be outraged if he learned of the man's rudeness. Despite her irritation, she smiled at such a prospect. "Perhaps, but not impossible."

Tillie brushed by Lord Grayson and positioned herself protectively beside Alexandria. The housekeeper's gaze bounced from the angry lord to her charge. Leaning over, she whispered, "I warned you."

At Alexandria's stern look, Tillie straightened and said out loud, "Shall I get some of the men?"

Thorne strolled further into the room. "By all means get whomever you wish, but I am not leaving until I've had my say."

Alexandria studied Thorne. His arms were crossed casually over his wide chest and he had a look of boredom on his handsome face, but she'd been taught to look beyond the obvious. Thorne was angry, but he controlled that anger. Once unleashed he would be a dangerous man. If any of the servants tried to throw him out, besides being subjected to charges because Thorne was of the aristocracy, they'd have a fight on their hands. From the looks of Thorne, he hadn't lost many fights.

"That won't be necessary, Tillie," Alexandria said, as she stood and placed her pen back into the crystal well. "I'm sure we can rely on Lord Grayson to try and act like a gentleman for the rest of his visit."

Black eyes narrowed. "Just as we can rely upon Miss Carstairs to try and act like a lady."

Alexandria's fingers curled into a fist. It was either that, or pick up the inkwell and throw it at Thorne. "That will be all, Tillie."

Tillie's shoulders snapped backward and a look of outrage crossed her narrow face. "I'm not leaving you alone with an unmarried man."

"Tillie, I am in no mood for this," Alexandria informed the housekeeper. "You, of all people, know that I can take care of myself. Besides . . ." She glanced back at Thorne. "The quicker he has his say, the quicker I can see the last of him."

"I'm leaving, but I'll be right outside the door." Giving Thorne a warning glare, the elderly woman did as requested.

Thorne noted the door left ajar and briefly wondered if the housekeeper actually thought he'd harm Alexandria. She hadn't pushed him that far . . . yet.

"I'm waiting."

A dark brow lifted at Alexandria's calm voice. She wasn't afraid of him. Not many people could say the same.

"Why did you refuse my sister's invitations?"

"I thought you were behind them."

His arms unfolded. "This may come as a surprise, but I do not wish to see you any more than you wish to see me."

Something like hurt flashed through Alexandria, but she firmly pushed it aside. When she spoke, her voice sounded indifferent. "Since we agree on that, at least, I'm sure you'll also agree that there's nothing we have to say to each other. You know the way out." She took a seat and reached for the smooth handle of the pen.

A large hand with long, tapered fingers moved the inkwell aside. Thorne intercepted and dismissed her glare as he planted both hands on top of the massive mahogany desk. "What I want and what my sister wants are two different matters. If she wants you for tea, then you're coming for tea."

"Not today. Not ever." Alexandria rose, her posture stiff, her voice cold. "You know the way out."

Thorne straightened. "When I go, you're coming with me."

"Was your sister's Season so unsuccessful that you have to threaten women to visit her?" Alexandria asked, regretting the spitefulness of her words almost immediately.

Thorne rounded the desk before the echo of Alexandria's voice had faded. "Go upstairs and change clothes and we'll be on our way."

"If I don't?"

"Either way, you're coming with me." His gaze swept her slim figure from her glittering blue-green eyes to the polished black boots peeking out beneath her tweed pants. "I simply assumed you would not wish to be seen in public wearing breeches."

Another snub. Grayson was about to get a lesson he'd not soon forget. "How can I resist such a kind invitation?" She came from behind the desk.

Just as her hand settled on the brass doorknob, Thorne said, "You have thirty minutes."

Alexandria's hand blanched as her grip tightened. Opening

the door, she stepped into the hallway. Her entire body vibrated with anger as she closed the door behind her.

"Did you hear that arrogant bastard giving me orders in my own house?" she asked Tillie. Before the wide-eyed woman could answer, Alexandria rushed on to say, "If it wouldn't give Father a heart attack, I'd shoot him."

Tillie gasped.

"Oh, Tillie, calm down." Alexandria wrinkled her nose. "I'm not to that point. Yet."

The door opened behind her. "Shouldn't you be getting dressed?"

Alexandria stiffened at Thorne's voice. He was getting closer to pushing her too far. She spoke without turning. "I was simply giving instructions regarding my absence." To an open-mouthed Tillie, she requested, "Please accompany me upstairs."

Once in her bedroom, Alexandria didn't stop until she'd raised one of the double windows on the far side of the room and stuck one long leg over the sill. "I'll stay at the cottage until nightfall."

"But—"

"I'll be safe. Wolf will find me." Alexandria lifted her other leg over the casement and stood with practiced ease on the foot-wide ledge. "I do hate that I won't be able to see Grayson's face when he learns I tricked him."

"But . . ." Tillie began again, but Alexandria grabbed a stout branch and quickly disappeared into a thick foliage of dark green leaves. The housekeeper held her breath until Alexandria appeared on the edge of the sprawling oak.

To Tillie's whispered question of "What will I tell his lord-ship?" there came no answer.

Moments later Alexandria was still smiling her pleasure at having outwitted Thorne when she rounded the house. Her smile died abruptly as she saw him less than ten feet away, arms folded, leaning negligently against a tree. To the casual observer, it might appear that he'd simply paused after a stroll, but the alertness of his body told Alexandria another story. He was livid.

"I see you've decided not to change." He pushed from the tree. "Shall we go?"

"How did you know?" she questioned sharply.

"Let's just say I have a good memory," Thorne explained, stopping inches from Alexandria. "And you were too agreeable." His hand circled her upper arm.

Alexandria resisted the gentle tug and the unexpected heat of his touch. "Let go of me."

Thorne gazed down at the belligerent woman whose eyes now matched the defiance in her beautiful face. "Don't try to fight me, Alex, you'll lose."

"You were not given permission to use my given name nor to shorten it," she tossed back, testing the strength of his hold. It was as unyielding as the walls surrounding the estate. "And I never lose."

Thorne flashed a self-assured smile. "Then this will be your first time because neither do—ahhh." Her fist to his stomach stopped his words and bent him almost double. Dropping her arm, he clutched his stomach.

"Consider this your first defeat," Alexandria told him. "Now, leave."

Thorne slowly straightened to his full height of six-feet-three. Anger emanated from him like a living thing. "You'll pay for that," he said with deadly quiet.

Unease slithered down Alexandria's spine. Thorne had proved he was no gentleman. Perhaps she'd pushed him too far. She took a step back without realizing it.

"Run, but it'll do you no good."

Furious with herself for showing her apprehension, Alexandria braced her body for the attack she was sure would come. "I won't run."

Her words made Thorne pause for a moment as something like admiration surfaced for Alexandria. Her feet were spread, her small hands fisted close to her chest. Few men were willing to face his wrath. Then he remembered Judith and her tears. He reached for Alexandria.

"Stop!"

A woman's high-pitched voice erupted from behind Alexandria as Thorne's unrelenting fingers closed around her forearm.

"Thorne, stop, please. Oooh!"

Alexandria heard the cry of pain, but she didn't dare take her eyes from Thorne. For a moment she wished she had as he looked behind her. A killing rage swept across his face. He shoved her aside.

Alexandria turned to watch him run to a woman sprawled on the cobbled driveway several feet from a crested yellow carriage. A coachman and a footman hovered over her. Seeing Thorne, they stood aside.

Going down on his knees, Thorne attempted to draw the woman to him. She pushed him away. Standing, he helped the black-haired woman to her feet.

The unknown woman was beautiful in a fragile sort of way. She was also in total disarray. Her straw bonnet was askew, her white gloves were soiled, dirt smudged her pale face, and more dirt was on her gray silk gown. From the way Thorne stood protectively over her, his intent gaze apparently searching for injuries, Alexandria guessed the strange woman was one of the few he'd not forgotten. Irritated by the thought without understanding why, Alexandria turned to leave, but the woman's shaky voice stopped her.

"Miss Carstairs, please wait."

Something compelling in the woman's cultured tones caused Alexandria to turn. "Yes?"

The woman didn't seem to notice the curtness in Alexandria's voice or the defensiveness of her posture. Instead, she appeared to gather her ruffled dignity around her small body like a cloak. Her chin lifted and she met Alexandria's hostile gaze without flinching. "Please forgive my brother. He meant no harm."

"Brother?" Frowning, Alexandria looked from one to the other and saw no resemblance, other than the black hair. The woman looked delicate and vulnerable. Thorne was bold and dictatorial. Her voice quivered. Her brother would walk unafraid through the fires of hell. But what else would one expect from the Devil's Angel?

"Don't apologize for me, Judith," he snapped.

Judith placed a hand on his chest, but her forlorn gaze remained on Alexandria. "Excuse our intrusion. Good day."

Alexandria watched Judith reach out to clasp Thorne's hand and start for the carriage. Her awkward gait caught Alexandria's attention. "You have injured yourself. Please come inside."

Judith's body jerked the same instant Thorne's brusque voice cut across the air. "You have done enough."

Ignoring Thorne, Alexandria easily positioned herself in front of the slow-moving pair. The paleness in Judith's face, and what might have been dried tears in the corners of her eyes, pricked Alexandria's conscience. "From the way your sister is limping, she must be in terrible pain."

"Shut up!"

Alexandria stiffened at the harshness of Thorne's tone. The anger she'd witnessed in his face earlier seemed minute in comparison to the rage she witnessed now. But she'd caused the problem, and she would not walk away. "I accept the blame for your sister's injuries. Don't punish her to get back at me."

A muscle leaped in Thorne's bronzed jaw. "Not your fault. Mine."

Alexandria heard the raw pain in Thorne's voice and didn't understand it any more than her inexplicable urge to soothe the hurt away. "The fault is mine," she said softly.

"The fault lies with neither of you." Judith lifted her head regally and squeezed her brother's clenched fist. "The injury happened as a child. Please don't distress yourself further, Miss Carstairs. Good afternoon."

Dismissed again, Alexandria stepped aside, then watched Judith's slow, halting steps and realized why her Season in London had been a disaster. English nobility admired only perfection. Enough of them had pointed in dismay to Alexandria's golden skin, her callused hands, and her crisp walk for her to know what rejection felt like. They'd made it clear that she was not welcomed as a friend to their daughters or as a suitable escort for their sons. In trying to get back at Thorne, she had rejected Judith the same cruel way.

Once again Alexandria rushed to Judith, ignoring the grim-faced man at her side. "I am sorry about refusing your invitations. However, I'm going to give you a chance to repay me in kind." Alexandria smiled despite her nervousness. "Lady Judith, would you care to come inside for tea?"

"No, she would not," Thorne snapped, trying to hand Judith into the carriage.

His sister refused to step onto the velvet-covered footrest. Instead, she asked, "Why did you change your mind?"

The question was asked lightly, but it was evident by the lines radiating around Judith's mouth that Allie's answer was important and dreaded.

"I realized how thoughtless I had been to you because I prejudged you. That was wrong of me, and I apologize."

"Is that the only reason?"

"We have something in common."

Puzzlement crossed the other woman's face. "What is that?"

"People judge us on first appearance and not on what we are inside. They see your limp and my unorthodox ways and choose not to look any further," Alexandria said bluntly.

Judith's thin shoulders relaxed. "You are the first person to acknowledge to my face that I have a limp. People chose to ignore me rather than look at my imperfections."

"They don't ignore me," Alexandria said with some satisfaction. "I am probably the talk from here to London, but I chose to ignore them. How about tea?"

"What about your busy schedule?" Thorne asked curtly.

Alexandria favored him with a hard glare. "Nothing that can't be rescheduled."

Judith shook her head, her disappointment easily read. "My aunt is expecting us to return home."

"Perhaps some other time?" Alexandria suggested.

"Is Friday too soon?" Judith asked, despite the sudden tightness of Thorne's fingers.

Alexandria smiled. "I'll expect you the day after tomorrow, at four."

"Let's go, Judith," Thorne ordered, finally succeeding in getting his sister inside the carriage.

Once seated, she pushed the curtain aside and leaned out the window. "Since we weren't formally introduced, I see no reason to stand on formality. If it is agreeable to you, I would like to call you Alexandria. Please call me Judith."

"Thank you, Judith, and everyone calls me Allie."

"Goodbye, Allie."

Thorne watched the coach pull away, then turned to Alexandria. "Do or say anything to me you wish, but harm Judith and you'll answer to me." Spinning on his heels, he walked to his curricle and climbed inside. Satin-skinned chestnut horses, their heads high, gracefully turned the hooded carriage and trotted down the driveway.

"I have no intention of doing anything to harm Judith. You, Lord Grayson, may not be so fortunate," Alexandria mumbled, and went back inside the house.

"By that scowl on your face, I see that Judith reached you in time," Lady Margaret said to her nephew. She looked at her niece standing beside Thorne in the foyer. "When she came downstairs and I told her where you'd gone, she insisted on going after you."

Thorne's scowl deepened. He kept walking.

Judith's dark eyes sparkled. "I'm glad I did. You should have seen—"

Thorne whirled. "I think the less said about this afternoon, the better."

Judith put her hand over her mouth to smother her laughter. Lady Margaret's ears almost twitched. "Tell me all about it this instant. However, I shall be ashamed of you, Thorne, if you acted ungentlemanly toward the chit, even though she deserved it."

"Oh, but she didn't. She was so nice to me when she thought I had injured myself," Judith cried, brushing her dress again. "She thinks Thorne is arrogant, and that is the reason she refused my invitations."

"The girl is beginning to interest me," Lady Margaret said.

"I thought you abhorred gossip," Thorne said, as he walked back to take both women's arms. "Our lunch is waiting."

"It is not gossip if the party involved is relaying the information," Lady Margaret explained. "Now, please let Judith continue. I'd hate to sneak behind your back later. Sneakiness is something I cannot abide."

Entering the elegant dining room, Thorne waved the footman aside and pulled out a chair for his aunt, knowing he was defeated. He was going to hear how a woman had doubled him over with one punch. A thoughtful frown crossed his face as he seated Judith. What if someone else beside Judith and his servants had seen the incident? He would be the laughingstock of England. He wasn't going within a mile of Alexandria again.

"She hit Thorne."

Thorne took his seat, ignoring his aunt's gasp of incredulity. His only consolation was that the servants had withdrawn from the dining room. The coachman and footman who drove Judith were on his staff in London and were completely loyal. Perhaps he should tell them not to mention the way Alexandria was dressed as well. If Judith insisted on cultivating the hoyden's friendship, he didn't want any gossip attached to his sister.

"I didn't expect it," he defended, and felt inexplicably worse. He disliked people who made excuses.

Judith sobered. "Of course you didn't. But apparently Allie has had to learn self-defense and used it without thinking. I'm sure she didn't mean to harm you."

Thorne's fork paused over his pork roast. "What do you mean, she has had to defend herself? Where was her father?"

"The same place I assume he was today when you arrived," Judith answered, her face as thoughtful as Thorne's had been earlier. "She is very beautiful, and men sometimes forget themselves with beautiful women."

Uneasiness moved though Thorne at the thought of any man touching Alex. He stabbed his meat. She would probably beat the poor man to his knees. His fork was an inch from his mouth when his head jerked up. "Has someone bothered you?"

Judith looked sad, almost wistful. "I don't think you have to worry about me."

Lady Margaret spoke up. "Because any fool would know that Thorne would call the bounder out."

Unconsciously Judith's hand moved back and forth across her left thigh. "I'm sure you're right."

Lady Margaret and Thorne exchanged knowing, helpless looks. "Aren't you going to tell Aunt Margaret about your invitation to tea Friday afternoon?" Thorne asked.

"Judith, I'm not sure you should accept," her aunt said. "She doesn't sound like a respectable young lady."

"Yes, she is." Judith pushed her peas around on her plate. "We could be friends."

"You don't know the woman. How can you think you would like to be her friend?" Thorne asked.

Judith's expression became mischievous. "Any woman who can get the best of you and walk away smiling, I want to know better."

Lady Margaret nodded. "You may have a valid point, dear."

"No, she doesn't," Thorne said, his eyes glinted. "The less we see of Miss Carstairs, the better for all of us."

"We shall see, Thorne," Lady Margaret said.

Thorne slumped in his seat. His aunt had that charging bull look again. Why the hell hadn't he taken Judith and Aunt Margaret to his lodge in Scotland?

Five

"You might have to marry the girl, sir."

Thorne arched a black brow at the small man seated across from his desk. Jeremy Peterson, one of the most respected solicitors in England, barely reached five feet. However, what he lacked in height he amply made up for with his sharp mind. "I don't consider that an option, Peterson. I sent for you to get me out of the contract, not bind me to it."

Used to being asked the impossible by Lord Grayson, Peterson understood the importance of his hasty summons to Grayson Hall. But this time he was unsure if he could deliver. "You won't get out of the contract without paying a great deal of money." He tapped the paper in front of him with his gold-rimmed glasses, then glanced up.

"The girl's father has everything on his side. If he wasn't an honest man, he could just demand the money and refuse your suit. You have nothing in your favor, according to the terms of the contract."

"In other words, my father sold me to get what he wanted."

Peterson didn't flinch. He'd been Thorne's lawyer for five years. In that time he'd learned to accept his bluntness. He replaced his glasses. "Perhaps he was not given a choice."

Thorne's voice harshened. "Everyone has a choice. It is just that some are too afraid to take it."

Peterson glanced once again at the papers he'd been studying for the last half hour, then brought his gaze back to his employer.

"Lord Grayson, the contract is legal and binding. Of course, if you wish another attorney to look—"

"If I didn't trust you and think you were the best, you wouldn't be sitting before me now," Thorne said, leaning back into his chair with a calmness he was far from feeling. "The only question now is, can I afford to pay the blood money?"

Shifting the contract to one side, Peterson stood and handed Thorne several sheets of paper. "When I received your message regarding the nature of the problem, I took the liberty of bringing your financial assets up to date." He pushed his sliding glasses further up his narrow nose.

"As you will note, you can pay the quarter of a million pounds and have ten thousand pounds left over for expenditures for the rest of the year, but it will leave you short if you have any unnecessary business expenses. Of course, you will have to forgo buying the railroad stock and the improvements on your three estates." Peterson glanced sideways, then returned to his seat. "And there is always the possibility of Countess Grayson asking for more funds."

Thorne's face became closed at the mention of the woman who had given him life and nothing else. "Has she?"

"No. However, her current companion, Lord Jiles, is a recent widower who is known for his reckless spending," Peterson answered, glad that at least in this he could give his employer the information he sought.

"No doubt he never had to earn a farthing of the money he spent," Thorne guessed, as he surged forward in his seat.

The solicitor nodded. "Five years ago he inherited his title and little else. He quickly married a wealthy matron and proceeded to spend her money with frivolous extravagance. After her death six months ago, he had to flee to Paris to escape creditors."

"Then he and the countess should make an excellent team, since they prey off others. I wonder who is going to use whom," Thorne said sarcastically, then glanced back at the papers in his hand. "What a pity I can't dismiss this as easily as I can dismiss the countess. It is almost as if Carstairs knew I couldn't pay him."

"Not many men could and still remain solvent," Peterson pointed out. "There is the hundred thousand pounds of Lady Judith's dowry over which you are trustee."

"No." Thorne shook his head. "I won't touch a sixpence of Judith's money. I'll either do this on my own or I'll sell Briargate." Even as the words formed, Thorne felt a twisting kind of anger. It was as abhorrent to him to sell his smallest estate as it was for him to sell himself to Carstairs. It had taken him four hard years of scheming and planning to buy back his heritage, and now he stood to lose it all because a father wanted a title for his daughter.

"It's a pity the young lady doesn't have an affection for someone else," the solicitor mused.

Thorne's gaze sharpened. "Why is that?"

Hearing the eagerness in Thorne's voice, the little man sat up straighter in his leather chair. "Since the money obviously isn't the reason for wanting to announce the betrothal, Squire Carstairs might be persuaded to let you out of the agreement with only the initial loan repaid if Miss Carstairs had an affection for someone else."

"I don't think the lady in question wants to marry anyone," Thorne said, annoyed in spite of himself that Alexandria thought him unsuitable.

"Perhaps she has yet to meet the right man. Would her father allow her to go to London for the Season?" Peterson asked hopefully.

"Why should he, when—" Thorne stopped in mid-sentence, a grin slowly forming on his face. "Peterson, you've done it again."

"I have, sir?"

"If the lady in question won't go to London, I'll bring London to her." Thorne stood. "I'll invite all the eligible young men down for a fox hunt."

"I beg your pardon, sir, but an invitation from you would

bring the ladies, not the men," Peterson reasoned. "Besides, even if you weren't against blood sports, the fox-hunting season is over."

"Only for two weeks. The men are probably so tired of balls and dinner parties they'll come to a hunt in droves. With any luck, the fox will stay in his burrow," Thorne said, warming to his plan. "Miss Carstairs is the best horsewoman I've seen, and despite her rough edges, she's beautiful and rich—qualities most eligible English bachelors can't resist. Men will be buzzing around her like bees to a honey pot."

"I hate to play devil's advocate, but what will make her interested in them if she turned *you* down?" Peterson asked.

"I don't know, but I intend to do my best to make sure someone offers for her before the weekend is over," Thorne said, taking Peterson's arm and showing him to the door.

"If this doesn't work, you can still marry the young lady and leave her in the country," Peterson reminded Thorne. "Her dowry would keep even the most lavish spender happy for two lifetimes."

"Miss Carstairs would reach London before I did, if that was what she wanted. Anyway, my wife and I will live together," Thorne said. At least until he could be sure all the children were his—something of which his father had never been certain. "Please see that my instructions are carried out immediately, and thank you for coming from London so quickly."

"My pleasure." Peterson clutched his brown leather case closer to his chest. "I'll see to everything personally. Any man in particular you wish invited?"

"Invite whomever you like," Thorne retorted.

"To serve your purpose, it must be someone in need of a rich bride immediately," Peterson reasoned thoughtfully. "Lord Harold is deep in debt and might suit your needs."

Thorne frowned. "The man's a compulsive gambler."

"Lord Gilbert?"

"Nearing his sixtieth birthday."

Undaunted, Peterson continued. "Viscount Simpson is thirty and sober."

"Too sober. The man spouts poetry at the slightest provocation," Thorne announced to Peterson. "Miss Carstairs wouldn't spend five seconds with him."

"Baron Frampton," Peterson said without a moment's hesitation. "Young, sober, and cuts a dashing figure on and off the dance floor. I'm told ladies find him vastly amusing."

"A womanizer is just as bad as the rest," Thorne put in.

Peterson wrinkled his nose to hide his smile. "Are you sure you are against this betrothal?"

Thorne looked thunderstruck. "Of course! I simply do not want the girl trapped into a marriage with some disreputable character. She is as innocent as I am in this." The words were barely out of his mouth before he realized he was making excuses again. He never made excuses before meeting Alexandria. He scowled. "Invite whom you choose. Just get it done and arranged for two weeks from today."

Peterson sobered. "Certainly, my lord. I shall see to it immediately."

Thorne watched the door close, then went to sit in his chair. He'd acted like a complete idiot with Peterson. This was what happened to an orderly life when a whirlwind like Alexandria entered it. Marrying her would be disastrous.

When Thorne married, he wanted a woman he could control, one who would be above reproach, and one who would keep out of his way. Alexandria would be none of these. The best way out of this was for her to marry and become some other man's problem. The thought made his scowl deepen and a muttered expletive slip past his lips.

Lady Margaret liked what she saw. Even in an out-of-fashion blue satin tea gown, Alexandria was beautiful. Lustrous dark gold hair was piled atop her head and allowed to cascade in thick curls down her back. The effect set off her delicate features and graceful neck. She would take London by storm in the right clothes and, of course, with the proper introduction.

But Lady Margaret was looking for something in Alexandria besides beauty. Thorne usually dismissed women, but for some reason he had not been able to dismiss Alexandria. It had surprised Margaret when he'd grudgingly agreed to escort them to the Carstairs' home, then left on his horse as soon as the coach drew to a halt, saying he'd return in an hour.

A beautiful woman might cause Thorne to take a second look; however, it would take more than surface appearance to sustain his interest. Watching Alexandria's animated face as she and Judith giggled over one of Alexandria's childhood pranks, Lady Margaret saw an openness and a gentleness that she couldn't help but like.

Alexandria didn't dither, either. Margaret detested anyone who couldn't make up her own mind almost as much as she detested the flirtatious ritual most women employed to attract men. Was it any wonder that men thought women's brains were the size of a hatpin? No man would think that for long about Alexandria. She would look him straight in the eye and tell him differently.

Margaret frowned. There might be a problem if that man were Thorne. After his mother had dominated and disgraced his father, Thorne didn't like outspoken women. Alexandria was definitely outspoken.

Lifting her delicate teacup, Margaret wondered not for the first time that afternoon if she should give Alexandria and Thorne a little push in each other's direction.

"Aunt Margaret, may I go to Allie's pond with her?"

"Please say yes, Lady Margaret," Alexandria said. "The warm water will be good for her. It's only a short ride from here."

Judith's cup rattled in the saucer. "I don't ride."

Alexandria glanced around sharply at the fear in Judith's voice, a fear that was reflected in her pinched features. "Then I shall teach you."

"Miss Carstairs, my niece doesn't wish to ride," Lady Margaret said crisply.

Alexandria frowned her puzzlement. "Why?"

"Young lady—" Lady Margaret began, only to be interrupted by her niece.

"It's all right, Auntie. Perhaps I should tell her." Carefully, Judith set the rose-patterned china on the table. "I was chasing Thorne on my pony when I was nine. He jumped a fence and I thought I could, too." Her hands clenched in her lap. "I was mistaken."

Knowing pity was the last thing Judith wanted, Alexandria offered none. But at least she now understood why Thorne had been so angry at her for jumping an unpredictable horse like Lexington. "Then we shall take the pony cart." Her hand closed over the fisted one in Judith's lap.

Margaret relaxed upon seeing Alexandria's concern for her niece. "I quite agree of the benefits of taking the waters for Judith, but it is not sea water, nor are there bathing machines here."

"Scientists in Germany are saying that ordinary water is just as beneficial as sea water," Alexandria persisted. "A bathing machine is unnecessary to take us into the water when all we have to do is step into it."

"Without a bathing machine you wouldn't have an assistant," Lady Margaret said worriedly. "What if you fell?"

"Stand up or swim, of course," Alexandria answered without hesitation, and pushed aside a distant memory when she could do neither and it had almost cost her her life.

Shock registered on Alexandria's guests' faces. Judith was the first to speak. "Do you mean you can swim?"

Too late Alexandria remembered that ladies did not swim. Telling the reason she had learned would only distress them more. She lifted her chin. "Yes," she answered, and waited for the condemnation.

Judith squealed and clasped her hands together. "Please teach me."

"There will be *no swimming,*" Lady Margaret said, before Alexandria could speak. "However, you may go wading—on the condition that Thorne accompany you."

"There is no reason for him to come," Alexandria said, caught between being happy that they hadn't been swept from the room and annoyed to have Thorne thrust upon her.

"It is the only way I will allow Judith to go."

Alexandria studied the implacable features of the older woman and realized she was as immovable and as stubborn as her nephew. Alexandria didn't want to see Thorne again, but she couldn't put her dislike of him ahead of Judith. The warm waters of the spring-fed pond would help the stiffness in her hip. "Very well."

"He is really very nice," Judith offered in a conciliatory manner.

"So is a bee, until he stings you," Alexandria muttered.

Lady Margaret cleared her throat. "When would you like to go? Judith didn't bring any bathing costumes and she'll have to have some made. Who did yours?"

"Mrs. Finch, but I don't wear—" The horrified expression on Lady Margaret's face stopped Alexandria's confession.

The older woman rose, her body as straight and unbending as forged steel. "What do you swim in?"

Alexandria felt the woman's disapproval and inwardly cursed her impetuous tongue. A knock on the drawing room door increased her anxiety. She would recognize those two quick taps anywhere. Visualizing herself under punishment until the pond was only a golden memory, she called, "Come in, Father."

"Good afternoon, ladies. Do you mind if we join you?" Squire Carstairs asked, as he strode into the room with a whiskered young man by his side.

Bloody hell, Alexandria thought. Of all the people for her father to have with him, Lord Billingsly was the worse. The man saw himself as a dandy and strutted like a peacock. He expected women to worship at his feet. From the glaring loudness of the yellow-and-black-checkered frock coat he wore today, looking at his feet might save the poor woman's vision.

"Hello, Father, Lord Billingsly," she greeted warmly. She might as well try to bluff her way through. "I don't believe either of you has met Lady Margaret and her niece, Lady Judith."

"Welcome to our home, Lady Margaret, Lady Judith," Oliver said warmly.

Lord Billingsly inclined his head. "On the contrary, Miss Carstairs, I have met your guests." Crossing his legs at the ankle, he leaned casually against a wing chair. "All of London wondered where you'd disappeared to, Lady Margaret."

Lady Margaret jerked her gloves tighter on her hands. "Now you may relate our whereabouts to them. If you will excuse us, we were about to leave." She draped her paisley shawl around her shoulders. "Come, Judith."

"Aunt Margaret, please . . . may we stay a moment longer?" Judith asked, her gaze imploring, her hand clenched atop her left thigh. After a few tense moments, her aunt sat, but her expression was dour.

The squire frowned. His questioning look at his daughter went unnoticed as she prepared another cup of tea. He spoke into the lengthening silence. "Lord Billingsly made a special trip from London to see Valiant."

"When I saw the Arabian for sale in the *London Times,* I came down immediately to make an offer. However, there was another reason." Lord Billingsly's approving gaze rested on Alexandria. "If I may be so bold, I was hoping Miss Carstairs might change her mind and return to London with me. Properly chaperoned, of course."

Alexandria coughed delicately into a lace handkerchief. "I'm afraid the London air might be too harsh for me."

Billingsly's smile faded. "I am sorry to see you ill. Perhaps we can go for a carriage ride while I am here."

"You do me a great honor, but my schedule is rather full," she said, handing her father a cup of tea.

"I can wait," he said tightly.

Alexandria gritted a smile. "As you wish."

"Have you ever been to Miss Carstairs's pond, Lord Billingsly?" Aunt Margaret asked suddenly.

Oliver choked on his tea. "Certainly not!" he shouted, forgetting to whom he was speaking.

"I am sure Lady Margaret meant no offense, Father. I offered to take Lady Judith there and her aunt was concerned," Alexandria explained, wondering how long she had before Lady Margaret told her father the real reason behind her question.

Oliver smiled sheepishly. "I'm sorry, Lady Margaret. I tend to overreact sometimes with regard to Alexandria. However, let me assure you that your niece will be quite safe. Wolf will see to that."

If anything, Lady Margaret's expression became more scandalized. "You approve of your daughter having a vicious wild animal for a pet?"

"I didn't at first, but after he saved Alexandria from a snake bite, then from a renegade wolf, I was happy she had Wolf."

Lord Billingsly spoke up. "I have to agree with Lady Margaret. The animal is dangerous."

"He is not," Alexandria defended hotly.

"He attacked me," Billingsly declared, just as hotly.

"Perhaps he had a reason," said a commanding male voice.

All heads turned as one to see Thorne standing in the doorway. Tillie stood beside him. Not to be outdone, she announced belatedly, "Lord Grayson."

Six

Billingsly's shoulders stiffened. His angular face flushed. "What are you implying?"

Thorne ignored Billingsly until he had nodded to the other occupants in the room. When he turned to the younger man, his gaze was chilling. "I wasn't implying anything. I thought I made myself quite clear."

Sensing undercurrents, Oliver sought to appease both men. "Lord Grayson, it's good to see you again. I was sorry I missed you the other day."

Thorne turned his gaze upon Alexandria, sitting stiff-backed with a becoming blush spreading from her slender throat upward. "Yes, it was most enlightening."

"Was there something you wished to speak with me about?" Oliver asked, his eyes speculative.

"No. I merely came to extend Judith's invitation to your daughter for tea, but as they are women, they changed their minds about the location," Thorne explained smoothly.

"I see," Oliver said, his disappointment obvious.

"Tea, anyone?" Alexandria asked abruptly.

"No, thank you, Miss Carstairs," Lord Billingsly said, his belligerent gaze intent on Thorne. "I mentioned to your aunt how surprised everyone was to see you disappear so quickly. We were concerned."

"I'm sure," Thorne said blandly. "Aunt Margaret, Judith if you are ready we can leave."

"Thorne, I . . . may we stay a moment longer?" Judith asked, glancing from Billingsly back to her brother.

Looking at the beseeching look in his sister's face, Thorne nodded. "I'll have a cup of tea."

"Lemon or cream?" Alexandria asked, leaning over to pour. Glancing up for an answer, she stared at the top of Thorne's dark head. His gaze was fixed on the revealing neckline of her gown. Stifling the impulse to cover her breast, she hissed between clenched teeth, "Sir?"

"Cream," Thorne answered, his unrepentant gaze still on the creamy smoothness of Alexandria's heaving breasts.

"Thorne, you like lemon," Judith reminded him.

Tea in hand, Thorne straightened and stared into Alexandria's stormy blue-green eyes. "I thought I might try something different."

"If you don't mind me asking, what brought you to the country?" Billingsly inquired tartly.

"The peacefulness," Thorne answered, and walked over to stand beside the couch Judith was sitting on.

His sister giggled, and Billingsly's shoulders became more rigid. "I daresay you might change your mind when you learn Lady Clarendon has decided to reenter society at a dinner party my parents are giving next weekend."

"I never change my mind about anything," Thorne replied, his gaze suddenly intent upon Alexandria.

Something about the chilling quietness of Thorne's voice piqued Alexandria's interest. If there was a possibility of a romantic liaison between Thorne and this Lady Clarendon, it would free Alexandria. There was only one way to find out. It was unthinkingly rude, but she was fighting for her life. Without further hesitation she asked Billingsly, "Who is Lady Clarendon?"

Billingsly's lower jaw dropped on receiving Alexandria's entrancing smile. Snapping his mouth shut, he sent Thorne a triumphant look before answering. "My widowed cousin. I would be delighted to introduce you to her if you come to the party.

During her Season three years ago, Rachel was known as "the Incomparable." She is also the only woman who ever tossed Grayson over," Billingsly said with unmistakable relish.

"Smart woman," Alexandria mumbled, and took a sip of tea. *Well, so much for that plan.*

A muscle leaped in Thorne's jaw.

Billingsly, who had been watching Thorne, missed what Alexandria had said. His thin eyebrows arched. "I beg your pardon?"

Oliver sent Alexandria a warning glance. "My daughter is overwhelmed by your invitation. You do her a great honor."

"It is your daughter who would honor me with her presence," Billingsly put in smoothly.

Knowing that some comment was expected of her, Alexandria set her cup down. "I'm afraid I already have an engagement for that weekend. Perhaps another time."

Thorne watched Billingsly grit his teeth and incline his head in acceptance, and tried to bring his temper under control. Alexandria was the most irritating woman he had ever had the misfortune to meet. No well-bred woman would have dared asked about another woman in mixed company. No wonder her father had decided to marry her off. Sitting there sipping her tea, she looked like an angel. Ha! And they called him "the Devil's Angel." She might lead Billingsly on a merry chase, but in Thorne she had met her match.

"Billingsly's loss is my gain. In two weeks I'm having a fox hunt at Grayson Hall." Thorne touched Judith's shoulder in silent reassurance, then looked at Oliver. "It would be a pleasure to have you and your daughter as my special guests."

"The hunting season is over," Lord Billingsly sneered.

"I just reopened it," Thorne said, hating that it appeared as if he and the fool Billingsly were fighting over Alexandria.

"What a splendid idea! I haven't ridden to the hounds in two years," Oliver said, with obvious pleasure. "We will be delighted, won't we, Alexandria?"

Alexandria's inclination was to decline, but one look at her

father and she knew she had pushed him enough for one day.
"Of course, Father. I think I'll remain behind with Judith and
the other ladies not joining in the hunt."

"You mustn't stay because of me," Judith said quietly.

Billingsly looked at Alexandria, his eyes filled with barely
concealed lust. "Do ride, Miss Carstairs. It will be my pleasure
to have you watch me catch the fox." He turned to Thorne.
"That is, if I have been invited?"

"Everyone is invited, but I wouldn't promise something that
you might not deliver," Thorne said casually.

"I always get what I go after, Grayson." Billingsly glanced
back at Alexandria.

"I once remember someone else being that confident," Alexandria told him. "However, the outcome depends on your
competition."

Billingsly's mouth curved into a cynical smile. "I know
you're an excellent horsewoman, but a woman has never won
the hunt before."

"Then it will be my pleasure to be the first." Alexandria
winked at a smiling Judith.

"Since you're so sure, would you care to make a small wager?" Billingsly asked, then quickly added, "With your father's
permission, of course, or were you simply teasing?"

"Whatever wager—"

"Miss Carstairs," Thorne interrupted. "I think you should
hear the wager before you agree to it, don't you, Squire?"

Alexandria started to tell him to mind his own business, but
something about his steady gaze made her keep silent.

"Very sensible, Lord Grayson," the squire said. "Although
I'm sure it will be an honorable wager."

Lord Billingsly nodded. "If I win, Miss Carstairs will return
to London with me and allow me to be her escort around the
city."

"No." Both Thorne and Alexandria spoke at the same time.

Billingsly's thin lips tightened. "I fail to see what you have
to do with it, Grayson."

"I agree with Lord Billingsly, Thorne," Lady Margaret said. "What Miss Carstairs does is none of your concern."

Hearing the censure in the voice of the woman she had wanted to call a friend, Alexandria glanced at Lady Margaret. It was not the first time Alexandria had been judged by someone and found lacking, but it was the first time in a long time she wished it could have been different. Firmly, she turned to Billingsly. "If I win, what do I get?"

Billingsly smiled with confidence. "Name it."

"Shadow Dancer."

His smile vanished. "My thoroughbred stallion!"

This time it was Alexandria who smiled. "It's that or nothing."

"Isn't there something—" A wolf's howl caused Billingsly to stop speaking. His head snapped from side to side as he searched the gardens beyond the blue-velvet-draped open double doors. His face paled. He swallowed loudly. "I find I'm late for a previous engagement."

"What about our wager?" Alexandria questioned.

"I—" the wolf's howl sounded louder, closer. Billingsly's eyes rounded. "All right."

"I promise to take good care of Shadow Dancer for you," Alexandria said, laughter in her voice.

"I'll show you out, Lord Billingsly," Oliver said. "Of course, I trust you to keep this wager a secret."

Billingsly looked as if he didn't know what had happened to him. "Ah, yes. Good day."

"Good day," Alexandria said, trying to keep the disgust from her voice. If Billingsly wasn't such a pompous coward she'd have told him that Wolf never announced his arrival.

"You shouldn't have made the wager." Thorne set his cup on the Chippendale table in front of Alexandria.

She dismissed Thorne with a look. "I told you once, you can't tell me what to do."

"I think we both know differently," Thorne said, his eyes challenging.

The truth of his statement sent Alexandria surging to her feet. No man was going to make her his chattel.

Thorne glanced at her balled fist. "Try it again and you won't be able to sit a horse for a month."

"Thorne," Lady Margaret admonished, her mouth gaping in shock.

Thorne gritted his teeth. What the hell was happening to him? For an insane moment his only thought had been to make Alexandria yield to him. He shut his eyes in denial of what he wanted and regret of what he could never have.

"Thorne, are you all right?"

His lids lifted to see Judith watching him closely. "Yes." Walking over, he touched her cheek and forced a smile, just as he forced his body to accept his control. "Maybe it's the fresh country air."

"Let us go then." Lady Margaret stood. "Goodbye, Miss Carstairs."

"I want to stay," blurted Judith.

"Judith." The crispness of Lady Margaret's tone had the desired effect. Judith's dark head fell, she retrieved her reticule, then stood.

Alexandria took the unhappy young woman's hands in hers and squeezed lightly. "I wish things might have been different. Goodbye."

Judith opened her mouth to speak, but nothing came out. Instead she nodded, her fingers tightening around Alexandria's.

Thorne glanced at the three women. Judith was near tears. Alexandria was spitting mad. His aunt's lips were pressed together so firmly in disapproval that he feared she might cut off her circulation. It didn't take a mind-reader to figure out the reason.

Alexandria.

Clearly, she had done or said something. Since he was reasonably sure she had not presented herself in breeches, it must be something else. Even before their heated exchange, his aunt had appeared stiff with reproach. Black eyebrows bunched as he sought the reason. He needed the three women to be friends in time for the hunt if his plan was to work. Once Alexandria was out of his life, he would stop dreaming about her in his bed and sleep peacefully again.

"Did you ladies have a nice visit?" Thorne asked, and watched three pair of startled eyes converge on him. "What did you talk about?"

Lady Margaret's gloved hands tightened on her shawl.

Alexandria's chin lifted.

Judith blushed.

"Sorry that took so long," Oliver said, as he reentered the room. Crossing to Lady Margaret, he continued the conversation they'd been having before Thorne's arrival. "As I was saying, I assure you that Lady Judith would be safe with Alexandria at her pond."

"I've decided against my niece going," Lady Margaret said coolly.

Disappointment sagged Oliver's shoulders. "I was hoping she and my daughter might become better acquainted. It isn't often that Alexandria has a chance to meet young women her age." He looked warmly at Judith. "Especially one so peaceful. Please reconsider. The pond is only five feet deep, and Alexandria is a good swimmer. I've watched her myself."

Lady Margaret gasped and pressed her hand to her ample bosom. "You've watched her!"

Oliver frowned. "Since she 'secretly' taught herself, how else was I to know that she was safe? The next time she went swimming I had two men try to sneak up on her." His frown changed into a grin. "Wolf had them running before they were within a hundred yards of the pond. They never even got a glimpse of her in her bathing costume."

"Bathing costume?" Lady Margaret repeated, turning to a blushing Alexandria.

Oliver's manner became jovial. "Forgive me, Lady Margaret, for not understanding your hesitation sooner. Alexandria has several costumes and I'm sure she can assist Lady Judith. If you remain concerned, Lord Grayson can accompany the ladies. Of course, Wolf won't let him near the pond, but he can fish in the small lake upstream that's stocked with trout."

Looking at the crimson stain in Alexandria's cheeks, Thorne finally understood the reason behind his aunt's hostility. His little hoyden didn't wear a bathing costume when she swam. He glanced at her and tried to picture her without clothes, her long, sleek body wet and tempting. He looked up and saw her furious eyes and smiled despite the jagged claws of desire ripping into him.

"Trout fishing sounds like an excellent idea, Oliver," Thorne said. "Although I regret not being able to see Miss Carstairs swim, I shall endeavor to bear up and enjoy fishing instead."

Judith gave an unladylike squeal of delight and hugged her brother.

Lady Margaret's lips became tight again. "Judith will not go in the water."

"Of course, Lady Margaret." Oliver quickly rushed to placate her. "Alexandria and Lady Judith can watch Lord Grayson fish."

"I won't—" Alexandria began.

"Alexandria," Oliver said firmly. "You will honor our guests."

Hiding her clenched fists in the folds of her gown, Alexandria managed a weak smile. "Yes, Father."

Lady Margaret nodded her approval. The chit might be wild, but she respected her father. Perhaps there was still hope. "Come, Judith. I think it's time we took our leave."

Outside, Thorne handed the women into the carriage, then gestured for Oliver to speak with him in private. They walked to the edge of the terrace flower garden. "Allowing your daughter to bet wasn't a wise decision."

Oliver shrugged. "Billingsly can open doors for her in London that would be closed to me."

"What if she wins?" Thorne asked, his irritation obvious.

"What man is going to let a woman beat him in a fox hunt?"

Oliver laughed, then pinned Thorne with a knowing stare. "Billingsly will try, but I think he'll lose to you."

Thorne finally understood the squire's reasoning. He sought to pit Thorne against Billingsly. If Thorne wanted Alexandria, the other man wouldn't have a chance. Thorne didn't, but Billingsly wasn't the one for her, either. Now, Thorne would have to win the damn hunt. There was no telling what mischief Alexandria would get into if she went to London with a fool like Billingsly. If her reputation was tarnished, there was no way Thorne could get her married off. "With your permission, I'd like to speak with your daughter."

"Under the circumstances, I see no reason why you shouldn't." Oliver glanced at Alexandria, who was waving at the departing coach. "Alexandria, Lord Grayson would like a word with you."

Alexandria's belligerent expression showed she'd rather do anything than talk to Lord Grayson. "I really need to look at the estate accounts."

"They can wait." Oliver turned to Lord Grayson. "Good day."

"Good day, Squire," Thorne said and watched the squire climb the stone steps and enter the house.

"What do you want?" Alexandria asked, her arms folded under her bosom inadvertently pushing their creamy smoothness over the lacy edge of the low bodice.

Thorne reluctantly lifted his gaze and wondered absently what she would say if he told her he wanted to lift her breasts out of her gown and stroke them until they both moaned with pleasure. "Alex, Judith doesn't ride."

Knowing that telling him to stop calling her "Alex" would do little good, she said instead, "She told me. We had already planned to take the pony cart. If there is nothing further, I shall say good day." Unfolding her arms, she started to leave.

Thorne smoothly blocked her path. "Why did Wolf attack Billingsly?"

"I don't see where—"

"Why?"

The determination in Thorne's voice warned Alexandria that he wasn't leaving without an answer. "He insisted on helping me from my horse and didn't release me afterward."

Thorne's face hardened into ruthlessness. "Did he hurt you?"

"No."

"Obviously, you didn't tell your father. Why?"

"For the same reason I didn't tell him you barged into the house. It would upset him, and I can take care of myself."

"I'll speak to your father," Thorne said, slapping his leather gloves against his trouser leg. "I don't want Billingsly anywhere near you."

Alexandria bristled. "What you want or don't want is of no concern to me."

Black eyes glinted. "Don't confuse me with a weakling like Billingsly."

"I won't." Her lips curled. "At least you didn't try to use me as a shield against Wolf." At Thorne's confused expression, she continued. "He was holding a riding crop, and Wolf wouldn't obey me to stay at first. I think someone once shot at Wolf and he remembers. There is a scar on his shoulder that could have been caused by a bullet."

"Billingsly?"

She was pensive for a moment. "I don't know, but if I ever find out, I'll take care of it."

"You'll do nothing," Thorne told her.

"I don't like being given orders."

Thorne gave a short bark of laughter. "That's putting it mildly."

"How would you like being told what to do all your life?" Alexandria asked heatedly.

"I wouldn't like it, but I'm not a woman," Thorne said.

The statement was so ludicrous that Alexandria was speechless for a moment. No way, not even in the darkest of night or from a hundred yards away, would even the most simple-minded confuse Thorne with a woman. He was too overpoweringly masculine. However, that was the last thing she intended to say.

"Women are not the brainless creatures men think we are," Alexandria said finally. "I can do anything a man can do and do it better."

Thorne looked thoughtful. "Anything?"

"Anything. Hunt, fish, ride, run an estate. Whatever you can do, I can do it better."

"Make love," Thorne murmured huskily.

Alexandria felt an unexpected rush of warmth in the pit of her stomach. The warmth intensified as Thorne brought his body closer. She felt confused. Not understanding what was happening, she raised her fist.

"Remember what I told you," Thorne warned.

"You are the most despicable man I know," she fumed, lowering her hand.

"I thought we agreed that that was Billingsly."

"You both are."

"Is that any way to talk to the man who is going to give you a chance to prove who's best?" Thorne asked, his voice a velvet whisper of huskiness.

His alluring voice disturbed her almost as much as what he said. "You mean to marry me?"

Thorne turned to leave. This time it was Alexandria who halted him. "Answer me."

He lifted her hand from his arm. "You don't have to be married to make love." Whirling, he walked leisurely to his horse.

"Do we have to kill it?"

Alexandria glanced from the two-pound trout flopping on the grassy bank to Judith's pale face. "We've already thrown back three others."

"I know." Judith twisted her hands. "But how was I to know they'd be looking at me?"

Bending, Alexandria picked up the trout, disengaged the hook from its mouth, then tossed the fish into the placid lake. "I'll let you explain to Father why he's not having trout for dinner." Alexandria stood.

"Maybe Thorne caught something," Judith said hopefully. "Let's go see."

With one hand on her wide-brimmed hat and the other holding her umbrella, Judith was off before Alexandria could stop her. Judith had such an eager look on her face, Alexandria didn't have the heart to try. However, she was slow to follow. She hated to admit it, but she was no longer sure of herself around Thorne. After he'd made his disgraceful remark to her yesterday, her body had reacted differently toward him, as if it was off balance.

A short distance away, Judith stopped. "Come on, Allie."

"Coming."

Alexandria's steps slowed ten feet from Thorne. Regardless of what she thought of his arrogant ways, there was no denying that he was a magnificent specimen of a man. Tan-colored trousers molded to his muscular thighs before disappearing into highly polished black boots. His white lawn shirt, open at the neck, fluttered in the same gentle breeze that ruffled his midnight black hair.

Bending, Alexandria pulled his fish line from the water. Holding up the flopping five-inch trout, she asked, "Were you planning on using this for bait?"

Thorne continued casting. "I don't see you with anything better."

"Because I asked her to throw them all back." Judith spread her hands a foot apart. "The last one was this long."

Finally Thorne turned. "How many did she catch?"

"Four," Judith answered. "I was hoping you'd caught something to take to Squire Carstairs. I forgot we promised."

"Give me time," Thorne told her.

"By all means. Let's go, Judith, and leave your brother to fish in peace," Alexandria said sarcastically. "Maybe he'll learn some things need skill and not force."

Thorne glanced around, his black eyes glittering. "Anytime you're ready to test your theory, Alex, I'm ready."

Throwing the fish back into the water, Alexandria turned and stalked off. Judith frowned at Thorne, then started after Alexandria.

Thorne raked a hand through his mussed hair. Why did he keep on taunting her? He had no intention of carrying out his challenge. He didn't seduce innocents, and he certainly wouldn't seduce one when he had his name on a betrothal contract. Watching the two women head further downstream, he focused his attention on the enticing sway of Alexandria's hips in her green velvet riding habit. Feeling the all-too-familiar tightening in his lower body, he turned his attention back to fishing.

It was difficult not to have a few lustful longings about a beautiful woman—especially since he knew he could slake his need on the woman in question. All he had to do was sell himself . . . just as his mother had done countless times to the highest bidder. But he'd sooner sell his soul.

The repeated peal of laughter drew Thorne from his dark musings. If Alexandria and Judith were fishing, then the trout must be as hungry as piranha and deaf as a post. Laying the rod on the grassy bank, Thorne went to investigate.

Five minutes later Thorne told himself that he shouldn't have been surprised. But he was. Gone were Alexandria's stockings, her jacket trimmed with gold braid, and the jaunty green hat with a plume. Gathered up in her hands was her riding habit skirt. Her shapely legs were bare to her knees as she frolicked in the pond. There was no other way to describe her prancing and kicking in the water to the enjoyment of Judith, who sat on the bank.

He was about to make his presence known when Alexandria pulled up her skirt to mid-thigh. Desire made him suck in his breath. Droplets of water slid down her long legs, making him wish it were his hand and lips instead. Sunlight glinted on her unbound hair, turning it into a golden halo that would never grace his pillow. She was the most desirable woman he'd ever seen, and he could never have her.

Unquenched need roughened his voice: "Get out of the water."

Alexandria whirled, lost her balance, and landed with a loud splash on her derrière in the water. *"AAhhh!"*

Thorne ignored Alexandria's language, which was better suited to the stables, and stepped into the water to help.

Alexandria pounded the water with her fists. She had wanted to show Thorne she was as capable as he in anything, and now she looked like a drowned cat. It was his fault.

"Allie, are you all right?" Judith asked, standing on the bank.

"Come on out before you upset Judith," Thorne ordered.

Anger coursed through Alexandria. She was sitting up to her bosom in water fully dressed and he was worried about upsetting Judith. She'd give him something to be worried about. Grabbing Thorne's hand, she jerked with all her strength. A small gasp escaped her: instead of Thorne falling headlong into the water, she was jerked against his wide chest.

Turquoise eyes met black ones. His arm tightened around her waist, pulling her lower body against him. She felt him everywhere. Her eyes widened in embarrassment and incredulity as her breasts swelled and her nipples hardened. Heat, unnerving and intense, rippled through her, despite the wetness of her clothes. She wanted to strike him; she wanted him to draw her closer. Flushing, she tried to twist free.

"Easy, Alex, I'm not going to hurt you," Thorne said softly, his hand gently stroking the elegant curve of her back. He continued until she stopped fighting. "Judith, please go upstream and get my jacket for Alex."

Alexandria heard Judith move away, but for some reason she couldn't take her eyes from Thorne.

Thorne saw the wild desperation in Alexandria's face, knew she didn't understand her awakening feelings for him any more than he understood his for her. "I think it's about time we came to an understanding."

"W-what kind of understanding?" Alexandria asked, her voice strange to her own ears.

Thorne felt her whispery-soft breath on his face and his lower body hardened. He sucked in his breath to gain control and instead almost lost it as he inhaled the lavender scent clinging to Alexandria. Unconsciously, his thumb stroked the inside of her wrist. Her pulse accelerated. With difficulty he tamped down the need surging through him and tried to forget that his little hoyden was a sensual woman waiting to be awakened. She wasn't for him.

"Why can't we be friends?" Thorne asked, his voice deep.

"I don't like you," Alexandria answered.

His lifted brow conveyed his disbelief in her words. "I thought you were too honest for deceptions, Alex."

Alexandria felt a strange fluttering in her stomach at his smile. He was aptly named the Devil's Angel. His middle finger touch the corner of her lip. Heat radiated through her body. She gasped and averted her head, but her lips parted. Her breathing deepened and roughened. She wondered if his mustache was as soft as it looked, if her touch could make him burn as his did her.

The silky texture of her skin lingered and teased his fingers. Awakening her to her own needs was easier than he'd anticipated, and it was harder on him to ignore the temptation to taste her lips and make her his. He might awaken her, but another man would satisfy those needs.

Alexandria's pink tongue circled her lip. He cursed his weakness even as his head dipped.

A man's terrified scream ripped through the air.

"Wolf!" Alexandria cried.

She shoved Thorne with all her strength and this time she was freed. Lifting her soggy skirt, she started for shore. She had taken only two steps before Thorne's hand clamped around her wrist. "Let me go! Wolf has someone trapped."

"You stay here. I'll see who it is."

"And then what?" Fear glittered in her eyes. "If it's a poacher, he may have a gun."

The man let out another chilling scream.

Thorne ignored Alexandria's frantic tugging and looked toward his sister, who was hurrying back to them empty-handed. "Judith, stay there until I come for you," he yelled. To Alexandria, he said, "Get your boots and jacket on and let's go."

Realizing arguing was useless, Alexandria did as directed. Finished pulling on her boots she glanced up to see Thorne staring at her stocking-clad legs. Their gazes met. Despite her wet clothes, she felt hot and flushed. Trembling fingers pushed her skirt down. Standing, she tugged on her jacket.

As soon as the task was completed, unrelenting fingers dug into her velvet-covered arm. She welcomed the distraction. Wolf needed her. This was no time for her body to turn traitor.

"Wolf?" A yelp sent her to the wooded incline behind the pond and to her right.

A few minutes later they broke into a clearing and saw Wolf with his hackles raised, his teeth bared. His quarry's back was pressed against a tree with his grubby hands raised.

The ragged man's bleary eyes widened and filled with hope when he saw Alexandria and Thorne. "H-help me. Shoot him!"

"Stay here until I quiet Wolf." Alexandria stepped out of Thorne's hold.

Thorne raised his hand to grab her arm again only to stop short of his goal. If he touched her without her permission, Wolf would attack him, leaving her at the mercy of the other man. Feeling helpless, Thorne lowered his hand and watched Alexandria approach Wolf and his prey.

At the touch of Alexandria's hand on his head, Wolf immediately sat on his haunches, his long tongue lagging. "What are you doing on Carstairs' land?"

The terrified man looked from Alexandria to the now docile Wolf. His mouth gaped, showing stained, broken teeth.

"Why were you on Carstairs land?" Alexandria repeated. The man swallowed loudly and his prominent Adam's apple bobbed up and down. "Sit down, and don't move until I tell you. Wolf, *guard.*" Wolf surged to his feet and a low, rumbling growl sounded from deep within his throat. The man sat.

Alexandria started walking in a wide circle. Fifty feet away, she found the bloody sack she'd been searching for. Inside were three freshly skinned rabbits. Wolf pelts were even more valuable.

Sack in hand, she whirled on the stranger. "Answer me." Dread roughened her voice.

"Don't hurt m' father," cried a small, dirty boy who ran from a clump of brush directly behind Alexandria. The blade of a knife gleamed in his uplifted hand.

Wolf surged forward to intercept the new danger posed to his mistress.

Thorne ran, remembering what Alexandria had said about Wolf not obeying her if someone had something in his hand, knowing he couldn't save Alexandria from the child or the child from Wolf.

Seven

Alexandria ran toward the child. That was the only way to save him. Wolf would go for his throat. Catching the uplifted arm with one hand, she applied enough pressure for the boy to release the knife. Quickly, she circled the child's waist with her arm, spun him around, then brought her other hand up to cover his face and bent her body protectively over him. "Stay!"

Wolf was leaping for the boy when Alexandria reached the child. The command came too late. One hundred and twenty pounds landed on her back, sending her to the hard-packed ground. The frightened wail of the child rent the air as all three went down.

Wolf scrambled from Alexandria's back, then whirled. He nudged her outstretched hand with his nose. Lying facedown on the ground, she didn't move. The child frantically struggled free from beneath the still body. One look at Wolf started the boy crying again. Ignoring the wailing child, Wolf licked Alexandria's face. She remained motionless. Lifting his head, he sent up a curdling howl.

The father took one step, then another, toward his son. Thorne's hand on his bony shoulder kept him from moving closer. "If you value your life or the child's, you'll stay."

"But . . ."

Increased pressure to the man's shoulder stopped his protest. Thorne's heart beat faster at Alexandria's stillness. Inching closer, Thorne picked up the ragged child and slowly began to step backward. Wolf never took his eyes from Alexandria. Giving the child to his father, Thorne knew the hardest task was ahead of him: getting Wolf to let him touch Alexandria.

A growl stopped him ten feet away. Wolf positioned himself between Alexandria and Thorne. "Wolf, I won't hurt her."

Thorne took another step. "Remember me, Wolf. I'm the one Alex protected last week." He lifted his hands. "I won't hurt either of you."

"Thorne, please stop."

Thorne jerked in mid-stride, but he never took his eyes from Wolf's yellow ones. That Judith had followed was obvious. "I've have no choice. If the knife . . ."

Dread crawled up his spine. Without realizing it, Thorne inched closer to Alexandria. His steps faltered only slightly as Wolf crouched and growled through barely parted teeth. "I only want to help, Wolf. Alex, wake up."

"Thorne, please stop," Judith bid. "Maybe he would let me near Allie."

"I'm not going to take the chance." Palms damp, Thorne inched closer. "Alex—wake up."

Alexandria moaned: her legs moved.

The constriction in Thorne's chest eased. "Alex, are you all right? Alex?" He took another step and Wolf crouched lower, his paws digging into the ground. "Damn it, Alex, wake up and call Wolf off, before one of us gets hurt."

"I . . . I . . . thought . . . you weren't afraid of him," came the breathy retort from Alexandria.

Relief coursed through Thorne. "I'm not. But if I hurt him, we'll never be friends."

"Wolf." The animal returned to Alexandria.

Dropping to his knees beside her, Thorne gently rolled her over, removed her hand clutching her stomach, afraid of what he would see. In war he had seen many stomach wounds, all of them fatal. Her white blouse was dirty, but not bloody.

"Tell me where you're hurt. I can't see anything but dirt."

Her lids lifted. "Isn't that enough?"

Shimmering turquoise eyes glared up at him. She was all

right. Unable to help himself, he pulled her into his arms. After a second of resistance, Alexandria relaxed and he drew her closer.

"Judith, she's all right." His eyes glinted as he looked at the poacher. "For that you can count yourself lucky."

"What are you plannin' ta do ta us?" the father asked, holding the whimpering child against his chest.

"Thorne, please tell the child that no one is going to hurt his father," Alexandria whispered.

Thorne wasn't so sure. Poaching was a serious crime. Besides, the man had almost gotten his son and Alex killed. Somehow, he didn't think the squire would be so quick to forgive. Thorne knew he wasn't, but if it would make Alex rest easier . . . "Don't cry, son, no one's going to harm your father. Judith, do you think you could bring some water?"

"Of course."

The man clutched the boy tighter. "I was hungry. I didn't mean no harm ta' your lady."

Thorne ignored Alexandria's sudden tensing in his arms. "There is always work."

"I lost my job when I had ta' sta' home with my wife after she 'ad the last babe and tuk sick."

"Where are they?"

The man's thin shoulders slumped. "Both gone a month ago. Me and my boy 'ave been livin' on 'andouts since." His bony shoulders straightened. "It ain't the kind of life I want for my boy."

"If you're telling the truth, it won't be," Thorne said. "Go help with the water; and if you run, I'll hunt you down."

Nodding, the man left with his son still in his arms.

"Poor little boy."

Thorne looked down at Alexandria. She had almost been seriously injured and she still thought of others. "Death is always tragic for the children."

Alexandria fought the sudden loneliness that overcame her. "Yes, it is."

Thorne studied the tenseness in Alexandria's face and knew it had nothing to do with her injury. "Your mother died when you were young, didn't she?"

"Yes." She tried to push away and a sharp pain in her chest stopped her. "Oh."

"Lie down," Thorne ordered.

"What do you think I'm doing?" Alexandria said, fighting a sudden wave of nausea.

"I should have done this first." Long, elegant fingers began to open the buttons on her blouse.

Outrage widened her eyes. "Stop that!"

Thorne gave her glare for glare. "I'm just checking your ribs. If they're broken—"

"If they were, I wouldn't be able to take a deep breath without a great deal of pain," Alexandria said, trying to sit up and re-button her blouse, and failing both. "They're just bruised."

Knowing she was probably right, Thorne brushed her hands aside and redid the pearl buttons. "How do you know about broken ribs?"

"I run the estate."

Sitting back on his heels, Thorne studied the woman before him. Each time he was with her, a new layer was revealed. She wasn't boasting; she'd simply stated a fact. She attempted to sit up again and bit her lip. "You're not going to ask for help, are you?"

"I told you, I can take care of myself." She hooked an arm around Wolf and eased to a sitting position.

"Sometimes we all need someone, Alex, it doesn't make you any weaker for asking." He held out his hand.

Alexandria looked at Thorne's hand and for a wild moment wanted to place her hand in his larger one. That thought gave her the courage to refuse him. "I can manage, Lord Grayson."

"Pride can lead to a mighty fall, Alex. If you get sick, how do you plan to beat Billingsly, or do you have a sudden urge to visit London?"

"I never lose. I thought I told you that."

Black eyes clashed with blue-green ones. "Let's call this a compromise. I don't intend to let you walk back to the pony cart, and the only way you're going to stop me is to put Wolf on me. As satisfying as that may be, your father won't be amused. So what's it to be, Alex—a compromise, or upsetting your father?"

Her body trembled, but she didn't move. "I won't be swayed by gallantry or pretty speeches. I intend to marry no man."

"Since I'm not in the market for a wife, neither one of us has anything to fear," he said. Not taking his eyes from Alexandria, he picked her up and stood.

"One of these days that confidence is going to get you into trouble," she said, her arms slowly going around his neck.

Thorne started back to the pond, noting absently that Wolf watched him closely. "Not today, it seems. Good thing, too. I'd have hated to miss you catch the fox."

"I know you're teasing me, but it won't be so funny when I win."

"Don't take any chances, Alex," Thorne said, stepping over a log. "No man there is going to be pleased to see you win."

Alexandria jerked her head up from Thorne's chest. The abrupt movement caused pain to lace through her and Thorne almost to drop her, but she had to ask, "Then you do think I can win?"

"What I think doesn't matter," Thorne said.

"Well, I will." She lay back. "The only thing I'm worried about now is what will father say when he sees me."

Tillie opened the front door, took one look at Alexandria, her face pale, her clothes wet, filthy and disheveled, and sent a nearby maid scurrying to bring the squire from his study. "What happened?" the housekeeper asked Lord Grayson, her tone accusing.

"I think it's better if you don't know," Alexandria said, her hand pressed against her bruised chest.

"The questions can wait. Miss Carstairs needs to rest." Thorne led Alexandria past the watchful housekeeper, then stopped upon seeing a stern-faced Oliver barreling down on him.

Oliver's searching gaze took in the entire scene, including Thorne on one side of Alexandria and Wolf on the other. Judith stood quietly behind the trio. "Allie, are you all right?"

"Yes, Father."

"I'm afraid my clumsiness caused Miss Carstairs to fall into the stream. Unfortunately, she seems to have injured herself," Thorne said.

Oliver's bushy eyebrows bunched. "I'd have bet everything I own that neither you nor Allie were prone to clumsiness."

"Perhaps under ordinary circumstances, but when Wolf captured a poacher, things became rather hectic," Thorne said, noting out of the corner of his eye Alexandria's rapt attention to his words. "In trying to protect Miss Carstairs, I made her fall in the pond."

Oliver nodded. "Knowing Allie, she tried to get there first. She dislikes poachers. Where is the man?"

"Outside," Thorne said, leading Alexandria to the stairs. "I'll be happy to explain everything once Miss Carstairs is allowed to go upstairs." He stopped at the banister. "Perhaps your daughter's maid can assist her."

"I don't have one," Alexandria said, straightening. "Besides, I feel much stronger now. You can turn my arm loose."

Thorne's fingers tightened fractionally, then he gently released her. Alexandria eased away from Thorne, missing the warmth of his body already. "Thank you, Lord Grayson." She glanced behind her. "Good day, Judith. I hope our next outing will be calmer."

"Good day, Allie," Judith said softly.

Alexandria started up the stairs, Wolf beside her. On the third step, she paused and looked back. Thorne must have sensed her gaze, because he paused and looked back. For once his eyes were warm and gentle, not arrogant and aloof. The familiar fluttering sensation returned to her stomach. Thorne had lied to protect her from her father's wrath and his aunt's censure. Why had he done that? They didn't even like each other. Alexandria continued to her bedroom. The last thing she wanted was to be grateful to an unpredictable man like Lord Grayson.

"Allie, you can't leave my bedroom dressed in breeches," Judith admonished. "Besides it's after midnight."

Alexandria continued to push her long braid under her hat. In the two weeks since her accident, this was not the first time Judith had tried unsuccessfully to deter Alexandria from her goal. Judith always lost, but she never ceased trying to teach Alexandria some propriety. Tonight was no different.

Although she was delighted they shared a bedroom because the house was full of guests for the hunt, she did wish Judith wouldn't worry so much. "I'll be gone for only a minute. Excalibur is in a strange stable, and I need to make sure he's all right."

"All right! I was there when Thorne said they had to separate him from the other horses because he was acting up. I can't believe you plan to ride a stallion tomorrow in the hunt." Judith's small hands clenched her dressing gown. "I agree with Thorne. He's too dangerous and it's not ladylike."

"One thing I've never been is a lady," Alexandria said teasingly. "I appreciate your concern, but I raised and trained Excalibur since he was a colt. He'd no more harm me than I'd harm Wolf."

"A-accidents happen," Judith whispered, her eyes dark with remembered pain.

"Yes, they do, but before I learned to ride, my father made sure I knew how to fall. I intend to win that race tomorrow, and the only way I can do it riding sidesaddle is on a horse strong enough to keep the pace and well bred enough to take the jumps smoothly." Alexandria wrinkled her nose. "Can you imagine me in London with Billingsly?"

Judith finally smiled. "I must admit, he's a bit of a bore."

"More than a bit, if you ask me," Alexandria quipped, and walked toward the bedroom door. "I'll be back before you miss me."

"I still don't like it," Judith said, peeking around Alexandria's shoulders into the dimly lit hallway. "If someone sees you, your reputation will be ruined."

"No one will see me."

"Where in the hell do you think you're going?"

Alexandria's hand froze on the stable door. Peering over her shoulder, she saw Thorne with a lantern in his hand, his eyes blazing just as brightly with fury.

"I asked you a question," Thorne demanded, as he advanced on her.

Alexandria straightened. "You have no right to ask me anything."

His eyes narrowed to slits. "Who is he?"

"He who?"

"Don't play innocent with me." Thorne grabbed her arm and entered the stable. "Let's not keep him waiting. Although I should tell you that men seldom marry the women they take liberties with."

"Liberties. What—" She stopped abruptly as she recalled what Judith had said about people assuming she was going to meet a man if she were seen. "You think I'm here to meet a man?"

Thorne sent another glance around the stable. "Why else would you sneak out here?"

"If I wasn't afraid you'd drop that lantern, I'd hit you," she hissed. "Do you ever tire of insulting me? I am out here to check on my horse. Why the hell would I want to be bothered by a man?"

Despite Alexandria's language and her anger, the knot in Thorne's stomach uncurled. Looking down into her belligerent face, he wanted nothing more than to take her into his arms and kiss her until she stopped spitting like a cat and began purring like a kitten.

Seeing her sneak from the house had been so reminiscent of the times he had seen the countess, then Rachel, sneak off to meet men that he had acted without thinking. His fingers uncurled from her arm. "I apologize, but if you wish satisfaction, I have a firm grip on the lantern."

An apology from Thorne was the last thing she expected and for a moment she didn't know how to react. "It's not your fault, I guess. Judith warned me. I just wanted to make sure Excalibur was all right."

"If you discount disrupting the entire stable and scaring some of the stableboys, I guess you can say he's fine," Thorne said, leading Alexandria around a stall and further into the stable.

"He is a little temperamental."

Thorne grunted. "I'd say—"

"Thorne? Thorne, are you in here?" came a woman's hesitant voice.

Alexandria stiffened. "No wonder you were worried. You wanted me out of the way to meet her?"

"Thorne?" The voice was closer.

"Stay here and keep quiet," Thorne ordered. Not giving Alexandria a chance to argue, he retraced his steps. Lady Clarendon stood a few feet inside the stable. "What are you doing here, Rachel?"

"I wanted to talk with you." She drew back the hood of her cloak. Lustrous black curls spilled over her shoulders. "We didn't have a chance during the party earlier."

"I'm rather busy, Rachel. We'll talk tomorrow."

"We've waited too long already," Rachel cried passionately, and stepped closer to Thorne. "I didn't have a footman watch you to give up so soon. Why must you continue to punish both of us? I was wrong to marry Harold when I loved you, but my father made me. He thought you weren't going to offer."

Thorne gazed down into the beautiful face full of entreaty

and lies, and felt growing distaste. "After seeing you making love with another man, I'd have been a fool to offer."

She blanched, her eyes widening in alarm. Thorne smiled coldly. "That's right, Rachel. I followed you the night of the Crandalls' party and saw you in the gazebo."

"I only went to make you *jealous!*" she cried, her voice as desperate as her hands clutching Thorne's coat.

Calmly, he pushed her away. "And lost your virginity to a man who later bragged about it. Your father married you to the first prospect he could."

"You're cruel to bring that up." Tears sparkled on her lashes and rolled down her cheeks.

"Remember that and stay away from me."

The tears stopped as abruptly as they had begun. Her eyes turned cold. "It's your 'Miss Nobody,' isn't it?"

"Be careful what you say, Rachel."

If she heard the warning in Thorne's voice, she didn't heed it. "Everybody is laughing at the Carstairs girl behind her back. She walks like a man, and her skin is disgracefully dark. One of the other women said her hands were rough as gravel—ohhh."

Holding Rachel's arm firmly, Thorne led her to the stable door. "Goodnight, Rachel." He closed the door and turned back to the darkness of the stable. Alexandria met him halfway, her head down, her fists clenched. She looked lost and forlorn.

"Goodnight," she mumbled, her voice reed thin.

He stepped in her path. "Rachel is a spiteful shrew." He reached for Alexandria's hands. She backed up and stuck them behind her. A sheen of moisture glistened in her eyes. Thorne wanted to curse; instead, he carefully set the lamp down. "Come here, Alex."

She darted around Thorne. He caught her in two running steps. She fought and twisted, but no sound came and her silent anguish tore at his heart more than anything else. "I'm not going to let you go, so you might as well stop and listen." He forced her hands open, then pulled her to him. They touched from waist to knee.

"You are the only woman here who threatens her vain need to remain the Incomparable, so she sought to discredit you." His thumb stroked her palm. "Don't let her win, Alex. Show her who is the stronger."

"I'd like to knock her teeth in," Alexandria said, feeling exposed and raw. From other women she'd heard all the words Rachel had said, but somehow it had hurt Alexandria more knowing Thorne was hearing them.

"If it wouldn't cause a scandal, I'd let you do it." Holding her hand, he picked up her hat, then placed it on her head. "On second thought, it might be worth it."

Smiling, Alexandria allowed Thorne to lead her out of the stable, wondering if he knew he still held her hand.

The morning of the hunt dawned clear. To the barking sounds of thirty-five excited hounds, everyone assembled in front of Grayson Hall. Alexandria was among the first to mount. Excitement flowed through her. Leaning over, she patted her Arabian's sleek neck.

"Good morning."

Alexandria straightened in her saddle to see Thorne walking toward her. Despite herself, her heart fluttered. Why did he have to be so handsome? "Good morning."

His hand closed on the bridle. "Be careful today. That fool Billingsly told some of the other men about your bet, and now half of them act as if you plan to lead women in a revolt against men."

Dread darkened her eyes. "Does my father know?"

"Not yet, and I didn't tell him."

She smiled. "Thank you, Tho—Lord Grayson. He'd take me out of the race and we both know Billingsly would claim victory."

Thorne nodded. "Just watch yourself. I'd hate to have to bust a few heads over this. You and your father are my guests."

Alexandria's excitement soared. No matter what, Thorne wasn't ashamed of her. "I'll be careful, but I intend to win."

The horn blew to assemble them. "Take care of her, you big brute, or I'll make a gelding out of you." Excalibur blew threw his nostrils and turned unflinching brown eyes on Thorne.

Alexandria laughed. "You can't scare him, Thorne, his blood-line is longer and better than yours."

Thorne's face became shadowed. "Anyone's would be better than mine." Turning, he walked away.

Alexandria opened her mouth to call Thorne back, but he was already mounting. Excalibur's ancestors had been bred for kings by kings, his bloodline kept as pure as theirs. Thorne knew that. She had meant it only as a jest. Why had he taken offense?

"Thorne is sensitive about his family, but even his is better than yours."

Alexandria slowly turned to see Lady Clarendon sitting imposingly on a bay mare. Granted, she was a beautiful woman in a blue riding habit a shade darker than her eyes, but she was also one of the most spiteful women Alexandria had ever met.

"Were you always this mean, or did you get this way after Thorne walked away from you?" Alexandria asked.

Lady Clarendon sucked in her breath. "I left him."

"We both know differently." Alexandria tilted her head to one side. "Thorne is no fool."

Lady Clarendon's hands tightened on the reins and her mare sidestepped nervously. "You have no right to call him by his first name."

"Wouldn't you be surprised if you knew what rights I have concerning Thorne?" Alexandria said, and watched the other woman's face turn purple with rage.

"To the fox."

Touching the stallion in the flank, Alexandria rode away. Going through the gate with the field of thirty riders, she cursed her impetuous tongue. She hadn't meant to say that, but she had wanted to pay Rachel back for last night. Alexandria had no intention of turning her budding friendship with Thorne into anything deeper. She urged the stallion into a gallop.

Fifteen minutes into the chase, she learned Thorne's warning was justified. Although there were five other women riding, her horse was the only one the male riders "accidentally" bumped into. She simply controlled her Arabian. In each case, however, it wasn't long before Thorne appeared and spoke to the man. Soon she wasn't being crowded. As she nodded her thanks to Thorne, he tipped his hat.

The sun soared higher in the sky and burned off the early-morning fog, yet the dogs had yet to catch the fox's scent. Alexandria was beginning to feel the effect of riding sidesaddle. Each time her determination slipped, she'd look into the smug face of one of the men who'd bumped into her and her resolve would strengthen.

Thirty minutes later, the dogs set up a terrible racket. The fox! Riders threw off their weariness and raced on. In front were Thorne, the Master of the Hounds, and Lord Billingsly. They veered to the left, away from a five-foot post fence to an open gate. The dogs continued toward the fence. Alexandria didn't hesitate. She followed the dogs. Never before had she attempted such a height on a sidesaddle and it would be risky, but it was the only way to reach the fox first.

"Come on, boy." Excalibur took the fence easily, but on landing, Alexandria had to scramble to right herself and stay in the saddle. Directly ahead, the dogs were clumped together, barking and digging.

The fox had gone to ground.

Dismounting, Alexandria waded into the pack of dogs and tried to scatter them. She was ignored. They had been bred to find, then kill the fox, and no one except the kennel master could control them.

A wolf's howl rent the air. On a rise Alexandria saw Wolf. He howled again, then charged for the dogs. "No, Wolf," she cried. Wolf kept coming until he was within twenty feet of the dogs, then veered sharply. One dog, then another, caught his scent, until they all were racing after him. Alexandria turned to mount until she heard Wolf's howl. He was having fun. Smiling, she ran over to the burrow.

She had just hunkered down on her knees when the fox stuck his head out. She grabbed. The young cub twisted and scratched, but Alexandria held on. "No you don't. I caught you fair."

Behind her, she heard the other riders approach and the faint yelp of the hound. Wrapping the cub with the tail of her skirt, she used a fallen tree trunk to mount, then put her skirt back in place.

"What took you so long, gentlemen?"

Thorne looked at Alexandria's hat and clothes askew and wanted to wring her neck. There was only one way she could have reached the fox first. "I thought I told you to be careful."

"If I had, I wouldn't have won," she said, holding up the squirming fox. "Lord Billingsly, you can deliver Shadow Dancer to me next week."

"Surely you knew I was just teasing you," Billingsly said.

"That's not what you were saying last evening, Billingsly," Thorne reminded him. "If you refuse to honor your wager, you'll become a laughingstock!"

Billingsly looked around at the others there and knew Thorne spoke the truth. "The horse will be delivered to you next week," he said grudgingly.

"I declare Miss Carstairs the winner," Thorne said. "The only thing is what do you plan to do with your prize."

"Turn him loose, once the hounds are back in the kennel of course," Alexandria said. "After all, I owe this fellow a lot of thanks."

Lady Clarendon approached and urged her horse beside Thorne. Her smile turned to fury when she saw Alexandria holding the fox. "She couldn't have won. She must have had the animal hidden."

Alexandria held her temper with difficulty. "If you'd get off your horse, Lady Clarendon, you'd see where the dogs were digging in the fox's burrow. I followed them over the fence and reached here first."

Lady Clarendon looked around at the milling riders and laughed. "Surely you don't expect anyone to believe such a preposterous lie!"

"Enough of this," Thorne said. "I've see Miss Carstairs' riding skills, and she is quite capable of taking such a jump. She won." His hard gaze touched everyone there. "No guest in my house is insulted. Is that understood?"

Lady Clarendon laid her hand on his arm. "Whatever you say, Lord Grayson."

Thorne moved his arm, dislodging her hand. "Call your dogs, Johnson, and let's get home." Wheeling his horse, Thorne started back, the others following.

Alexandria watched them leave and her fury grew toward the spiteful creature. How dared she call her a liar and a cheat! Then, simpering and touching Thorne as if he were hers. What had he ever seen in the woman? Well, she was going to show them all. She wanted no doubt that she'd won fairly.

Catching up with the Master of the Hunt, Alexandria thrust the fox into the startled man's hands. "Take care of my fox. Lady Clarendon," she yelled, and waited until all heads had turned toward her. "Now we'll see who's the liar." Wheeling Excalibur, Alexandria raced toward the disputed fence.

"Miss Carstairs," Thorne shouted, but he knew it was useless. Whirling his mount, he started after her.

Twenty feet from the fence, Excalibur shied as a rabbit ran from his hiding place. The stallion lost his stride and turned aside. Alexandria pulled him back using all the strength in her slim arms. He obeyed, but they had lost their momentum. All she could do was hope they had enough speed and power to clear the fence.

Perspiration beaded on Alex's brow as the horse left the ground. Her breath caught and held, her ears alert for the sound of the horse's legs against the top rail. There was only the sound of her own heartbeat. Then, his powerful hooves came down on the other side. She slipped in the saddle and grabbed his silky mane to remain seated.

Thorne was by her side almost immediately. Dismounting, he pulled her from the saddle. "You little fool! You could have gotten yourself killed!"

Grinning, Alexandria ignored his angry face. "I think I'm beginning to learn that your growl, like Wolf's, doesn't always carry a bite."

Thorne blinked. She wasn't intimidated by him. One look usually sent most women running. He knew if she could read his thoughts, she would. It was becoming harder and harder to remember the reason she couldn't be his. At the moment, he wanted nothing more than to drag her into his arms to keep her safe, then make love to her until neither of them could lift their head. "Get on your horse."

Alexandria lightly touched his rigid shoulders. "If I hadn't taken the jump again, no one would have believed me."

"The ones worthwhile would have; the rest don't matter. Nothing is worth risking your life for. You're not invincible, Alex, and it's time you understood that. Let's go."

Alexandria stepped into his hand and mounted. In silence they rode back to Thorne's house. Winning didn't matter anymore. She realized that she wanted Thorne's approval, and somehow she had lost it.

Eight

"Close the ledgers, Alexandria, I wish to speak with you," Squire Carstairs said, as he entered the study.

Doing as her father had bidden, Alexandria watched him walk to the open double door and look out, his hands clasped behind his back, a sheet of paper held tightly in his fist. He was angry with her. Ever since the fox hunt a week ago there seemed little that she could do to please him.

Somehow, her mother's older sisters, Beatrice and Helen, had heard about what had happened and had promptly arrived to tell her father again how he'd failed in rearing Alexandria and that she and her father were both a disgrace to the family. They took special exception to her clothes and to her being called "Allie."

By the time her aunts left two hours later, her father had sent for a seamstress and ordered all her clothes to be given to the poor. That done, he assembled the household staff and told them to address her as "Miss Carstairs" from that moment on. She had never seen him so upset by his sisters-in-law. At another time Alexandria and her father might have laughed at Beatrice and Helen, but her father was strongly feeling the weight of his responsibility toward his daughter.

The next night, Lord Wilson came to dinner and the next as well. His nasal voice and his clammy hands made Alex shudder, but apparently her father liked the man. Her time was running out to choose a husband and there was nothing she could do to save herself. Thorne certainly showed no sign of offering for her.

She hadn't seen or spoken to him after the night of the hunt ball, when he had formally presented himself before her to lead her to the dance floor. When she had refused, as she had all other offers, he had stated it was tradition for the winner to dance. He held her in his arms as if she were a life-sized doll, his displeasure with his duty evident.

"In my hand is a letter from Beatrice suggesting I send you to them for instructions in becoming a lady. A lady!" he shouted, as he turned to face her, his face ruddy. "She also hints that her husband's cousin, Lord Mauldin, would be amicable to having you for a wife."

Alexandria rushed to her father. "You can't! Lord Mauldin is a cruel man much like my aunt's husband. He has already buried two wives because of his abuse. All he cares about is the dowry I'd bring."

"Don't you think I know that? But the fact remains that you *must* have a husband. I told you, Alexandria, your aunts will do everything they can to get your inheritance. Their husbands might have bluer blood than I, but their pockets are tattered. I'll not have anyone shame the memory of my dear Elizabeth. You will act like a lady, and you'll marry someone of importance. If you can't choose, I'll choose *for* you."

She paled and staggered back. "Father, no!"

"I leave for London this morning. I shall return at the end of the week. You have until then to name your future husband. Think carefully, Alexandria, because if you don't choose, I shall."

She swallowed a lump of growing fear. "Has Thorne, I mean, Lord Grayson, indicated that he might ask for my hand?"

Her father's features hardened. "No."

Alexandria didn't understand her small stab of disappointment, but her father wasn't finished.

"However, Lord Wilson, among others, has asked to be given permission to call on you. I thought to have you get to know each other slowly, but after this letter from your aunt, we must proceed with all due haste. You have five days." He strode from the room.

Alexandria closed her eyes. "This can not be happening to me. Father loves me." Her eyes opened and she glanced around the silent room. Her father loved her, but he had never gone back on his word. She knew with a chilling certainty that he would do exactly as he'd said because he did love her. This was one time that she was not going to be able to talk him out of what he wanted. Yet there had to be some way out of her problem. She needed to think. Her pink organza dress rustled as she ran from the study.

"Nora, I need your help," Alexandria told the young woman dusting a lamp on a hall table. Grabbing the startled woman's hand, Alexandria continued up the stairs. Inside her room, Alexandria presented her back to the servant. "Unbutton me, quickly. Then, go tell Kent to saddle Excalibur for me."

"Miss All . . . Miss Carstairs, you can't . . . I, er, mean you, er . . . shall I lay out your riding habit?"

"Since my father had my breeches burned, there is nothing else I can wear."

Nora quickly began to work on the twenty-eight buttons in Alexandria's dress. "I meant no harm, but the squire did threaten to fire us all if you left the house in breeches again."

"I heard him, Nora, and I'm sorry. I didn't mean to involve the house staff in my problems. I am just as confused as you about the changes going on."

"Pardon me for saying so, but marriage ain't so bad, if you find the right man."

Nora had married one of the footmen in the past month, and she now spouted off to anyone who stood still long enough to listen about the joys of married life. Nora had never traveled more than twenty miles from the thatched-roof house on the estate where she was born, and neither had her husband. They were both kind people who were immensely well suited for each other.

"Ah, but that is the problem, Nora. How does a woman find the right man?"

An hour later Alex sat by her pond, no closer to the answer to her question. She admitted that if she'd had the answer, she still wouldn't want a husband. If she'd ever been in doubt, the married couples at the hunt had made them fade. Fidelity was not a common trait among the *ton*. Husbands and wives freely chose other mates, and everyone acted as if it was expected.

If they had married for love, they had long since forgotten. They stayed together because to do otherwise would cause a scandal. Any woman brave or foolish enough to petition for divorce in the secular courts would be ostracized and would possibly lose her children. Once again, the man, no matter what his misdeeds, was always in the right.

If she married, it would be to a man who loved and cherished her—and appreciated her intelligence. Yet did such a man exist?

A slow smile formed on her face. Her father had told her to choose her future husband; he hadn't mentioned a wedding date. All she had to do was get a man to pretend he wanted to marry her, a man of social position who would appease her father. Thorne's face materialized.

Despite their differences, she trusted him. Then, there was the marriage contract. Thorne was the perfect choice. He might still be angry with her, but he had been angry with her before. He obviously didn't want to marry her, and she didn't want to marry him. The ruse would harm no one, and it would gain her some time. Getting up, she dusted off her skirt and mounted.

She had chosen.

Alexandria was sure of herself until she stood before Thorne. Lean, rugged, and handsome, he exuded a strength that somehow soothed and irritated her. He wore an aura of power and assurance as effortlessly as he wore his brown riding breeches and frock coat.

Setting his book aside, he rose from his chair and came around his desk. "Alex, I'm afraid you just missed Judith. A friend of Aunt Margaret's took ill suddenly and they left for London yesterday."

Hearing her name on his lips somehow boosted her courage. "I know, she sent me a note." Alexandria took a deep breath. "I came to see you."

Dark eyebrows climbed over fathomless black eyes.

"May I be seated?" Alexandria asked.

"Forgive me." Indicating a seat in front of the desk, Thorne folded his arms across his chest and leaned against the desk.

"I know we haven't always gotten along very well, but I need your help."

"In what way?"

She moistened her lips and blurted, "I want you to agree to the betrothal contract."

"What?" His hands snapped to his sides.

Not liking Thorne towering over her, she stood and moved out of his reach. "If you don't, Father is going to give me to Lord Wilson."

Thorne opened his mouth to tell her the squire couldn't because of their betrothal contract, then remembered that he definitely could, and at the same time ask Thorne for a quarter of a million pounds. "What makes you think your father is going to give you to Lord Wilson?"

Reassured that he at least had not said no, Alexandria relaxed and explained. "For the past two nights he has been to dinner, and this morning Father received a note from my aunt regarding another potential suitor." She stopped and looked at Thorne. "My father has given me until he returns from London to choose. If I don't, he'll choose for me. He returns in five days."

She looked so beautiful and helpless that Thorne seriously considered helping her. Then he remembered that nothing about Alex was helpless. Her win at the hunt had proved that and scared the hell out of him. He had wanted to turn her over his knee as much as he had wanted to hold her in his arms and berate her for being so reckless. Being formal with her the night of the hunt ball after the hunt was the only way to keep from doing either. "Alex, I don't want a wife."

"You won't help me?"

Exasperation roughened his voice. "Your father is only trying to scare you and probably me as well. It's just a game he's playing—you'll see."

"That's easy for you to say, but I'm the one having to watch Lord Wilson's hands."

Thorne tensed, his black eyes glittered dangerously. "Has he done anything improper?"

"Not since I threatened to sic Wolf on him."

Thorne eased back against the desk. "Perhaps I should have a talk with Wilson."

"No. Then he would wonder why. I have enough to worry about without it being known that you refuse to marry me."

Thorne almost smiled. "I believe it was you who refused first."

"That was before I saw Lord Wilson."

Thorne laughed out loud. "Alex, you certainly know how to wound a man's pride."

"Apparently not enough for you to pretend to court me." Her head fell.

"Pretend."

Her head lifted. "Didn't I mention that? Father said choose, so I figured once I chose, he'd be content and I'd be able to go back to the way I used to be." She lifted her riding skirt. "He burned my breeches."

"So I court you and you get to wear breeches again. What do I get out of pretending?"

"Anything," she said quickly.

"I think I've warned you about agreeing to something without knowing what it is."

"But you don't try to touch me the way Wilson and Billingsly do."

The wishful note in her voice twisted through him like a serrated knife. He wanted her probably worse than the others combined, but he controlled his need better. There couldn't be a courtship, pretend or otherwise. Sooner or later, he'd make her his and he'd have to marry her. That couldn't happen. He didn't plan to marry anyone he couldn't control.

"What's it to be, Lord Grayson?"

"That depends on what you're willing to give." Closing the distance between them, his finger lifted her chin as the pad of his thumb skimmed lightly across her lower lip. Her sharp intake of breath was expected, his desire to draw her into his arms was not. His hands fell.

"You have no idea of what I want or how to give it to me, Alex. I, on the other hand would be expected to stop seeing other women and devote myself to you. You probably haven't had your first kiss yet."

She hadn't, and the thought that he had judged her and found her lacking angered Alexandria as nothing else had. Grabbing the lapels of his frock coat, she stood on tiptoe and pressed her lips against his, imitating what she had seen Nora and John do.

Thorne's hand hesitated only a fraction of a second before he pulled Alexandria to him, fitting her to his hard length. He leaned his head back, away from Alex's unpracticed assault, and began to softly kiss her mouth, showing her how to be gentle. When she began to follow his lead, he began to nip her lips. He wanted more.

"Open your mouth, Alex."

She did, then jerked as Thorne's tongue touched hers. But she didn't retreat. Instead, she followed his lead. The hot glide of her tongue against his made her shiver. Without thought she pressed closer, needing more. Her arms circled his neck, drawing him closer. His hand slid up from her waist and settled on her breast and lightly squeezed.

Passion fled. The full impact of what she was doing came to her. Frantic, she pushed out of his arms, her breathing as ragged as his, her cheeks crimson.

Trembling fingers touched her kiss-swollen lips. "I . . ." With a choked cry she whirled and ran from the room.

Thorne took a step to bring her back, then stopped. What would he say? "I'm sorry?" He wasn't. "It wouldn't happen again?" It would. He had deliberately baited Alex, but he hadn't expected need to hit him so quickly or so powerfully. He had wanted, from the first moment they met, to feel her mouth on his, to unleash the wild hunger he sensed within her. Now that he had, he knew if he touched her again, they would both pay dearly for it.

Not even Wolf's yelp stopped Alexandria in her headlong flight from Thorne. She kept on riding, jumping any obstacles in her path, until Excalibur was blowing loud and hard. Reining in, she slid from the saddle. Her body still trembling, she pressed her head against his sweaty flank.

"I'm sorry. I tried to use you to run from myself and the truth. Thorne doesn't want me, and I just made an utter fool of myself. How can I face him again after acting so shamelessly?" Her hands touched her lips, felt their tenderness, and the unquenched need making her body shake.

"What am I to do?"

Wolf nudged her leg. She reached down and stroked his head. Mournful yellow eyes stared up at her. "Wouldn't it be tragic if I was stupid enough to fall in love with the Devil's Angel?"

Wolf yelped.

"Glad you agree. I'm not that stupid. I still have until Friday to think of something. Come on, let's walk Excalibur and cool him off, then after he's rested we can start home." She glanced around. "Just my luck that I raced further onto Thorne's property instead of away from it. We won't get home until dark."

Alexandria had been riding for five minutes when she heard the first rumble of thunder. Glancing up at the gray clouds racing across the darkened sky, she groaned. Within minutes she was soaked by the hard-pounding rain. Urging Excalibur faster, she leaned low over the horse's neck.

Just as they were passing a huge oak, lightning lit up the sky seconds before it struck the tree limbs directly overhead, sending a shower of sparks spilling over horse and rider. Frightened, Excalibur reared, almost sitting on his haunches. Alexandria had automatically thrown up one hand at the deafening sound and, riding sidesaddle, had no way to control the powerful Arabian.

She felt herself falling and tried to tuck her head to roll. Her booted heel caught in her habit skirt and she landed with a thud, facedown, her arms outstretched. Dazed, she tried to draw her hands under her to sit up. The cracking of the limb splitting drowned out her screams as the branch plummeted on top of her.

A wolf had been howling for the past hour. Thorne heard it, tried to ignore it, and couldn't.

"More wine, your lordship?"

"No, thank you, Benson."

"Very well, sir." The butler turned to leave.

"Benson."

"Yes, your lordship?"

"That wolf—have you ever heard one howl this long before?"

"Can't say that I have, sir. Perhaps he's caught in a trap."

"A trap." Thorne whirled from studying the relentless rain hitting the windowpanes.

"Yes, the groundskeeper reported some chickens and sheep being killed. Traps were set."

"Have the man sent to me immediately."

It wasn't long before the man entered. "You sent for me, your lordship."

"Did you set wolf traps on this property?"

The gamekeeper twisted his hat and let his gaze skirt away from Lord Grayson's. "No, but I'm going to in the morning."

Thorne relaxed against his chair. "There will be no traps, Jamison. Nor do I want you to shoot any wolves on this property. Is that clear?"

"Yes, your lordship, but if you're concerned about Wolf, Miss Allie taught him about traps already."

Thorne came out of his seat. "What?"

"Yes, sir." The man's shoulders relaxed in his ill-fitting jacket. "Wolves are territorial. Me and Miss Allie had our, er, talk, sir, about a year after she got Wolf. If there's any damage, she pays.

"You mean, he hunts on our land?"

Jamison tensed again. "I don't know, sir. No one ever seen him. I just send her a bill if anything looks suspicious, and she pays."

"If there is no trap, then why is that wolf howling?"

"Don't rightly know, sir. Maybe it lost its mate. Heard tell that they mate only once. Maybe the mate died."

Thorne ran his hand distractedly through his hair. The sound, mournful and eerie, came again. Thorne walked to the window and looked out. A black sheet of rain fell.

Alex was all right. She and Wolf were probably nice and warm and safe. But he couldn't forget the one other time he'd heard the sound and Alex had been hurt.

He turned. "Saddle my horse and one for you. We're going to investigate."

"Yes, your lordship." If Jamison hated going into a rainstorm, he wisely didn't show it.

Thorne watched the man go, then turned once again to look outside. "Be home, Alex. Be home and safe."

A short time later Thorne knew his feeling had been right. Lightning illuminated Excalibur, his head down against the driving rain. But it was Wolf, standing by the fallen tree limb, that cause Thorne's heart to stop, then pound heavily in his chest.

Dismounting, he didn't think, he just ran toward Wolf. He was on his knees, reaching under the branches trying to feel for a pulse when he heard the first growl.

"Damn it, Wolf, I don't have time for this," he said, never taking his fingertips from Alexandria's neck until he found a pulse . . . slow, but steady.

Thorne sat back on his heels. "She's alive, but I'm going to need your help to move the tree limb. Find something to use as leverage."

"But Wolf."

"If I'm not mistaken, as long as you don't get too close to Miss Carstairs, you'll be safe. We'll work from the trunk, and I'll stay closer to her. Just walk in a wide circle and come up from behind."

"I hope you're right," Jamison muttered. Tying the reins of the horses to a bush, he started to circle Thorne.

"Wolf," Thorne said. The animal didn't turn until Jamison had disappeared. "You trust me because Alex told you to once. Now you have to trust me again." He rose and pointed downward. "Stay."

Wolf growled low in his throat. He had caught Jamison's scent.

Thorne felt the gun in his pocket, then moved his hand. Wolf wasn't vicious. "Stay." He walked toward Jamison, who remained in the shadows and took the stout branch from him.

"Stay close to me. If he attacks, don't run; step behind me."

The man's eyes rounded. "Your lordship, I can't—"

"Do as I say." Thorne wedged the four-inch-thick branch midway up the fallen limb. "Grab hold, and whatever you do once it starts to move, don't let it fall."

The tree branch used for leverage crept upward. Several inches off the ground, Thorne heard the branch cracking and cursed. "Hurry!" Gritting his teeth, he pushed with all his strength. The final cracking of the branch sent terror coursing through him.

Wolf barked and Thorne looked up, fear twisting his insides.

Alex lay facedown, free of the fallen limb. Wolf stood over her, alternating licking her face and yelping. He had pulled her free.

Thorne ran to them. Taking off his coat, he wrapped Alexandria in it, then stood with her. "Hold on, Alex." Walking to his horse, he mounted awkwardly. The horse shied. "Wolf, you're scaring him."

Wolf stepped back.

"I'll be. He's almost as smart as a human."

"Tie Excalibur's reins to his saddle, then get Dr. Keller and bring him back to Grayson Hall." Wheeling, Thorne started for home at a brisk trot. He wanted to race as fast as he could, but he couldn't risk the wild ride without knowing the extent of Alexandria's injuries.

Reaching the manor, he wasn't surprised to find Excalibur had followed. Wolf materialized out of the darkness as soon as Thorne's booted foot struck the front door.

Benson opened the door. His disapproving expression changed to one of surprise as he saw his master holding something in his coat, then fear took hold as Wolf growled.

The butler's eyes bugged in his thin face. He grabbed his throat as if to protect himself.

Thorne brushed past the frightened man. "Miss Carstairs has been injured. Send the carriage for Tillie, her housekeeper, send a maid to me with one of Judith's nightdresses, have another one heat water and bring it to the gold bedroom, then have someone take care of the horses."

Elbowing open the door to the mentioned bedroom, Thorne lay Alex on the bed. Drawing his coat away, he again felt for a pulse and found it remained steady. Sitting her up, he drew off her jacket.

"Your lordship?"

Thorne heard the quaking female voice behind him. He didn't turn. "He won't hurt you. Just come around to the other side of the bed. She has to get out of these wet clothes."

A growl followed by a terrifying scream told its own story.

Thorne straightened with Alexandria's ruined riding boot in his hand: "Wolf, stop that! I can't undress her."

The butler stuck his head inside the door, followed by a bucket of water. "They are afraid of the wolf, sir."

"Everyone?"

Keeping his gaze on Wolf, Benson set a second bucket of steaming water by the first. "Yes, your lordship. That is why I brought the water. I haven't asked the stable—"

"Damn it, what good will a stableman do helping me un—" Thorne's mouth snapped shut. "Close the door and bring the physician as soon as he arrives."

"Thank you, sir."

Thorne couldn't help but hear the relief in the man's quivering voice. He threw a look at Wolf. "This is your fault." He tossed the ruined things aside and took off a stocking. "If Alex finds out I undressed her, she'll have my head."

Wolf barked.

Thorne began unbuttoning her blouse. He did reasonably well until he drew off her camisole. The sight of the creamy swell of her breasts started a deep ache in his groin. The ache worsened as he completely undressed her, then gave her a bath. By the time he'd removed the soiled counterpane, put on her night-dress, and tucked Alexandria under the covers, he ached like hell. It was relief to hear the soft knock. Now, his mind could think of something else beside lust.

"Come in."

Gray hair, a forehead, and a nose appeared until the entire face of Dr. Keller had poked around the door frame. His neck swiveled until he saw Wolf. The animal growled. The head disappeared behind a closed door.

Thorne had had enough. "Another sound out of you and I'll throw a net over you and put you in the kennel." Snatching the door open, he dragged the doctor inside the room, then slammed the door shut on the servants standing in the hall. He didn't stop until he and Dr. Keller were beside the bed.

The man kept looking over his shoulder.

"Damn it, man, where's your backbone? Miss Carstairs may be seriously injured and all you can think about is your own skin. I'll pay you double or triple."

Dr. Keller's backbone snapped ramrod-straight. "Money isn't the problem. If that animal decides to have me for a meal, he'll do it. Yes, I'm frightened, but I'm the only doctor around here. I've got two women nearing term."

Thorne plowed his hand through his hair. "I apologize, Dr. Keller. It's just—" he looked at Alexandria, touched her cheek.

Dr. Keller opened his bag and reached for his stethoscope. A strong hand stopped him from completing his task. "Wolf doesn't like anyone to touch her with something in their hands."

"Then, how am I going to listen to her lungs?"

"The old fashioned way I guess."

The doctor sighed and closed his bag. "Just keep an eye on him or you'll have to deliver two babies."

"I will." Thorne walked over to Wolf. "Be a gentleman and let him take care of Alex. I know you don't like it, but she'll be fine."

Wolf's eyes followed the movements of the man touching Alexandria, but he made no move to go near.

"Finished."

"How is she?" Thorne asked, going to the bed and unconsciously smoothing Alex's forehead.

"Slight concussion, but otherwise she seems all right. She'll be fine unless she gets lung fever. Keep her warm and quiet. If she wakes up, give her something to drink, but nothing heavy." He picked up his bag.

Thorne held out his hand. "Thank you."

"You are welcome." He shook Thorne's hand firmly, then looked at Wolf. "I had always heard he'd take a man's hand off if he got too near his mistress, but I didn't believe it. How come he trusts you?"

"Because she once told him to."

The doctor nodded. "Be glad she did."

Thorne opened the door. Milling servants parted to let the

doctor pass. For the first time Thorne noticed they held knives, clubs, guns in their hands. "Were you planning on protecting yourselves or me?"

Benson's shoulders straightened. "You, your lordship, of course."

"I told them I didn't think you'd come to harm, but we thought we'd listen and see," Jamison pointed out.

Thorne, who had never noticed the people who served him, did so for the first time. They cared about him the person. "Thank you, but Wolf won't harm me. Did someone go for Tillie."

"I'm here," said a puffing voice. "If you've touched a hair on my baby's head, you'll answer to me."

Nine

I've touched a lot more than the hairs on her head, Thorne thought. Wisely, he said, "Dr. Keller just finished his examination and Miss Carstairs is going to be fine. See for yourself." Opening the door, he stood aside. "She's in here."

Thorne and Tillie both stopped a foot inside the room.

"The wolf is in the bed," Benson whispered. "What are you going to do now, sir?"

All Thorne's good thought about his loyal servants vanished. Wolf had let him care for Alexandria because he sensed she needed help. Now Thorne didn't know how to approach the animal, who had some very sharp teeth. "Go to bed, all of you."

Closing the door, he looked at Tillie. "Well, you were so anxious to see your baby. Tell him to get down."

"How did you get her here?"

"I carried her, of course," Thorne said as if the answer were obvious.

Tillie took a step closer to the bed. "Wolf let you?"

"Yes."

"Then tell him to get down."

Thorne walked to the bed. Wolf's jaw was atop one of Alexandria's hands. "Down, Wolf." The animal didn't move. "I guess my telling you what to do is over." Gently disengaging her hand, he checked her pulse, nodded his approval, then put it under the covers. "Sorry, she has to stay warm."

"You're just like her."

Glancing up, Thorne frowned at the awe in the housekeeper's voice. "I beg your pardon."

"She mumbled to herself when she was frightened or upset, and Wolf is the one she usually mumbled to."

Somehow, Tillie's words irritated Thorne. He didn't want to be like Alexandria in any way. "I was simply trying to get Wolf to cooperate."

Tillie walked to the other side of the bed, the furthest from Wolf. "Yes, I'm quite sure it's natural for you to tell a wolf why you plan to do something." Slowly she reached out to touch Alexandria's pale face.

A low rumble from Wolf's throat vibrated against the bed.

The housekeeper looked at Thorne. "Well, tell him it's all right."

"Wolf, you know Tillie, and I told you, I'm getting tired of all this growling. Alex must have taught you some manners."

The noise stopped. Tillie touched Alexandria's face, ran her hand over the purple bruise on her head. "Is the doctor sure she'll be all right?"

"He's sure. He said to keep her warm. It's a good thing the covers are thick, or Wolf would soak the bed." He started toward the door.

"Where are you going?" Tillie asked anxiously.

"I need to change clothes."

Tillie looked from Thorne to Wolf. "Don't be long."

"I won't."

True to his word, Thorne returned shortly dressed in brown pants and a white lawn shirt. "I've prepared a room for you if you want to rest."

"I'll not leave her with you." She looked at Alexandria. "I won't ask who undressed her, since you're the only one who can get close to her. But I'm here now and I plan to stay. Don't think I missed you calling her Alex."

Thorne's bland expression didn't change. "That chaise longue should be very comfortable. I'll take the other chair."

After a final check on Alexandria, Tillie reclined in the chair

Thorne had drawn near the bed. Her eyebrows arched when he placed a blanket over her. "I don't know about the devil, but you certainly can be an angel."

"Goodnight, Tillie."

"Goodnight. But you just remember Allie might make you a real angel once she learns you undressed her." Thorne whirled. Tillie closed her eyes and said, "If she don't, the squire might."

"Why doesn't she wake up?" Thorne impatiently asked Dr. Keller the next morning.

"She's running a little fever," the doctor said. "I listened and I didn't hear anything in her lungs." He glanced over his shoulders. "How did you get him to let me listen with my stethoscope?"

"I told him to," Thorne said tightly. "You were standing here. Why is everyone asking me these idiotic questions?"

A moan from the bed drew everyone's attention.

Tillie quickly rewet the cloth she had been sponging Alexandria's forehead with and repeated the motion. "Hush, Allie. You're going to be all right." Alexandria's moan deepened and she weakly tried to push the cloth away. Predictably, Wolf jumped on the bed and showed his displeasure with white fangs.

"Down, Wolf," Thorne ordered. Taking the cloth from the motionless Tillie, he sponged Alex's forehead. "Alex, you're all right. Wolf here is making a nuisance of himself, and Excalibur is disrupting the stables again."

The thrashing stopped; Alexandria moaned once again and was silent. Thorne kept repeating the motions, unaware of the looks between Tillie and the doctor.

"I'll check on her again this evening if those babies don't decide it's time to see the world. Keep sponging her, and try to get some liquids down." Dr. Keller picked up his bag and started for the door.

"If her fever worsens?" Thorne asked.

"We'll just have to wait and see. But she is strong, and a fighter." The doctor walked from the room.

Thorne glanced up to see Tillie watching him intently. "Well, what is it now?"

"You tamed her just like she tamed Wolf." It was a statement.

"Be careful, Tillie. That tongue of yours may get you in trouble. I'm simply here to control her pet, nothing more."

"I never doubted it for a minute."

Thorne's hand tightened on the cloth. "Tillie."

"I'll go fix some nice broth in case she wakes up."

Alex didn't wake up. The chicken broth grew cold sitting on the table. Thorne stood over her bed, Wolf by his side. Hours later, Tillie was asleep.

Thorne stared out the window, trying to remember how to pray. She had to be all right. Nothing as filled with life and carefree as Alex could die.

Something wet and rough lapped across her face. Alexandria turned her head to one side and a dull ache shot through her head. She moaned.

"Alex?"

Fighting through the darkness, she opened her eyes and saw Wolf, his paws on her pillow, then lifted her gaze and saw Thorne. Puzzlement drew her brows together.

"You fell from your horse and I brought you to my house two days ago."

She looked to Wolf with his paws on the bed, then back to Thorne again. "He didn't bite you?"

Thorne felt something like happiness that Alex was concerned for him. He brushed her hair from her forehead. "No. He remembers that I helped you before."

She smiled. "I guess it's a good thing I didn't sic him on you, then."

Thorne smiled in return, his hand still on her face. "I guess it is."

"Remember me?" Tillie said from the other side of the bed. Alex flushed. "Hello, Tillie."

"It's about time you woke up," she said, brushing moisture from her eyes. "That animal of yours has been a menace."

"Wolf?"

"Who else? Growled at anything that came near you, except his lordship."

"He was only trying to protect her. Weren't you, fellow?" Thorne ran his hand across Wolf's head.

Alexandria noted the action, and somehow it didn't set right with her. "Go hunt."

Wolf didn't move. "I told you to go." His paws hit the floor and he walked to the door.

Thorne frowned at the harshness of Alexandria's voice. "If someone had watched over me the way Wolf has you, I don't think I'd be so harsh." He walked to the door. "Come on, Wolf. I'll send up the maids to assist you."

Alexandria felt her eyes mist. "I didn't mean to sound like a shrew," she mumbled, as the door closed.

"You've done it now," Tillie said.

"What are you talking about?"

"If you don't know, then I'm not going to be the one to tell you." Tillie said cryptically, and left the room.

Later in the evening a knock sounded on the door.

"Come in," Alexandria said softly.

"Wolf wanted to come back." Thorne opened the door for the animal, but obviously didn't plan to enter.

"Lord Grayson, please come in. I'm sorry about this morning. I wasn't intentionally mean to Wolf. It's just that my life has been changing so much lately. I thought I was the only one Wolf would obey. When I learned I wasn't, I felt," her shoulder shrugged, "betrayed and bereft." She looked up and tears glistened in her eyes. "Have you ever wanted something or someone that would be there just for you, no matter what?"

Thorne sat on the side of the bed and took her hands in his. "Very much."

"After my mother died, I tried to be the son Father wanted. It seemed I failed at that and at being his daughter."

Strong fingers lifted her chin. "You haven't failed. There aren't many women as strong as you, or as beautiful."

"If you think I'm beautiful, why don't you want to pretend?" she asked.

"Because before long it wouldn't be pretending?" His lips closed on hers; the kiss deepened into passion. Her arms slipped around his neck.

"Take your hand from my daughter!"

Thorne sprang from the bed to face Squire Carstairs, his hands clenched, his face flushed with rage. "It was only a kiss."

"Is that what you're calling it with my daughter in her nightdress?"

"Father, please."

"Quiet," Carstairs stormed, turning on her. "I expected better than this of you." He looked at a docile Wolf a few feet away. "Obviously Grayson's attentions were welcomed, otherwise Wolf would have attacked him."

"He didn't attack because nothing happened," Thorne explained.

"My daughter has spent two nights with you unchaperoned and I find the two of you in bed and you say nothing has happened," Oliver cried incredulously.

"Tillie was here."

"She isn't here now and I daresay there've been other times she's been absent. Deny it, if you can."

Unable to deny the charges, Thorne simply repeated, "Nothing happened."

"You expect me to believe that, after what I just saw with my own eyes?"

"Father, it's the truth."

Squire Carstairs ignored his daughter and asked Thorne, "Do you plan to honor the betrothal contract?"

Thorne refused to look at Alexandria. "No."

"You have ruined my daughter's chance for a decent match. Now you don't want her." The older man's hands clenched. "Please leave and send Tillie to me at once."

Only then did Thorne look at Alexandria. Her eyes were closed, but the tears seeped from beneath her lids. "I'm sorry, Alex." The door closed softly behind him.

"Father."

"Silence. You have done enough."

Tillie rushed into the room. "Squire—"

"I blame you for this as much as I blame them. You will go down and make the coach ready to take us home, then come back here. I will carry her downstairs."

For once, Tillie said nothing.

Squire Carstairs picked up Alexandria. For a moment he held her to him, his hold tightening, then he straightened, and for her, it was like leaning against a tree trunk: no give, no warmth.

Downstairs, the butler held the door open and Thorne walked out with them. Oliver quickly discovered he could not put her in the coach unassisted. Thorne stepped forward. One look from the squire and he stepped back.

"Henry." The footman, thin and barely eighteen, jumped from the back of the coach. "Hold her."

The young man looked startled, then did as bidden. Since she weighed almost as much as he did, he staggered. Thorne took Alex. This time it was he who glared at the squire.

"I appreciate you trying to spare my strained back, but I assure you, I'm much better," Thorne said.

Without another word, the squire got inside the coach. Thorne sat Alexandria on the other seat. For a long second their eyes locked and held. Regret mingled with tears in her shimmering eyes, tears he knew she would never have shed if she hadn't been so weak. He shouldn't have kissed her. Even as he thought the words, he remembered the sweet taste of her mouth, the softness of her body. "Goodbye, Miss Carstairs." Stepping from the carriage, he assisted Tillie inside.

"Thank you, Lord Grayson."

"The door, Henry."

The footman looked at Thorne still holding the door, then at the squire. Thorne stepped back. Henry closed the door and Oliver yelled, "Drive on." The footman jumped on just as the coach passed.

"I should have warned you, Alex, that you can't pretend with the devil."

"Lord Wilson has asked for your hand. He's coming tomorrow for dinner for my answer."

Alexandria lifted puffy, red eyes to her father. "It's yes, isn't it?"

"You only have yourself to blame," Oliver defended.

"We only shared a kiss. It was as Thorne said."

The squire's mouth tightened. "You expect me to believe that when even now you call him by his given name, as he called you?"

Alex flushed, but her gaze never wavered. "I have never lied to you."

"I've never caught you in such a position before, either," he said tightly. "But even if I were to believe you, no one else in England would. You have to be wedded before the story can circulate. I'm surprised it hasn't already."

"It's been a week. If my reputation was going to be ruined, it would be already," she said, praying she was right.

Oliver shook his graying head. "I won't take that chance. Tomorrow, when Lord Wilson comes to dine, you'll be cordial and receptive. Defy me in this and you'll wed your aunt's cousin by marriage."

Alexandria paled. "Why won't you believe me?"

"Why did you let him touch you?" her father countered.

A strange heat spread through her body. Afraid her father could see her apparent wantonness, she lowered her head.

"You've brought shame to your mother's memory, Alexandria, but by God, you'll make amends."

The library door slammed and she jerked. Unshed tears stung her eyes. Angrily she brushed them away. Tears were a waste of time. There had to be a way out. Pacing the length of the room, she could think of nothing to save her except a proposal from Thorne. He wasn't likely to ask. She couldn't blame him for not wanting to be married to her.

It appeared she did not employ loyalty. Even Wolf had deserted her. Since her accident, he had been back once, and then only for a couple of hours. Her life was changing, shifting, and things would never be the same again.

A brief knock sounded on the door before it opened. Tillie stood in the doorway. "Lady Judith to see you."

Judith's name was barely out before both women rushed to embrace. Alexandria held tightly to the smaller woman, not realizing until that moment how much she needed to see someone who didn't condemn her.

"Oh, Allie," Judith said. "Thorne said you'd been ill. Are you feeling better?"

Alexandria tensed. "Is . . . is that all he said?"

Judith's beautiful face creased into a frown. "Yes. Is something the matter?"

"No, everything is fine," Alexandria said. Obviously Thorne felt ruining her life after he'd saved it was his due. She winced inwardly at the unfairness of her thoughts.

"Forgive me for saying so, Allie, but you don't look fine." Judith turned Alexandria to her as she started to walk away. "I know we haven't known each other for long, but I consider you my friend, and I hope you consider me yours."

"I do, but—"

"No 'buts.' Tell me what's the matter. Everything seemed to have changed since we left. The servants are acting strange, and Thorne spends most of his time riding. Does your illness have something to do with Thorne?"

Alexandria bit her lower lip. "Why do you ask that?"

"Because he's changed since we left. He not as quick to laugh or to bait me. The servants scurry around him like . . . like . . ." Her hands waved in the air. "Like they're in awe of him as if he's invincible and can do the impossible."

"Like tame a wolf," Alexandria said softly, her anger at his accomplishment no longer eating at her soul.

Judith's black eyes rounded, then she caught Alexandria's hands and pulled her down on the couch. "Tell me everything."

With a heavy sigh, Alexandria did . . . at least the parts she remembered, filling in with what Tillie had told her. She finished by telling Judith about waking up and Thorne kissing her.

Instead of the condemnation she expected, Judith's eyes grew misty and wistful. "Just like in a fairy tale."

"Not quite. There is no Prince Charming for a 'happily ever after,' " Alexandria said, standing. "There'll be no happy ending. Unfortunately, my father saw us and thought the worst. Since Thorne refused to offer for me, my engagement to Lord Wilson is to be announced tomorrow night."

Judith looked stricken. "No. It can't be!" Awkwardly she came to her feet. "Thorne would never compromise a lady's honor and do nothing."

"It's not Thorne's fault. The . . . the kiss meant nothing to either of us. If my father hadn't seen us, we'd have forgotten it happened," Alexandria said, knowing she lied. Thorne might have forgotten; she never would. It was like stepping into the light after a hundred years of darkness. Light and textures teased and seduced the senses and your body ached and craved for more.

"Allie, a gentleman lives by his code no matter the circumstances," Judith said, snatching her wrist-length gloves tighter on her hands.

Alexandria didn't like the glint in her friend's eyes. "Please don't interfere. Thorne won't appreciate it, and he might think I put you up to it." She tried to smile and failed miserably. "Besides, I can always run off and live in the woods with Wolf."

"No, you won't. You love your father too much to do anything to disgrace him," Judith said with certainty.

"Thank you for believing me."

"You're too straightforward and honorable to lie. Now, I must return home," Judith said, going to the door and opening it. "Aunt Margaret is taking a nap, and Thorne is out riding again."

Now it was Alexandria's turn to appear surprised. "You came alone?"

"My maid is waiting in the carriage. I have two footmen, an outrider, and the driver." She laughed. "That should satisfy my aunt. Have heart. Some of us have to wait longer for our Prince Charming than others." Squeezing Alexandria's hands lightly, she left.

"I'm afraid mine won't be in this lifetime," Alexandria said softly to herself. This time when the tears came, she had no hope within her to stop them.

"Thorne Graham Blakemore, you're a cad. An out-and-out bounder. You should be called out. Drawn and quart—"

"Judith, I think I get the gist of your displeasure," Thorne said, his feet propped up on a hassock as he sipped his port.

"Obviously not enough for you to do the gentlemanly thing and offer for Allie," Judith said, glaring down at her brother.

"I have done nothing that warrants such a drastic measure." He lifted the glass toward his mouth. Judith snatched it from his hand. He arched a brow. "If you wanted a glass, why didn't you say so?"

"Oh. You make me want to stamp my foot. You ruined my best friend and all you can do is sit there and make jokes."

Black Hessians hit the floor. "I assure you, putting my name and 'matrimony' in the same sentence is not a joking matter."

"Thorne, she'll have to marry Lord Wilson." Judith shuddered. "Didn't you see the way he looked at her at the hunt? His eyes were so . . . daring. I'm not sure the man is well balanced."

Thorne, who understood the lustful gleam in Wilson's eyes, scowled and came to his feet. "Carstairs is bluffing. He wouldn't give Alex to someone like Wilson."

"Are you so sure of yourself that you'll let Allie be punished for something you both did?" Judith asked softly. "I thought you were a better gentleman . . . no, a better man than that. I guess I was wrong. I guess the Grayson family's honor has been found lacking once again." She sat the glass on the table.

Thorne jerked around, his gaze hard and cutting. "You don't know what you're saying, Judith."

"Unfortunately, I do. You see, I know why you were racing away from the house on your horse the day I was hurt. I . . . I also saw Mother and her friend in the library."

"Judith, don't."

As if it had been held too long, she continued. "I thought he was hurting her, but I was too afraid to move from my hiding place behind the desk. I'd been playing with my dolls. Then you came in and I knew what they were doing was wrong." She looked at him with sad eyes. "That's why I wouldn't turn around. I needed to be with you. Because I always felt safe with you. I always could count on you to do the honorable thing."

"Judith, you don't understand."

"What if I were in Allie's place and you were in her father's place, what would you have done?" She didn't wait for an answer. "We'd either be attending a wedding by now, or a funeral. The latter is more likely."

"Nothing happened," he gritted out between clenched teeth. "Carstairs is only trying to scare Alex."

"What if you're wrong, Thorne? What if Squire Carstairs is serious? Do you really want to see Allie married to someone like Wilson?" Turning, she left the room.

Long after the door closed, Thorne remained unmoved. That was his problem; he didn't want to see Alex married to anyone, including himself.

Emotions he thought long buried fought and clawed their way to the surface. He didn't want to feel any of them, but he did.

Desire, jealousy, need, and they all had one name: Alexandria
Elizabeth Carstairs. She was nothing like the woman he envi-
sioned for his countess. She'd smile sweetly in compliance, then
do as she damn well pleased. He'd never have a moment's peace.
He'd always be afraid of never fully making her his. But would
he have a moment's peace if she became Wilson's or any other
man's wife?

"It's about time you showed up."

"Good afternoon, Tillie. Please announce me," Thorne told
the older woman.

Tillie's impudent gaze swept the dark earl's rigid posture, then
she folded her thin arms across her frail chest and said, "And
what name might I use? I've heard so many in connection with
you lately."

"Whatever you wish."

"I guess it's Lord Grayson for now." She stepped aside.
"They're in the library." Opening the heavily carved door, Tillie
stepped inside to announce him, but the frigid words of her
employer stopped her.

"What the he—! Get out of my house, Grayson," Oliver ordered, his face red with anger.

Thorne glanced at Alexandria sitting in a chair, her hands
clasped in her lap, her head bowed. He never thought he'd see
her so subdued, and the thought angered him.

"I'll go as soon as I talk with Miss Carstairs."

"You have nothing to say that either of us wants to hear. Now,
leave. I should think you've caused enough of a blight on this
house's honor."

"That's why I've come. To correct the problem."

"There's only one way to correct the problem."

"I am aware of that. If I may, I'd like to talk things over with
Miss Carstairs."

"You'll talk now or take yourself off."

Thorne's gaze didn't waver. "I intend to speak with your

daughter alone. I prefer it to be with your permission. I'll do it without, if necessary."

The squire studied the implacable set of Thorne's jaw, the rigidness of his body. "You have five minutes." The door slammed behind him.

"Alex," Thorne called softly. She remained as she had been, head bowed, hands clamped, since he'd entered the room. He took a deep breath and plunged ahead. The next few minutes weren't going to be easy on either of them.

"Alex, I have a proposition for you. A bargain. I'll get you out of your predicament if you agree to marry me, produce an heir, and obey me in all things. In return, you'll act as befitting my countess. There will be no breeches or unladylike behavior. I demand loyalty and honesty. If you have any notion about being unfaithful, forget them. I do not plan to be a cuckolded husband. Well, what is your answer?"

When no answer came from her bowed head, he stepped closer until his black booted feet touched the hem of her moss green gown. "Did you hear me? I'll marry you."

Her head lifted, and instead of the gratitude shining in her eyes, Thorne saw a burning rage. Unconsciously, he stepped back. Alexandria rose regally and looked at Thorne from head to toe.

"I heard you, my lord, and you can take your proposal and go straight to hell."

Ten

Thorne blinked. He couldn't have heard what he thought he had heard. Alexandria should have been down on her hands and knees, thanking him for saving her from a perverted weakling like Wilson. Or at the very least, she should have fallen upon his neck with profuse thanks. Instead, she looked as if she wanted to punch him in the stomach again.

"Alex, perhaps you misunderstood. I said—"

"I heard your ludicrous proposal," Alexandria snapped. "I trust you heard my reply. Now, take yourself from my sight before I forget you saved my life."

Thorne didn't move. He only studied the sweeping anger in Alexandria's face, then his own anger took over. He, one of the most sought-after bachelors of the *ton,* had been turned down by an irritating hoyden masquerading as a lady. "Am I to understand that you prefer Wilson to me?"

Alexandria would have laughed if her situation hadn't been so dire. Thorne looked down his aristocratic nose at her as if she'd lost her mind. For one insane moment she allowed herself to think he might be jealous, then admitted the obvious truth. Thorne just didn't think any woman in her right mind would choose Wilson over him. He was right, of course, but she wasn't going to give him that satisfaction.

"I prefer not to get married at all," she reminded him.

"The ability to make that decision was taken from you five days ago. Now, stop acting like a spoiled child. I won't beg for your hand."

"I'm enormously pleased." She looked, with obvious disdain, from his intricately tied white cravat to his tailored frock coat and trousers emphasizing his superb build. "I would rather be shackled to Lord Wilson than to a narrow-minded aristocratic snob like you, who is arrogant enough to think he is doing me a favor by treating me as if I have no sense and no honor. What occurred the last time we met was due to my illness, not to a flaw in my character." She lifted her chin. "There will be no bargain."

She'd done it again—caught him off-guard and made him feel foolish for treating her like other women. Alex was an Original. Her standard of honor was as high as his own. She might be over exuberant at times, but he had seen at the hunt that she could hold her own with any other woman or man.

Her ability to do the unexpected, her spontaneity, was one of the reasons he didn't get tired of being around her as he did with other women. As he looked at her lush breasts rising and falling over the modestly cut bodice of her gown, his loin tightened. He wanted her. Lord help them both, he was going to have her. He'd be less than a man if he couldn't control a woman. His face softened into the smile that had helped earn him the nickname "Devil's Angel."

"Forgive me, Alex, for stating things so badly. I did not mean to imply you were dishonorable or senseless. In fact, the opposite is true. If it were not, we both know I would never have allowed Judith to associate with you."

Thorne's unexpected smile and the caressing note of his deep voice took the fight out of her. No matter how much she tried to deny it, she wanted Thorne's approval, his friendship. Neither was possible. "I accept your apology. Now, please leave." She started for the door. "My father has been upset enough lately."

Thorne matched her step for agitated step. "Then your answer is no?"

She stopped. The abrupt motion causing her skirt to swirl around Thorne's legs. "That is the only possible answer. We'd both be miserable."

"And Lord Wilson would make you enormously happy, I suppose." She blanched and looked away. Seeing her reaction, Thorne used all his bargaining skills to correct his earlier blunder. "Of course, as in any agreement, you may wish to have conditions of your own."

Alexandria looked into Thorne's handsome face, his black eyes intent, and wished for the ability to be able to sweep from the room, her nose in the air. Marrying Thorne would be disastrous. Both of them were too used to being in control. He wasn't about to relinquish that control, and neither was she. They'd clash at every turn.

However, as gratifying as leaving might be to her wounded pride, it would certainly leave her no escape from marriage to Lord Wilson. Perhaps there was a way to set Thorne back on his heels and save herself at the same time.

Tapping one slender finger on her chin, she leisurely circled Thorne and tried to keep from smiling as his body stiffened in obvious disapproval. Facing him, she said, "Are you sure you wish to hear them?"

He nodded curtly for her to proceed. "Well, then I believe I have a few. First, you are to act as a gentleman befitting your rank. Second, you are not to be unfaithful. Like you, I do not wish to be cuckolded."

Thorne stared at Alexandria a full five seconds, then burst into laughter. She had deftly turned the tables on him. With her he would never be bored.

Alexandria watched in fascination at the change laughter brought to Thorne's face. He was always handsome. Laughter added another dimension to him, making him less remote, more approachable. Her lips curved into a smile. "Does that mean you agree to my terms?"

"It does if you agree to all my terms," Thorne countered.

Laughter vanished from her face. "Could . . . could we leave out the part about an heir?"

"No," Thorne said flatly. "Despite what you may think of me, I believe in the sanctity of marriage. I need an heir. I hate to be blunt, but a celibate marriage is out of the question for me. Our time is almost up. What is your answer?"

Dread knotted her stomach. She turned away from him to hide her terror. The marriage bed was something she feared more than being subservient to a man. She still remembered the terrifying screams of one of the mares as she was impaled by a stallion to breed. She chewed her lower lip. Nora didn't seem to mind. "Do you have much experience getting heirs?"

"I have no bastards, if that's what you mean."

She flushed and shook her head. "I . . . I mean . . . experience with the . . . process."

"I know young women are told all sorts of wild stories, but you have no reason to be afraid."

She whirled. His patronizing tone irritated her. "I'm not afraid. I simply wished to know if it would take you long to get this heir you want."

Thorne's smile was slow and full of teasing sexual promise. "If it does, we'll simply have to keep on trying."

Her blue-green eyes widened.

"Your answer."

Her head lifted. Somehow, she'd endure mating with Thorne. At least she could stand for him to touch her. She barely tolerated being in the same room with Lord Wilson. "I accept the bargain."

Thorne let out a breath that he hadn't been aware he was holding. "Then let us seal the bargain with a kiss."

She quickly stepped back to avoid his hands. "That is what got us into this predicament."

"Come here, Alex." He held out his hand. "You have nothing to fear from me, and it's time you began to trust me. If we're to make the bargain work, you have to be willing to meet me halfway."

She looked into Thorne's black eyes and again felt the strange heat centering in her lower body, remembered his lips on hers and the forgetfulness that followed. She didn't want that.

"Alex, come here," Thorne gently coaxed.

Swallowing the lump of fear in her throat, she took the few steps that would bring them together and placed her hand in his. The heat of his body was unexpected and so was the trembling in her legs.

"A kiss is nothing to fear, Alex. Let me show you." Gently, he took her in his arms. His mouth brushed across her lips, teasing them apart. When he felt her body softening against his, he released her arms, then circled her waist, bringing her closer. Her breasts swelled, her nipples strained toward him. The kiss deepened until he felt his control slipping through his hands. Abruptly, he set her and temptation away.

Dazed, Alexandria slowly lifted her heavy lids, then touched her tingling lips. "Do married couples kiss often?"

Hot desire shot through Thorne. "The happy ones do."

"Shall we be one of the happy ones?" she asked, her voice breathless.

He recognized the hunger in her wide eyes and soft trembling lips, a hunger he knew he mirrored, a hunger that was becoming more difficult to control. He swore he'd never give any woman the kind of power his mother had had over his father. Something hard flashed across his face. "I don't expect happiness; contentment is enough."

Taking her arm, he went to the door and opened it. He was not surprised to find the squire standing there, nor to see Tillie several feet behind him, pretending to dust a table in the hallway.

"Squire, I have the pleasure of informing you that your daughter has done me the honor of consenting to be my wife."

Oliver's gaze slid to Alexandria's, then steadied on Thorne. "What changed your mind?"

"What does his reason matter?" Alexandria asked tightly. "It's what you wanted, isn't it? He's saving the family name— and me—from being ruined and disgraced. Now you won't have to give me to a man like Wilson."

Oliver paled visibly. "I did what I thought was best."

"Best for whom, Father?" Alexandria asked softly, the hurt visible in her voice and in her face.

"Perhaps we should discuss this in the library," Thorne suggested, reopening the door, then closing it behind them. He noted with some pleasure that although Alexandria pulled her arm from him, she remained by his side. "I think six months is long enough for the engagement. In the meantime, Alexandria can stay with my aunt and Judith while the fittings are done for her trousseau."

Alexandria stiffened. "I appreciate your kindness, Lord Grayson, but I need no assistance in such matters."

Thorne merely lifted a brow. "As you wish."

"The marriage will be in a month," Oliver stated flatly.

Both Thorne and Alexandria stared at him in amazement. Thorne was the first to recover. "Surely, you can't be serious."

"I've never been more serious about anything else in my life," Oliver said. "We have very few relatives as have you, and I see no reason to wait."

"You hate me that much?" Alexandria asked, her voice a strained whisper.

Oliver seemed to waver. "I'm doing this for your own good, Alexandria. Don't forget you made this necessary."

"How can I, when you remind me often of my sin?" She clutched her stomach. "If you'll excuse me, I think I'll go to my room. Convey my apologies to Lord Wilson."

As soon as the door closed, Thorne rounded on Oliver. "You, of all people, should know that Alexandria isn't a liar. Why are you treating her like one?"

"I don't have to explain myself to you," Oliver said.

A brief knock sounded on the door before Tillie entered. "Lord Wilson's coach just pulled up. Shall I send someone for Miss Carstairs?"

Oliver straightened his coat. "That won't be necessary, Tillie." He glanced at Thorne. "Do you wish to stay or go?"

"I'll stay. He deserves to confront the man who's marrying the woman he wanted."

Oliver nodded. "Please show Lord Wilson directly into the library."

Tillie looked at Thorne and smiled warmly. "I never doubted you for a moment." The door shut.

"What do you plan to tell Wilson?" Oliver asked.

"The truth," Thorne said, and had the satisfaction of seeing Oliver blanch.

"You can't! I'll not have Allie disgr—"

"Lord Wilson," Tillie announced.

A portly, middle-aged man stepped into the room. His whiskered face lost its smile when he saw Thorne. He glanced at Oliver, then back at Thorne. "Squire, Lord Grayson. Am I too early?"

"You're punctual, as usual," Thorne said. "I wanted to speak to you."

The man frowned. "Me?"

"Yes," Thorne said. "I don't know how to put this delicate—"

"Lord Grayson," Oliver interrupted sharply.

"I demand to know what is going on," said Lord Wilson, his beady brown eyes scurrying from Thorne to Oliver.

Thorne raised a dark eyebrow at the impudent man. "It has come to my attention that certain men might be paying too much attention to my fiancée, Miss Carstairs."

"Your *fiancée!*"

"Yes. We've been betrothed for the past ten years. Of course, she didn't know anything about the betrothal until I made my intentions known this afternoon." Thorne's smile was feral. "She led me to believe you might have aspirations in that direction. I reassured her and asked her to let me talk with you privately."

Thorne's hands on the man's shoulder tightened a fraction. Wilson winced. "I'm sure now that you know of the betrothal contract, you'll understand that Miss Carstairs is lost to you or any other man. Of course, if you wish to persist, I'll have to call you out."

Wilson staggered back until the bend of his knee caught the back of a chair and he plopped down like a sack of oats. His mouth opened and closed like a fish gasping for air on a bank before he could speak. "I . . . I didn't know . . . the squire didn't—"

"Don't blame the squire. He sought the best man for his daughter," Thorne said, and watched as the color gradually began to seep back into Wilson's face. It wouldn't do any harm to feed Wilson's inflated ego. "I hope there are no hard feelings." Thorne extended his hand.

Wilson hastily rose. "Of course. I am something of a catch. But if I had to lose, I'm glad it was to you. May I be the first to offer my congratulations?"

"Thank you," Thorne said, barely managing to keep the distaste from his face at the self-effacing man. How could Oliver have thought of marrying Alex to such a weasel? "I hope I can count on you not to mention your suit to anyone. I won't allow the slightest hint of scandal to touch my fiancée."

"Of course, of course." Lord Wilson tugged on his black cravat, completely destroying the intricately tied knot. "I'll be the soul of discretion."

"Good. Now, if you'll please excuse us, there are a great many details my future father-in-law and I still have to discuss."

Wilson backed toward the door. "Certainly. Good day."

The vibration from the closing door had barely died before Oliver said, "That was a foul thing to do."

Thorne flicked at his impeccable coat sleeve with long, elegant fingers. "I thought I handled things quite nicely."

"I mean, about threatening to tell Wilson the true reason for you marrying Alexandria," Oliver shouted.

Thorne's jaw tightened. "I *did* tell him the true reason. And if I ever hear you say differently again, I'm going to forget you're her father." Turning on his heels, Thorne strode from the room.

Learning that she was right held no satisfaction for Alexandria.

Just as she had always known, marrying into the aristocracy

instantly and irrecoverably cut her off from all she held near and dear. The servants, already in fear of her father, became even more distant after he announced her betrothal to Thorne. She had to threaten to fire every last one of them if they didn't stop bowing whenever she happened to come upon them. She wasn't a countess yet.

If that wasn't enough, some of the aristocracy who'd always stuck up their noses in the air when she walked by now came calling to pay their respects. Despite Thorne and his grandfather being estranged, the duke was a powerful man, and that power would be Thorne's one day. No one doubted that he would forgive or forget.

Then there was Lady Margaret and Judith. Alexandria had been afraid that Lady Margaret might be adamantly opposed to their marriage, but the older woman was determined to make the wedding the social event of the season in spite of the short time period. There were lists for guests, food, flowers, and travel arrangements, and always there were people coming and going.

At the end of the first week, she was restless. After the second week, she was ready to call off the wedding. She told Lady Margaret as much. She promptly attributed Alexandria's mood to wedding jitters.

At the end of the third week, she felt closed in, restless, and scared. No longer was she allowed to ride. An estate manager had been hired by her father. She had seen Wolf only twice, and then from a distance. Life for her had irrevocably changed, and there was nothing she could do about it.

"Perhaps I should have run away," she mumbled to herself, as the white satin wedding gown Judith had helped her choose was drawn upward over her head. Judith had a natural talent for the cut and style of clothes that Alexandria had no desire to emulate. "Or shoot Thorne."

"What did you say, Miss Alexandria?" Nora asked, as she carefully folded and put away the fifty-foot white lace train.

Sighing, Alexandria stepped off the small stool. "Nothing," she said, standing quietly as she was stripped of the yards and yards of white petticoats. She had tried to help once and had been sternly reprimanded by Lady Margaret. A lady did not assist in her toiletry. Judith, to Alexandria's horror, didn't even know how to comb her own hair.

"Miss Allie."

Alexandria looked around and found Tillie staring at her strangely. She was the only one brave enough to continue calling her by her nickname. "Is something the matter?"

"Not with me, but I've been calling you for over a minute and you've been staring into space and mumbling," Tillie told her.

"I'm listening now."

"Don't bite my head off. If I was the one marrying his lordship, I'd certainly be pleased."

Alexandria lifted her chin. "You're not me."

"Then I guess his lordship will have to go riding without you," Tillie said, then turned to leave.

Strong fingers caught her arm. "Thor—Lord Grayson wants to take me riding?" Alexandria cried, unable to keep the eagerness from her voice.

"What do you think I've been trying to tell you?" Tillie said. "He's downstairs, waiting."

"Oh, Tillie." Giving the housekeeper a brief hug, she ran toward her armoire and jerked open the door. "Where is my riding habit?"

"I'll get it," Tillie said. "Sit and let Nora redo your hair. You don't want to keep his lordship waiting."

Alexandria sat. Thorne was giving her a reprieve. In less than thirty minutes, she was rushing from her room, the feather in her hat swaying. Her father's stern look and Thorne's unintelligible gaze slowed her pace until she reached the bottom of the stairs, where they waited for her.

"Good afternoon, Lord Grayson."

"Good afternoon, Miss Carstairs. May I say you look lovely?"

"Thank you, your lordship, may I say you look quite fit."

He offered his arm. "Shall we go?"

"Oh, yes," Alexandria said, placing her fingertips lightly on his sleeve and looking longingly at the front door.

"Lord Grayson, I trust your groom will be with you at all times," Oliver stated.

Thorne's jaw hardened as he felt her hand clutch his arm. "I don't hold the reputation of my future wife lightly." They walked from the house.

Seeing Excalibur saddled, Alexandria gave a cry of delight and raced down the steps to hug the horse's neck. He nickered, nudging her chest. "I missed you. I don't have a carrot to give you."

"Allow me," Thorne said, handing her a carrot.

Her eyes misted. "Thank you." The stallion finished off the carrot in two greedy bites.

"Shall we go?" Thorne inquired, wondering why he had felt such joy in giving her pleasure. Cupping his hands, he helped her to mount.

"Where shall we ride?" Alexandria asked, feeling better than she had for the past three weeks.

"I thought we might go to your pond, if you don't mind."

"No," Alexandria said, and smiled. "In fact. I'll race you." With no more warning than that, she took off. Excalibur went from a standstill to a gallop in four long strides.

Thorne watched his future bride race away and saw her hat bounce up and down, then come loose. Alexandria never checked her headlong race. He took after her. Thank goodness they hadn't managed to cower her. He wanted an obedient wife, not a quaking child. Passing the hat, he leaned over and snatched it up without breaking the horse's stride. Today, he'd let her win. After they were married was soon enough to let her know who was in charge.

"I won," Alexandria cried, jumping off her horse, her face flushed, her tawny hair hanging in becoming disarray down her back.

Thorne dismounted and handed their reins to the groom who'd ridden up behind them. "Only because you cheated."

She looked affronted. "I never cheat."

Thorne grunted. Taking her hand, he started toward the pond. "My aunt and Judith informed me that you were feeling rather closed in."

She sighed deep and long. "Everything changed. Being a countess is going to be a lot more boring than I imagined."

"I wasn't aware that being married to me could be considered boring."

"It wouldn't be if I was allowed to think, dress myself, or do anything besides sit, sip tea, and listen to people who've never liked me tell me how pleased they are at our betrothal." She looked up at him. "I bet nothing in your life has changed."

Thorne chose not to comment. Everything in his life had changed. Alexandria took over most of his thinking. His nights were haunted with visions of her. He had purposely stayed away until his aunt and his sister had commented how depressed she was.

"Well, has it?" she asked, stopping on the grassy bank in front of the placid water.

"Nothing ever stays the same," he said, then gestured behind her. "Someone is here to see you."

She glanced over her shoulder. "Wolf!" Going down on bended knees, she opened her arms wide. He knocked her back on her derrière. Laughing, she hugged him. "I thought you didn't love me anymore. I'm sorry I acted so stupidly. I missed you so." She looked up at Thorne. "How did you get him to be here?"

"I didn't. Come on, our food is waiting."

She stood, still stroking Wolf's fur. "Food?"

"I thought to surprise you with a picnic." He glanced at Wolf. "If he hasn't decided to eat without us."

"Wolf is very well-mannered."

"That's debatable. Come on, I'm starving." The three of them started toward the pond.

Everything was as Thorne had left it. Spreading the blanket, he helped Alexandria to sit and placed the basket between them. Resting on his haunches near Alexandria, Wolf looked on. Alexandria realized she was hungry herself. They ate in companionable silence, both throwing Wolf bits of food.

Finished, Alexandria said, "Thank you again. This was very nice of you."

"You seem surprised to find that I can be nice."

"You must admit, it's a side of you that I haven't seen very often."

"Whose fault is that?" Thorne asked.

Alexandria had the grace to flush. "You seem to bring out the worst in me."

"That is not my intention," Thorne said, taking one of her wind-tossed curls and twirling it around his long finger.

Alexandria fidgeted on the blanket. Thorne's deep voice stroked across her nerve endings like velvet, soft and inviting. She steeled herself against succumbing. "Perhaps it's because we do not know anything about each other. You know about my family, but I know nothing about yours. Judith said your mother is in Paris. Will she be coming?"

"No," he said, his voice harsh.

"Perhaps if I wrote—"

"No." His face hardened into unrelenting ruthlessness. "You might as well know that the woman who bore me has no more love for me or Judith than she does for last season's gown. Furthermore, I don't need you interfering in my life."

For a moment, Alexandria was too stunned to respond to the savage intensity of his voice, but she had only herself to blame. Theirs wasn't to be a real marriage. Thorne only wanted her to supply an heir, not to be a part of his life. Why hadn't she remembered the bargain? "Of course. Shall we go?" Alexandria stood, her voice tight.

Thorne rose in a single graceful motion. His hand clamped on her arm before she had a chance to leave. He saw her retreating and cursed under his breath. He would not lose any more because of a woman who was better suited to the gutters than the drawing rooms. "It's best for everyone that she not come."

"I heard you the first time." She glanced at his hand on her arm.

Thorne muttered under his breath. It seemed impossible, but even in another country, Marianne continued to over-shadow his life. "I don't want us to part angry. We have enough against us."

Alexandria gave him a long, hard stare. "It's not my fault. You become annoyed at the least thing. I'm beginning to wonder if Judith imagined that you have a best friend."

Thorne almost smiled. His posture did relax. "When Stone-well's ship docks in a few weeks, I'll be happy to introduce you to him. After two years in India his enlistment is up." He smiled ruefully. "Actually, Stonewell will probably be more shocked to see that I have a wife than you'll be to see him."

She made a face. "Hard to believe a kiss could cause such a fuss."

"I find it harder to believe that we had waited that long," Thorne countered softly.

Alexandria turned away from the compelling truth in his eyes. "It's getting late, I think we should return."

"Not until I do this." With those words he leaned forward and took her lips. She stiffened, but she didn't pull away. As the kiss lengthened, she leaned into Thorne. When he lifted his head, she was surprised to find herself on the blanket again, her arms clutching his. She was even more surprised to find that she wasn't afraid.

Thorne looked into her wide, dazed eyes. Alexandria didn't know it, but she was learning to enjoy his touch. Their time spent making love would be wild and passionate. His thumb stroked her slightly swollen lower lip. She inhaled sharply.

"There are so many things to teach you," Thorne said huskily. "And I shall do them all with pleasure."

Kissing was one thing, mating quite another. She struggled to get out of his arms. "Thorne—"

"Remember the bargain, Alex. There is no going back for either of us. In one week you'll become my wife and I have every intention of sharing your bed. Often." Setting her away, he stood. "Shall we go?"

"I knew I should have run away," Alexandria mumbled.

Thorne came down on his knees so fast that Wolf jumped up, his hackles raised. Neither Alexandria nor Thorne noticed.

"Run from me and I'll find you." He gripped her chin between his thumb and forefinger. "I'll not be made the laughingstock, as my father was. Disobey me, Alex, and you'll regret it until your dying breath. Be at the church on time or suffer the consequences."

"Yes, Lord Grayson."

Thorne released her chin, then helped Alexandria to her feet. She was doing it again—smiling with her face, though her eyes promised retribution. How could he keep forgetting that she didn't scare, she simply smiled and did what she bloody well pleased? He'd be lucky if she didn't show up at the church with Wolf as the ring bearer.

Thorne's irritation hadn't abated by the time he dismounted in front of Grayson Hall. The unmarked coach in the driveway caused his jaw to tighten. He, like Alexandria, was getting tired of people telling him how pleased they were while their ears twitched for any hint of gossip. Today, however, he was in no mood to be sociable.

Benson opened the door seconds before Thorne reached the heavily carved portal. His dour face put Thorne on alert. "What is it?"

"Countess Grayson is in the study."

Rage swept through Thorne and this time he let it take over. "Where is Judith?"

"Upstairs with Lady Margaret," Benson told him. "Lady Margaret thought it best Lady Judith remain there until you came home."

Thorne nodded, then handed Benson his hat and gloves. His
booted heels pounded on the floor as he headed for the study,
already calculating how much it would take to send Marianne
back to Paris.

He opened the door. His searching gaze spotted the countess
almost at once. She sat behind his desk as if she belonged. He
made a mental note to have the chair redone. "How much will
it take this time?"

Marianne Constance Blakemore, Countess of Grayson,
slowly turned from looking out the window. Dressed in a blue-
and-white striped traveling gown, she looked every day of her
fifty-two years and then some. The slight downward tilt of her
chin could not completely hide the second chin. Skin that had
once been smooth and supple now seemed too tired to resist
gravity's pull. The woman who in her twenties and thirties could
have had her choice of men to choose from was irrevocably
gone and in her place was a woman who paid for her choices.

"You're still a nasty man, Thorne."

"I wonder why." He advanced to the desk. "Name your price,
but know this is it. I won't have my marriage disrupted nor
Judith disturbed. But of course you knew that."

Marianne smiled. "The thought had crossed my mind when
your wretched little solicitor refused an advance." She fluffed
the ruffles over the daring décolletage of her gown. "I find
myself short of funds."

"Why not let Jiles pay?"

Marianne blinked and averted her eyes. In that instance
Thorne had the answer to the question he had posed to his
solicitor. After years of using men, Marianne was now the one
being used. Disgust overrode every other emotion. She didn't
have to end up this way; she had run headlong into it, thinking
only of herself and that her beauty would last forever. Picking
up a pen, Thorne quickly dipped it into the well and wrote a
note to his solicitor.

He tossed the paper to his mother. His disgust grew when

she quickly picked it up. "This is all. I won't take care of you and your paramour."

She blanched. "You bastard."

His smile was cold as ice. "We both know that's entirely possible." Spinning on his heels, he walked to the door and opened it. "Goodbye."

Slowly she rose and crossed to him. "I wonder if you know how much I despise you?"

"I wonder if you know how much I don't care. I'll see you to the door. I wouldn't want you to make a detour."

She stuffed the note into her reticule. "Don't worry. I have no use for a crippled daughter."

Thorne's hands fisted and he looked at the woman who should have loved him, but instead hated him from his earliest memories. Even when she had hit and riled at him, he had thought it was somehow his fault. His weak father had never objected . . . not even when her wrath turned on them both.

"Your loss." Whirling, Thorne didn't stop until they were outside. His entire body stiffened as a blond man who appeared to be in his early thirties meandered slowly from the back of the house. "Is that Jiles?"

Marianne jerked the drawstrings tighter on her purse. "You don't expect me to travel alone, do you?"

Jiles approached, holding out his hand. "Good day, Lord Grayson, I'm—"

"Get the hell off my property."

Anger, hot and violent, erupted in Jiles's green eyes. His grip on his cane tightened.

Thorne looked from the man to the cane, almost wishing he'd try to use it. Jiles was the first to look away. Thorne turned to Marianne and for the first time noticed the dark spot on her cheek. Under his intense stare, she touched her face and turned away. For a moment he felt like unleashing his fury on her as much as the man she let abuse her.

"How could you let . . ." Stopping, he drew a calming breath. "Your life is your own, but if you ever bring this filth or any of your friends anywhere near Judith or my wife, I'll cut you off without anything, and damn the consequences."

"Now, see here," Jiles said hotly. "Marianne has a right to come here, to her share of—"

Thorne's fist landed with a solid whack under Jiles's jaw. He fell like a stone. Marianne swooped down upon the unconscious man like a giant bird, yelling obscenities at Thorne and trying to revive Jiles. Thorne stared at the screeching woman a long time, then calmly walked back into the house and closed the door. He only wished he could close out the past as easily. A past, no matter how hard he tried, was destined to disrupt his life.

Slowly he climbed the stairs. Judith met him on the landing. Taking her into his arms, he promised everything was fine. Yet somehow, he knew that even as he spoke the words, Marianne wasn't through disrupting their lives.

Eleven

To Thorne's immense relief, Marianne didn't show up at the small parish church for his wedding, and Alexandria did show up . . . without Wolf. The first sight of her in satin and lace, her tawny hair caught up in orange blossoms and white roses, took his breath away. As the organist began to play Mendelssohn's "Wedding March," Alexandria's chin lifted. A reverent silence followed as she slowly made her way down the aisle of the church, filled with white heather, red and white roses, orange blossoms, leaves, and berries.

For a long moment he could hardly believe the beautiful woman coming toward him would soon belong to him. She looked like a fallen angel. Then, she neared, and in her eyes he saw something he never expected to see . . . fear. No spirit, but a flesh-and-blood woman, who, despite her misgivings, kept her word with a strength and a courage he had known in few men.

Without thought, he broke tradition and went to her. Her white-gloved hand clasped in his, he led her the last few steps to the altar. To his great pride, she answered the minister in a strong, clear voice. For better or worse, they were pronounced man and wife.

After the wedding breakfast Thorne walked beside her on the front lawn of her father's estate as she accepted gifts and good wishes from the tenants and servants. He didn't know another woman in her position who'd have taken the time to show her appreciation for such an outpouring of respect and love. By the time they went inside, her arms overflowed with flowers and several footmen were equally weighed down with packages. She conducted herself with grace and ease and affection. An angel for the Devil's Angel. Only he knew her serene smile was a mask.

As the day progressed, he watched her grow paler and paler each time she glanced his way. It didn't set well with him to know that his wife obviously dreaded the coming night as much as he relished it. There was nothing he could do to quell her fears until the time came. He wasn't worried about changing her mind once they were in bed. Their few shared kisses had shown him that with patience and gentleness, she would turn to liquid fire in his arms. What worried him was what she might do afterward.

His new wife was predictable only in her unpredictability. He hadn't lied when he'd told her he believed in her honesty. But honesty alone wouldn't keep her from the unscrupulous men and women who might try to use her. The secluded life she had led in no way prepared her for the aristocracy of which she was now a part. Much too often lies and liaisons, not honesty and faithfulness, were the rule.

For the time being, he would have to keep a close watch on her. Alexandria wasn't going to be pleased to have to check all her movements with him first. She'd do everything in her power to thwart him, but he was sure he would come out the victor in any skirmish.

If she wasn't the type of wife he might have chosen, she had proved her loyalty and trustworthiness. Regardless of what her father had done, and her anger and hurt because of it, her love hadn't wavered. Yet her father's lack of trust had taken the spontaneity from her spirit. Since she was now his wife, she was now his responsibility, and thus it was his duty to make her as happy as possible.

Locating Oliver in the crowded room, Thorne started in that direction. It was time they had a talk. Accepting congratulations and good wishes, he easily moved through the milling crowd of over two hundred people. Nothing the *ton* liked better than being where a scandal might be in the making. Thus far, they had not gotten what they had hoped for.

Nodding to the men standing around Alexandria's father, Thorne said, "Oliver, I'd like a word in private with you."

If the squire heard the commanding note in his new son-in-law's voice, nothing showed in his jovial face. "Certainly." His gaze encompassed the men with him. "Please excuse us."

Moments later they were alone in the study. Thorne was the first to speak. "Now that Alex is my wife, she is also my responsibility. What concerns and affects her affects and concerns me as well. Her honor is linked to mine. Before we leave, you will apologize to her. We told you the truth."

Oliver looked at Thorne's unrelenting gaze, then walked over to the open double doors to gaze out. The spring wind brought the scent of roses. "Perhaps I acted too hastily, yet the reason behind notifying you of the betrothal was a valid one. She needed to be married, and now she is."

Something inside Thorne twisted violently. "Are you saying Alex has already been compromised in some way?"

The squire turned, his face as hard as his voice. "If you didn't touch my daughter, then no man has."

Thorne's steady glare was his answer.

Oliver nodded, his relief obvious. "Then there is still time for an annulment."

"Annulment?"

"The only reason I sought you out was because I wanted to see Alexandria safe from her malicious aunts if something happened to me before her twenty-first birthday. Now they can't touch her. If you live apart, an annulment can be secured."

"Alex is my wife," Thorne said tightly.

"In name only," Oliver reminded him. "We both know the circumstances under which you married my daughter. Despite what you may think of me, I won't have her hurt. I forced her into marriage to protect her reputation and to protect her from her greedy aunts. Now that she is Lady Grayson, no one will talk. They will be too afraid to offend you. Everything I wanted has been accomplished."

With difficulty, Thorne clamped down on the rage building within him. "Am I to understand that after everything you have put Alex and myself through, the accusations, the rushed wedding, you expect me to marry her in the morning and give her back to you this afternoon?"

"I do," Oliver answered without hesitation.

"Then you're a fool." Thorne started for the door.

Oliver was on his heels. "Just tell me one thing. Did you marry my daughter because you didn't want to pay the quarter of a million pounds a year, or did you think to gain more by the marriage?"

Never braking his reckless pace, Thorne jerked open the door and came to an abrupt halt. Alexandria, pale and shaking, stood in the doorway. Obviously, she had heard the conversation through the door. Her eyes searched his for the answer he refused to give her father.

"We're leaving," Thorne said, and grasped her arm. Not giving her a chance to answer, Thorne started for the front door. Seeing the stricken look on Alexandria's face, he whispered harshly in her ear, "Smile, damn it."

Somehow Alexandria managed to smile as Thorne rushed her past the curious guests and to the waiting carriage. The driver leaning against the crested coach, straightened to his height of six feet, took one look at Thorne's face and shoved his glass of punch into the hands of the buxom woman standing by him and opened the door.

As soon as the door banged shut, the coach lurched forward. Hands clasped tightly in her lap, Alexandria stared out the window and tried to tell herself that she didn't feel betrayed by Thorne. It didn't matter if he had married her to keep from paying the money her father spoke of or not. She had agreed to the bargain. Her fate had been sealed the moment she had been foolish enough to let Thorne kiss her.

"You have nothing to say?" Thorne asked, pulling a slipper

from beneath him and crushing it in his hand. Judith's handiwork. He'd need more than luck to make his marriage work.

"What would you have me say?" she questioned softly.

Her calm answer irritated him. He knew any other woman would have questioned him or at the very least gone into hysterics if he had dragged her past their wedding guests. As it was, within the hour, he'd be labeled either a lusty brute or an insensitive cad. The gossipmongers would have a field day and Alexandria had to know that. Yet she had not said one word to rebuke him.

Instead, his new wife simply looked out the window instead of at him. And it was all Oliver's fault.

If the squire hadn't been her father, Thorne would have called him out. Either her father thought very little of his daughter or very lowly of Thorne. Staring across at the stiff-backed composure of his wife, Thorne knew with a certainty that it was the latter. Alexandria was a woman a man could tousle at night and hold in the broad light of day. She deserved to know the truth.

"I didn't think of the betrothal contract when I asked to marry you."

"It doesn't matter." Her voice was flat, indifferent. She watched the passing countryside.

"It does to me," he said, with more force than necessary. "I don't care what your father thinks, but I don't want our marriage to begin with you thinking I married you to keep from paying the contractual agreement our fathers made. If I hadn't wanted to marry you, I would have sold everything I owned to remain free."

Finally Alexandria looked from the window, her eyes haunted. "That's just it, Thorne. By virtue of being a man, you are free. I, on the other hand, became your chattel the moment I said, 'I do.' " She looked back out the window.

Something hard flashed in Thorne's eyes, then he turned and stared out the window. Neither spoke again during the ride to Grayson Hall. As soon as the carriage rocked to a halt, Thorne stepped out to assist Alexandria.

A stunned Benson greeted them at the front door with disbelief. "Your lordship! We didn't expect you back—"

"Have someone show Lady Grayson to her room," Thorne snapped.

The butler's gaze bounced between his lord and his new lady. "I'll see to it personally." He lifted his black-coated arm toward the spiral staircase. "This way, your ladyship."

"Where is the maid assigned by my aunt for Lady Grayson?" Thorne asked impatiently, glancing around the foyer.

"At your wedding celebration, as are most of the servants. However, I'm sure once it becomes known that you have returned, they will also," Benson explained.

"I'm sure I can manage by myself until then," Alexandria said, and headed for the stairs.

"In the past, perhaps, but you are a countess now. Benson, find someone to assist my wife." Spinning on his heels, Thorne went back out the front door.

Benson looked from the retreating back of his master to the tightly set mouth of his new mistress, then momentarily glanced heavenward. "This way, Lady Grayson."

Alexandria flinched at the name, but said nothing. She had made a bargain with the Devil's Angel, and she was honor-bond to keep it.

Ten minutes after the butler left, the maid arrived. Her hair was windblown, her pink muslin dress mussed and wrinkled. On seeing her mistress still in her wedding gown, words of apology tumbled from the servant's mouth. "I'm sorry, your ladyship. I came as soon as I heard his lordship and you had left." She rushed across the room. "If you will turn around, I'll unbutton your dress. His lordship said you wanted to rest. The cook is preparing a tray."

Already it had started, Alexandria thought, as she presented her back to the flustered young woman. Thorne gave the orders and expected his wife to obey. "What is your name?"

The woman blushed and paused in pushing a satin button through a loop. "I'm sorry. Mary is my name. The head groom, Simon, is my father. I've never been a lady's maid before, but I'll serve you well, your ladyship, I promise. I know it don't look good being late the first time, but my father brought me in the wagon as soon as he heard."

Alexandria glanced over her shoulder into the worried face of her maid. "I have never been a wife or had a maid. It looks as if we both have a great deal to learn."

Night had long since fallen and Thorne had yet to come and claim his husbandly rights. Alexandria, dressed in a flowing white nightdress that revealed the slender curves of her body, waited on the far side of her room. Her ears were alert for any sound to indicate Thorne was in the connecting bedchamber. Thus far there had been no sound. She bit her lower lip. She did not know how much longer she could maintain her courage.

"Are you doing this on purpose? Why don't you come and have done with it?" Hearing the words out loud shook her already dwindling composure.

"Why did I agree to this?" For the hundredth time, she wished her mother had lived to advise her. Tillie told her the bedding hurt, but it was her duty to submit and give her husband an heir. There were three basic things wrong with Tillie's advice: unmarried and unbedded and childless, Tillie had no experience of her own, and Alexandria wasn't sure that submission was in her nature.

In the mating ritual of the animals she had seen, the female had quickly been dominated and overpowered by the male. Instinct drove the male with no thought of tenderness for the female. She might be able to get through it if Thorne showed some compassion or tenderness. Her hands clenched in the folds of her gown. The face she had seen just before he'd left her in the foyer held not one shred of compassion or tenderness.

The door across the room opened. Thorne, in a blue velvet

dressing gown, was framed in the flickering candlelight. Her throat dried, her heart thudded in her chest. Whether from fright or from the almost overpowering masculine picture he presented, she didn't know.

His eyes boldly touched her everywhere, lingering first on her barely concealed breasts, then on the dark triangle below her waist. Her body grew hot, then cold. Fighting the urge to cover herself and run from the room, Alexandria crossed to the high four-poster bed and lay down.

Walking to the bed, Thorne cursed softly under his breath. His temper had caused this. Alexandria lay like a virgin ready to be sacrificed. Her eyes were tightly shut, and so were her hands. He wanted more than a body. He wanted Alexandria to share in the passion he knew he could bring to them both.

One finger grazed her lower lip. She gasped, her lids flew upward. "We have all night." Without another word, he slid his hands under her shoulder and legs and picked her up. Her breast nudged his arm and his hands tightened. "Mary tells me that you didn't eat."

Alexandria swallowed.

"We can't have you not eating." Going through the connecting door into his room, he sat her on the blanket-covered floor in front of the fireplace filled with flickering candles. "I thought a picnic might be nice."

Curling her feet under her, Alexandria pulled her sheer robe together with one hand and accepted the plate of cold chicken with the other. "Th-thank you."

"Are you cold?"

How could she be cold with her entire body burning?

Shrugging off his robe, he draped it around her shoulders. The sight of his bare chest did nothing to stem her anxiety. Hair as black as midnight swirled in thick profusion downward to his pants. She noticed the prominent bulge and quickly jerked her gaze upward.

Thorne watched her with a stillness that unnerved and confused her. Heat flushed her cheeks. Then she felt another kind of heat. The lingering heat in his robe burned through her night-dress, and his nakedness disturbed her in ways and places she didn't want to think about.

"Aren't . . . aren't you cold?" she asked.

His questing fingers reached out and brushed a stray lock of hair away from her face. "No. Eat your dinner."

Alexandria never felt less like eating, but she picked up the chicken and began to nibble. Soon she began to enjoy the food and remembered she had been too nervous to eat all day. Trying to ignore the man mere inches away, she finished her meal, then set her plate aside. "Thank you."

"My pleasure."

Alexandria twisted on the blanket. The deep rumble, almost caressing note in his voice brought her tension back. Valiantly she sought a safe topic of conversation. "I-I hope Judith and Lady Margaret had a safe trip back to London. Judith told me that she doesn't live far from you and we can see each other every day."

"Hmmm." Thorne leaned over, picked up a lock of her thick hair, and rubbed it between thumb and forefinger.

Instead of his hand retreating, it hovered above her breast. Unobtrusively, she tried to avert her head and found to her horror that Thorne's hand followed. His knuckles brushed against her skin. Heat flared to her belly. Air hissed through her teeth. Wondering what was happening to her, she pulled his robe tighter and insinuated her hands between their bodies. Thorne smiled lazily, his eyes still on her.

"I-I haven't seen Wolf since we were at the pond. I'm worried about him."

"Don't be. I think he has a mate."

Shock straightened her spine. "A mate? He can't."

Thorne twirled her hair around his hand. "Why? It's natural for him to seek one out. Wolf is only obeying the instincts that assure his species will last."

Alexandria's lips tightened. "By dominating and hurting a female."

Thorne frowned. "Is *that* what you think about mating?"

Alexandria spat out the answer in one clipped word. *"Yes."*

"Then I shall have to show you differently." Before Alexandria had time to protest or to be frightened, Thorne leaned over, brushed his lips gently across hers, then sat back. He was pleased to see her eyes were still wary, but no fear showed in their blue-green depths.

"We'll take this only as far as you want to go. I won't force you or hurt you, but I do want you to trust me in this. You did enjoy the kisses we shared, didn't you?"

"They didn't repel me the way Lord Wilson's lips on my hand did."

Thorne lifted a heavy brow. Alexandria certainly knew how to cool a man's ardor and put him in his place. Fortunately, he knew a thing about her as well. "Well, at least we're getting someplace. I wouldn't want to frighten you."

Her head snapped back. "I'm not afraid of anything."

"I'm glad to hear that, but if you were, it would be all right. Most women fear their wedding night."

"I'm not most women." Her eyes glittered in the firelight. "I'll show you." Quickly, she brushed her lips across his. "See?"

"Good. Then we shall begin with the kisses and proceed from there." Once again he leaned forward and tasted her lips. The pressure was warm, gentle, teasing, learning the shape and texture of her mouth as she learned his. Soon she wanted a deeper union and pressed against him. This time when his tongue met hers, she tentatively responded.

His robe dropped from her shoulders, the warmth of his hands seemed to be everywhere. He encouraged her to touch him as well. Her breasts felt heavy, tight. His lips closed over one rosy tip and heat splinted through her body. A moan erupted deep in her throat. Protest stumbled and died as sweet sensations flowed through her. The touch of his hands became something she longed for and wanted, not something she feared.

His lips returned to hers again, his hands stroked her from

breast to thigh. She felt herself being lifted. Moments later she was pressed against the softness of the bed. Thorne's face filled her vision. He nudged her legs apart. For a wild moment she felt vulnerable again, but his mouth and his hands quieted her.

"I'm here, Alex. We're going through this together."

She felt the bluntness of his manhood against her and closed her eyes and concentrated on his hands which moved seductively over her belly. She jerked as his fingers slid into her femininity. His tongue matched the same erotic rhythm and resistance fled as she lifted her hips to meet his hand.

She didn't realize until it was too late that he had replaced his hand with what she feared most. By then she wanted him so badly the tightness and the dull pain seemed a small price to pay.

With exquisite gentleness, he eased into her, making them one. For one brief moment Alexandria knew he had complete control of her body, yet she didn't care, only the intense pleasure sweeping through her mattered. She rose to meet his thrusts, no longer afraid of what was happening to her because she was safe in Thorne's arms. At the shattering end, she clung to him, crying out her fulfillment. Moments later, she realized her arms were wrapped tightly around him and pushed away. She had to remember, they had a bargain, nothing more.

In a sensual haze, Thorne resisted Alexandria's attempt to separate them. Rolling over, he pulled her more securely against him and drew up the sheet. Never had he experienced a more intense union nor a more satisfying one. For the first time after making love to a woman, he had no desire to leave. Brushing his lips against her temple, he fell asleep.

Twelve

Alexandria couldn't move! Heat surrounded her. Her eyes flew open. A blue and gold brocade canopied ceiling was overhead. The events of the night came rushing back and she realized where she was and in whose bed she lay . . . worse, what she had done in that bed. Snapping her eyes shut, she tried to make the picture of her wanton display the night before in Thorne's arms go away. It would not. The image was as real as that of Thorne, his arm thrown possessively across her waist as he slept. She had to get away to think.

Slowly removing his arm, she got out of bed. The sheet slid down over her naked body. Knowing that her husband was equally unclothed, she hurried to the connecting door.

Once in her room, she quickly poured a basin of water and washed, unmindful that water pooled at her feet. It was imperative that she wash away any trace of Thorne. She might as well have been trying to wash her skin away. Each touch to her sensitive skin only made her remember his hands, his lips. Flinging the towel away, she ran to her drawer and pulled out her underclothes. She had to get away.

In less than ten minutes she was dressed in a new garnet riding habit. Opening the door, she didn't stop until she reached the stables. It took her only one look to pick out the horse she wanted to ride. She was searching for the harness room when she heard a noise behind her.

"Good morning, your ladyship," the gray-haired man said,

his tweed cap in his callused hands. "I'm Simon, the head groom. Can I do something for you?"

"Saddle this horse."

Simon glanced at the high-spirited black stallion and frowned. "El Cid doesn't have a good temper, Lady Grayson. I'm sure Lord Grayson can help you pick out another horse."

She struck her riding quirt against her billowing skirt. "I need no help in picking out a mount. Now, saddle that horse, or would you rather work someplace else?"

Her threat obtained the correct response. "Yes, Lady Grayson."

Leaving, he returned shortly. On seeing the sidesaddle, Alexandria opened her mouth to protest, then snapped it shut. Lord Grayson's wife would not ride astride. The damn bargain again. She should have shot Thorne while she'd had the chance.

As soon as the girth was tight, Alexandria stepped forward. Once in the saddle, she held out her hands for the reins. "If you please."

With obvious reluctance, he placed the leather strips in her gloved hand, but the groom's hand slid to the horse's silken mane. "If your ladyship will wait a moment, I'll saddle a horse and go with you."

"That won't be necessary. Neither will it be necessary to inform Lord Grayson that I have gone." The black Arabian pranced. Alexandria easily held the animal under control. "Now, please release my horse."

"Lady Gray—"

"You have until the count of three."

"It won't take but a moment to sad—"

Her booted heels touched the horse's flanks. El Cid answered the command and jumped forward. Instantly the groom jerked his hand away. The stallion hit his full stride thirty feet away.

Simon watched the pair, and despite his initial misgivings he had to admire the way her ladyship sat a horse. Excalibur wasn't the only stallion she could control. He did not look away until they were out of sight, then he glanced back toward the manor, hoping Lord Grayson would appear and solve his problem. No one came.

Sighing, the groom went to saddle his master's horse. Lady Grayson was going to know he informed the master and she was not going to be pleased. A spiteful mistress could make his life hell . . . if she didn't fire him. Yet something told Simon that his lordship was going to be equally displeased to learn his new bride had ridden out alone and that Simon had let her.

Thorne stretched his hand out. Instead of the velvet softness of his wife's skin, he encountered a cold sheet. He came awake in an instant and sat up. He glanced toward their connecting door. Last night's pleasure was more than he had allowed himself to expect. Perhaps the bargain wouldn't be as bad as he had thought. All he had to do was tame Alexandria's more impulsive nature and things would be fine.

Getting out of bed he started for her room, recalled that he was naked, then went to put something on. He didn't plan to keep his robe on long, but if she saw his chest and blushed, seeing him fully aroused might send her into a swoon. He grunted. On second thought, Alexandria didn't impress him as the swooning type. He pushed open the connecting door.

The room was empty. Clothes littered the floor in front of the wardrobe.

Obviously, she had dressed by herself. But why had she not called her maid and where had she gone? He dismissed the idea that she had gone back to her father. They shared too much for her to leave.

A frantic knock on his door drew his attention. Since he had left specific instructions that he not be disturbed, he had a feeling it had something to do with his missing wife. He reentered his room and said, "Come in."

Benson, Corbin, and Simon entered, each looking at the other as if gathering strength in numbers. Corbin, his valet, detached himself from the group and started laying out Thorne's riding clothes.

"If this concerns my wife, I suggest someone starts talking, and quickly," Thorne said.

Simon stepped forward. "Lady Grayson rode out on El Cid a few minutes ago." He looked at Benson, who favored the groom with a slight nod for him to continue. "She didn't want a groom."

"And you didn't insist?" Thorne thundered.

Simon didn't flinch from the hard gaze of his master. "Her ladyship isn't easily persuaded."

Knowing the man to be right, Thorne cursed under his breath and threw off his robe. "Saddle my horse."

"Montclair is waiting for you downstairs."

"You may have saved your job," Thorne said, blindly shoving his arms into the sleeves of his shirt held by Corbin. "Did she say where she was going?"

"No, your lordship."

Brushing away the valet's help with his boots, Thorne pulled them on and stood. "Lady Grayson is not to leave the estate unattended."

"If she wishes otherwise?"

"You have your orders."

Simon bowed his head in understanding. "Yes, your lordship."

Thorne was halfway out the door before he turned. "Why did you come to tell me this, knowing it might cost you your job?"

Simon looked uneasy. "Because not telling you would have displeased you more, and possibly caused harm to her ladyship. I know she's a good rider, but El Cid can be stubborn."

"In her ladyship he may have found his match." Thorne turned, and continued down the stairs. Outside he mounted and rode in the direction of her swimming pond. He wasn't worried about her handling the Arabian, she could handle anything on four legs.

What bothered him more was that she had ridden out alone. He had hoped that once they married, her independent, head-strong nature would curb itself. Obviously, he had been wrong. From the obvious reluctance of the groom, the man had held something back. Knowing Alexandria, she had probably forbidden the man to tell her husband she had left unescorted. It was a good thing the groom feared the master more than the new mistress.

A short distance from the pond Thorne leaned over and picked up a lady's riding hat. The ostrich plume lay at an odd angle. Alexandria. Urging Montclair on, he saw soon El Cid tied to a bush and peacefully munching grass. Dismounting, he walked over the short hill.

Alexandria sat quietly against the trunk of a tall oak with her arms folded across updrawn knees. She didn't appear to notice the wind tossing her tawny hair around her slumped shoulders or that she was no longer alone.

Her eyes, always so full of life, looked lost and desperate. His irritation at her abrupt departure vanished, leaving in its place an unexpected need to take the shadows from her eyes and have her smile at him again. His heels snapped a twig as he took a step toward her to accomplish just that.

Her gaze found him immediately. Eyes that moments ago were shadowed became defiant and accusing. She scrambled to her feet. "What do you want?"

He stiffened as though he had received an unexpected blow. The belligerent woman standing before him didn't need his or anyone else's reassurance. She had almost made him forget how deceitful women could be. He would not forget again.

His face settled into a mask of indifference. "To remind you of your duty and your position. You are my wife now, and therefore you must adhere to decorum. You are never to ride unescorted again."

Alexandria welcomed the curtness in Thorne's voice. If he had been gentle she might have cried out her confusion at what happened between them last night. That would have been a costly mistake. Thorne must never know his power over her. "The man who saddled my horse must have run to tell you as soon as I left. First the maid, now him. Are all your servants going to spy on me?"

His eyes hardened. "Your foolish actions this morning showed someone needs to keep an eye on you."

"I can take care of myself."

"Perhaps, but you will return with me now to Grayson Hall."

Although Thorne didn't move, Alexandria stepped back. Her involuntary response to his implied threat angered her as nothing else could. "I'm not one of your servants that you can order around. Last night I submitted to your vileness because of the bargain. Today, I want to be left alone." She turned and began to walk away.

Pure rage swept through Thorne. In three long strides he reached Alexandria. Unrelenting fingers clamped on her forearm and pulled her against his hard chest. When he spoke, his face was as cold as his voice.

"I don't take orders, Alex, I give them. Therefore, you will do as I say, when I say. You may be safe from Wilson, but not from me," Thorne said fiercely. "I rule your life now. It can be pleasant or unpleasant. Do I make myself clear?"

Knowing he wasn't going to release her, and feeling the heat of his body reach out to hers, she glanced away from his compelling maleness and said, "Yes."

He released her arms. "Good. I hope the occasion doesn't arise where we have to have this discussion again. So you know that I can be lenient, I'll give you an hour to return."

"You're too kind."

His face clouded in anger. "Keep pushing, Alex, and you're going to push me too far." Spinning on his heels, he walked to his horse and mounted. "Don't make me come after you. I might have to prove your words a lie about the hatred of my touch."

Alexandria watched Thorne ride away and felt raw fear for the first time in her life—not physical, but emotional. Even when he was threatening her, her body responded to his touch.

Nothing in her life had prepared her for something that she could not control, could not understand. Falling under the spell of the Devil's Angel would be sheer madness. Knowing his intrusion had made it impossible to find the peacefulness she'd once enjoyed at the pond, she walked toward her horse.

Untying the reins from a shrub, she glanced around, her eyes searching for Wolf. "Where are you? I need something to be as it was before." Putting two fingers together in her mouth, she blew. A shrill whistle was the result. Nothing. She whistled again. Fighting the stinging in her throat, she used a tree stump to mount.

Arriving at the stable, she dismounted and handed the reins to a stableboy, thankful that at least she didn't have to see Simon. The man was probably laughing up his sleeve.

Entering her room, she saw that her clothes had been put away, and Mary stood over a bathtub of steaming water.

"Oh, Lady Grayson," the servant said, and rushed over to Alexandria. "Forgive me for not being here to assist you this morning. I know it doesn't speak well of me to be late yesterday and this morning, but I promise to do my best."

Allowing the young woman to help her out of her jacket, Alexandria said nothing.

"I have your bath ready." Urging Alexandria to sit, Mary began to pin up her mistress's hair. "What would you like for breakfast?"

"How did you know when I would return from my ride? Have you talked with your father?" The thought that the servants were discussing her made her feel exposed.

"My father? No, my lady, he seldom comes into the house," Mary said, her nimble fingers shoving in the last hairpin. "It was his lordship. He said I was to keep everything ready for the next hour."

Thorne again. Was there nothing he did not have a say in? He wanted to rule her life as surely as he ruled the estate and the people upon it. She had little to do or say about anything.

A spurt of anger shot through her. Standing, she reached to unfasten her skirt. Mary's hands were there first.

"Did you decide about breakfast? Lord Grayson requested you join him if you returned in time."

"I have a slight headache, Mary." Alexandria stepped out of the skirt. "The cook can prepare anything for breakfast. Please bring all my meals to my room today."

"Dinner, too? The cook has prepared something special. She—"

"All my meals. Please extend my apology to the women, and my regrets to Lord Grayson." Alexandria stepped into the tub. "You may go. I'll ring if I need you."

"Shall I get a powder for your headache?"

"All I require is peace and quiet."

"Yes, your ladyship."

Alexandria slipped further down into the soothing waters of her bath. If only Thorne was as easily dismissed.

"I'll go mad if I have to do this day after day," Alexandria cried, looking about her gold and white bedchamber. Night had long since fallen and she had dismissed Mary for the evening after she'd delivered the dinner tray. During the hours of her self-imposed sanctuary, she paid dearly for her impulsiveness.

She threw a cutting look at the closed door connecting their bedchambers. In the future she must weigh her options. She was as smart as Thorne; it was about time she acted like it. She had only hurt herself with her ride this morning, as she had by refusing to go down for dinner. Thorne was free to do as he pleased. The word "free" resounded in her brain. Her eyes filled with determination. "I'll beat you yet, Thorne."

With renewed determination, Alexandria crawled into bed and gave the door one last look. She almost wished he would walk through it so that she could refuse him. He might be lord of everything else, but he was not lord of her body, and from now on she was going to stop acting like a witless ninny and prove it to him.

Alexandria awoke feeling tense and miserable. One look at the closed door didn't help her disposition. Ignoring Thorne was going to be harder than she thought. Riding had always helped her work things out in the past. It wouldn't be the same without Wolf and Excalibur, but it was all she had.

Throwing back the covers, she rang for Mary. She didn't need the girl, but it seemed important to her that she assist her. Alexandria was almost sorry she had rung for Mary when the young girl had insisted on doing her hair in an elaborate coiffure despite the fact that a hat would cover it anyway.

Impatient steps carried her to the stable. Simon appeared before she got within twenty feet of the door.

"Good morning, your ladyship. The groom and the horse Lord Grayson picked out for you will be ready shortly," he said, his gaze uncertain.

Alexandria pressed her lips together and said nothing. With obvious relief, Simon went inside the stable and returned moments later with a horse that looked as if she were better suited to a plow than to a saddle. Thorne was clearly showing that he was indeed master of his house.

Standing next to the head groom, and holding another horse, was the poacher Wolf had caught. The man looked almost as scared now as he had then. She started to ask about his little boy, then decided against it. He was a male, and males always survived.

Ignoring both men, she mounted. The slowness of her mount irritated her almost as much as the man following behind. The urge to race away lasted only as long as she remembered his son's cries for her not to hurt his father.

The child's courage had said something about the man, as had the father's fierce hold on the child. They loved each other. The need to see her own father, for him to hold her, shook her to the very core. Before she could change her mind, she turned the slow, plodding horse toward the Carstairs estate.

Joyous shouts, smiles, and waves greeted Alexandria as she rode into her father's stableyard. Throwing the reins to Peters, she dismounted and ran to see Excalibur. The Arabian nickered and tossed his magnificent head. Alexandria threw her arms around his neck and just held on.

"You still love me, don't you? You haven't changed," she said, not feeling the tears sliding down her cheek. Time passed as she just held on.

"Allie."

She whirled on hearing the familiar sound of her nickname. Her father in his dressing gown stood a few feet away. He hadn't called her "Allie" since the morning he'd discovered her and Thorne together.

"Allie, are you all right?" Oliver asked, uncertainty and longing mixing in his voice. A sob erupted from her. He opened his arms and she flew into them. "It's all right, honey. You're home now."

Alexandria's arms tightened. She needed his reassurance. She hadn't realized how much she'd missed her father until that moment.

After one last hug, Oliver pushed his daughter away. Taking a handkerchief from his pocket, he dried her face. "I bet you haven't eaten. Mrs. Swanson has probably heard the news of your arrival and is in the kitchen preparing your favorite breakfast." He laughed. "Although I hope, unlike me, she took time to get dressed first."

Alexandria finally managed a wobbly smile. "You'll never live it down if the aunts hear that you were running around in your robe."

"As you have pointed out in the past, our people are completely loyal." Circling her waist, Oliver started out of the stable. Excalibur nickered in protest. "You'll get your chance. Right now, I want my daughter to myself."

Oliver and Alexandria were a short distance from the stable

when a gray streak materialized out of nowhere. Dogs started yelping, horses neighed, chickens ran for cover. Alexandria barely had time to turn before a hundred and twenty pounds hurled itself at her. The only thing that saved her from falling was her father.

"Wolf. Oh, Wolf. I've missed you so," Alexandria cried, going down on her knees, grinning as Wolf gave her face a tongue bath. "Let me look at you." Wolf sat, his tongue wagging, his intelligent yellow eyes alert. "Obviously, you've managed well without me." The last words were shaky. "I wish I could say the same about me."

"What did you say, Allie?"

Startled, Alexandria glanced up into her father's frowning face. She realized she had spoken her doubts, as usual, to Wolf, but this time her father had heard. Trying to bring a smile to her face, she stood, her hand still stroking Wolf's fur. "Thorne says Wolf has a mate. I was simply inquiring about her." She leaned her head on her father's shoulder. "It's good to be home."

Oliver's pudgy hand tightened around her waist. "Always remember that this is your home, Allie—no matter what. Now, let's get you some breakfast."

Later that morning, Alexandria finished her third helping of ham and muffins. "I can't eat another bite, Mrs. Swanson," Alexandria told the smiling woman. "You're the best cook in the country."

Mrs. Swanson beamed with approval. "I have poached salmon for dinner, and those tarts you like so much."

"I don't know if I'll be here that long," Alexandria said.

Protests littered the dining room. Tillie had found a reason to return every few minutes, as had the butler and Nora. Her father's was the loudest.

"Nonsense. Grayson has you for the rest of your life; he can't begrudge your father one day."

"That's just it, Father. No one knows where I am," Alexandria pointed out.

"Lord Grayson is a smart man," Oliver said. "He'll figure it out."

Having Thorne come and drag her back to Grayson Hall was not something Alexandria relished. "Perhaps I should send him a note."

"All right, if it would make you feel better," Oliver said.

"It would, and thank you, Father," Alexandria said. "It appears you have a lunch guest."

"Excellent. Nora, please send Peters to me. We'll be in the library," Oliver said, rising to assist his daughter.

Smiling, Alexandria rose. Thorne couldn't object to her staying this time.

Yet as the day lengthened, Alexandria wasn't so sure about her decision. Worse, she wasn't able to relax. Perhaps her two-word note had been a bit brief. If he dared embarrass her in front of her father and staff, she'd let Wolf loose on him. She glared down at Wolf, sitting by her feet. *And you had better bite him, too.*

"Allie, why are you frowning at Wolf?"

Alexandria sat back in her chair and looked at the chess board with disinterest. "Perhaps I should have gone home."

"You sent Grayson a note."

"I know, but Thorne was rather displeased when I rode off yesterday without a groom or without telling anyone where I was going. I'm not sure a note will pacify him."

"Are you afraid of Grayson?"

Alexandria jerked her head up. "Of course not."

"Then why did you feel the need to leave Grayson's estate the morning after your marriage, and this morning, as well?" Oliver persisted.

Abruptly coming to her feet, Alexandria walked over to the open door. "I was restless."

Wolf and Oliver were right behind her. "You aren't the restless type. I demand the truth, Allie. Did I make a mistake in choosing Grayson for your husband?"

Alexandria turned, loving her father, yet not knowing how to tell him of her problem. She gave the only answer she could. "I guess I'm not cut out to be a wife. Perhaps you knew that. Perhaps that's why you had to buy me a husband."

Oliver flushed to the roots of his thinning hair. "I did no such thing! I'd give anything for you not to have heard the conversation between Grayson and myself. Betrothal contracts are not unusual; I only sought to make sure that once Thorne's father had the two hundred thousand pounds I'd lent him, neither Thorne nor his father would back out of the contract."

"Why didn't you wait and let me pick my own husband? Was I so lacking in sense that you thought I could not?"

"Never. You're the most level-headed woman I know." Sighing, Oliver walked into the gardens. "Thorne was different then. Quiet, intelligent, loyal to his family. I thought it would be a good match."

"What about my feelings?"

He turned, his eyes pleading for her understanding. "If you'd been violently opposed to the match, I'd have sought another way to protect you. But after I saw you two together . . ." He glanced away. "I assumed things would work out. Never would I have let Grayson near you if I thought he would act in a manner not befitting a gentleman. In the past he had always been careful of the reputation of young innocents."

"He hadn't changed in that respect. We shared a kiss, nothing more. However, in your need to see me wed, you married me off to a man who doesn't love me and never could," Alexandria said, defeat heavy in her voice.

"Allie, forgive me," Oliver cried. "I only wanted to keep you safe."

"I know, Father. I only wish you'd have trusted me more."

Pain whipped across his face. "I can make it up to you. To both of you. The marriage can be annulled, and—"

"There can be no annulment," she said quietly, studying the pieces on the board to hide the flush in her cheeks.

"Then you and Grayson can live apart permanently," her father persisted. "It's done all the time. You don't have to run from him each day. Think on what I'm saying."

Alexandria did think. Her father was right: she *had* been running from Thorne. No, from herself. She couldn't make herself indifferent to his touch, and she had tried to run from that. Only she couldn't run far or fast enough. It was time she faced Thorne and kept her end of the bargain. If her father realized she was running from her husband, so would everyone else. To a proud man like Thorne, that would be humiliating.

"I'm going back to Grayson Hall." Rising, she picked up her gloves and hat.

"Stay, Alexandria. Don't make a bigger mistake by going back. Grayson has served his purpose. Things can be as they were before."

Alexandria smiled sadly. "Things can never be as they were before. I made a . . . a vow." Putting her hat on her head, she tried to pin it into place. "Could you help me, Father? I lost a hat yesterday. I don't want to lose another one."

With a defeated sigh, Oliver moved to help. "Hold still," Oliver said, sticking a three-inch pin slowly through the purple velvet. "That thing could kill a person." Finished, he stepped back. "Allie, I wish things could have been different for you."

"So do I, Father. Unfortunately, neither of us counted on dealing with the Devil's Angel." She looped her arm into his, then glanced down at Wolf. "You can see me off, but I want you to stay clear of the horses. They aren't used to you."

Outside, Wolf stayed clear, but he refused to leave Alexandria's side. He matched her step for step. She had yet to get within fifteen feet of her mount. It was all James, the groom, could do to control the frightened horses.

With an abrupt motion of her open palm against her thigh, Alexandria gave the signal for Wolf to stay. She started toward the horses; he was right behind her. The animals' eyes were white, their ears were sticking straight up as they fought to be free. Alexandria came back to the front steps on the house.

"What is the matter with you?"

"I don't think he likes you riding off with someone he isn't sure of," Oliver said.

Hands on hips, Alexandria glared at Wolf. "Your concern is a little late."

"Showing a person you love them is never too late," her father said softly.

"I guess not," she said, then turned to the groom. "Go on without me. I'll follow on Excalibur. He's used to Wolf."

"I can't leave without you, your ladyship," the groom said, eyeing Wolf.

"You have your orders."

He shook his head. "It will mean my job. Lord Grayson warned us all. My boy finally has a home."

Alexandria now understood why the man had looked so frightened this morning, but she had had enough of people not obeying her. "It will mean more than your job if that stupid horse throws me and I fall and break my neck. I don't suppose his lordship will be too pleased to learn you caused the death of his wife."

The man paled beneath his leathery skin.

Oliver coughed into his hands to conceal his laughter.

"You have your orders, James. If my husband fires you, then you can work here," she told him.

"But—"

"One more word and I'll fire you here and now myself."

The man looked as if he wanted to cry. "Yes, Lady Grayson." The groom left, pulling the horse behind him.

"Nicely handled, daughter. I'll send someone to saddle Excalibur for you." Oliver reentered the house.

Alexandria turned to Wolf. "Now, see what you've done." He barked and sat back on his haunches, watching her with intelligent eyes. "I wonder if you're worried about me or if you just want to see him?"

* * *

Thorne walked to the stable at a fast pace. He needed to get away. If one more person asked where her ladyship was, when would she be returning, should her bath be kept ready, what food did she like, he was going to lose the temper he was holding by a strand. And if that wasn't enough, he had to deal with their sympathetic looks. He didn't need any sympathy.

Why weren't his servants like everyone else's, unobtrusive and blank? He didn't know if they took more than a proper interest in his and Alexandria's marriage because it had been hasty or because he had taken care of her. Either way, he didn't like it.

Halfway to the stables, he heard the sound of horses and turned. He was unaware of how much he hoped to see his wife until he saw James without her.

Fury race through him with the speed of lightning. A riderless horse might have caused another man to be alarmed, but Thorne knew his wife's riding skills. The docile horse he had given her couldn't have thrown a child. More important, he reasoned that if the horse had accomplished the impossible and thrown her, the groom wouldn't have bothered catching the horse. There was only one logical explanation for Alexandria not being on the horse: she had chosen to remain with her father.

Seeing Lord Grayson, the groom paled. His explanations began several feet before he halted in front of his lordship. "I know your orders, but—"

"Where is Countess Grayson?"

The man swallowed loudly. " 'er father's. That wo'f of hers was barkin' and she sent me back. I wanted ta stay, but she—"

Angry at his own miscalculations, Thorne walked off while the groom was still talking. Thorne had purposefully appointed James to be Alexandria's groom because Thorne hadn't thought she would risk the man's dismissal. She had seemed so concerned for his child that day. His wife was a better actress than he imagined. But if she thought she was rid of him, she was mistaken. For better or worse, Alexandria was going to remain his wife.

Thirteen

"This is not going at all the way I planned," Alexandria mumbled to herself, as she paced the length of her bedchamber. Three hours ago she had come home, her apology rehearsed, only to find no husband. No one seemed to know where Thorne was. From the covert glances the servants gave her, she knew they thought her marriage wasn't a normal one.

Determined not to let them know anything was amiss, she had calmly asked the servants, inside the house and on the grounds, to line up in small groups to meet Wolf. That in itself, she thought, would give them enough to talk about, instead of the unusual lives of their employers. Especially when Wolf knew they were frightened of him and went from bared teeth to complete disinterest as the mood struck him.

By the time she'd finished, several of the female staff were hysterical or threatening to quit. Alexandria hadn't heard from the male servants yet, but she had no doubt her errant husband would. In this, however, he would stand behind her. As much as she hated to admit it, he and Wolf had connected in some way during her illness. Wolf obeyed Thorne, yet he would look at her father as if he were speaking gibberish. Apparently Thorne had a way with animals as well as with women.

After having his fun and eating half a ham, Wolf had vanished an hour ago as quietly as he'd come. She'd glanced up from reading and seen he'd slipped away.

"He probably didn't go back to Mrs. Wolf, either." Alexandria kicked at a hassock. "I don't know about you, but when my husband finally gets home, I'm—"

The connecting door opened. Thorne, in a white lawn shirt and buckskin breeches, took two steps into the dimly lit room, then came to an abrupt halt. His head lifted; his gaze instantly found her. Even in the dim candlelight, she felt his eyes touch her. To her utter shame, her nipples hardened and her belly caught fire. How could she talk to him when all she wanted to do was . . .

Eyes shut tightly, she turned away, hoping by not looking at him she could recover herself.

Thorne was stunned to see his wife. He heard something and had come to investigate. His errant wife stood framed in the high arched window with the moonlight flowing over her shoulders. The need for her was deep and sharp and unexpected. No woman had ever affected him this way, but he learned from his father that desire made fools of men. He didn't know what her game was, but he wasn't playing.

"So you decided to grace me with your presence?" he tossed sarcastically.

Her eyes opened. "I've been here for hours; it is you who have been absent."

His brow arched at the sharp tone in her voice. "I assure you that one gets used to the partner being gone on the honeymoon."

She turned. "I-I had things to do?"

"Was running to your father to see about an annulment one of them?"

Heat climbed up her cheeks. "You know that is impossible after . . ."

"Annulments have been obtained after a marriage has been consummated," Thorne pointed out, walking further into the room.

"We made a bargain."

"Apparently, one you now regret."

Her shoulders squared. "I'll keep my end of the bargain."

"How very noble," Thorne said harshly. "But I'm afraid I

don't want a wife who flees from my presence at the break of dawn."

"I only went to see my father."

"And who had you planned to see tomorrow, and the day after that? I was a fool to think a woman would honor her part of the bargain."

Turquoise eyes flashed. "Don't you *dare* call me dishonorable. I'm here."

"For now." Two steps brought him so close to her he could feel the heat of her body through her thin nightdress. "Can you deny that your father asked you to file for an annulment?"

"He only wants what's best for me. He presumed you had acted dishonorably and thought to correct matters," Alexandria defended.

Thorne snorted. "He wanted you to have a title, and he chose me as the victim."

"Victim? I didn't want to marry you any more than you wanted to marry me." Hands on hips, she glared at Thorne. "The only reason my father wanted to see me married was that several of his friends had died recently and he thought he might be next. He remembered the betrothal contract and believed you might be able to protect me from my greedy aunts until I'm twenty-one. If anyone is a victim, it's my father and me. Your father received two hundred thousand pounds he never intended to repay, and now you have everything that once belonged to me. We received nothing."

"Wrong, Alex. *I'm* the one who received nothing. Now that your aunts have been taken care of, your father thought to do away with me. But I won't be dismissed, and neither will I be the laughingstock of England. There are going to be a few changes, and you will heed them."

She snatched her hands to her sides. "There isn't too much more you can do to make my life miserable."

Thorne continued as if she had not spoken. "I will not be embroiled in an annulment suit. It is enough to know that I made a mistake without telling the world as well. Despite what you or your father wants, you will remain my wife. In the remaining two weeks of our supposed honeymoon, we will have our meals together and spend our time together. We will retire to our separate chambers. At the end of two weeks, I will return to London alone. You will remain here and act with decorum; otherwise, I shall return. Don't make me come back." He walked to the connecting door. "Breakfast will be at ten." The door closed.

A myriad of emotions coursed through Alexandria. The first was rage, pure and raw. Her fingers closed round a brass candlestick before she had a chance to think. It landed with a solid, satisfying thump against the connecting door.

She turned to look for another object, saw a small Meissen vase, and picked it up. Her arm was arched in the air when the connecting door opened.

Thorne looked at the yellow and gold vase, then back at Alexandria. "I know it's difficult, but try to remember that you are a countess now."

"I know exactly who I am, you pompous jackass. I almost went insane yesterday with nothing to do," she said heatedly. "You are not leaving me in this house to rot!"

"You sulked in your room by choice, as you chose to leave each day," Thorne pointed out. "Throwing things is just as childish. I can see why your father wanted to get rid of you."

Alexandria hurled the vase.

Instead of dodging it, as she'd expected, he caught it. "You little hellion! You need to be taught a lesson." Setting the vase aside, he advanced on her.

"Ha! You tried to teach me a lesson before, remember?"

Black eyes narrowed. Alexandria's fist shot out. Thorne caught one of her hands, then the other. Barely swerving to keep from being kneed, he fell back on the bed, taking Alexandria with him. She twisted and bucked, trying to get him off her.

His body hardened. "Be still, you little fool, unless you want me to assert my husbandly rights."

She stopped thrashing instantly. Thorne knew the second she

became aware of him sexually. Her breath tangled in her throat, her body softened, her nipples hardened against his chest. He gritted his teeth against answering the call of her body with his.

"Not this time, Alex." At her questioning look, he continued, "You won't trade the use of your body to get your way." He rolled to his feet. "The bargain is over." The door closed behind him.

Alexandria struggled to her feet, trying to deal with her body's swift response to Thorne and his refusal to take advantage of it. But why? The answer came swiftly: if she didn't want to honor the bargain freely, Thorne would not force her. He had the right of the church and the right of honor, but he hadn't taken his rights.

Instead, he had released her and in the process made her see how she had hurt his pride because she had been afraid to face the truth. No more. If their marriage was over, so be it; but they both were going to know the reason why.

Without bothering to knock, she entered Thorne's room. "I'd like a word with you."

Thorne walked to the window and looked out. "I can't think of anything we need to say to each other."

"My riding each day has nothing to do with trying to get out of the bargain," she told him quietly.

"I told you, the bargain is over. Now, you'd better leave. I'm going to bed and you know how the sight of me offends you." He pulled the shirt out of his breeches.

Alexandria's gaze followed his movements. "I wouldn't have this problem if you did," she muttered.

Thorne's hand paused in the act of undoing a button. "What did you say?"

She lifted her gaze and found him watching her with a predatory stillness that made fire lick along her nerve endings. The tip of her tongue moistened dry lips. "I don't find you offensive."

"Then why did you take off each morning?" Thorne asked.

Alexandria wanted to run from the answer, but knew she

couldn't. "Because I can't be indifferent to your touch. You make me feel things I shouldn't, and I don't like them. That's why I went riding, why I sent you away from the pond. Why I visited my father today," she finished, her body trembling.

He crossed the room, his eyes never leaving hers. "Then you weren't planning to take your father's advice and get an annulment?"

"No, we had a bargain. Unless that is what you want."

"This is what I want." Thorne pulled her into his arms and kissed her, his mouth moving lazily over hers. Finally he lifted his head, his breathing loud and raspy. "You see, I'm not indifferent to your touch, either."

"You aren't?" Surprise and wonder laced her voice.

"No." His lips nibbled on her ear.

Alexandria shuddered. Thorne almost smiled. "See how your body responds to mine?"

"I-I know, and I'm not sure I like it," she said.

Lifting his head, Thorne studied the belligerent thrust of his wife's chin, her fear mixed with desire. "Give me your hand."

Taking her hand, he placed it over the wild beating of his heart, then on hers. Watching her eyes widen in understanding, he moved to her taut breast. She flushed and tried to withdraw her hand, but he had already moved to her nipple. When their entwined hands covered her womanhood, she started as much from unexpected heat as from the sharp increase in her desire. He moved to his hard arousal. She moaned in the back of her throat.

"I want you as much as you want me. My body can't hide it from you any more than yours can." His voice deepened. "We're one of the lucky couples to be able to enjoy each other's bodies and give so much pleasure," Thorne explained, gently circling a rosy-tipped breast with his fingertip and watching it perk up. His head dipped and his teeth closed around the taut peak.

Air hissed though Alexandria's teeth. "Thorne, I'm not sure I can stand this much pleasure."

"Why don't we find out together?"

* * *

From one second to the next Thorne was awake. Morning sun filtered through the partially drawn drapery. A sweeping glance of the room confirmed what he already felt: Alexandria was gone. Cursing his stupidity, he threw back the covers and got out of bed. He didn't need two guesses to know she'd gone riding.

Well, she wouldn't be able to go off again. This time when she came back, all her clothes would be in his room. He smarted because twice she had managed to leave his bed without his knowledge. It was a good thing he had retired from his work for her Majesty's spymaster four years ago. He had definitely lost his edge. He strode into her room and stopped.

Alexandria lay in the middle of the bed, her body curled into a ball, her tawny hair spread over her pillow. Thorne relaxed. He climbed into bed with her and drew her to him. Warm lips brushed across her ear. She smiled, then tried to burrow deeper under the covers.

Thorne smiled in return. Perhaps he should be a gentleman and let her sleep. They'd made love for most of the night, and each time had been more powerful than the last. And each time Alexandria had met him with an eagerness and desire that made him want her as he had no other woman. He kissed her again. He'd never said he was a gentleman.

Alexandria's eyes opened. She smiled and blinked, then her eyes widened. Grabbing the sheet, she scooted away. "What are you doing in here?"

"I might ask you the same thing," Thorne said. "I went to sleep with you in my arms and woke up to find you gone."

Her gaze snapped up toward his chest dusted with swirls of black hair. "It's daylight."

"So it is." Thorne reached for her and she scooted away again.

"It's indecent. What if the servants come in?"

"No one would dare set foot in either of our rooms without knocking or being summoned."

"Thorne, it's daylight."

Slowly, gently, he pulled the sheet from her hands. "There's no rule that a man and a woman have to make love only in the dead of night."

"I'm not sure this is right."

"I am." His eyes ran the length of her body. "I can't think of anything more right." His lips touched hers and he pressed her into the mattress.

By the time Thorne escorted Alexandria downstairs to eat, it was nearly one. Despite the twin spots of color in her cheeks, Alexandria held her head high as Thorne seated her in a chair next to his. She had wanted to eat in her room, but Thorne had refused. Sleeping late was normal for newly married couples; a wife riding off each morning was not.

After lunch, Thorne took her with him to his study to take care of his business affairs. Alexandria looked at Thorne, his head bent, then down at the book she had aimlessly picked up. She put it back on the shelf. Whatever Thorne was studying so intently would be infinitely more interesting. She walked behind his chair.

"Are you going to buy that railroad stock?"

"I might," Thorne answered absently.

"It's a good investment," Alexandria ventured. Perhaps if he knew she was knowledgeable, he might let her help. "I think the railroads are a thing of the future."

Thorne leaned back in his red leather armchair, his gaze skeptical. "What do you know about investments?"

"Enough. Father always discussed his with me." She picked up his papers and began to glance through them. "I liked running the estate, but Father thought I should be prepared for anything."

"May I have that back?"

Reluctantly, Alexandria handed them back. "I'd go with Rockmore instead of Pemberton."

"Why?" Thorne asked, only half listening to her answer, more compelled by her lavender scent, the rounded swell of her breasts.

"More established, better run, more routes," she answered without hesitation.

"I'm thinking about investing ten thousand pounds."

"Good. I'll invest—I don't have any money to invest, do I?"

Her voice sounded so forlorn, he said without thinking, "How much did you want to invest?"

"Since I don't have any money, there is no use discussing it," she said, trying and failing to keep the hurt from her voice.

"Alex, I know it's not easy, but I want you to know that your father was wrong," he said, watching her closely. "Furthermore, I don't plan to touch your money."

Disbelief widened her eyes. "Why?"

He turned back to his papers. "As you pointed out, my father borrowed money he never intended to pay back. Taking your money would make me as dishonest as he was," he finished tightly.

Alexandria felt his pain as if it were her own. "Thorne. Sometimes I . . . I say things without thinking." Tentative fingers touched his rigid shoulders. "Father says it's one of my worst traits."

He glanced up. "One? How many do you have?"

"I'm sure you'll find out," she said, laughing.

Thorne watched her face light up and couldn't help but laugh with her, enjoying the sound and trying to remember if he'd ever heard his parents laugh together. He hadn't. They hadn't cared enough for each other to try. But his wife of a few days cared enough.

The knowledge both humbled and annoyed Thorne because her caring shouldn't have mattered, shouldn't have made him feel good inside. Worse, it shouldn't have made him want to wrap himself in her smile and never let go. It seemed he had gotten more than he'd bargained for. He reached for his wife.

With a squeal, she scurried behind the chair in front of the mahogany desk. Thorne casually leaned back in his chair. "Is there a problem, my sweet?"

Her eyes rounded at the endearment. "Yes. I mean no."

He didn't miss her quick glance at the door. Perhaps it would be best to wait. His hunger for her wasn't going to be satisfied quickly. "Good. Do you think you might check with the cook to see why the food tasted so horrible this morning?"

"I already know," came the soft reply.

"Do you mind sharing the knowledge with me?" asked Thorne, a black brow arched.

She straightened and stepped to the front of the chair. "I introduced Wolf to the staff. I wanted to make sure if he decided to pay us a visit, he would be safe." She wrinkled her nose. "Unfortunately, Mrs. Hinton had a rolling pin. He growled and she became hysterical, then a couple of other women became frightened. Some of the men weren't much better."

Thorne heard the scenario, but what stuck in his head was "visit us." If Alexandria could learn to share Wolf, the odds of the bargain lasting would increase. "I guess we should be thankful the food this morning was edible at all. Perhaps you should inquire if anyone can take over her duties until Mrs. Hinton has recovered."

"Yes, of course." Alexandria was out the door in a flash.

"Run while you can," Thorne said softly.

Fourteen

What number was she on? Alexandria wondered, as she waited for Mary to finish her morning and evening ritual of brushing Alexandria's hair one hundred times. Striving to keep from fidgeting, Alexandria tried to pay attention to the constant chatter of her maid and listen for Thorne at the same time. Surely he wouldn't come in this morning, as he had done for the past week, and embarrass her.

Heat climbed up from her throat as she recalled Thorne's bold entrance into her room, his dismissal of the maid, then his taking her back to bed. The heat centered much lower in her body when she recalled what they had done . . . what she had enjoyed doing so much.

It was one thing for Thorne to be able to make her want him, quite another for her to enjoy it so much. Worse, there were moments lately when she looked at him and wished he would take her then and there. There had to be something wrong with her. No decent woman enjoyed lovemaking. Nora didn't count because she was in love.

Alexandria fidgeted on the stool, barely hearing Mary's promise to be finished soon. There was no love between her and Thorne, only an excessive need to mate. She had to put an end to it. Wanting something that much wasn't healthy. Besides, it made her too vulnerable.

His touch made a mockery of her control, and when he looked at her a certain way and called her his sweet, her knees actually trembled. Damn, she starting to tremble just thinking about it. This had to stop.

"That will be all, Mary."

The young maid looked stricken. "It's still tangled."

Remembering who had tangled her hair less than an hour ago, Alexandria surged to her feet. "Please lay out a gown. I have an appointment with Lord Grayson at twelve."

As expected, at the mention of Thorne's name, the maid hurried to the wardrobe across the room. Opening the carved door, she glanced back at her mistress. "What type of dress will you require?"

"Just pick anything," Alexandria said. Bending from the waist to let her hair fall, she began to brush her hair.

"Lady Grayson, I could finish your hair—"

"Please, just lay out a dress. I have brushed my own hair since I was five," Alexandria said, pulling the brush faster and faster through her snarled hair, disregarding the number of times the brush snagged.

"Yes, your ladyship."

Alexandria tried not to let the dejected sound of her maid's voice change her mind. If Thorne caught her in her chemise and pantalets, Alexandria knew exactly where they would end up. She was like a candlewick waiting for the touch of a flame, and Thorne was that flame. He easily knew how to get past her feeble objections. A brush of his lips, a nip of his teeth, a caress of his sensitive hands . . . her belly flared.

The sterling silver brush moved faster and faster through her hair. "You won't catch me this morning," she muttered, closing her eyes against the pain and brushing harder.

Her hand was in mid-air over her head when a comb started through her hair. "Mary, I told you I'd do this."

The comb continued from the nape of her neck to the crown of her head. Thoroughly irritated, Alexandria brought her head up and encountered a pair of intense black eyes in the toilet mirror. Open-mouthed, she stared at her husband.

"Was my touch too heavy?" he asked mildly, his dark head tilted to one side.

Abruptly turning, she looked wildly around the room for Mary.

"I dismissed her," Thorne said casually, and tossed Alexandria's silver comb on the top of the dressing table.

Alexandria's gaze ran the length of her husband in his dressing gown and back up. "Stay away from me."

Thorne matched her steps. "Why, my sweet, one would think I meant to do you harm."

"We both know exactly what you plan," Alexandria said, trying to resist the tantalizing voice. "Today I'm going downstairs before one o'clock."

"Surely you don't intend to go down dressed as you are?" His fingers teased the pink ribbon tie on her chemise.

She batted his hand away. "Neither do I intend to waste any more time in bed with you," she said, then blushed at her own frankness. "Please leave so I can ring for Mary."

Thorne walked over to her flounced petticoat, picked it up, and waited for Alexandria. She stared at him skeptically. "I assure you I know how to assist you."

"How do you know?" she asked tightly.

"Come here, Alex."

Alexandria didn't budge. The thought of Thorne helping any other woman sent a surge of unexpected jealousy though her. "There is only one way you could have learned. It only remains for you to tell me the number of women who have preceded me."

All playfulness left Thorne. "Past liaisons are not a topic to discuss between man and wife."

"So you say. You say a lot of things, Thorne. You would not take it so lightly if *I* was the one with the experience."

Thorne's face harshened. "We both know that is not the case."

"I am beginning to think my inexperience may be to my disadvantage," she said, wanting him to feel a small fraction of the hurt she felt. "All I have is your word about what goes on between a man and a woman. Suppose I wanted to test your theory?"

Tossing the petticoat aside, he crossed to her in seconds. Alexandria didn't cower, she simply continued to glare at him, her eyes flashing angrily. "You won't test any theory unless you want me to warm your backside."

Lifting her brush, she shook it threateningly. "If you dare lay—"

"I dare because you are my wife. I will not have to because you honor yourself and your vow too much to be dishonest." Removing the brush from her unresisting fingers, he pulled her into his arms. "I dare because I took the same vows."

She sighed and relaxed against him. "You got out of that one."

"I wonder how long it will take me to get you out of these," Thorne said.

Alexandria gasped as she felt her pantalets sliding down her legs. Thorne had undone the backstring tie. Grabbing the undergarment, she scurried away. "Thorne Graham Blakemore, if you embarrass me again, I'm going to start locking that door," she threatened, pointing toward the connecting door.

He looked at her a long moment. "We made a bargain."

"One time is all that is required to produce an heir, and we've certainly gone far past that." She retied her pantalets. "Now, do you behave and help me dress, or do I find a locksmith?"

Thorne became deathly still. "You would lock me out of your bedroom?"

She lifted her chin and disregarding the anger and something else lying just beneath the surface of his voice. "Only if you force me to do so. We've been up here long enough. At least if I come downstairs dressed, that will say something."

"There will be no locks on that door," he said tightly.

"There will be if I say so," Alexandria insisted defiantly. "Now, what is your decision?"

His eyes widened in accusation, then he picked up the petticoat. When he turned, his face was as emotionless as his voice. "Hold up your hands."

Glad to have won one battle, Alexandria pushed aside her uneasiness and did as he'd requested. After all, she reasoned, she had a right not to be embarrassed each morning. He'd be all right by evening. At least, she hoped so. She didn't want them in bed all the time, but neither did she want them at odds again.

Pushing the last pearl button through the loop of her plum-colored taffeta gown, he stepped in front of her and asked, "Shall I do your hair?"

Her mouth gaped. "You did their hair?"

"Do you need assistance with your hair?" His face remained impersonal and detached.

Unexpected pain lanced through Alexandria. She turned away. "No. Please leave."

Thorne didn't move. Instead, he studied the dejected look on Alexandria's face, watched her hold a clutched fist to her stomach. "I helped Judith with her hair after her accident."

Her head snapped up. "Why did you let me think otherwise?"

"Because I don't like ultimatums, especially in the bedroom. My father had to beg for every moment in his wife's bed." His eyes narrowed. "I swore I'd never beg a woman to share her bed. I'll meet you downstairs."

Alexandria caught his arm. "I wouldn't do that to you, Thorne. But I can't help wondering afterward if they know what we've been doing up here."

Some of the tension left Thorne's body. "It's only afterward that you start thinking?"

Her face flamed. "Thorne!"

"Come on and let's get your hair done, then you can help me dress."

She groaned as he sat her at the dressing table. This wasn't turning out as she had planned.

"Don't worry. I'll behave for now because I'm taking you to

a place where you won't have to worry about the servants, and I plan a lot of 'afterwards.' "

Fifteen minutes later they were downstairs. A smiling maid met them at the foot of the stairs with a picnic basket. Alexandria was sure Thorne meant to take her to her pond until they took a path around the side of the house. "Thorne, where are we going?" she asked, her hand planted firmly on the crown of her wide-brimmed hat.

"You showed me your pond, I thought I would share mine with you."

The adventurist spirit in Alexandria surged. "I bet mine is better."

"Not even close," Thorne said, as they came over a small hill. "What do you think?"

She halted, her lips slightly parted as she gazed at the wide expanse of water below. A stream snaked from the lake to disappear into the woodlands. "Does a teacup in a bathtub give you an idea?"

He favored her with a smile. "That's the same way grandfather must have felt on seeing the lake for the first time. The story goes he told the man who widened the lake to make it the biggest and the best for miles around. Apparently, the man only heard miles. It's over a mile to the other side, where we're going."

"The other side!"

Thorne's brows knitted. "Does that bother you?

"No," Alexandria quickly assured him. "Why should it?"

"For a moment, I thought your voice sounded strange. I know it's bigger than your pond, but if it frightens—"

"I'm not frightened of anything," she said, trying and failing to keep from remembering the last time she was on a lake. Only because of Wolf had she kept from drowning.

"Everyone is fri—"

"We're wasting time." She started down the sloping hill. One weakness was enough for Thorne to know about. He didn't have to know that after three years she still was afraid to be in water over her head. She had taught herself to swim so that she wouldn't ever feel that helpless in the water again. But she had always known that she could touch bottom anytime she wished.

Thorne caught up with Alexandria several feet away. "I'm the one leading this expedition, remember?" Not giving her a chance to answer, he grasped her arm and continued down the hill to the grassy bank.

"I haven't been across the lake in years. Through those crop of elm trees and evergreen shrubs on the other side is a garden with a gazebo and stone statues that grandmother designed before she knew the width of the lake. I don't believe she ever went to the other side. The boat is over here."

Alexandria watched Thorne put the basket in the small craft no more than ten feet long and tried to swallow the knot in her dry throat. It wasn't any larger than the one she and her cousins had sneaked onto the lake, and their boat had capsized less than five minutes after they were in the water.

Turning, Thorne held his hand out to her. "Come on. I'll help you in."

Damp fingers closed in the billowing folds of her skirt. She glanced down, then back at the boat. Perhaps there was a chance she didn't have to go. "It appears you were too good a ladies' maid. I won't fit."

Seeing the skirt of the dress span a good seven feet wider than the boat, Thorne arched a brow. "It seems I'll have to undress you again."

"You'll do no such thing," she said indignantly. Thorne's taking her clothes off was just as dangerous as her getting in the boat.

"It's your fault, you know," he said, coming to stand in front of her. "If you hadn't started an argument this morning, I'd have remembered to have you wear something else."

"Why is this suddenly my fault?"

"Because I am never at fault." Ignoring her belligerent expression, Thorne led her behind a clump of trees to a small clearing.

"I will not undress out here," she told him, refusing to let him touch a single button.

Folding his arms across his wide chest, he stared down at her. "Do you want to go for a boat ride or return home?"

Alexandria looked across the lake. If they didn't go, she'd spend another day watching Thorne work in his study and be miserable. The most he would let her do was read some of his correspondence, and only if she badgered him. On the other hand, if they did cross the lake, there was a strong possibility that she might panic and embarrass herself.

She touched her throat, remembering the sting of water in her nostrils, the helplessness of not being able to touch anything solid, fighting to stay afloat only to sink beneath the surface again and again until she came up and grabbed something solid. Wolf. Her cousins had swum away and left her to drown.

She glanced at Thorne watching her, his black eyes speculative and oddly patient. He was arrogant and dictatorial and possessive. Like Wolf, Thorne would fight with all his considerable strength to keep her safe. Unlike Wolf, who had rescued her because he loved her, Thorne would do so because he considered her a possession and the future mother of his heir. She could trust him with her life; it was her emotions she had to worry about.

"You probably planned this to get me out of my clothes again," she said, trying to keep her voice light.

He chuckled. "Alex, you do have a suspicious mind." Quickly he undid buttons and untied strings. Alexandria shrugged out of her underthings until she wore only one petticoat under her dress. Draping the excess of material over her arm, she went to the boat before she could change her mind.

Pushing the boat off the bank, Thorne jumped in and grabbed a paddle. His even, controlled strokes sent the boat gliding through the water. Alexandria's fingernails biting into the wooden seat relaxed somewhat. "How long will it take to reach the other side?"

"Not long, but I thought we might explore more of the lake.

I told Benson not to expect us back until late this afternoon," Thorne said.

A shaft of fear laced through her. Looking at the quickly receding shore, she realized if she didn't get her mind on something else, she was going to make a complete fool of herself by demanding they return. It had to be something that would pique Thorne's interest and possibly his anger. "Then that should give me time to talk with you again about my duties?"

Placing the paddle across his lap, he leaned forward. "We already discussed your duties," he said, his voice as seductive as his fingertips tracing her lips.

Alexandria barely caught herself from tilting her head and nipping his fingers with her teeth. Jerking upright, she fought to get control of her emotions. That wasn't the type of conversation she had in mind. "I require something to do besides that. You must admit, I know how to run an estate—and about investments."

"I have an estate manager and I've done well without your help," he pointed out.

Alexandria was not to be put off. "You call losing five thousand pounds by investing in a coal mine that closed two weeks later doing well?"

Thorne frowned. "I don't recall giving you papers that contained that information."

"You gave them to me yesterday and told me to read them and stop bothering you."

"If I remember, you were talking so I couldn't think, just as you are now," he said, unwilling to admit it had been that or pull her down on the floor. God. He was turning into a rutting fool. "For your information, I closed the mine so some safety measures could be instituted. I have told you before, a woman does not conduct business."

Alexandria's shoulders stiffened as if readying for battle. "What do you call running a ten-thousand-acre estate if not conducting business? And if I do say so, I ran mine much better than you are running yours. You have ground lying fallow on which you could plant or run sheep and make quite a profit with selling wool. Your stable, although adequate—"

"Adequate?" His paddle came out of the water.

"Could be turned into a profitable business with the right guidance. You may not realize it, Thorne, but an estate should take care of itself, not require money from your other ventures."

"You seem to have made a judgment very quickly on the productivity of the estate," he said brusquely.

Alexandria looked uneasy for the first time since starting the conversation. "From force of habit, I pay attention to things."

The paddle went back into the water. "I'll think about what you said."

"But—"

"We'll discuss it later, Alex." After all he had done to buy back the estates and make them successful, his wife of nine days found his efforts lacking. No matter how he tried to ignore her words, her criticism bothered him. In the past he hadn't cared a damn what anyone thought.

"Thorne?"

"Not now, Alex."

"Thorne."

Something about her voice brought his head around. "What is it?"

Reaching under her dress, she pulled out a plum-colored slipper. Purplish water streamed from the toe. "Are we sinking, or does your boat leak?" Her voice trembled.

"Damn." Laying the paddle aside, he handed the basket to Alexandria. A steady trickle of water bubbled up through the seams at the bottom of the boat. It took only a minute to determine that he couldn't repair the damage. "I'm not going to be able to stop the water."

Biting her lower lip, she looked at the receding shore, then to the other side of the lake. They were an equal distance from both. "Can we make it back?"

"No," he said, searching her eyes. "If I capsize the boat and we stay here, there is no guarantee someone will see us. We'll have to swim."

Alexandria closed her eyes for a moment. When she opened them, Thorne was still watching her. A portion of her fear receded. Thorne wouldn't let anything happen to her. Setting the basket aside, Alexandria removed her hat with unsteady fingers, then presented her back to Thorne. "You better get me out of this unless you want me to sink along with this boat."

Thorne glanced at the swiftness of the water rushing in and ripped the dress and petticoats away. He turned her to him. "Can you make it to shore?" he asked urgently.

She glanced at the bank, then back at Thorne. "I've never swam that far," her voice was faint, unsure.

His hands tightened. Then, lowering his head, he pulled off his boots. He didn't want her to see the fear in his face. He was a fair swimmer, but he wasn't sure he could make the distance himself. If Alexandria became frightened and tried to struggle . . . He lifted his head.

"Get to shore safely, and you can discuss the improvements with the estate manager."

Her eyes remained solemn and watchful. "We're in that much trouble?"

Ripping off his shirt, he tossed it away. It sank almost immediately. Alexandria shuddered. Thorne pulled her to him and kissed her long and hard. "We're going to be all right. If you get tired, just rest and float."

She nodded.

"You first."

She looked over the side of the boat, then back at Thorne. "Do you think you could lift me over the side?"

Picking her up, he hugged her to him, then lowered her over the side. Her hands clutched his neck as her feet touched the water. Reluctantly, he released her legs. Removing her hands, he placed them on the side of the boat and slipped into the water beside her. "You'll soon get used to the coldness of the water.

Don't try to swim fast, just slow, steady strokes. I'll be right beside you."

"I wish Wolf were here," she murmured.

"Swim," Thorne ordered.

Alexandria began swimming. Thorne matched her stroke for stroke, praying neither of them tired or got leg cramps.

"You're doing fine. It looks like the estate manager will have a new assistant."

"Tho—"

"Swim."

She swam, listening to Thorne's voice, one minute encouraging, the next minute making nonsensical comments about her having pink sheep or knitting blankets for the horses. She wanted to tell him to save his strength, but somehow her strength was connected to his voice. Closing her mind to her own fear, she concentrated on Thorne's voice and nothing else.

The instant Thorne's feet touched bottom, he picked Alexandria up in his arms and carried her to shore. He had almost lost her. His hold grew fiercer with each step. Unexpectedly, she struggled to be free.

"P-please put me down."

Hearing the desperation in her breathless voice, he resisted the urge to keep her in his arms and lowered her to the bank. "Are you all right?"

She nodded and curled her toes in the grass. Angling her head slightly, she looked back at the lake. The boat was gone. She shuddered. "I knew you wouldn't be like the cousins."

His fingers dug into her soft flesh as he pushed her away from him. "What are you talking about?" he asked, his voice as savage as his face.

"I can't imagine my cousins trying to rescue me. In fact, they and the aunts will be most unhappy to learn you did," she whispered.

He felt the tremor that went through her and pulled her to him, knowing he was holding her too tight, knowing he didn't intend to stop. Perhaps feeling her warmth would help him control the rage building inside him. He had ordered the estate manager to check the boat the week before the wedding, then Thorne had checked the craft yesterday himself. It had been sound.

His jaw tightened with the knowledge that someone had tried to kill them.

Fifteen

Questions without answers swirled in Thorne's head. The only thing he knew for sure was that he couldn't let anyone on the estate know that someone had tried to kill them. "Come on, we have to get you into something dry."

Alexandria evaded his reaching hand. "And how do you propose to explain when we arrive back and I'm wearing a dry petticoat?" At his puzzled expression, she continued, "People will think that . . . that we were doing something unmentionable to have left them here in the first place. We both know Mary can't keep a secret."

"Married people make love, Alex."

"In the proper place and at the proper time." Going to the clearing, she returned with her petticoat. "Please sink this in the water. Hiding it is too risky."

"Alex—"

She started for the water.

Jerking the ruffled undergarment from her, Thorne did as she'd asked. When he turned, she had the crinoline. Seeing the determined thrust of her chin, he sank it also.

"Satisfied?" Thorne asked, wondering if Alexandria realized her rosy nipples were clearly visible, as was the tawny delta between her thighs.

"A lady must protect her reputation."

Thorne thought of what they had just gone through and wondered at the calmness in his wife's voice. She was almost too calm. It appeared she could handle any situation without him.

Somehow the thought bothered him. Wading out of the water, he picked her up. After a brief hesitation, her arms circled his neck.

"That made number three."

He frowned down into her forlorn face. "Number three?"

She pointed in the general direction where their boat had sunk. "Hat number three. Although Father shares the blame for hat number two. He did help me pin it."

"This time you could have lost more than a hat," Thorne said, his voice tight with suppressed rage.

"I'm sorry about your boat."

"I'm the one who is sorry. My carelessness almost got you killed. I wasn't thorough enough when I checked the boat yesterday," he gritted out the distasteful lie.

"I do believe you have admitted your first mistake," Alexandria pointed out with obvious relish.

Thorne grunted and started for Grayson Hall.

She frowned. "If you're worried about what people will think, then I can say that I stood up and the boat capsized."

"The blame is mine. I won't have people thinking that you're foolish."

"Would you rather have them think that you tried to kill me?" she asked mildly.

Thorne stopped in his tracks. His gaze darkened as he stared down at Alexandria. "Is that what you believe?"

"If you wanted me dead, all you had to do was push me overboard instead of freeing me from my death trap." She wrinkled her nose. "The aunts would have shouted with joy in the streets if you had."

His face twisted into grim lines. "They are that malicious?"

"Greed does strange things to people. I know you don't like Father putting you in the position to offer for me, but he only did what he thought best. Despite everything he loves me." Alexandria pushed her damp hair out of her face. "If the aunts use this accident to put doubts in my father's mind, he will do everything in his power to dissolve this marriage."

Unconsciously Thorne's hold tightened as he reached the crest of the hill. "Not if you won't let him."

She looked away from his intense stare. "I'll stick by the bargain, but I see no sense in playing into the aunts' hands. Once I ran away from them in London when I was ten and they didn't notify Father until two days later."

He stopped abruptly. "God. Where were you?"

Alexandria grinned impishly. "I bribed the downstairs maids to let me stay in the servant's quarters. When Father arrived, the aunts were weeping and hysterical until I showed up. Both of them swooned. Father and I both agreed it was because they knew they had missed out on getting his money."

"They remind me of one of my relatives," Thorne said caustically, and began walking again. "You were very resourceful."

"I'm glad you agree. I hope you will also agree on what I have planned."

"I gave you my word, but I would like for you to discuss your plans for the estate before you implement them."

"If I didn't know how distraught you were, I'd ask you to put me down, and then I would hit you again."

Thorne halted. He didn't know if he wanted to take umbrage at her calling him distraught or the fact that she wanted to hit him.

"Why must you always discount my honor?" Removing her arms from around his neck, she glared up at him. "I fully plan to take part in running the estate, but not by asking you to keep a promise you made to take my mind off the danger we were in."

"You continue to amaze me," he said frankly.

Alexandria made a face. "Considering the women you have been around in Society, it's no wonder. Now, what kind of story do we tell? A monster would give the lake a sort of mystery."

"I told you, Alex, we are going to tell the truth. I was careless."

"My father isn't going to like that."

"I can handle your father."

"That's what you think," Alexandria muttered.

* * *

Several hours later, Thorne stood with his shoulder braced against the bedpost in Alexandria's room and watched her pretend to be asleep. To his displeasure, she had actually told that idiotic monster story. For a moment he had actually thought she might have lied to help him and placate Oliver until he remembered how much she liked being in charge.

Not surprisingly, Oliver had scoffed at his daughter being so easily frightened, and actually looked with suspicion upon Thorne. He didn't have to be a mind reader to know that if her father had any idea Thorne was being stalked by a killer, the squire would never let his daughter leave for London in a few days, as originally planned.

Thorne had to be the target. Alexandria might think her aunts greedy, but her death would accomplish nothing unless Oliver was dead also. If the aunts were going to resort to murder, it would have made more sense to do it before the wedding. No, he was the one the killer was after. After four years, his past had caught up with him.

His superior had warned him that it was difficult for a government agent to retire, but especially one of Thorne's caliber, for he had earned the name of *Jaguar*. The enemies of England had been handed swift and merciless punishment. There were many ways to kill a man, and he had used most of them.

Now, someone wanted to collect the twenty-thousand-pound bounty on his head, and that someone didn't care who else died.

Thorne's hands fisted on the polished mahogany bedpost. To keep Alexandria safe, he needed her absolute trust and obedience. He didn't have either. He thought she had begun to trust him until her father had told Thorne about her earlier boating accident. Once again he learned that a woman could give her body and nothing else; yet this time he wasn't able to dismiss it from his mind so easily.

"Why didn't you tell me about the boating accident?" The

curved shape beneath the counterpane didn't move. "You had a great deal to say an hour ago. Are you afraid now?"

Alexandria sat up like a spring, her tousled tawny curls tumbling around her shoulders. "I'm not afraid of anything."

Thorne looked at the belligerent thrust of his wife's chin and wished she wasn't so easily baited. "Then why didn't you tell me about your boating accident?"

"It didn't matter," she said, her fingers tightening around the covers.

Thorne walked to the side of the bed. "I suppose it didn't matter either that you disobeyed me tonight."

"What was I supposed to do, let you and Father come to blows?"

"You were supposed to let your husband handle things."

"Why, because I'm a woman? I'm as smart as you are, but the only time you pay me any attention is in bed." She blushed fiery red, but held his gaze.

"And that displeases you?"

"How would you like someone using a weakness against you?"

"What you see as weakness I see as strength."

"You'd say anything to get what you want."

His face darkened. "I don't use lies and threats to get what I want, Alex. I won't use you. Perhaps it's about time you learned that."

"What are you going to do?" she asked, wearily watching him untie his robe.

"I'm going to bed." Blowing out the lamp, he crawled beneath the covers. Pulling a stiff Alexandria into his arms, he said, "Goodnight." It was a long time before Thorne felt Alexandria relax with her back pressed against his chest. Getting her to trust him was going to be harder than he'd thought.

Night shrouded the streets of London and Alexandria had never been so miserable in her life. With each roll of the carriage wheel taking her further from all that she knew and loved and closer to Thorne's townhouse, the ache in her throat increased. If the trip hadn't been planned, she might have thought Thorne had brought her to London to punish her for her accusation. Surreptitiously, she stole a glance at him on the other side of the coach.

His face was grim, and he looked as if he didn't know she was in the carriage. He had been coldly polite since the night of the accident four days ago. Each night he came to her bed, took her in his arms, and went to sleep. For her, sleep now became almost impossible. She hadn't known her body could crave his so much that she wanted to scream in fury and frustration. Even now, she wanted nothing more than to have him hold her and make love to her. That shameful knowledge kept her pressed in the corner of the seat. But how much longer could she hold out?

The coach stopped in front of a brightly lit four-story house. Three footmen bounded down the steps. One opened the coach door, the other two began to unload the luggage.

"We're home, Alex." Rising, Thorne stepped down, then assisted her.

Benson, riding in the carriage following theirs, hurried to them. "Everything should be in readiness. I know the trip must have been tiring to her ladyship."

"Thank you, Benson," Alexandria said through stiff lips. At least Benson thought of her comfort, even if her husband didn't.

In the foyer, Benson motioned for a stout, matronly woman. "This is Nelda; she will be your maid."

"Welcome, Countess Grayson. I'll show you to your room."

"Thank you," Alexandria said, her steps slow and heavy, inwardly dreading another night of torture of Thorne holding her and nothing else.

Thorne studied the slump of Alexandria's shoulders beneath her cloak as she climbed the stairs. He didn't like seeing the unhappiness in face. She could end their torture with one touch of her hand. Reluctantly, he turned away. He didn't know how much longer he could wait until Alex realized that she could trust him enough to come to him again. Yet he had to. She had to make the first step. They'd both lose too much if he took the choice away from her.

Opening the door to the study, he crossed the room to his desk, then reached for the globe of the oil lamp.

"That won't be necessary," said a voice as smooth and as dark as night.

Thorne's fingers tightened for a fraction of a second, then set the globe back in place. He turned toward the voice. "One of these days you're going to skulk around in the dark and be surprised . . . with a bullet."

"Perhaps," the voice said, this time several feet away from the original sound.

"Will you stop moving? You know it isn't necessary."

A laugh, low and husky, floated across the room. "Force of habit. You don't easily forget the things that kept you alive. Apparently, someone is hoping you forgot your training."

Thorne came to attention. "Have you found something?"

"Nothing definite, but the answer may be in the report Ann is bringing. There is a problem, however," the man said.

Thorne heard a clink of glass. "Help yourself, and what is the problem with Ann?"

"Seems she won't give the report to anyone except you. And since I need that report to fit the final pieces to identify that double agent, I am calling in that little debt you owe me."

Thorne had always known the time would come to repay *The Shadow,* but not this way. "I'm married. You know what Ann expects."

"That's your problem," the voice took on a ragged edge. "You owe me a favor. I won't lose another agent because you can't handle your wife."

"How well did you handle yours?

"Careful, *Jaguar,* or we may have to test which of us is the better," he snarled.

Thorne brushed a hand wearily across his face. *The Shadow*

could learn things it might take Thorne weeks, if not longer, to uncover. Each of them had been betrayed by a woman. But at least he hadn't been marked on the inside and outside by one as *The Shadow* had. For now, being away from Alexandria might ensure her safety. "I'll meet Ann."

"You'll receive instructions later." The door leading to the formal gardens opened. The man silhouetted in the moonlight weaved like a specter, then was gone.

Thorne leaned against the desk. So the lies begin. He had asked Alex for honesty and he would be unable to give it in return until whoever was after him was caught. He was balanced precariously on a two-edged sword. He would never let harm come to Alexandria because of it. He left the study.

Without knocking, he entered her bedroom and stopped short. Alexandria, a towel in her hand, was stepping from the tub. Seeing him, her eyes widened. Instead of covering herself, as he had expected, she kept her gaze on him and began slowly to run the towel over her body. Need shot through him.

Finally she came to him. "I want you."

"Be sure, Alex."

The towel fell from her hands.

Thorne's lips took hers in a ravenous kiss. She clung to him. He didn't question her sudden change. All he could think of was how much he needed her and how much he'd lose if she ever turned against him.

Early the next morning Thorne reached for his wife and felt a cold sheet. Memories of her running away from him at Grayson Hall sent him to her room. Empty. Whirling, he reentered his room and jerked on the bell pull. By the time his valet arrived, Thorne was almost dressed.

Corbin rushed over to assist his master with his frock coat; Thorne waved him aside. "Have you seen her ladyship?"

"Yes, she is in the drawing room."

Thorne didn't question the slight easing in his body, just went to find his wife. Opening the door to the drawing room, he saw her staring out the window.

"Alex."

She whirled in a rustle of mauve taffeta. Her turquoise eyes were large in her pale face. For a moment he thought she might bolt from the room. He remembered another time when she had run away from him to the pond. Last night, for the first time in their marriage, Alex had been the aggressor; knowing his wife, the idea probably did not set well with her in the light of day.

Yet instead of running, she held her arms stiffly to her sides and jutted her chin at a defiant angle. "What are you doing here?"

He lifted a dark brow. "Looking for you. Breakfast should be ready shortly."

"I'm not hungry. Now, if you'll excuse me, I'd like to be alone," she said, and sat behind a small writing table.

"Not until you tell me what is going on in your head," Thorne said. "If it is about last—"

"I don't wish to discuss last night." She began stacking the already neat papers. "If you must know, my father's solicitor, Mr. Anderson, is coming."

Thorne tensed. "Apparently this is not a social call."

"No, it isn't, and therefore, your presence is not needed," Alexandria said.

"Alex, if you expect to see Anderson this morning or any other time, you had better offer me an explanation and do it quickly."

She surged to her feet to tell him he had no right to tell her what to do, then realized he did . . . just as he had the right to use her body. He had everything, while she had nothing. Her hands curled into tight fists. "Why can't you let me run my own life?"

"Because, like it or not, your life is now tied irrevocably with mine," Thorne said. "You should know that it's against all propriety for you to see Anderson alone."

"I've been seeing Anderson alone for the past three years."

"You weren't Countess Grayson then."

"I wish I wasn't now," she flung.

"What you wish is that you didn't enjoy our lovemaking so much," Thorne said softly.

The truth of his words sent an unwelcoming ripple of need rushing through Alexandria. The knock on the door was a welcomed intrusion.

"Come in," Alexandria ordered.

The door opened and an elderly man entered. The smile on his bearded face disappeared as he looked first at the tight-lipped Alexandria, then at her husband's stoic face. "Good morning, Lord Grayson, Lady Grayson. May I again offer my wife's and my congratulations on your marriage."

"Yes, you may; however, Lady Grayson brought you here for nothing."

Anderson's bushy eyebrows bunched. "I don't understand."

"It is my husband who doesn't understand," Alexandria said, coming from behind her desk. "Mr. Anderson is going to act as my agent in my investments, and there is nothing you can do to stop me."

"What do you plan to use for money? You have nothing unless I give it to you."

Her face paled slightly, but her gaze never wavered. "I once told you that I will be no man's chattel. The day before I left, Father gave me a letter stating I have complete access to his banking account."

"Your father forgot one detail—me." His face thunderous, Thorne turned to a wide-eyed Anderson. "You will inform Carstairs that I take care of my own and that if he tries to undermine my authority in any other way, he won't like the consequences."

"You can't do that!" Alexandria cried.

Thorne ignored her. "Good day, Mr. Anderson."

After throwing a quick glance at Alexandria, the man left. Locking the door, Thorne leaned against it. "Now, tell me why you wanted to use your father's money and not mine."

"Your money. Ha! It's *my* money."

He pushed away from the door. "I haven't touched your damn money, nor do I intend to. If I wanted a rich wife, I didn't have to marry one who gets angry everytime she enjoys herself in bed."

Alexandria flushed. "Stop saying that!"

"You're the one who is going to stop this nonsense," Thorne said, jerking off his cravat. "I can't be worried each time I hear you cry out in pleasure that when I wake up, you're going to be gone or doing something to get the upper hand."

She backed up. "What are you doing?"

He lifted a brow and pulled off his frock coat.

She looked at the window.

"You'd never make it. And I assure you, you don't want to be stuck in such a precarious position."

"You are mad."

"And you are behind on getting undressed," Thorne said, coming toward Alexandria.

She skirted around the back of a couch. "Stay away from me."

"In a couple of hours I'll be happy to."

Stopping, her eyes widened. "Hours!"

"Longer, if necessary."

"Thorne, you can't. The servants will know."

"I told you, they already know. The thing for you to do is accept that, as you accept my authority."

"I can't." Her voice quivered.

"You can if you stop thinking that you have to be better than I am."

"I *am* better."

"We're about to find out. I'll even let you be on top. You enjoyed that position last night. And if it will make you feel any better, you can try to persuade me about Anderson. You may as well get something out of your defeat."

Her eyes sparkled. She accepted his challenge. "Don't be sure about who will be defeated."

Thorne snorted at such an idea and reached for the buttons on her dress. Three minutes later he gritted his teeth to keep from moaning as Alexandria's teeth tugged on his nipple. Five minutes later he was trying to count sheep when she brushed her cheek against his belly. Ten minutes later, he found himself saying yes and he didn't know what she was asking. Giving up, he caught her hips in the palm of his hands and enjoyed his defeat.

He didn't know how long it was before reality returned. "What did I promise?"

"Hmmm," came the soft reply.

"I said, what the hell did I promise?"

Lying on top of Thorne, Alexandria raised up. "Why are you yelling—" She stopped abruptly as she realized they were still joined and Thorne was still hungry for her.

"Bloody hell," he said, and pulled her beneath him.

A long time later, he rolled to one side, taking Alexandria with him. Thank goodness this time he had the presence of mind to keep his mouth shut . . . at least he thought he had. "I didn't make any more promises, did I?"

Alexandria shook her head, her silky hair brushing against his naked chest.

"Alex." His fingers lifted her chin for him to see her face. She looked sated, beautiful, but a hint of a frown still touched her face. He didn't want that. Leaning over, he brushed his mouth against hers. "Did I hurt you?"

"No. Did I hurt you?"

His eyes widened, then he burst out laughing and pulled her to him before he had time to think why he shouldn't. "All right, tell me what I promised."

"Nothing."

"Nothing?"

She sighed deeply. "I forgot to ask. Foolish wasn't it."

"But I remember you saying something."

She hid her flaming face in his shoulder. "You must have been mistaken."

Thorne wished with all his power to be able to remember, but he couldn't. "In that case, I think it's only fair that Anderson be allowed to come once a week during my presence and let you invest with my money."

"Twice a week, and use both our monies."

"Deal."

Shortly after lunch four days later, a knock sounded on the drawing room door. Alexandria glanced up from writing in her ledger. Mr. Anderson had just left and Thorne never knocked. "Yes?"

A footman in blue-and-gold livery opened the door. Lady Margaret in a vivid red taffeta dress entered. "Good afternoon, Alexandria."

"Lady Margaret, this is a surprise." Rising from her desk, Alexandria went to the older woman and frowned as the door closed. "Judith isn't with you?"

"No," Lady Margaret said, her face shadowed. "I wanted to speak with you in private."

"Is Judith all right?" Alexandria waved the elderly woman to a silk brocade settee and took a seat in a straight-backed chair in front of her. "Would you like a cup of tea?" She gestured to the tea service on the table.

"Thank you. As I was saying, physically Judith is fine, but . . ." Lady Margaret shrugged her shoulders and took the cup of steaming tea. "Judith has always been shy, but she has gotten worse since we returned from Grayson Hall. I think you can help."

"Me?" Clearly taken aback, Alexandria set her cup down.

"You have a certain way of challenging life that Judith lacks. Those days she spent with you were the happiest I've ever seen her," Lady Margaret said, looking wistful.

"You'll forgive me, Lady Margaret, but I thought you didn't like me for being exactly that way."

Lady Margaret had the grace to look uncomfortable. "At

first; then I realized you were just being headstrong, not improper. Judith needs more confidence."

Alexandria nodded her agreement. "How can I help?"

"By letting Judith stay with you and Thorne until she acquires that confidence." Lady Margaret set her cup on the gateleg table. Eagerness shone in her gaze. "As long as she is with someone of my age, she will never have the opportunity to blossom. I thought of claiming to be ill, but we both know Judith would see it as her duty to stay with me. The only thing I can think of is to say I am going on a Continental Tour with Lady Elleby to aid in her recovery. But instead of touring, we'll be at her estate in the country."

"Is there a reason for not going on the tour?"

Lady Margaret looked uncomfortable again. "In case something should happen, I'll be able to return quickly."

"You mean, if I create a scandal," Alexandria said bluntly.

"If I didn't trust you, I wouldn't ask," Lady Margaret pointed out.

"I guess not." Alexandria grinned. "When can I expect Judith?"

Lady Margaret relaxed. "Not until we do something about your wardrobe. Yours is as atrocious as Judith's."

"We cannot all wear red, as you have today."

"I agree, but while Judith wears browns and dark grays, you are nearly as bad with those dark colors you picked out for your wardrobe," Lady Margaret pointed out.

Alexandria looked down at her plum-colored gown. "My father picked out the colors to make me appear more subdued."

The elderly woman nodded. "I think we both know why, but now you're married. And frankly, if you keep on wearing those dreary gowns, Judith will also. You are one of those rare women who shines in whatever she is wearing. Judith could shine as well if she had the self-confidence you possess."

"I don't know if it's self-confidence or that I just don't care what others think of me," Alexandria confessed. Except Thorne, she thought, and wondered why his opinion mattered so much.

"From now on you must," Lady Margaret said, then leaned her considerable bulk forward in her chair. "Your beauty and Thorne's name will gain you entrance into the elite circles, but it will be up to you to become accepted, not just tolerated." She sat back in her chair. "And, quite bluntly, if you're not accepted, then I couldn't possibly leave Judith in your care."

"Then I'm afraid you have wasted your time. You saw the disaster at Grayson Hall," Alexandria said. Even Thorne had disapproved of her.

"You acted with charm and dignity. The mark of a woman of character is to look adversity in the face and smile," Lady Margaret pointed out.

"I have had a great deal of practice," Alexandria said dryly.

"No doubt you will gain more being married to my nephew," Lady Margaret said with all honesty.

"No doubt."

"Then you agree to the wardrobe as well?" Lady Margaret asked hopefully, and picked up her cup. "Thorne will not mind the expense."

Alexandria thought of the countless hours of fittings and twisted uneasily in her seat. She wanted to help Judith, but . . . "Do you really think another wardrobe is necessary?"

"I do. The women of the *ton* like fashion almost as much as gossip. You must make a statement your first night. I hope you will use some of Judith's sketches for a gown. I know Thorne received an invitation to the Duke and Duchess of Singleton's ball next week. You must plan to dazzle them. Your acceptance will be as much to Thorne's benefit as Judith's."

"Thorne's benefit? From what I have seen, women flock to Thorne," Alexandria said caustically.

"Now, but not always. Their mother—my sister, Marianne—went to Paris two years ago because of certain . . ." Lady Margaret paused, her hands tightening on the cup before she continued, "unpleasantries. I won't go into details, but suffice it to say that Thorne and Judith have both had to live with the whispers and sly looks. Your success would end the stigma to one Lady Grayson and begin the reign of another."

The protective spirit in Alexandria surfaced. No one was going to treat Thorne or Judith badly. "When can we start?"

"I knew I could count on you." Lady Margaret's round face broke into a relieved smile. "We'll visit every modiste in London until we find what we are looking for. Remember, Judith and Thorne aren't to know a thing about our little discussion."

"I'll remember."

"Now that that is settled, I'd better go home."

Alexandria stood and followed Lady Margaret into the hall. "I will call on you tomorrow."

"Excellent. I think you and I shall make a great team."

"A great team to do what?" asked a deep male voice. Both women turned and watched Thorne approach. "Good evening, Aunt Margaret, where is Judith?"

"Resting," Lady Margaret said.

Alexandria spoke up. "Your aunt was kind enough to point out that my wardrobe is a bit drab. She is going to help me do something about it."

"There is nothing wrong with your clothes," Thorne said.

"Spoken like a husband." Lady Margaret tugged her gloves tighter. "I'll expect you tomorrow."

Thorne's searching gaze went from one woman to the other. "Expect her where?"

"I just told you, Thorne, we're going shopping," Alexandria said.

"I'd prefer you wait until I can take you," Thorne told her, his body tensing.

Alexandria gave him a questioning look. "If you are worried about the money, I can use some of my investment money."

"I was not worried about the money," he said tightly. Letting Alexandria loose in the city was asking for trouble. He needed to be able to make sure she was safe. "Why don't you wait until I can take you?"

Her lashes flew up in surprise. "When would you find the

time? Besides, you'd probably hate shopping with three women."

"The child is right, Thorne. You know she'll be perfectly safe with me," Lady Margaret said.

"That may be, but during the Season most of the modistes are booked," Thorne pointed out, although his aunt had that confident look in her eyes again. "Where will you find one to make a new wardrobe?"

"We'll manage," Lady Margaret said, in a voice that left no doubt as to her ability or that the conversation was over. "I'll expect to see you tomorrow, Alexandria." Without another word she left.

Thorne damned his inability to keep his wife at home and safe. If she'd been any other woman, he'd have ordered her to stay home. Ordering Alexandria to do anything was like asking a wild stallion not to try and jump the fence: a waste of time and a direct challenge. "I'm sending two footmen with you."

"Two?"

"If you have another mishap while in my care, your father will be upset," Thorne reminded her, knowing that at least in this he spoke the truth.

She wrinkled her nose. "I suppose you're right."

"No argument?"

"The conservatory and gardens are nice, but I'm not sure how much longer I could have stayed inside," she confessed. "I'm sure people must think us snobbish for refusing all the invitations we've received."

"We're still on our honeymoon." Thorne repeated the story he had used to keep them home. "People expect us to stay home."

"Not Lady Margaret! I can't wait until tomorrow."

Thorne frowned. "I want you to be careful, Alex. London can be dangerous."

"We're only going shopping. What can happen to us with two footmen?" she asked, tilting her face up to his.

He didn't answer, just drew her into his arms.

* * *

Two hours after Alexandria got out of bed the next morning, she was sipping tea in Lady Margaret's drawing room. "I hope you will forgive me for my unannounced visit, but I need your assistance and Judith's if I am to present myself properly at the Singletons' ball next week."

Judith frowned and lowered her gaze. "I don't know what I could do to help."

Alexandria's gaze met Lady Margaret's. Judith was shutting herself away again. "I do. I am in need of a new dress for the ball. I want to use one of your designs."

Judith looked astonished. "Mine! They are just fanciful drawings."

Alexandria warmly took Judith's hands in hers. "They are more than fanciful. They are the most beautiful drawings of gowns that I have ever seen. In fact, I remember one in particular that I want made for my ballgown. If you don't mind?"

"I would be honored, but do you really think my drawings are any good?" Judith asked, her tone a mixture of fear and hope.

"I do. So much, in fact, that I'll wear one of your gowns or I won't go," Alexandria said adamantly. "I have heard that the *ton* likes a little mystery. What better way than with a new look and a gown by a secret designer? They will fight for the name."

"I don't know, Allie," Judith said, her hands clenched in her lap. "I hate for people to think badly of you because of something you wore."

"They won't," Alexandria said with supreme confidence. "I want to make a splash in your design. All I need is your permission."

Judith's back straightened. "You have it."

"Good. One last thing . . . I'd like for you and Lady Margaret to accompany me to the modiste to select the right material."

Lady Margaret frowned on cue. "I don't want Judith tired."

"I'll be fine," Judith rushed to say. "If Allie needs my help, then she shall have it."

"Splendid," Alexandria said. "When do we start?"

"Right after breakfast," Lady Margaret told them. "One should never go shopping on an empty stomach."

Three hours later, Alexandria found that Thorne had been right as they emerged from another dress shop. All the reputable modistes were already booked and the materials spoken for. She didn't mind that so much as she minded seeing the light in Judith's eyes grow dimmer and dimmer with each refusal. "Lady Margaret, who is the most prized of all the modistes?"

"Madame LaRauche, but if the others are unavailable, then so is she," Lady Margaret said, looking almost as sad as Judith.

"We shall see." Alexandria turned to one of the footmen who were always within arm's reach. "Please tell George to take us to Madame LaRauche."

Lady Margaret didn't speak until they were in the carriage. "I'm not sure about this, Alexandria. She is said to be rather difficult."

"So am I," Alexandria said, and sat back in the seat. She wasn't her father's daughter for nothing.

Ten minutes later, the Grayson's crested carriage pulled in front of a shop that bore the name "Madame LaRauche, Modiste" in discreet gold script. The fact that carriages were two deep didn't seem to bother Alexandria, who asked one of the footman to bring Judith's drawings.

As soon as the shop door opened, Alexandria strode inside, whipped off her shawl, and flung it to the floor. "I refuse to wear anything so distasteful again."

All eyes in the shop turned. Alexandria advanced further into the crowded dress shop. "I must see Madame LaRauche. No one else will be able to comprehend his designs."

Judith and Lady Margaret stared open-mouthed at Alexandria because she had spoken in flawless French.

A tall, regal woman in a dove gray silk gown detached herself from two women who were looking over several bolts of colored satin. "I am Madame LaRauche. Who are you?"

The words were spoken with such haughty disdain that Alexandria knew her plan was going to work. "At last I have found you." Quickly, she went to the woman and stared at her with total reverence. "He said that no one would be able to make his designs come to life, but I refuse to listen. The future Duchess of Ashton cannot shame her husband in these rags."

Discerning eyes flicked over Alexandria's gown. Alexandria knew, like the modiste, that although the magenta did nothing for her coloring, it and the lace at her cuff and sleeves were the finest available.

"I have just come from Paris, and he . . ." Alexandria's voice trailed off as she lowered her head briefly. "He became angry because I would not wait as others must for their gowns. Such a temper for one no higher than this." She held up a hand to her shoulder. "He looks like a child with that drooping mustache and reclining in his chair. I told him to give me the sketches I had sent for him to draw the gowns on and I would come to you. He laughed. But I know you can make them come to life."

The name of Worth ran through the shop like a wildfire. The noted designer couldn't draw, so he had lithographs made of heads and arms, then he sketched the dress. His temper was legendary, as was his high-handed manner of treating even the most aristocratic woman. It was not unusual for him to refuse to speak or to ask them to sit. However, in the case of her aunts, Alexandria could hardly blame the man.

"Are you saying that Worth—"

Alexandria screeched and threw her arm across her face. Her two footmen, Judith, and Lady Margaret rushed to her side. "Say no more." Removing her arm, she uncovered the sketches. "All I need to know is, can you bring to life what he envisions? If not, I must seek someone who can."

The modiste looked momentarily taken aback by such a blatant challenge. Neither woman had to look around to know that they were the center of attention. If Madame LaRauche refused to accept the assignment, she was saying that she doubted her ability and before the day was out all London would know it. From the way the modiste looked at Alexandria, she knew she had been trapped. Her expression promised retribution.

"Look before you decide." Alexandria thrust the sketch at the woman and sought to soothe her anger. "I'll pay whatever price you want. I implore you, Madame."

Slowly the woman's gaze moved to the design. The simple ballgown left one arm bare and was held up by delicate netting. All the attention would center on the woman wearing the creation.

She looked at Alexandria. "Anyone can do this," the modiste said with a Gallic shrug, her disinterest obvious.

"But can they do these?" Alexandria said and began to show the more intricate sketches of gowns that boasted netting, lace, ribbon, or flounces to be worn with embroidered or fringed cloaks. Alexandria breathed easier as interest shone in the woman's eyes. "I require the best for the Singleton ball, and I am told that *you* are the best."

Madame LaRauche lifted her gaze, her black eyes openly speculative. They both knew that regardless of who designed the gowns, Worth's name would be attached to them and if Madame LaRauche created the gowns, her fame and income would soar because of it.

"The best costs."

Alexandria smiled, and shrugged as only the exceedingly wealthy can do, those privileged few who considered it vulgar to know how much money one had. "And I can pay for it. What good is money if not to buy the pleasantries of life?"

Turning, the modiste walked to the curtain separating the room, then looked back. "Then let us get started."

Sixteen

Alexandria stood in the middle of the room wearing a shimmering gold dress that caught and reflected the light like a thousand candles. Her face glowed. A gold feather soared from the loose bun and curls at her nape. The daringly cut neckline bared the creamy whiteness of her shoulders and the swell of her breasts. Madame LaRauche had brought to life Judith's sketches as Alexandria had known she would. It hadn't been easy.

The woman was as difficult as Lady Margaret had said she could be. Everything had to be exact or with an outburst of French she would rip away whatever had offended her. Sometimes Alexandria thought Madame LaRauche was paying her back, because the modiste always treated Judith with the utmost care.

Alexandria had never remembered being so tired. More than once Thorne had mentioned that he'd come to see her and she'd been asleep. The connecting door to their bedchamber opened and she turned in expectation.

Thorne stood in the doorway.

"Do you like my gown?" she asked huskily. Her voice held both an invitation and a challenge.

For a moment, Thorne was speechless. She was the most beautiful woman he'd ever seen. She looked ethereal and innocent and seductive at once. Men would flock to her. Women with more poise and experience than Alexandria had been caught up in the dangerous games played by the *haute ton* and come to ruin. That thought helped him regain his voice.

"The neckline is a bit too low."

Her smile faltered. In the past week of peace she had forgotten how abrupt Thorne could be. "Lady Margaret approved of the dress."

"We both know my aunt has strange tastes in clothes." He tried to tell himself that he wasn't jealous. He only thought of her safety. In that gown she would stand out like a candle in a dark room . . . easily located, easily harmed.

The fan in her hand snapped open. "Perhaps, but we also know that she is the soul of discretion. She would do nothing that might bring a hint of gossip to you or to Judith." Alexandria took a deep breath and the rounded swell of her breasts drew Thorne's eyes. "I am sorry the gown does not meet with your approval."

The hurt in Alexandria's voice jerked his head up. He resisted the urge to soothe her. She was his wife and he didn't want every popinjay salivating at the sight of her.

"I'll ring for Nelda to help me out of this." She reached for the gold feather in her hair. "I wouldn't want to shame you."

Thorne's hand caught hers midway to its target. He inhaled her lavender scent and gritted his teeth. Lord, he wanted nothing more than to drag off her clothes, then drag her into bed. Her lips parted and trembled, and he knew she felt the same way. He released her arm and stepped away from temptation. "You don't have time to change. You'll have to go as you are."

Alexandria tamped down her anger and showed the barest hint of teeth in her smile. "How kind of you to allow me to do so."

"The coach is waiting."

Both were silent as they went downstairs and got into the carriage. Pulling her fringed shawl around her bare shoulders, she glanced out of the window. She was silly to feel hurt. It was not a part of the bargain for Thorne to hand out compliments. She had to remember. Just as she had to remember that her conduct tonight would not only affect her relationship with

Thorne, but determine if Lady Margaret would leave Judith with them.

If Lady Margaret was right and Judith did want to be married, then Alexandria was going to help. Although she didn't see why any woman would willingly want a man cluttering up her life, changing it.

"I hope you remember that you are my wife and a countess now."

Thorne's words brought her out of her musing. Her back stiffened. "If you thought I might embarrass you, why did you have me accept the invitation?"

"Just remember what I said, Alex," he repeated, as the coach pulled to a stop in front of a brightly lit mansion. The door opened and he stepped down. "I'll be watching."

"Of that I have no doubt." Alexandria muttered, wondering if she could perhaps talk Judith out of marriage.

Fifteen minutes later they were still waiting in the entrance to the ballroom to be announced. Thorne frowned down at Alexandria's décolletage. "Can't you pull that thing up?"

Alexandria lifted a brow, watched Thorne grit his teeth as his eyes stayed on the swell of her breasts. Comprehension dawned. He was jealous! He had to care a little bit. Her smile rivaled the sun for brightness. She lifted her hands. One held a hand painted silk fan, the other a gold reticule.

"It appears, my lord, that my hands are occupied. Would you like to try?" Alexandria laughed as his mouth gaped. They were announced and her laughter floated out to the crowd. Thorne urged her forward, his scowl as evident as her radiance. They stopped under the brightly lit chandelier.

A hush fell over the crowd for a full ten seconds. Even the music stopped as everyone turned to see what was going on, then Thorne and Alexandria began to move toward their host and hostess.

"Grayson, how good to see you, my boy," said an elderly man, his brown eyes direct, his bearing regal despite the thinning gray hair on his head.

"It was kind of you and your duchess to invite us," Thorne said. "May I present my wife, Lady Alexandria Grayson, our hosts, the Duke and Duchess of Singleton."

"She's lovely, Thorne. No wonder you rushed her to the altar," the Duchess of Singleton said. Her gaze swept Alexandria's gown. "A golden angel for the Devil's Angel. How appropriate."

Alexandria curtsied, inadvertently displaying her charms. Out of the corner of her eye she saw Thorne's face darken. "You are too kind."

The Duke of Singleton watched the byplay and choked back his laughter. Finding Thorne's gaze on him, he coughed as he tried to smother the sound. He turned to Alexandria. "You'll find that my wife rarely is kind."

"Really, Charles, you'll have Lady Grayson think ill of me," the Duchess of Singleton pouted.

"Only an unsighted and deaf person would think that," Alexandria said truthfully. "Your husband's delight in you is in his voice and in his face. You are a fortunate woman, and from what I have heard from Lady Margaret, one who is very deserving."

The duke and duchess looked fondly at each other. "I think Thorne is the lucky one," the duchess said. "If you don't mind, Thorne, I am going to take your countess and introduce her to some of our other guests."

"I'm afraid I can't, your grace, my husband has bidden me to remain by his side."

A muscle leaped in Thorne's jaw. "I am sure our hosts do not want to hear our domestic discussions."

"On the contrary, I can't wait to whisk her away and hear every delicious detail." The Duchess of Singleton looped her arm through Alexandria's. "Imagine a rogue like Thorne being so possessive he doesn't want his wife to leave his side. How did you tame him, dear?" she asked, leading Alexandria away.

"With a whip and a chair." Alexandria answered.

The Duchess of Singleton laughed. "My dear, you are a breath of fresh air. You'll be the talk of the Season."

"I hope not. Thorne would be furious," Alexandria said, then grinned mischievously.

"From the possessive way he looks at you, he already is." The duchess glanced at Alexandria's gown. "Your dress is exceptional. I wouldn't mind having one similiar. You must be aware that there is a great deal of speculation regarding who the designer is."

"I am, but for the present I am sworn to secrecy," Alexandria answered, with what she hoped was just the right amount of regret.

The older woman sighed remorsefully. "Just as well. I would never be able to carry off that dramatic look."

Alexandria caught the wistfulness in the duchess's voice. "Only because the gold would not be suitable for your lovely translucent skin. But I'm sure one of the other sketches would be to your liking. To prove it, I insist you look over my sketches and pick one out. It will be my gift to you for making me feel so welcome."

Pleasure lit the duchess's face. "I accept before you change your mind. By the way, I'm having a garden party on Thursday around two and I'd love for you to come. Of course, Lady Margaret and Lady Judith are welcome."

"I don't know their plans, but I'm sure they will be as delighted by the invitation as I am," Alexandria said, excitement ringing in her voice. If the duchess accepted her, then everyone else would.

The matronly woman patted Alexandria's gloved hand. "Excellent, let me introduce you to some of the other guests."

For the next thirty minutes, Alexandria met the *haute ton* of Society. Some faces were new, others she had met at the fox hunt or at her wedding. However, the women who had been less than enthusiastic in meeting her before, were now overly friendly. Alexandria knew the reason was a combination of the duchess's backing and her new gown. Everything went well until Alexandria mentioned that Judith was also having her gowns made by Madame LaRauche.

"I assumed with her affliction she wouldn't go out," said Lady Dalton.

Alexandria turned on the horse-faced woman so fast she gasped and stepped back. "Judith has a slight limp, she has no affliction."

"I . . . I meant no offense," the older woman sputtered, looking wildly around her.

A hand tugged her skirt and Alexandria realized the duchess was trying to caution her. Around her were the grande dames of Society; if she alienated them, she might as well leave London.

"Please forgive me, Lady Dalton, but your remark unintentionally reminded me how imperfect I am and how others judge me because of it." The women looked at her as if she had sprouted wings. "I would give anything for your complexion or to have beautiful blond hair like Lady Ashcroft or to be demure like the duchess. Instead, I look like this." Alexandria spread her arms wide. She sprouted another wing and a horn.

"On the other hand, men don't have to be perfect. I'm sure you know my husband, Lord Grayson. He is said to be rather difficult, but no one seems to mind. If a woman were to act that way, it would cause a stir." Her voice lowered. "Men, however, expect nothing less than perfection from us." The women slowly nodded in agreement.

"I think you are beautiful the way you are," whispered Lady Caroline, the daughter of the horse-faced marchioness. Fortunately, the younger woman did not favor her mother in looks or temperament.

Alexandria saw the sincerity in the young girl's face and returned the compliment in kind. "Thank you. Only a moment ago I was admiring your pretty blue eyes and thinking they would go well with a light blue gown Madame LaRauche insists is wrong for me. I suppose I am vain to want it anyway."

"Not in the least, Lady Grayson," the marchioness hastened to say, her greed for the gown obvious.

"Thank you," Alexandria said. "You ladies have been so kind to me. I don't know how I can repay you."

Alexandria saw the greed on the women's faces and knew all of them wanted to mention the designer, but none were so bold. Her smile broadened.

"Come, my dear," the duchess said. "We must discuss the sketch you plan to give me."

Several pairs of eyes widened. Alexandria could have kissed the duchess for her help. "Of course. Women must stick together. I do believe in rewarding my friends." Alexandria turned with the duchess, then glanced over her shoulder. "Lady Caroline, we must talk again sometimes."

The young woman smiled for the first time that evening and Alexandria felt the light squeeze on her arm by the duchess. Perhaps being in Society wasn't going to be so difficult.

Later, sipping a glass of warm lemonade, Alexandria noticed that a man across the room boldly watched her. "Your grace, who is the man with the monocle by the buffet table? He has been looking at me for the longest time."

"I wondered when you would notice," the Duchess of Singleton said, and smiled to an elderly couple passing by. "I also wonder when Thorne will put a stop to it."

Alexandria frowned. "The man is being insolent, but there is no reason for Thorne to interfere."

"You don't know, do you?" the duchess asked.

"Know what?"

The older woman refused to meet Alexandria's gaze. "Nothing. I believe your partner is coming for the first set. Enjoy the dance."

Before Alexandria could protest, an eager looking young man bowed and led her onto the dance floor. Having little choice, Alexandria dismissed the incident and smiled.

From the far corner of the room, Thorne watched his wife, the ex-hoyden, waltz by on the arms of yet another man. The duchess had made sure Thorne knew his wife's dance card was full and wasn't it a pity he had waited so long to ask. It had taken considerable willpower and all his love and respect for the duchess not to tell her to mind her own business. The rest of his waning willpower was being expended not going on the dance floor and tell the grinning fop to stop trying to look down the front of his wife's dress.

A passing woman caught his furious expression and hurried away. Thorne hardly noticed. His attention was centered on the swirl of gold and the enchanting woman in it. He didn't have to look to know that most of the people in the room watched the same woman. How was he going to protect her when she drew attention like a magnet drew metal? And it was only going to become more difficult.

With her obvious approval by the duchess and the sour bunch across the room, by tomorrow afternoon he and Alexandria would have more invitations than they could possible accept. And as impossible as it seemed, Alexandria had turned into a social butterfly. If he didn't know better, he'd have sworn she'd been in Society all her life.

Laughter floated to him. Alexandria. He couldn't see her face, but he didn't have to. The tightening of his body was all he needed to recognize his mate. *His mate.* Realizing his idiotic thought, Thorne went in search of something to drink with a kick to it. Then he would come back to keep an eye on his wife.

An endless hour later, Thorne accepted another man's congratulations on his good fortune. They didn't seem to run out of words to praise the Golden Angel.

"I guess we all know now why you went to the country, Grayson," Lord Holden laughed, his eyes on Alexandria as she whirled across the dance floor.

Viscount Osborne by his side nodded. "There hasn't been an Original like her since Lady Clarendon." The words were barely out of his mouth before the sudden tension in the small group of men alerted the slightly inebriated man that he had made a faux pas. He swallowed loudly. "I meant no offense."

Thorne looked at the man with indifference. "Why would you think I was offended?"

"I . . . er . . . I," the gray-haired man sputtered, "there was talk of you and the . . . er . . . lady making an announcement before she married Clarendon."

"Unfortunately, there is always talk of something or another. Personally, I deal only in facts." Thorne looked at each of the four faces surrounding him and knew his words would be repeated many times before the night was over.

"I have only asked one woman to marry me and I have committed myself to protect her with my life. Any harm or the slightest cause of unhappiness done to her I will look upon as done to me." He smiled and it was glacial. "I have a long memory." Nodding abruptly, he left.

Easing his way through the jovial crowd, Thorne hoped the threat of retribution was enough to keep Alexandria safe. He wanted the would-be killer to know that no power on earth would protect him if something happened to Alexandria. But was it enough?

"Thorne."

Glancing around, Thorne saw the last person he wanted to see, Rachel Clarendon. Only because she held his arm did he stop. "Good evening, Lady Clarendon. If you will excuse me."

"Thorne, you were going to walk past me," she said reprovingly, her hand clutching his arm.

"I am in a hurry."

"To get your wife, I hope." She released his arm. "She is making a spec—"

"Be careful, Rachel." His soft voice held a subtle warning.

"Thorne, she is a disgra—"

"Be quiet!" he hissed. "You thought to ruin Alexandria's reputation at the hunt. I said nothing because I thought you would have enough sense to stop on your own. I was wrong. Alex is my wife. Say or do anything that might cause her embarrassment and when I get through with you, you won't be able to appear in public."

Rachel paled, her hand circling her bejeweled throat. "What are you talking about?"

"Cuckolding your husband. Be thankful you married Clarendon. I would have killed you if you had raised your skirt to so many men."

She gasped. What little color she had left drained from her face, leaving it pasty white.

"Set your sights on someone else, Rachel. I will take no man's leavings." Whirling, he stalked away.

A few minutes later Thorne slipped quietly into the duke's dark library. With practiced ease, he crossed the room to a curtained alcove. Two men waited for him. "Have you learned anything?" Thorne inquired.

"No. My people are still working on it," said one of the men, his voice deep.

"Damn. What am I supposed to do in the meantime?" Thorne questioned. "Alexandria must be kept safe."

"Be patient, my boy," the Duke of Singleton said. "You know *The Shadow* is the best there is."

Thorne snorted and looked in the direction of the first man who had spoken. "Forgive me if that doesn't give me any great comfort."

"Don't worry, *Jaguar.* If he or she gets to you before we get to them, I will consider it my duty to comfort your wife in her time of need," *The Shadow* said, his voice dry and cynical.

With a curse, Thorne moved, his hands outstretched, only to meet thin air. "Stand still."

"My face is scarred enough." *The Shadow* said from across the room, his voice flat and indifferent.

Fist clenched by his side, Thorne didn't move. What was the use. *The Shadow* was gone by now.

"None of that, you two," the duke admonished. "Thorne, you know he was only joking."

"I wasn't amused."

"Sorry. I didn't know you had finally met someone you cared enough about to fight for."

The voice was within a few feet of Thorne. He could strike out if he wanted. Both men knew that. Both men knew Thorne wouldn't. "Just keep her safe."

"You take care of Ann and I'll take care of your wife." The double doors opened, the curtains billowed.

How could you be lonely with hundreds of people surrounding you? Alexandria answered the question before the question formed completely. Because none of them was the person she wanted to be with. Despite his ability to make her want to push him over a cliff, she missed Thorne. The feeling was not mutual, however. He had yet to seek her out for a dance. But not more than ten minutes ago he had walked off with that snobbish Rachel. And he was the one who had talked about propriety!

Her young dance partner finished the set with a flourish. "Thank you, Lady Grayson. May I escort you back to the duchess?"

"I think I'll get a breath of fresh air." She didn't want to face anyone.

The young man hesitated. "Would you like me to accompany you?"

"No. I will be fine." Not giving him a chance to say anything further, she walked into the gardens. Cool breezes touched her flushed cheeks. Gripping her fan, she walked away from the sound of music and the voices of other people who had sought the solitude of the garden.

"Grayson is a fool to leave a beautiful woman like you alone."

Alexandria whirled. A few feet away stood the man who had watched her so insolently. Tall and impeccably dressed, he might have been handsome if not for the cruel set of his generous lips. If Thorne didn't like the man, there must be a reason. "Fool is not a word one would associate with my husband, and as for leaving me, I expect him shortly."

The man laughed, a hollow sound like wind blowing through

a canyon. "Nicely done, but if I know Rachel, she is using all her considerable charm to correct her mistake of letting Grayson slip through her fingers."

"I'd say she has an impossible task, since Thorne is my husband," Alexandria said with asperity.

"You really are an Innocent." He took a step closer. It was all Alexandria could do not to step back. There was something intrinsically evil about this man. "Thorne could establish her as his mistress and there would be nothing you could do."

Irritation turned to anger. "I won't stand here and listen to you insult me and my husband." She started to step around him.

"Not even to know why Rachel is so intent on attracting Grayson's attention?"

Knowing the man was baiting her, she was still unable to keep going. She knew part of the story; she wanted to know all of it. "Obviously, you think you know a great deal about my husband."

"I make it my business to learn about those things which interest me. Allow me to introduce myself, Simon Seaton, Earl of Kendricks, at your service." He bowed.

Alexandria lifted a brow in acknowledgment. "You were saying."

Kendricks looked momentarily taken aback by her abruptness. "Because of my intervention, Grayson did not marry Rachel."

"If you have something to say, please do it without the dramatics."

Cruelty flattened his mouth. "Rachel tried to use me to make Grayson jealous. I used her instead for my pleasure. He learned of our little rendezvous and refused to offer for her."

Alexandria kept the revulsion from showing in her face only because she knew Kendricks expected to see it. She disliked Rachel, but no one deserved to be used for another person's selfish pleasure. So this was the man Rachel had been foolish enough to meet.

"Grayson should be thankful I took her off his hands. I was

only amusing myself. With you, however, it would take more than one night to satisfy me." He reached for Alexandria.

"Touch my wife and I'll kill you."

Hands fisted, Alexandria spun to see Thorne step out of the shadows. Relief coursed through her until she saw for one split second that the rage in her husband's eyes was directed at her.

"Don't be so touchy, Grayson," Kendricks said, adjusting his monocle. "Your wife and I were simply getting to know each other better."

Alexandria gasped at the implication. Her balled fist came up. Catching her hand in his, Thorne stepped between them. "If you continue to cross me, Kendricks, I'll have to kill you. This is your first and last warning."

Without a word, Kendricks walked away.

Thorne whirled on Alexandria. "What in hell do you mean, coming into the gardens with a debaucher like Kendricks?"

"I did not come into the gardens with him, he followed me."

"You should have foreseen that and stayed inside."

"I needed some air."

"So much that you risked your reputation being alone with Kendricks."

"I am surprised you noticed that I was gone. You and Rachel appeared to have a great deal to talk about."

Thorne's face hardened. "Stay away from Kendricks."

"I can take care of myself."

"Rachel probably thought the same thing."

"Are you angry because of what might have happened to me or what did happen to Rachel?"

A muscle leaped in his temple. "We are going back inside to say goodnight to our hosts, then we are going home. You will smile and appear happy."

"Are you going to answer my question?"

"Don't push me, Alex, you might not like the answer you get."

Seventeen

Thorne woke in a foul mood. That mood worsened as he dressed and went downstairs to his study. Nothing had gone the way he had intended in the last few days. If it wasn't enough that he still had no idea who or why someone was trying to kill him, he had spent the night in his bed. Alone. That was not what he had intended.

Yet once they'd arrived home the evening before, Alexandria had gone straight to her room, her question still hanging between them. He hadn't given her an answer, but he knew.

When Kendricks had taken Rachel's innocence, Thorne was only mildly irritated at her stupidity and Kendricks's coldheartedness. Last night, seeing him near Alexandria, Thorne had wanted to tear him apart. The only reason he didn't was the knowledge that an altercation would have damaged Alexandria's reputation and given Kendricks a perverse sense of pleasure.

With a disgusted snort, Thorne sat back in his chair and admitted his old nemesis and friend *The Shadow* was right. Thorne had found something he couldn't walk away from. But caring made a man weak and he had no intention of allowing Alexandria to lead him around with a ring in his nose. He was in charge of his household and today she was going to know it once and for all time.

A impatient knock sounded on the door. Alexandria. Thorne glanced at the clock on his desk. He had requested her presence exactly an hour ago. Folding his arms across his chest, he waited. The knock, louder and more impatience came again. The lessons had begun.

"Come in."

"You sent for me," Alexandria said, before she completely entered the room and before the footman had time to close the door.

Thorne slowly sat upright to give himself a chance to regain his composure. His wife might want to make him shake some sense into her stubborn head, but she also made him want to drag her off to the nearest bed. This morning, however, he doubted if he touched her they would get a foot away. Of course, she didn't look as if she was in the mood to be touched, much less made love to.

Her eyes sparkled like diamonds in the sun. She'd fight like a lioness if he touched her. From the way she looked down her pretty nose at him, she didn't want to listen to a thing he said. At least this morning, her peach silk dress didn't display the creamy curves of her breasts and tempt him so.

"Are you finished sulking?"

A tawny brow lifted. "I am not sulking. It is you who gave orders to the coachman not to take me anywhere this morning, thus making me a prisoner in this house."

"You are not a prisoner, Alexandria," Thorne pointed out. "I am simply concerned with your welfare."

"Certainly. Then will you have the carriage brought around? I wish to leave."

"Where are you going?"

"I don't question you when you leave."

This wasn't getting him anyplace. "A man's reputation is not as easily tarnished as a woman's."

"Are you accusing me of being dishonorable again?" Alexandria said, taking a step closer. "Because if you are, I am—"

The door behind her opened abruptly. A tall woman, dressed in a mauve silk gown, glared at the footman who sought vainly to stop her entrance into the study. "I'll have you fired for daring to try and stop me. I need no permission to enter this room."

Thorne slowly came to his feet, his face devoid of expression. "That will be all, Jeffries."

After one last look at the satisfied face of the intruder, the footman closed the door.

Swirling in a swish of satin and lace, Dowager Grayson touched one side the brim of her large straw hat topped with birds and flowers, then walked straight to Thorne's desk. "I need more money," she said, and fingered a large ruby pendant hung around a neck that had begun to wrinkle and sag.

Thorne looked at the necklace, then back at the older woman. "I see you found the necklace. I wonder if perhaps the other pieces were found as well."

"The jewelry was given to me as part of my dowry," she snapped.

"Not given—*entrusted* to you, as the wife of a Grayson," Thorne said. "You dishonored him and you dishonor the family heirlooms by wearing them."

"I suppose you want them for her?" Dowager Grayson sneered, inclining her head toward Alexandria, who hadn't moved since the woman's entrance.

"They are hers by right, if she wants to have them. However, after seeing one of the pieces on you, I doubt if she wants to wear it," Thorne said, taking his seat.

Dowager Grayson advanced on him. "You always were a nasty boy. You turned into an even nastier man."

"The apple doesn't fall far from the tree." Thorne's expression remained unchanged. "Now, you barged your way in, I'm sure you can find your way out." He picked up his pen.

"Didn't you hear me, you imbecile? I need more money. When I signed those papers for you to have guardianship of Judith, you promised to take care of me," the dowager countess cried.

Thorne didn't look up. "Eight thousand pounds in the past three months is more than enough to take care of you if . . ." He glanced up, his gaze hard and cutting. "If you didn't have to pay Jiles to be your . . ." he paused. "What do you call a man who lives off a woman who lives off her son?"

The older woman gasped. "What a foul thing to say!"

"The truth is sometimes unpleasant."

"Don't speak to me that way. I'm your mother."

"How unfortunate for both of us." He picked up the paper on his desk. "You know the way out."

She didn't move. "I wonder if you know how much I loathe and despise you," Dowager Grayson sneered. "No one likes you. I hear the rumors. You're tolerated now only because of your wealth. You and that crippled sister of yours who disgraces me each time she is seen in public."

"Madam, I believe my husband asked you to leave."

The dowager whirled, her eyes were cold and forbidding. "So you decided to speak to your betters." She sent a cutting glance toward Thorne. "Why did you chose some ill-bred commoner when you could have married Rachel?"

"I am sure you and Rachel know all about being ill-bred," Alexandria said, then smiled into the woman's suddenly startled face. "How fortunate for me that the Duchess of Singleton overlooked Judith's and my faults and invited us to tea. It is puzzling, however, for one so highly respected that you were not on the guest list. Stranger still that at the Singleton ball last night no one inquired about you."

Thorne's mother raised her hand. "You little—"

Alexandria's smile widened. "Please."

The dowager jerked her hand to her breast as if it had touched a snake. "You are mad."

"Then I am sure you want to leave with all due haste." Thorne stood. "Don't come back."

"You can't throw me out. This was my home and you owe me some respect."

"I owe you exactly what you gave me and Judith: nothing. As for this house, if it hadn't been in the family for so long, I'd have sold it instead of having everything you purchased removed before moving in." Thorne's hands rested palms down on his desk.

The dowager jerked her shawl tighter. "You haven't heard the last of this. Jiles has friends in high places. My solicitors will be in touch."

"Waste money, if you choose, but you'll not receive one farthing more until August. In case you are thinking about charging things to my name, don't. I am sending notices to your creditors, as well as mine, publicly announcing that I will not be responsible for your debts."

The woman's face ashened. "That will ruin me."

"You have already done that to yourself."

Suddenly, she clutched her chest. Her eyes shut tightly, she swayed. Alexandria quickly went to the dowager's side and helped her to a chair, then rushed to pour a small portion of wine. Out of the corner of Alexandria's eye, she noticed that Thorne had not moved from behind the desk.

Alexandria held the glass to the woman's lips. Putting her hands over Alexandria's, the dowager drained it. Her eyelids fluttered opened. "Th-Thank you."

"Are you feeling better?" Alexandria asked, taking the glass and setting it on a small table. She couldn't explain, but the woman's hands on hers made her feel as if she were betraying Thorne.

"A little. If I could be allowed to rest." A single tear rolled down her cheek. A laced-edged linen handkerchief dabbed the moisture from the corner of her eye. "You don't know how humiliating it is to have to beg for money from a man who hates you."

Alexandria refrained from saying the feeling appeared to be mutual. Having shared a close relationship with her father, she couldn't imagine such hate. Even when her father was angriest, she never felt he hated her. Once again she glanced over at her husband, who had a look of bored indifference on his face. "Thorne, perhaps we should send for a doctor."

"I have already had a doctor examine her," Thorne said.

Abruptly his mother jerked upright. The tears and sniffling stopped just as abruptly. "According to the doctor, she is in excellent health."

"No doctor has examined me," she yelled with amazing strength.

"You know him as Scanlon, your footman," Thorne said mildly. "I believe you employed him in Paris when Jiles had to make himself scarce because his creditors were hounding him for money."

"You are lying," she said, but her voice lacked conviction.

"Unlike you, I have no reason for lying. I don't like being made a fool of. After the second heart seizure and your quick recovery, I became suspicious." Thorne's jaw tightened.

He hadn't asked *The Shadow* how far the examination had gone and he hadn't volunteered any information, except that his mother was in excellent physical condition. Thorne had used the only man with the expertise and the ability to keep his mouth shut after the assignment was over. He owed *The Shadow* a debt, and the only way he was going to be able to repay it was to be dishonest with his wife. If for no other reason, the woman before him would receive no pity.

"You should have been content with the two hundred pounds I gave you less than a month ago. According to my calculations, you are eight thousand pounds over your allowance already," Thorne told her. "Part with some of your jewelry, if you're so desperate. From me you'll get nothing more than the agreed-on amount. The well, as the saying goes, has gone dry. I suggest you pick your lovers better or get rid of the present one."

Marianne surged to her feet. "You'll regret this." The door slammed.

"I didn't know she was faking."

Thorne brought his attention back to an uncertain Alexandria, who stood in the middle of the room. "That woman has just insulted you and you rushed to her aid."

Alexandria wondered if Thorne realized he referred to his mother as "that woman." He was too much in control not to know exactly what he was doing at all times. Unlike her, he had no weaknesses. "I thought she was ill."

"And that, in your mind, obliterates all that has gone before?"

He looked at her as if she was slightly weak in the mind. "Not exactly, but it makes it less important."

"I shall have to remember that." The tension seemed to go out of him.

"Does that mean our fight is over?"

A dark brow climbed upward. "We were having a discussion."

Alexandria screwed up her face. "We never discuss anything. You give orders and you expect me to obey them."

"You're my wife. You are supposed to obey me," Thorne said and came from behind his desk. "It is my right by law."

Alexandria had enough. "What about my rights? I told you I will not be treated as if I am too stupid to know my own mind."

"I will not have my name dishonored," Thorne shouted.

His mother again. Trying to remember that Thorne's first experience with a woman had been with a mother who'd despised him, and knowing a proud man like her husband wouldn't have wanted her to witness their disharmony, Alexandria reined in her temper. "There will be no reason to be displeased by me tonight at Lord and Lady Whitehall's party."

"Wasn't last night with Kendricks enough, or did you find you like flirting and being accosted by strange men?"

"No man is going to touch me unless I wish. Including you." She whirled to leave the room. The palm of a hand slammed shut the door she'd opened.

"Challenging me again, Alex?"

The emotionlessness in Thorne's voice caused a chill to race up her spine. She slowly turned. His face, like his voice, was devoid of all warmth.

"Well, you should think twice before answering." He pressed closer until their bodies touched.

The arousing heat of his body was in direct contrast to his

chilling gaze. This was not the man she knew. "I wish to go to my room."

"What if I don't want you to?"

"Thorne, I—"

Her words were silenced by his punishing mouth. His lips slanted across hers, opening her mouth and allowing his tongue to thrust inside. At the same time he ground his lower body against hers, his arousal evident. Need clamored in her lower belly. She couldn't let him do this to her.

The knee she brought up proved useless when he moved to the side, then with his leg pinned the lower half of her body against the door. He captured both her hands in one of his and held them behind her back; his other hand cupped her breast.

Need became hunger. A broken cry erupted from her lips. Alexandria didn't know if she whimpered from pain, fear, or arousal. She only knew that he had proved her desire for him once again and in so doing had taken something from her she had no way of getting back.

"Are you going to challenge my authority again, Alex?" Thorne questioned. When moments passed and no answer came, he lifted her chin and cursed under his breath. In her eyes he saw fear and uncertainty, and he had put it there.

He had proved she was no match for a determined man, showed her helplessness, and somehow defeated the proud woman who, minutes ago, had defended him and his sister. The woman who matched his passion with an honesty that undid him. The thought sickened him. His body lifted from hers.

"You may slap my face."

Alexandria looked away. "May I leave now?"

"Damn it, Alex, you needed to learn men like Kendricks and others won't care that you say no."

"In other words, they'll treat me just as you did." Her shoulders stiffened. "Thank you for teaching me about men and honor."

He jerked as if she'd slapped him. "That wasn't what I was trying to teach you and you know it."

"No? Then what? That women aren't to be trusted? That every man who sees me will try to dishonor me? Or were you taking out your anger against your mother on me?"

His hand shot out and grabbed her arm. She met his gaze without flinching. "Be careful of that sharp tongue of yours, Alex. One day you may regret using it."

"I already do. I was a fool to agree to this bargain," she spat, her own anger overruling caution. "You disgust me."

His eyes gleamed. "Challenging me so soon, Alex. If I didn't have an appointment, I'd make you take back those words." His fingers uncurled. Opening the door, he stepped into the hallway.

His entire being vibrated with anger. How had he let things get so out of hand? Alexandria didn't deserve the way he had just treated her; no woman did. But damn if he would be told by his wife when he could touch her. She was his and his alone, and it was past time she realized that. Halfway to the foyer, he met the butler.

"Pardon me, your lordship," Benson said. "I was just coming to tell you that I was informed the wheel is loose on your carriage and your departure will be delayed."

Not wanting to stay in the house and be reminded of his loss of control, Thorne said, "I'll hire a hansom. Send the carriage to my club when it is ready."

"Yes sir."

Long, deliberate strides carried Thorne to the foyer. Benson turned from giving an order to a footman to hand Thorne his walking stick, gloves, and top hat. Too impatient to pull on his gloves, Thorne stepped into the mid-morning sunlight. He noticed none of its brightness. Alexandria's face still haunted him.

How could he have stooped so low? She needed to show more caution, but he needed to show more compassion. She was not like his mother or Rachel. Putting on his hat, he bounded down the stone steps.

Waving a flower seller away, he started across the busy street, his mind still on Alex. She might be angry, but he had no intention of spending another night alone.

Halfway across the street, the loud rumble of metal wheels against the cobblestone streets reached his ears moments before someone cried out a warning.

Looking up, Thorne saw a team of four horses pulling a water wagon heading straight for him. The driver was leaning out of the box as if trying to stop the wild dash of the team. He yelled something to the horses. Thorne couldn't hear for the increasing noise of the wheels and the screams of people trying to get out of the way of the wagon.

Thorne whirled just as the horses thundered past. He came to rest on his hands and knees. He watched the rear of the wagon turn a corner, sending a barrel out the back. The wooden barrel shattered, spilling water the moment it hit. The wagon never slowed.

"Your lordship, your lordship, are you all right?" Corbin cried anxiously, going down beside Thorne.

"Of course, he's not," Benson said, from the other side of his master.

With the men's help, Thorne stood. Thankfully, nothing appeared broken. The street was littered with goods as people had fled to get out of the way of the wagon.

The valet picked up Thorne's hat and cane. His white gloved hand came away soiled as he brushed off his master's pants.

"I'll need more than that," Thorne said, looking down at his stained pants and ripped jacket.

"If his lordship is recovered, I'll go attend to laying out your clothes," the valet said, and went inside.

Thorne and Benson followed. Entering the house, Thorne was surprised to see what he thought must be the entire house staff hovering near the doorway. Seeing that he was unharmed, they bowed respectfully and left.

"Does everyone know of the accident?"

"It is very possible, sir," Benson told him. "It was I who shouted the warning. Most of the staff was in the house, and Lady Grayson was about to go up the stairs."

Unconsciously, Thorne glanced toward the stairs, then beyond.

Benson followed the direction of his master's gaze. "I thought she was behind me when I rushed outside. Probably seeing you lying in the street gave her such a fright that she had to take to her bed."

"Probably," Thorne said lightly, despite the unexpected pain he felt. He didn't know one thing that could give Alexandria a fright . . . until he had overpowered her in the library and shaken her confidence.

"The streets are getting more and more dangerous," the butler said, breaking into Thorne's thoughts. "If a man cannot handle a team, he shouldn't be allowed to drive."

"You think it was a runaway?"

Benson frowned. "Why else would a team of horses run through the streets like that?"

"Why indeed?"

Continuing up the stairs, Thorne went to his room. As expected Corbin had things ready. All the time Thorne bathed, then changed clothes, he kept glancing at the closed door.

"I do hope her ladyship is all right," Corbin said, helping Thorne with his coat.

"I'm sure she is."

"I saw her maid when I was coming upstairs." Corbin smoothed the jacket over Thorne's broad shoulders. "Said she had gone to check on her ladyship, and was told by Lady Grayson that she didn't want to be disturbed."

At Thorne's continued silence, the valet continued.

"The maid thought her voice sounded strange," Corbin said, picking up the ruined clothes. "I told her that you would take care of things." After one meaningful look at the closed connecting door, the valet let himself into the hallway.

For once, Thorne didn't try to reason things out, he opened the connecting door. Alexandria reclined on a small couch, her eyes closed, her head resting on the padded armrest.

To think he had needlessly worried about her. He started to

leave, then saw a tear roll unchecked down one cheek, then the other. He stepped further into the room.

Something in his gut tightened.

The only time he had seen her cry was when her father had accused her and Thorne of acting improperly. He was sure the only reason she'd cried then was her weakened state. Yet she was crying for him and he had just shaken her to the core. No one except Judith had ever cried for him, not even Aunt Margaret.

Stepping into the hallway, he stopped a passing servant and advised her that under no circumstances were he or Lady Grayson to be disturbed for the rest of the day. With a quick curtsy and a fervent thanks that he was well, the woman left.

Reentering the room, Thorne removed his jacket, then knelt and gently pulled Alexandria into his arms. "It's all right, Alex. It's all right. I guess being in an accident counts as much as being ill?"

She clutched him to her. "You were just lying in the street. So still . . ." her voice trailed away.

"It was my own fault. Instead of paying attention, I was thinking about what a bastard I had been to you."

She sniffed and pulled out of his arms. "Are you trying to apologize?"

"I guess I am. We both know you'd have fought a lot harder if another man had touched you," Thorne said, his thumb brushing the moisture from her cheek. "I had an unfair advantage."

Alexandria's hand touched his, then fluttered away. "Thank you for coming to assure me that you are all right and for the apology, but I shouldn't keep you from your appointment."

"I'm where I want to be." His lips brushed against hers with a feather lightness. Picking her up, he placed her in bed. "Would you be disappointed if we didn't attend the Whitehall party?"

"It depends on the reason," Alexandria said, worry obvious in suddenly pinched features.

Thorne smiled and began to undo the buttons on her dress. "I'll give you one guess, my sweet."

Eighteen

"Aunt Margaret, surely you can't be serious," Thorne said, disbelief widening his eyes. Just when he was congratulating himself on two days' peace with Alexandria, another problem occurred.

"I've never been more serious about anything in my life," Lady Margaret told her nephew. "My ship leaves on the morning tide, and I plan to be on it. Unless, of course, you refuse to take Judith in."

"Of course, he won't refuse," Alexandria rushed to say, as she patted Judith's hands. "Will you, Thorne?"

"Of course I won't refuse. But that doesn't mean I approve of Aunt Margaret touring the Continent with only a female companion. Lady Elleby is at least sixty years old."

"Sixty-one, to be precise," Lady Margaret said, drawing herself up straighter in the wingback chair. "The same as I. So you see, if we're ever going to go on this tour, it has to be now. Evelyn's sickness last month made us realize that."

"But anything could happen," Thorne stated, worry evident in his face.

"London is as dangerous as anyplace," Alexandria chimed in again. "Your-your mishap the other day proved that. You also insist that I have two footmen with me whenever I leave the house."

Thorne threw Alexandria a look that sent most men running from the room, Alexandria inched her chin higher. He turned to his aunt. "You will not go, and that is final."

"I don't need your permission, Thorne. I only need to have you look after Judith. Alexandria was a great success at the Singletons' ball and she assures me that Judith has an invitation from the Duchess of Singleton to a garden party tomorrow afternoon. I believe you have plans for the opera later that night." Lady Margaret smiled warmly at Alexandria. "I'm leaving Judith in good hands."

Thorne thought of the danger stalking him. "She cannot stay here."

All three women started at the vehemence of his voice. Judith bit her lower lip. "I understand, Thorne. You are on your honeymoon. I can retire to the country until Aunt Margaret returns." She tried to smile and failed. "After all, it's not as if my reputation would suffer. I was becoming bored with the Season anyway."

Alexandria glared at her husband. "I am sure Thorne didn't mean it that way."

He shoved four fingers through his hair. "Of course I didn't." Looking at the sadness in his sister's face, Thorne added one more score to settle with the attempted murderer. "All right, Aunt Margaret. But I want a letter from every port."

Lady Margaret looked stunned for a moment. "I-I may be too busy."

"I can't think of anything more dull than writing instead of enjoying life," Alexandria said helpfully.

"Nevertheless, I want a letter and an itinerary," Thorne said sternly. "Otherwise, I will assign someone to go with you."

"Oh, dear," Lady Margaret said, her gaze finding Alexandria.

"The thought of writing all those letters might upset anyone, Lady Margaret," Alexandria said, her head tilted to one side as if she were deep in thought. "Why don't you write me and include a letter to Judith and Thorne? I'll see that they receive theirs. After all, you did plan to send me information on animal husbandry in each place you dock."

Lady Margaret relaxed in her chair. "A splendid idea, Alexandria. I knew I was leaving Judith in good hands."

He glanced at the three expectant women, then sighed loudly. "Have a good trip."

The ladies jumped up, hugged each other, and giggled like schoolgirls. Thorne watched as Alexandria and Lady Margaret kept throwing each other side glances and frowned. If he didn't know better he'd think they were up to something. But that was idiotic. Alexandria might be impulsive, but his aunt was the soul of discretion. Perhaps his imagination was running away with him. Still, the idea of sending someone to watch over his aunt and her companion was a sound one. There was no reason for her to know.

"Now that's settled, there is no reason to delay your moving in," Alexandria said, as she hooked her arm through Judith's. "I'll have Benson get Henry and Mason, my two footmen, and we'll have you moved in by nightfall. Lady Margaret I insist we have your farewell dinner here."

In a matter of hours Judith was settled in the opposite wing from Thorne and Alexandria's bedchambers. His mouth tightened only fractionally when he saw that Lady Margaret's trunks were already packed. The farewell dinner was a mixture of sadness and joy.

When Alexandria insisted Lady Margaret spend the night to keep from being alone, Thorne was pleased and felt guilty that he had suspected something was going on. He wasn't pleased on learning the ladies planned to continue their conversation in Lady Margaret's room.

He wanted Alexandria in his bed. The thought that he desired her so much gave him the needed push to wish the ladies a good night and retire alone. Needing someone too much was the first step to being used. He went to bed missing Alexandria and wondering how could he have misjudged his wife and aunt.

An hour after awakening the next morning, Thorne knew he should have trusted his instincts. His aunt was gone, and his wife would only say that she was safe.

"Alexandria, you will tell me this instant which vessel my aunt planned to sail on," Thorne ordered. "There isn't enough time to find the answer on my own. It is too dangerous. Some-one should guard her."

She shook her head, sending the soft curls framing her face bouncing. "I gave my word, but if it will make you feel better, she did hire a man to take care of things."

"Who?"

"I can't tell you."

"Alex, I don't plan to ask you again."

"Good, this was getting so tedious." She stood. "The Duch-ess of Singleton's garden party is this afternoon and I promised to help Judith with her gown."

"Alex," Thorne growled.

"I gave my word, Thorne. Lady Margaret is safe." Alexandria edged toward the door. "You know how you can be such a stickler on honor. You shouldn't ask me to break my word."

"I could catch you, you know?" Thorne said darkly.

"I hope you won't," Alexandria said, reaching behind her to grasp the knob. "I'd probably do something foolish, then you'd do something foolish. Believe it or not, I don't like it when we argue."

"This isn't another of your attempts to prove you're the better man?"

"I only try that with you," she told him. "This has nothing to do with us. I am following Lady Margaret's wishes."

"Are you sure she's safe and well?"

"You have my word." Alexandria pulled the door opened, then paused as Thorne sat in the chair behind his desk. "Thank you."

He glanced up. "For what?"

"For trusting me," she said, and then was gone.

Thorne knew she had not given him much choice. There was no reason to suspect that the man after him meant any harm to his aunt or Judith. Now that Judith was living with them, it was going to be more difficult for him to protect them all. Alexan-dria seemed to have decided she liked Society and was determined to drag Judith with her. What a time for her to test her wings.

Later that afternoon, Thorne looked up from his cluttered desk as a knock sounded on the study door. "Yes?"

The door opened and Alexandria sailed in wearing a light gold taffeta gown. She looked beautiful and tempting. "I see you are ready to go," Thorne said.

"Yes, we just wanted to say goodbye." Smiling, she turned toward the open door. "Isn't that right, Judith?"

Judith, in a light pink organza tea gown, her hair in ringlets, framing her heart-shaped face, looked beautiful and uncertain. As she stepped through the open doorway, her questioning gaze searched Thorne's face. "Please say something."

Thorne slowly rose from his chair and went to her. "Sleeping Beauty finally woke up."

Her smile wobbled. "I had to. Frankly, I'm afraid my Prince Charming has climbed up the wrong trellis and rescued some other woman."

"His loss." Thorne gently touched her cheek. "You look beautiful."

"Doesn't she?" Alexandria said beaming. "Wait until you see her tonight dressed for the opera. Her only problem will be deciding who Prince Charming is."

Thorne, his throat tight, caught Alexandria's hand in his. "Thank you."

Alexandria flushed. "I didn't do anything. Now, we'd better be off. It's unfashionable to be late for tea."

Thorne lifted a heavy brow. "When did you start caring about being fashionable?"

"Why, Thorne, you'd think I was a complete hoyden. Come, Judith, before Thorne issues more insults." She started from the room. "I'd have you know I had the best instructors in England."

"And ignored them all," Thorne said softly.

* * *

"Let's hurry, we don't want to be too late," Alexandria said, pulling her gloves past her elbow.

"You planned on being late?" Thorne asked, leading the two women down the stairs.

"Of course," Alexandria confessed. "I had a long talk with the Duchess of Singleton about the best way to make an entrance and be seen and she said to arrive shortly before the curtain goes up. We'll be the center of attention."

Thorne glanced at Judith, whose fingernails dug into his coat sleeve. Ignoring the butler holding the door open, Thorne stopped and gently took Judith's arms. "Are you sure this is what you want to do?"

"No, I'm not." Judith said, her eyes direct. "But as Alexandria has pointed out, I have to make do with what I have. I must face my fears in order to conquer them. Otherwise, I'll always be a prisoner. I'm wearing a beautiful dress and I have both of you with me. It's now or never."

"I'm very proud of you." Holding out his arms, he waited until Judith, then Alexandria, each took an arm. Once again his wife had surprised him. He wondered if there would ever be a time in their marriage when she didn't. Handing her into the carriage, he honestly didn't think so. He looked at his wife, beautiful and golden, and decided for tonight he was going to try and forget about the danger and enjoy the changes in Judith.

An hour later, Thorne knew he had partially succeeded in one and completely failed in the other. He had never been so tired of people stopping by to say hello. Glaring at the latest duo to pay their respects, he barely held his peace. Judith, it seems, was learning from Alexandria, who wasn't afraid of the devil.

"Applegate, the curtain is about to go up for the second act," Thorne said mildly,

"Oh, quite, Grayson. One tends to forget the time in such pleasant company," the young man gushed.

"My wife and my sister thank you," Thorne said mildly, but there was no mistaking his possessiveness.

Flushing to the roots of his blond hair, the man took himself off, his friend snapping at his heels. As soon as the red velvet curtain closed, Alexandria said, "Thorne, you could have been more civil to the man."

"He's lucky I didn't throw him over the balcony, the way he was ogling the necklines of both your gowns. In the future you will see that your bodices are raised."

"Yes, Thorne," Judith said, drawing her shawl over her bare shoulders.

Watching Judith withdraw into herself once again made Alexandria want to hit her husband. Instead, she said, "I told you once, Thorne, if you think my gown immodest, you can pull it up yourself."

His eyes darkened. "One of these days you will push me too far."

" 'One day' is not tonight," Alexandria said, then turned to Judith, who sat next to her. "If your brother has a problem with the cut of our gowns, it is his problem, not ours. Lady Margaret approved of these dresses before she left. Do you think she would have if they were immodest?"

Judith's gaze went from brother to sister-in-law. Her head lifted regally, slim fingers released the shawl.

Alexandria nodded her approval.

Thorne gritted his teeth. If Judith decided to follow Alexandria's lead, he had better assign another man to watch them. His wife had a knack for turning an ordinary day into an event. Of all the time for Ann Masters to be arriving, now was the worse. Trying to escape her advances was going to be annoying as hell. Ann considered any man fair game, but a man who told her no she considered a challenge.

In some ways, she and Alexandria were a lot alike. Both were defiant and proud. Yet Alexandria had a seductive innocence that Ann had lost long ago. He wasn't sure if she'd ever possessed the loyalty Alexandria had.

He glanced over at Alexandria, then lower, to the rising swell of her creamy breasts. She glanced up and had the impropriety to turn one shoulder slightly toward him and smile challengingly.

"There is an old saying that you should never tease the lion with the cage door opened."

"What does that mean?"

"Someplace it is day, and this night is a long way from being over."

Thorne watched with satisfaction as Alexandria read the promise of his words and quickly gave her attention to the stage. Feeling better than he had since this morning, he sat back in his chair and thought of his hands inside the bodice of his wife's gown. His fingers would stroke her breast, feel the creamy flesh blossom at his touch, feel her nipple harden. Knowing Alexandria, she would do her best to avoid him once they arrived home. Even as his loins tightened, he smiled. In some things he was a patient man.

Arriving home two hours later, Alexandria insisted on making sure Judith was settled and comfortable for the night. Thorne said nothing, merely went to Alexandria's room and dismissed her waiting maid. Undressing, he climbed into her bed and waited.

Fifteen minutes later, Alexandria entered with the housekeeper's keys jingling in her hand. After locking her door, she went to the door connecting their bedchambers and locked it. "The lion is safely locked in his cage. Try and get me now?" she laughed, a full throaty sound of triumph.

"I'll do more than try," Thorne said, from the shadows of the canopied bed.

Alexandria whirled in a rustle of silk.

Throwing the covers back, he started toward his wife. Her eyes rounded at his nakedness and obvious arousal. "I believe you wanted some assistance with your gown." Long, elegant fingers rimmed the bodice of the gown, then slipped inside.

Alexandria gasped and grasped his hands. "Th-Thorne, I don't need your help now."

"But I need the practice in assisting you. Twice you have

requested my assistance and twice I have failed you." His thumb grazed her nipples. They hardened immediately.

She swallowed. "Judith—"

"If you think I plan to remain chaste while Judith is here, you are sadly mistaken." His lips grazed the top of her breast, then he lifted and took the pouting nipple between his teeth.

"Bloody hell," she mumbled, holding his hands more for support than to stop him.

Thorne managed a smile. "Not hell, paradise. And morning is a long time away." A tearing sound was heard, but neither noticed.

Alexandria's last coherent thought was that perhaps teasing a lion wasn't a good idea, but the results were very pleasurable.

"I have never done anything like this before," Judith said in a hushed voice.

"Well, I say you are long overdue," Alexandria replied, dragging her sister-in-law by the hand down the back stairs.

Judith almost smiled. "Clearly, this is not your first time."

Alexandria threw a smile over her shoulder. "Clearly." Opening the kitchen door, they walked past the wide-eyed servants. "Good morning, everyone," Alexandria greeted. "No need to stop working. Lady Judith and I will soon be out of your way." At the door, she stopped. "Benson, his lordship is busy in his study, and I know he wouldn't wish to be disturbed. Is that clear?"

Benson's face took on what was becoming a familiar pained looked. "Quite, your ladyship."

Grinning, Alexandria continued with Judith out the door. As ordered, the barouche awaited them. The driver stood by the chestnuts, the two footmen on either side of the doorless carriage. All were six feet tall and looked amazingly fit in their topcoats of vertical blue-and-gold-striped livery. "Good morning, George, Henry, Mason."

Quickly doffing his hat, George, the coachman, gained his

seat while one footman let down the padded footstep and the other moved to assist Judith, then Alexandria inside the carriage. As soon as the ladies were seated, the footmen jumped on the back of the carriage and it took off.

"May I ask where we are going?" Judith inquired.

"Rotton Row," Alexandria answered, lifting her umbrella. "I understand from the duchess that it is a place for women to go and be seen.

"I must confess, that I, like Thorne, am surprised by your sudden interest in Society."

Alexandria took an inordinate amount of time unfurling the tiny bit of lace and ribbons. "I want to make Thorne proud of me."

"I don't think the right way to go about it is to sneak out of the house while he is having a meeting in his study," Judith pointed out drolly.

"I know it may not sound right, but you will see. Anyway, he has become too protective lately." She shrugged her shoulders beneath an apricot gown. "I plan to show him that I will be safe."

"Why wouldn't you be safe?" Judith asked, nodding to a matronly lady in a passing carriage.

"I didn't say that I wouldn't be safe, he is just *afraid* that I won't be," Alexandria corrected. "There was a mishap at Grayson Hall, and if another one occurs, your brother is concerned that it might upset my father."

"Will it?"

"Most assuredly," Alexandria said, then sat back in her seat. "Therefore, it is up to me to prove to Thorne that I can go out without his knowledge and return home safely."

"I see your point, Allie. I only hope my brother sees it as well," Judith said ominously.

Alexandria chose to ignore her sister-in-law's warning, and instead, enjoyed the sheer freedom of being out and making the decision to do so. She understood Thorne's reasons to be protective, but she had to show him there was no need. She could take care of herself.

The carriage turned into Hyde Park and Alexandria thrust Judith's prediction out of her mind. Nothing could keep her from enjoying today.

"Look at that strange dog beside that carriage," she told Judith.

"The latest fashion accessory to an afternoon outing. Soon no well-bred lady will be without her dog trotting beside her coach in perfect harmony," Judith said sarcastically.

"Wolf would send the whole lot of them running for their lives." Alexandria's face saddened. "I worry about him. I hope he is all right."

"He is," Judith reassured, then nodded to another lady driving her own gig. "Allie, you didn't speak."

"Sorry, I was admiring her horse. Do you think Thorne might let me drive myself?" Alexandria mused.

"I don't know, but I do know that you just snubbed Lady Gilbert."

Alexandria managed to look suitably horrified. "I was paying more attention to her horse."

Judith nodded her understanding. "I know it may appear strange, but there is as much protocol while riding in the carriage as in leaving your card or proceeding to dinner."

"Please, can you help me? Thorne would be devastated if I offended anyone," Alexandria asked, hoping she looked sincere.

"Whatever you do, don't speak to someone above you in peerage unless you know them, and be sure and speak to those beneath you so they can speak to you," Judith explained.

Alexandria frowned. "How am I supposed to know who is who? I don't know these people."

"Just watch me," Judith advised. "I'll use my umbrella. If I lean it forward, it means they are above you, backward means beneath you."

"Splendid. Judith, I am so glad you are with me," Alexandria said, this time telling the truth. Her father had made sure she knew how to conduct herself with the aristocracy. That knowledge had honored her mother's memory and protected Alexandria against the aunts. Judith didn't have to know that Alexandria had a selective memory. Her sister-in-law needed to be needed and Alexandria was going to make sure she was. "We shall make a splendid pair."

"Here comes your first test." Judith tilted the umbrella forward.

Alexandria waited until the woman and her two daughters nodded, then nodded in return.

Judith glanced at Alexandria. "The Duchess of Winston and her two nieces. All three are sticklers for protocol. You did excel—" She stopped abruptly, her face tautening.

Alexandria followed the direction of her gaze and saw the Earl of Kendricks approaching on a prancing gray mare. Alexandria tensed. Of all the people Thorne might object to her meeting, Kendricks had to be at the top of the list. Telling the driver, who had slowed down at Kendricks's signal, to continue would cause too much gossip. She didn't care for herself, but now there was Judith to consider.

"Good afternoon, Lady Grayson. Lady Judith."

"Lord Kendricks," Alexandria said. Judith gave the briefest nod, then turned her shoulder to stare at a couple strolling on the footpath.

Kendricks, his gaze fixed on Alexandria, didn't appear to notice. "Once again I see you have slipped away from your husband."

Alexandria repressed her guilt and lifted her chin. "And once again you don't know what you're talking about."

Kendricks's hands tightened on the reins and the horse fought the bit, then neighed in pain. Flecks of foam in the animal's mouth became red-tinged. Concerned for the horse, Alexandria overrode her disgust for Kendricks. She leaned forward in her seat to get a better look at the animal. "Your horse seems to have a tender mouth."

"Her own fault. Like most females, she doesn't like to be ridden," Kendricks said snidely.

Before her marriage, Alexandria would have been ignorant of Kendricks's insinuation, but no longer. Her temper flared even as she realized the real reason for the horse's pain. She came to her feet. "My God! You're using a harsh bit! What kind of barbarian are you? If you want to show your horsemanship, don't cut your mount's mouth to pieces doing it."

Kendricks's handsome face darkened in rage as he glanced around. "Be careful of your accusations."

"I can prove what I'm saying." She reached for the footrest. Henry was there in a matter of seconds. The footman looked from Kendricks back to his mistress, then beseechingly at Judith.

"Allie, no," Judith pleaded, as she glanced around at the people stopping to stare. "Please do not create a scene."

"I'm sorry, but I won't let anyone abuse a horse in my presence. Henry," she said, extending her hand. The footman helped her down. As soon as her foot touched the ground, Mason, the other footman, stepped on the other side of her to put her between the men.

"Well, Lord Kendricks, are you so little a man that you're afraid of a woman showing you up for the barbaric coward you are, or will you let me remove that bridle?" Alexandria taunted, one hand on her hip.

"No one is going to touch my horse," he warned.

"Spoken like a true coward," she shot back.

"If you were a man, you'd pay for that," he said menacingly.

Alexandria sneered. "If I were a man, I'd make you pay for what you're doing to that horse. Anyone who has so little respect for a defenseless animal while prancing around deserves to be horsewhipped."

"It seems Grayson needs help in teaching you your place." Kendricks edged his horse closer.

Nineteen

"Stop!"

Heads turned toward the commanding voice, then bowed. Thirty feet away the Prince Regent sat atop a gray gelding. He looked stern and forbidding with his monocle and long mustache. With him was a guard unit of ten soldiers and two men in civilian clothes. One of the men rode to them.

For a moment Alexandria had eyes only for the prancing black Arabian stallion the stranger rode. Sixteen hands tall, his steps were quick and graceful as he trotted to them. He would run for miles and never tire.

"What is going on here?"

Alexandria finally looked at the rider. He was dressed in black, except for his white cravat, and his face was set in harsh angles and hard planes. A scar ran from his earlobe to the cravat as if someone had attempted to cut his throat. Alexandria looked at the gray eyes that held no warmth, and shivered. Somehow, she knew the person who'd attempted to harm the stranger had not lived.

"I am not in the habit of asking a question twice." The stranger spoke with such menacing quietness that for a moment Alexandria felt uneasy.

Kendricks's mouth tightened. "This is none of your concern, Radcliffe."

"Would you like me to relay your words to the Prince?" Radcliffe asked, his voice faintly taunting.

Kendricks's gaze lowered. "I meant no disrespect. I didn't know you spoke for Prince Albert."

Radcliffe's eyes remained glacial. "Now that you do, perhaps you'll explain why you would abuse this woman?"

"A misunderstanding."

"There has been no misunderstanding," Alexandria quickly said. "If you will check his horse's mouth, you'll find a harsh bit."

Radcliffe fixed his gaze on Alexandria. "You created this scene and risked a scandal to help a horse?"

If she could stand up to Thorne, she could stand up to this cold stranger. "Yes."

For a long moment he studied her, then his attention shifted to Kendricks's horse. "Take off the bridle."

"You can't be serious," Kendricks cried, wildly glancing around him at the milling crowd just out of hearing distance.

"Take off the bridle and proclaim aloud your thanks to the lady for calling your attention to the matter. Do it or I will take off the bridle myself," Radcliffe said, his voice as cold as his eyes had been earlier.

Kendricks didn't move until Radcliffe made a motion to dismount. Quickly getting off his horse, Kendricks tied the reins around the horse's neck then took off the bridle. His entire body vibrated with anger. His gaze promised retribution. "Thank you, Lady Grayson, for calling my attention to my horse's sore mouth." He spun on his booted heels to go.

"Kendricks," Radcliffe called and the man stopped. "Twice you chose to question me. For your sake, I hope there is not a third time."

Fear, stark and vivid, widened Kendricks's eyes. His gaze swiveled from the Prince to Radcliffe, who watched him with unblinking gray eyes. With one last hard look at Alexandria, Kendricks turned and continued on foot down the lane.

"Thank you, Lord Radcliffe."

"You can thank me by going home and taking your second-in-command with you," Radcliffe said.

Alexandria glanced around to see Judith behind her, her gloved hand wrapped around her umbrella. She blushed. "I thought you might need some help."

Alexandria grinned. "Kendricks didn't stand a chance."

"You have made an enemy in Kendricks. I advise you to stay clear of him," Radcliffe warned.

"You sound like a man used to giving orders," Alexandria said lightly.

A shadow of annoyance crossed his face. "Stay away from Kendricks, and tell your husband what happened."

Alexandria lifted her chin. Men must start giving orders from the cradle. "Thank you for your assistance, but you have no right to tell me what to do."

"Tell Grayson or I will," Radcliffe warned, then looked from the coachman to the footmen. "I'm sure Grayson will want to have some words with your servants as well."

"It's not their fault," Alexandria cried.

"No, it's yours, and what you do affects those around you," Radcliffe said. "If you can't learn caution, at least learn wisdom." Whirling his horse, he was gone.

Uncharacteristically stung by his words, Alexandria watched as he rode back to the group of men. The Prince listened as Radcliffe spoke to him, then they both started toward her. Knees trembling, Alexandria curtsied. Hearing Judith's "Oh, dear," didn't help.

"Lady Grayson, we would welcome you and yours at court," the Prince said, his black silk top hat, cigar, and reins in his left hand.

"You do me a great honor," she said, glad her voice sounded sure and strong.

Nodding, he rode on with Radcliffe by his side. Somehow, Alexandria knew he was behind the invitation. He had sternly reprimanded her, then gained her a high honor by getting the Prince to speak with her. But why?

"Judith, is Lord Radcliffe a friend of Thorne's?" Alexandria asked, climbing into the carriage.

"Not that I know of. But very little is known about the man. Most people try to stay away from him. People see him, I'm told, and turn in the opposite direction." Judith's face saddened. "He came to one of the parties I attended at the beginning of the Season, and people almost tripped over themselves getting out of the way."

Frowning, Alexandria said, "The scar is not that deforming."

"It's not the scar. It's something about the man, the almost palpable danger about him, as if he's glimpsed death and conquered it. Kendricks probably regrets his hasty tongue. Radcliffe is not a man one would want for an enemy." Judith looked thoughtful. "I wonder if that is why he doesn't have many friends. Even being accepted at court, he must be very lonely."

"I don't think a strong man like Radcliffe would let himself be subjected to any emotion that might make him vulnerable," Alexandria said tartly.

"Do you think admitting to loneliness makes you vulnerable?" Judith asked, watching Alexandria intently.

Alexandria opened her mouth to say yes, any weakness made you vulnerable, then stopped, remembering the passion she and Thorne shared. In his arms, she felt many emotions, but since that day in the drawing room, vulnerability had not been one of them.

"Allie?" Judith prompted.

"No. I don't," she finally answered. "However, I'm sure Radcliffe does. I wonder if the scar on his face has anything to do with his irritating manner."

"If I were you, I'd start worrying about Thorne. This outing definitely won't please him," Judith reminded Alexandria.

Her sister-in-law was right. Thorne had been adamant when they'd made the bargain about her acting befitting a countess, and no matter that people probably hadn't heard what was said; the rumors associated with it would probably be much worse. "I'll tell him in a way that he won't be upset."

Judith's dark eyes widened. "I have the greatest respect for

your abilities, but that is something I will have to see to believe."

"There is no need for you to come with me."

"I'm going."

"Do you think I need protection?"

"Thorne has been known to be unreasonable on certain occasions," Judith said frankly.

"Your point is well taken," Alexandria said.

Arriving home, Alexandria assured the coachman and the
footmen of her intervention with Thorne, then went straight to
the study. Lifting her hand to knock, she paused in mid-air when
she heard the muffled sound of angry voices. Lowering her hand
and ignoring Judith's gasp of incredulity, she pressed her ear to
the door.

One word rang clear. "Murder."

Frightened beyond belief, she opened the door. What she saw
chilled her to the bone. Thorne had his back to a strange man;
the man reached into his pocket. "Thorne, a gun," she yelled,
and started forward, umbrella raised.

What she saw next stopped her as effectively as if she had
run into a brick wall. Without turning, Thorne's left arm came
up at a right angle the same instant he back kicked with his left
foot. Her eyes widened larger as the stranger, moving with star-
tling speed, blocked both blows with his forearm.

Thorne spun and both men faced each other in a slightly
crouched position with their feet spread apart and their unclenched hands raised. To her utter astonishment, the strange
man smiled. Thorne hissed a guttural curse that made her ears
burn.

Straightening, Thorne looked across the small space separating him from one of the few men he called friend and cursed
again. Richard Barrows, Third Earl of Stonewell, appeared
amused at this turn of events. As usual, a smile lurked at the

corner of his mouth. Coming upright, he straightened his un-ruffled cravat.

"I assume the umbrella-brandishing lady is your wife," Stonewell said, his lips twitching.

Thorne was livid. He had lost control. Damn it. He never lost control. If Stonewell hadn't been trained by *The Shadow,* as Thorne had, he might be seriously injured, instead of fighting to keep from laughing. And what made Thorne angrier was that he had reacted to the panic in Alexandria's voice and not to what he knew. Stonewell posed no threat to Thorne.

Yet, when he had heard Alexandria yell a warning, he had reacted instinctively. But even as he sought to subdue the attacker, he had fought the fear for Alexandria that gripped him. All his years of discipline vanished the moment he thought she was in danger.

And there she stood, with a damned umbrella in her hand, ready to defend him from someone she thought had a gun. While he admired her courage, he couldn't help but worry that if the threat had been real, she might have been seriously injured. He had to make sure that that didn't happen. To do that, he had to control his emotions.

"Alexandria, I assume you have an explanation for your warning," he asked, walking to her.

Alexandria peered around Thorne as if to make sure the stranger presented no threat. His upper body appeared to be shaking oddly, but otherwise he remained with his back to her. "I heard the word 'murder,' then he reached into his pocket."

"Alex, you heard incorrectly. As for reaching into his pocket, he was simply checking the time. Let me point out that you entered without permission. Otherwise, such an erroneous assumption would not have occurred," Thorne advised her. "Also, while I commend you for your courage, you must allow me to take care of any situations which may arise regarding either your safety or mine."

She sighed. "I suppose we're back to the better man."

A heavy brow lifted, but his face remained impassive. "It does seem to be where all of our conversations generally lead."

"If I promise to try and remember, will you teach me how to fight like that."

Thorne wasn't surprised by the request. In fact, he was beginning to know his impulsive wife quite well. Her face and eyes glowed with excitement. Of course he had no intention of teaching her to fight, but a straightforward "no" would mean he'd never hear the end of it. As much as he hated to be evasive, in this case he had no choice. "Your skirts would get in the way. Now, if you will excuse me, I was just about to go to the club."

"The club?" she shouted.

He turned at hearing the panic in her voice. This time he allowed his gaze to go further than the umbrella. His eyes narrowed slightly, taking in Alexandria's slightly askew wide-brimmed straw hat. "Why were you coming to talk to me?"

She took a deep breath. "It wasn't my fault, Thorne."

He made an impatient sound. "It never is."

"Grayson, aren't you going to introduce me to your wife?" asked the elegantly dressed stranger, a smile curving his lips.

Thorne threw his best friend—they'd been at Eton together—a look that would have sent most men running for cover. Stonewell smiled, showing even white teeth in a sun-bronzed face. Thorne admitted defeat . . . for the moment. "Lady Alexandria Grayson, Richard Barrows, the Third Earl of Stonewell. Once, he was a close friend."

Stonewell's blue eyes twinkled. "I'm honored, Lady Grayson. You'll forgive me for not taking your hand, but I'm not sure if you're convinced yet not to use that umbrella on me."

Alexandria liked the brash man immediately. "Good afternoon, Lord Stonewell. I've heard so much about you. Please forgive me."

"For wanting to protect your husband? I hope I shall be fortunate enough to win a wife such as you, Lady Grayson," Lord Stonewell said, taking her hand and kissing it.

Thorne grunted and pulled Alexandria's hand away. "That's enough of that."

"I see you're as protective of her as she is of you," Stonewell told them.

Thorne and Alexandria looked startled at such an announcement.

"Isn't that the way it should be between a man and his wife?" asked a softly modulated voice.

Stonewell's entire body tensed. The teasing smile vanished as his gaze sought and found Judith standing in the doorway. "Lady Judith." The name was spoken with reverence and awe.

Judith smiled shyly. "Welcome home, Lord Stonewell."

In several long strides he stood in front of her. Taking her hands, he kissed both palms. Judith felt the rush of warm air graze her skin and shivered.

"Your letters kept me sane," Stonewell declared, as he continued to hold her hands.

Red stained Judith's cheeks. "It was the least I could do for someone serving his country so far away in India."

"Now that I am out of Her Majesty's service, I hope I can repay you in some small way for your kindness," Stonewell told her.

"Stonewell, if you keep acting the fop, I'm liable to think you got too much sun in the desert," Thorne said. "Turn Judith's hand loose. We have to leave."

Reluctantly, Stonewell bowed over Judith's hand. "I have not been under your brother's command for four years, yet he still gives me orders."

Judith smiled. "I think he likes giving orders."

"You know him too well." He kissed her hand and turned back to Thorne. "At your service."

"Alex, you and Judith must excuse us."

"Thorne, I—"

"We'll discuss it later," he interrupted, starting toward his desk.

"All right, but don't get angry with me when you hear about

what happened in the park with Kendricks this afternoon," Alexandria mumbled.

Thorne spun and grasped Alexandria's arms. "What happened?" he asked anxiously.

"So now you have time to talk with me."

"Damn it, Alex, I want to know exactly what happened. If that bastard touched you, he's a dead man."

Alexandria blinked at the deadly promise in her husband's voice. "H-he didn't touch me."

Realizing he had almost lost control again, Thorne loosened his grip. "I want to know what happened, and I want it now."

"All right." Alexandria gave Thorne a very abbreviated version of what happened, leaving out Radcliffe's name and ending with the quickness of George, Henry, and Mason to protect her and Judith.

"Do you have any idea of the danger you put yourself or Judith in?"

"There was no danger, Thorne," Judith rushed to say.

"Did Kendricks bother you?" Stonewell asked her, his tone as deadly as Thorne's had been earlier.

"I didn't think he even knew I was there. I was watching him. He never took his eyes from Alexandria until Radcliffe and the Prince Regent arrived," Judith said thoughtfully.

"Radcliffe and Prince Albert were there!" Thorne thundered.

Alexandria thought of running, but knew she wouldn't get ten feet in her cumbersome dress. Knowing she had little choice, she told Thorne everything.

"My God," Thorne said, and closed his eyes.

For the first time Alexandria regretted not handling the situation with more decorum. The one thing she hadn't meant to do was cause a scandal.

"I don't think the Prince Regent thought it bad of me or he wouldn't have invited us to court," Alexandria reasoned. She wasn't about to tell him Radcliffe's opinion of her.

Thorne opened his eyes. "He invited you to court?"

"*Us* to court. He's a chivalrous man, and his love of horses is well known," Alexandria said. "So you see, no harm was done."

"No harm! No harm!" Thorne yelled. "Not only did you disobey me, but you managed to embarrass Kendricks in front of the Prince and only God knows who else. The story will be discussed for weeks. Kendricks will not forgive or forget, no matter how smoothly you say Radcliffe handled things."

"The hor—"

"Be quiet. The horse is nothing compared to—" His words stopped abruptly.

"I would never put Judith in danger, Thorne," Alexandria said softly, sure he had been about to mention his sister's name. Her hand rested lightly on his arm. "You must know that."

Thorne studied Alexandria's worried face and felt a strong urge to drag her into his arms and keep her safe. Didn't she realize what a challenge she presented to a jaded bastard like Kendricks? Thorne met Stonewell's gaze and knew their thoughts were the same.

"If you ever disobey me again or do anything so foolish, Alex, I'll do something we'll both regret," Thorne promised.

"I shall be the soul of discretion."

"Somehow I doubt it," Thorne told her. "However, at the Hartworths' party tonight, please try to curb your impulsive nature. If I don't miss my guess, you will be even more the center of attention."

"I will be above reproach," she promised.

To Thorne's great relief, Alexandria kept her word at the party. She smiled, dazzled, met vague innuendo and outright rude questions with a look of boredom, then quickly changed the subject. Those thoughtless enough to repeat their questions found themselves staring after her.

At the moment, she sat across the brightly lit room sipping champagne punch, looking beautiful in what was becoming her signature color, gold. Judith, who was seated next to her, glowed. Stonewell stood nearby. Nodding to Stonewell, Thorne slipped into the gardens and waited.

After leaving the house this afternoon, he had gone to see the Duke of Singleton. Ann Masters had arrived the day before from France and they wanted Thorne to meet her tonight. His refusal stunned Singleton and earned a nod of approval from Stonewell. Alexandria needed her husband more than Ann needed to rekindle an affair with Thorne that had burned to ashes years ago.

Thorne had agreed to meet *The Shadow* at the party, but that was all he'd agreed to. Through the windows he caught a glimpse of gold and knew he had purposely positioned himself where he could watch Alexandria. Stonewell was a good man, but Thorne understood Alexandria better than anyone, and as irrational as it seemed, he knew he could protect her better.

An evergreen bush rustled, then a shadow materialized by his side. "So she has put a ring through your nose."

Thorne tensed at the cutting words. "I will protect what is mine. Think what you will."

"Six men have died, and I intend to see that none are added to their number." *The Shadow* bit out each word. "If you are so worried about your wife, perhaps I should make sure she is no longer a distraction."

Thorne turned on the man whose gray eyes were bottomless pits of nothingness. "You can die as easily as another man."

"Death means nothing to one who has no life. Yet we both know if I give the order, your wife will be kidnapped, even if I die." The voice carried absolute conviction. "Perhaps separating the two of you is best in any case. If we kept her, at least you'd know she was safe."

"She stays with me." Thorne said each word distinctly.

"Then I shall tell Ann to expect you at nine tomorrow night," *The Shadow* said. "Instead of sending men for your wife, I will send them to protect her. Kendricks went to his estate in the country for a couple of weeks. Is that out-of-the-way enough for you?"

That was as good as Thorne would get. "It's not as permanent as I'd have liked."

"Killing him would have solved nothing. The man I knew as *Jaguar* would not have caused so much confusion because he feared for a woman."

"Perhaps because he had yet to meet the right woman," Thorne retorted.

"Your affection for this woman could be costly. You wanted to wait until Stonewell could be with her; now that he is here, you still refuse to leave her. She is becoming a liability."

"Harm her in the slightest way and I'll hunt you to the ends of the earth."

"Yes, but who can find a shadow?" Turning, he faded into the night.

"You heartless bastard," Thorne mumbled. Yet not so long ago, he'd have readily agreed with *The Shadow.* Everything and everyone was dispensable for the good of England. But that was before a turquoise-eyed spitfire had come into his life. He had a sudden need to be with his wife, to hold her and make sure she was safe. He didn't question the urge, simply acted on it.

Reentering the ballroom, he collected Alexandria and Judith, then bade their host and hostess goodnight and went home. Taking only enough time to undress and put on a his brocade robe, Thorne entered Alexandria's bedroom, words of dismissal already on his lips for her maid. They were never uttered.

Alexandria, in her chemise and drawers, stood in the center of the room, whirling and kicking, clearly practicing fighting techniques. "I wonder if you will ever cease to surprise me."

She flushed but met his gaze. "I thought you had retired for the night."

"Obviously. Do you mind if I watch?"

"There is nothing to watch unless you teach me."

Shaking his head, he walked to her. "I will not."

"Why?"

"Because the only man who will ever see you dressed this way is me," he said possessively, his finger grazing the curve of her breasts.

"Of-of course, but if I had on breeches—"

"You will never wear breeches again," he told her, kissing the soft curve of her shoulder.

"Thorne, you have an annoying habit of telling me what to do."

"You have an annoying habit of talking when I'm trying to make love to you." His lips took hers, his thumb grazing her nipple. "I like your moans better. Much better." Lifting her in his arms, he carried her to the bed.

Twenty

"Mr. Anderson, I'm sure Lady Grayson will be down shortly," Judith said, then glanced once again at the closed drawing room door as if expecting it to open and reveal her tardy sister-in-law. "She was looking forward to discussing her investment in the tin mines with you."

Anderson's brown eyes narrowed behind wire-framed glasses. "It isn't like her to be late." His gaze strayed to the gold inlaid clock atop a neat desk, then to the pocketwatch in his hand. Both said a quarter to eleven. His appointment had been for ten.

"Grayson is probably detaining her," Stonewell offered. His explanation was met with a deep blush from Judith and a look of reprimand from the solicitor. Stonewell resisted the urge to grin and tried again. "Lady Judith and I were discussing only yesterday how her brother likes to give orders. He's probably discussing with Lady Grayson her agenda for the day. Lady Judith, I'm delighted you escaped such an ordeal."

"Lady Grayson does require a strong hand sometimes," Mr. Anderson admitted thoughtfully.

Judith rushed to defend her friend. "Allie just knows her own mind."

"Sharp mind it is, too." Opening his satchel, the solicitor took out a sheet of paper, then stood. "I don't think she'd mind me telling you first, since you also invested. They struck another vein of tin. You both stand to double your investments. Of course, as you agreed, you'll have to repay your loan to Lady Grayson out of your first returns."

A squeal of unladylike delight erupted from Judith. Realizing what she'd done and that Lord Stonewell knew she had entered into commerce, she looked at the paper that was being handed to her as if it were a snake. What must he think of her? Why did she have to be an early riser and agree to come down to meet Lord Stonewell and Mr. Anderson?

Each had arrived within five minutes of the other and both had appointments with Thorne and Alexandria, who showed no signs of coming downstairs. Under strict orders never to disturb them when their doors were closed, no matter the occasion, Benson had sought Judith's assistance. Now, she had shamed herself.

Clearly puzzled by the distress on Lady Judith's face, the solicitor hesitated. "Is there a problem?"

"She's probably stunned with her good fortunes," Lord Stonewell put in. "You and Lady Grayson have my congratulations. If she agrees, perhaps you'll let me sit in on some of your investment talks."

"You . . . you don't think it unladylike?" she questioned softly.

Lord Stonewell gave an inelegant snort. "No. I think a woman should learn about finances. Especially since some women spend money so recklessly."

Judith brightened. "Allie is teaching me about commerce. I must admit, I never thought about it before."

"If nothing else, Lady Grayson will make you think," Mr. Anderson said.

"I couldn't agree with you more," said Thorne from the doorway, his arm possessively curving the waist of a blushing Alexandria. "Good morning."

"Good morning, everyone." Her cheeks were as rosy as her gown. "I'm sorry that I'm late, Mr. Anderson."

He waved her apology aside. "Your sister-in-law took very good care of me."

"I don't plan to be as gracious, Grayson. I'll have to think of some way suitable to repay you," Stonewell said sternly, a twinkle in his blue eyes.

Judith looked stricken. "I-I'm sorry, Lord Stonewell. I didn't mean to bore you. I didn't realize . . . that . . ." She stammered to a close.

Disregarding propriety, Stonewell crossed the space separating them and took her hand in his large one. "It is I who should apologize. I forget you are not used to our barbs. Please forgive me. It was my intention to bring a smile to your face, not a frown."

Judith's anxious expression dissolved into a shy smile. "It is I who should apologize for my hastiness."

"Why don't we forgive each other?" Stonewell kissed Judith's hand.

"Stonewell, if you're finished, we can go into the study," Thorne said, his tone caustic.

No one missed the change in Thorne's voice—least of all, the man it was directed toward. Stonewell's shoulders snapped back and the smile slid from his handsome face. "By all means. Good day, ladies, Mr. Anderson." Briskly he walked from the room, Thorne on his heels.

As soon as the study door closed behind him, Thorne spoke. "What the hell was that all about?"

"I have no idea what you are talking about."

"Kissing and simpering over Judith," Thorne said through clenched teeth. "I won't have you treating her like the rest of your women."

Blue eyes glittered. "By that, I assume you mean kissing her hand. If you mean anything else, I'd advise you not to say it."

"I'll say what I damned well please," Thorne roared. "Judith isn't like the other women you've met. She has no more defense against you than a baby chicken against a fox."

"She doesn't need any," Stonewell said, his voice rising. "God, what kind of friend do you think I am to take advantage of an innocent like Judith? She's had enough in her life to contend with."

Instead of soothing Thorne, his words angered him more. "Yes, and it's my fault. That's why I won't let anything or anyone hurt her again."

"I could never hurt Lady Judith; you should know that," Stonewell told him.

"I know you wouldn't do it intentionally, but you know the effect you have on women. How is she supposed to know it's just your way?" Thorne walked to the window and looked out on the cloudless day. "She asks so little of life and gets nothing in return. Not even the simple pleasure of dancing."

"What are you talking about?" Stonewell asked, his entire body coming alert.

Thorne whirled, his hand gripped the back of a wing chair. "You were at the party last night. Did you see one man ask her to dance? Didn't you think it strange? Alexandria refuses to accept dances so Judith will not feel alone, but it has to be tearing her up inside. She is just beginning to have enough confidence to go out with us. I won't have you destroying that and adding more pain."

"She will dance," Stonewell said softly, his voice ringing with absolute conviction.

"What?"

"Judith will dance," Stonewell said.

Thorne studied the closed face of his friend and knew he would get nothing else from him. When Stonewell was in one of his intractable moods, no one was able to budge him. It was almost as if two men resided in the same body: one affable; the other brooding.

Thorne felt an unexpected moment of unease. Stonewell could be singularly driven when he put his mind on something. For whatever reason, he had decided to champion Judith. Judith needed a friend. Stonewell's charm was legendary, but so were his fighting skills. "I need your help, but not if it might hurt Judith."

"Then I suggest you get on with whatever it is you want me

to do." Stonewell sat in a chair and crossed one leg over the other.

After studying the direct gaze of his friend for a long moment, Thorne sat behind his desk. "I have to see Ann tonight, and if I know Ann, once she sees I'm not going to crawl back into bed with her, she'll want to have me dancing on her string for amusement."

"What do you want me to do, wait until the lights are out, then take your place?" Stonewell asked, his usual humor having returned.

Thorne lifted a heavy brow. "Somehow I think she would notice the difference."

"Probably." Stonewell shrugged broad shoulders beneath a dark blue frock coat. "I assume you have another job for me."

Thorne nodded. "My 'no' is not going to stop Ann. She'll keep trying, enjoying having me pay attention to her. Consequently it will take time to get the information *The Shadow* wants. But I'm hoping it will also keep the killer's attention solely on me. I don't want Alexandria or Judith getting hurt by being too close to me. Ann's little game may prove useful." He drew a deep breath.

"My wife, however, is not one to stay indoors, and where she goes, Judith goes. I'm betting the man is after me, but I don't want to take a chance on being wrong. I wanted you to escort them wherever they go—that is, until what just happened in the drawing room."

"I thought we were finished with that topic," Stonewell said mildly, studying the shine on his black boots.

"You hurt her, Stonewell."

Stonewell glanced up. Something flashed in his light blue eyes, then was gone. "It was never my intention."

"That is what I was trying to make you understand earlier." Thorne's mouth compressed into a tight line. "Judith doesn't have the confidence of other women because she can never forget she has a limp."

"Don't you think it's time she forgot?"

"Yes, but not because of a man who will expect more than she is able to give," Thorne said with brutal honesty.

Stonewell's hands opened and closed in a helpless gesture. "Where were you planning to go tonight?"

Thorne waited a long moment before he spoke. "To the theater."

"I shall be here at eight." Stonewell put on his top hat. "I will protect both of your ladies." Opening the door, he started down the hallway. Head down, his thoughts dangerous, he almost missed her. Something caused him to look up. What he saw caused his chest to hurt more than he thought possible and allow a man to remain living and sane.

Judith, beautiful and uncertain, stood at the top of the stairs. Her lower lip quivered. She tucked it between her teeth, then blurted, "Did you and Thorne have a disagreement because of me?"

The pain in his chest intensified. He'd rather walk through fire than give her one moment's unhappiness. "If that were true, would he have asked me to escort you and Lady Grayson to the theater tonight?"

Surprise and elation flashed across her face, then it was gone as if it had never been. "I guess not."

"Neither your brother nor I wishes you the slightest worry. You must forgive our bad manners." He smiled. "Did you make any other investments?"

"No. I was too upset to remain." She flushed. "I mean—"

"You mean you were concerned about your brother and couldn't concentrate," Stonewell offered helpfully.

Straightening her shoulders, she looked straight at him and said, "I mean I was concerned about both of you."

Stonewell started up the stairs. Before he had taken two steps, she was gone. His hand clamped the banister. "You won't be able to run forever."

"Lord Stonewell, do you also talk to yourself?" Alexandria asked coming up behind him.

Turning, he bowed. "Not that I am aware of. Good day, Lady Grayson. Mr. Anderson."

"A likable young man," the solicitor said, watching Stonewell leave through the door Benson held open.

"Yes, he is." Alexandria shook Anderson's hand. "I am sorry to rush you off."

"I understand. Good day, Lady Grayson."

Going down the hall, Alexandria knocked on the study door. After a brisk command to enter, she did so. The frown on Thorne's face slowly disappeared. His broad shoulders, however, remained rigid. She felt a strange and unexpected need to make everything right for him and bring the smile back to his face.

"I see brothers are just as protective of their sisters as fathers are of their daughters."

Thorne sent her a skirting glance. "Are you going to tell me I overreacted?"

"We were condemned, yet we were innocent," she said, coming to stand by his side. "Judith needs to feel as if she is worthy to be a woman. I can't imagine you having a friend who'd take advantage of her need."

"I only did what I thought was right."

"So did my father," she said softly.

"Humph," Thorne said, not liking the comparison. "However, unlike your father, I'm willing to give Judith and Stonewell the benefit of the doubt. I've asked him to escort you and her to the theater tonight."

"Why can't you take us?" Alexandria asked, her hand resting on his shoulder.

"I have things requiring my attention," Thorne said, hating the deception.

"Then we won't go," Alexandria said.

"I would like for you to go. In fact, this may take a few evenings to finish, and I don't want you and Judith becoming bored."

"You mean, you don't want me getting her into trouble," Alexandria said dryly.

"The thought had occurred to me."

"I'll go—if you take me riding in the morning."

Thorne's smile was pure male. "You're beginning to like being on top."

She punched him on the shoulder. "On a horse."

He pulled her onto his lap. "I like my idea better."

"Well, I like mine," she told him.

"All right, my sweet. But don't be surprised if we do both."

Alexandria blushed. Thorne laughed and pulled her into his arms, loving her softness and the sweet smell of lavender that always seemed to be on her skin. The word "loving" brought a frown to his face. Although it wasn't the same as "in love," he had better watch himself. Falling in love wasn't part of their bargain.

Thorne stepped with obvious reluctance from the hired conveyance. Black eyes scanned the foggy streets before he walked up the six steps leading to Ann Masters' front door. It opened on the second rap of his silver-tipped cane.

"Good evening, your lordship," the butler said, standing aside so Thorne could enter. "Miss Masters is waiting for you upstairs. If you will please follow me." He reached for Thorne's hat and cane.

"I'll keep these," Thorne told the man who was on the early side of twenty. "Please tell Miss Masters if she is not downstairs within ten minutes, I am leaving and not returning."

The six-foot-plus butler blinked. "I-I beg your pardon, sir?"

"You heard me. Ten minutes." Thorne pointedly took out his watch.

The uncertain servant stared at Thorne for a full three seconds, then started for the stairs. Once he was at the top, he stopped and looked back as if to make sure Thorne was still there.

Replacing his watch, Thorne leaned against the gold and blue wallpaper in the entryway, crossed one leg over the other at the ankle, and prepared to wait. He had no doubt Ann would come down in less than ten minutes, if nothing else, to berate him for not rushing to her bed. She might as well learn he had no intention of taking any other woman to bed but his wife.

"How dare you?" Ann screeched from the second floor. Grabbing the folds of her transparent nightgown, she rushed down the stairs. Lustrous, fiery red hair flowed around her shoulders and fell over one lush breast. With each angry step she displayed long, bare legs.

Behind her on the stairs, the butler looked lustfully at the near-naked splendor of her backside as he followed her. Reaching the bottom of the steps, he tripped, glanced guiltily at Thorne, then hurried away.

Thorne looked at the beautiful woman rushing toward him and felt not the slightest twinge of desire. He'd thought he wouldn't, but it was gratifying to know he'd met the challenge.

Ann stopped mere inches from him, her ample breasts heaving from exertion. "I've waited two days for you, and this is the way you treat me."

"If you were cooperative, you wouldn't have to wait at all," Thorne said mildly.

"You know why I sent for you." She brushed her hair impatiently over her shoulder.

"Yes, to play the stallion to your mare," Thorne said, not even trying to hide the irritation he felt.

Ann's red lips parted in an inviting smile. With a practiced shrug, the negligee slipped over her shoulder. The material hung on an uptilted nipple. "Would that be so bad?" Her hand reached for him.

Knowing her usual habit, Thorne caught her wrist inches from his groin. "It won't work, Ann. Nothing you can do is going to get me back in your bed."

She jerked her hand away. "Is your wife that good?"

His face harshened. "Mention my wife again and I'll leave."

"You wouldn't dare. Do you have your orders?"

"You should know I never bluff."

She glanced at the gloves and hat he held. "Oh, Thorne, I don't want to fight with you. I just want you to remember the good times we had," she said cajolingly, her finger tracing the intricate folds of his crisp white cravat. "After me you didn't have another mistress."

"Because I found the trouble far outweighed the pleasure," Thorne told her.

She jerked her hand back as if she had touched fire. "You will regret that."

Thorne sighed impatiently. "Ann, the name."

"I seem to have forgotten. Perhaps after we have visited Lady Addison's salon I'll remember." She started toward the stairs.

Thorne frowned. Lady Addison's salon was the center of the literary and artistic avante garde. It was also the center for open liaisons. The women who came were in the company of their protector or looking for one. "The moment we enter you know what they will think."

She glanced over her shoulder. "Yes, they'll think you have finally come back to my bed."

"Then I shall have to make sure they know differently." Steel rang in Thorne's voice.

"You do and you'll have the death of three men on your conscience." Thorne's eyes narrowed. "That's right, three men have been marked for death. Only I know when their deaths are to be and who is the assassin."

"You would see three men die because I refused to bed you?" Thorne asked, appalled at her callousness.

"You won't refuse for long." Turning, she walked up the stairs, her derrière swaying in wanton invitation.

"I could beat the answer out of you."

Her shoulders tensed, but she didn't turn. "You could, but

then, who would you send, the next time you needed information? I won't be long."

Thorne gritted his teeth to keep from following Ann up the stairs and carrying out his threat. But for now it suited his purpose for her to think she was in charge. He only hoped he didn't have to keep up the pretense for long. He had an idea keeping Alexandria from becoming suspicious was going to be the hardest task of all.

Something was bothering Thorne and she was going to find out what it was Alexandria thought as she watched the house her husband had entered moments earlier. Shifting restlessly in the seat of the hansom cab, she tried to figure out what was going on.

Since he had asked Lord Stonewell to escort her and Judith five days ago, Thorne had become tense and silent. To her questions of what was bothering him, she received an abrupt answer of, "Nothing." Only in their lovemaking was he the tender and passionate man she remembered. If Thorne was in some type of trouble, it was her duty to help him.

She hadn't missed the glances he and Lord Stonewell exchanged nor that, despite Thorne's anxiety about Judith, he permitted Stonewell to escort them. He was with them more than Thorne was. Knowing asking Lord Stonewell was futile, she had decided to get the answers for herself. After all, she reasoned, Thorne had helped her out in her hour of need and she was going to do the same for him.

Obviously, he labored under the erroneous opinion that all women were created equally useless. Well, he was about to find out how ingenious and creative his wife was. Glancing down, she smiled at her breeches-clad legs.

Since she couldn't travel freely as a woman, she had decided to do so as a man. It had been simple to send the measurements she'd obtained from her dressmaker to a tailor. The clothes arrived that morning and by afternoon she was pleading a vague illness and requesting to be left to rest in peace. She had slipped out of the house by the servant's entrance minutes before Thorne had entered a hired cab.

Adjusting her black wig, she tried to think of all the things that might disturb Thorne. Was his mother behind his nightly meetings or was he in some sort of financial trouble? Whatever it was, she was going to find out the reason.

The front door of the house opened and two people emerged. Alexandria felt the air leave her chest. On her husband's arm was a woman.

The hazy illumination from the gaslight almost directly in front of them left no doubt of her beauty or of her lush figure. Brazenly, the woman pressed against Thorne before he handed her into the carriage.

Alexandria hardly noticed that as she'd instructed, her cab started to follow them. Anger quickly escalated into rage. Lies . . . all lies. He had used her and like a . . . a woman, she had let him.

Lost in thought, she almost missed what the driver hollered. " 'ey, you in there. I can't follow 'em no further."

Finally looking out the window, Alexandria saw a large wooden gate open and Thorne's carriage enter, then the gate close. Putting on her top hat, she stepped onto the cobbled street. "Why? What is that house?" she asked, pitching her voice to make it huskier.

"Where a gent can take 'is lady friend an' not worry about no wif'," the driver explained, envy and relish mixed in his words. "No one gets in 'cept he's known. Many 'v' tried."

"We'll just see about that," Alexandria mumbled, and started toward the gate.

Twenty-one

Five minutes later, Alexandria knew her driver had spoken the truth. The rude man guarding the gate refused to allow her entrance, although she assured him she was a late-arriving guest of Lord Grayson's. The servant then had the unmitigated gall to look her straight in the eye and say, "Never 'eard of 'im."

Pretending to leave, she waited in the shadows of the leafy branches of a big elm tree growing over the six-foot brick wall. Without anything to stand on, she couldn't scale the wall or reach the limbs, but the tree might serve as a way out . . . if she ever got in.

A red carriage trimmed in black lumbered down the street and stopped in front of the carriage gate. Watching the guard wave to the coachman in greeting, she quickly came up on the guard's blind side and slipped in beside the carriage.

Once inside, she ran into the dense foliage of the garden. Looking from her hiding place, she saw a footman in gold and green livery open the coach door while another footman opened the front door. When all were gone, she followed the bricked path to the back of the house. Open double doors allowed laughter, voices, and music from the crowded room to flow outside.

Hiding her hat behind a rhododendron bush, she straightened her wig, adjusted her black and gold embroidered waistcoat over her bound breasts, then casually walked into the house, hoping her face showed boredom and not the rage she felt. Keeping to the wall, her head slightly bent, she didn't stop until she was partially concealed by a two-foot wide pillar. Her gaze searched the yellow-and-white room until she found them.

The woman wore a loud red dress the bodice of which tried, without success, to conceal her ample breasts. With each calculated sweep of her oriental fan, each twist of her bare shoulders, each movement against Thorne's arm, the material lost more of the battle. Alexandria expected her nipple to pop out. Apparently, so did several men in the room, because they also stared at the woman.

Gradually, Alexandria's gaze moved to Thorne. Nothing could have prepared her for the anger shimmering in his black eyes. She closed her eyes against it. He was jealous of the woman's displaying herself. All his words of a bargain and being faithful were nothing but lies.

"Quite something, isn't she?"

Alexandria's eyes snapped open to see an elderly gentleman standing by her side. In his blue-veined hands was a brandy snifter. His gaze was fixed on the woman by Thorne. "Who is she?"

"Ann Masters, an actress. By the sound of your voice I'd say she had added another heart to her collection," the man said, turning to look at Alexandria.

Her eyes widened for a second until she realized that anger and strained had roughened her voice and made it thready. "Does that include the tall gentleman by her side?"

He swirled the brandy, then sipped. "Who can tell about him, but there is talk he might." He leaned over and whispered in a conspiratorial tone. "Recently married to a woman who is reported to be stunning, yet, since Ann returned from France a week ago, he has been with her five nights straight." The balding man sighed. "To be young." He glanced down toward his pants, then sighed again, then looked at Alexandria. "You are young, find another woman to bed. At least you can."

Finally understanding the elderly man's problem, she coughed to hide her blush. "Perhaps you're right. Please excuse me." She didn't stop until she began to climb the elm tree beside the outside wall. Landing lightly on the sidewalk, she continued toward the carriage.

"Lost your 'at?"

"Take me back to where you picked me up," she told the driver. Inside, she closed her eyes against the pain and anger seeping through her. When the pain came, it knotted her stomach and stung her throat.

"I will not cry. I will not cry," she repeated over and over, like a litany. Clutching her stomach, she rocked back and forth.

Arriving home, she took the back stairs and entered her room. Opening the wardrobe, she began dragging out clothes. She was leaving, the hussy was welcomed to Thorne. How dared he make her trust him, then take that woman to his bed. Her hand was on another dress when she stopped.

Thorne came to her bed each night and they made love, often into the early morning. Afterward they would be exhausted and fall asleep in each other's arms. The staff no longer expected them downstairs until after eleven. Was it possible a man could make love so many times and with such enthusiasm to two different women?

She looked down at the dark rose dress in her hands, the same dress she had worn the day in the study Thorne had taught her to trust him. A pungent ache filled her heart as she remembered their lovemaking and Thorne's tender teasing afterward. She remembered Rachel's lies of Thorne wanting her. Perhaps the Masters woman wanted Thorne as well.

"No woman is taking my husband," Alexandria said, rehanging her dresses. Afterward, she undressed and stuffed the man's clothes in the back of her wardrobe. Pulling on her nightgown, she crawled beneath the covers. Blowing out the candle, she prayed her instincts were right.

Hours later, she heard the connecting door to Thorne's bedroom open. Tightly shutting her eyes, she pretended to be asleep. A short time later, she felt his presence as clearly as if she could see him.

Warm lips grazed her forehead. Instinctively, her body

heated. How could her body react to him after what she had seen? What if he really was playing her false? Her balled fist connected with the side of his head. His yowl of pain didn't ease her anger.

"Damn it, Alex, wake up. You almost maimed me."

Be thankful it wasn't a couple of feet lower. Her eyelids fluttered upward. Thorne stood by her bed with a candle in his hand. "Thorne?"

Scowling down at her, he gingerly rubbed the side of his head. "You hit me."

"Why would I do that? You haven't done anything to deserve to be punished, have you?" she questioned, hoping he would take the opportunity to tell her about Ann Masters.

He straightened. "Never mind. I just came to check on you."

Alexandria spoke past the lump in her throat. "I'm feeling much better now. I'm so fortunate to have such a caring husband."

"Goodnight." He left.

Rubbing her hand over her bruised knuckles, she looked at the closed door. For a moment, he had looked desperate, unsure. Those emotions didn't fit a man like Thorne. Perhaps she was right. There was only one way to find out.

"As I told you, Miss Livingston, Miss Masters is not receiving any visitors."

"Did you tell her I was from the newspaper?" Alexandria asked the young man who stared at her with anything but the studied indifference of a butler.

His eyes lifted from her bosom. "Yes."

Her sigh was eloquent and long. "I was so hoping our readers could hear firsthand from a woman who is a connoisseur of men. We were willing to pay a hundred pounds for—"

"A hundred pounds!"

"Yes, didn't I mention that." She looked flustered. "What must I have been thinking of?" Opening her reticule, she pulled out a fistful of bank notes. She pressed one into the butler's white-gloved hand. "Please be so kind as to inform Miss Masters and tell her if she doesn't wish to be interviewed, then I will have to ask the next woman on my list."

Pocketing the money, the servant mounted the stairs. Less than two minutes later he was back. "Miss Masters will receive you in her bedroom."

Greed had opened another door. Keeping the growing distaste from her face, Alexandria mounted the stairs. Receive, ha! Who did the woman think she was, the queen?

Stepping inside the lavishly appointed bedroom, Alexandria thought perhaps the woman did. Gold was in the oriental rug, the velvet chair coverings, and the heavy damask draperies. The redheaded woman reclined indolently amid several pillows in an enormous four-poster bed. Her thin gown clearly revealed her large breasts.

Alexandria glanced at the butler; he licked his lips, then left.

"You said something about a hundred pounds," Ann said, her voice husky and deep.

Walking to the bedside, Alexandria laid the money on the night table. Perfume bottles, jewelry, and several books stretched from end to end. So did a thin layer of dust.

Slender fingers grasped the money, then stuffed it behind the pillow against her back. "What can I do for you, Miss, er—"

"Livingston," Alexandria finished. "Since there has been so much on, shall we say, the other woman in well-placed men's lives, I wanted to do a column on a single woman who captured the hearts of legions of admirers. Of course, I shall keep your name and your protectors a secret."

Ann picked up a bottle of perfume and dabbled some on her wrist. "Why me?"

"Your name came up the most often when I was making out the list, and," Alexandria decided to flatter her, "You were said to be the most beautiful and the most successful. Your talent as a great actress is known at home and abroad."

The woman preened and Alexandria thought of Billingsly.

Thrusting her breasts out, she ran a hand through her thick, curly hair. "I wasn't aware that I was so famous."

Infamous, Alexandria thought, but held her tongue. "If I could use your writing table, we can get started." It was already past nine and she needed to be back home before Thorne checked on her.

"How do I know you're not a wife?" Ann asked, her gaze suddenly suspicious.

Alexandria gave her a level look. "Because I have paper in my reticule instead of a gun."

Ann blanched. Alexandria had said the words with so much conviction the other woman shrank against the pillows. Cursing inwardly for allowing her anger to show, Alexandria continued to the writing table and took out her paper. "I assume there are a great number of wives who are unhappy about, shall we say, your expertise?"

Ann relaxed and looked smug. "Enough."

"Miss Masters, I paid you for information. If you do not wish to give me that information and do it to my satisfaction, perhaps I should go to the next person on the list." Alexandria stood.

Ann pressed against the pillow. "No, sit down. I just don't know how many. I've been an actress for five years, but before that men liked me."

Alexandria sat. Picking up the pen from the brass well, she poised it over her paper. "Why?"

Ann blinked. "Why?"

"To be blunt, you're a beautiful woman, and although your bosom might cause second looks, what is there about you that makes a man risk scandal and an irate wife to become your protector?"

Throwing back the covers, Ann got out of bed. The flimsy material clung to her curves. "Because unlike those simpering aristocratic wives, who are more interested in the latest fashion and gossip, I'm not shy about showing a man I like what he

does to me. And he likes what I can do to him. I'm very ver-
satile."

"In what way?" Alexandria persisted.

"Are you sure you want to hear this?" Ann asked, her hands
on her hips.

"Quite."

"I can do things to a man that will make him scream or pass
out with pleasure by using my tongue and hands." Her voice
dropped to a husky purr. "I can keep a man on the edge for a
long time and make him sweat and yell for more."

Alexandria swallowed. "I-I'm sure wives could learn to do
the same things."

Ann arched a perfect brow. "Are you married? I can see by
your attitude that you are. You're blushing now, so what would
you do if he asked you to do this?" Taking a leatherbound book
from her night table, she brought it back to the desk and opened
it. "Would you do that with your husband?"

Alexandria's eye's widened at the picture of a naked woman,
her hips raised in the air, with a man's—She looked away.

"If you can't look at it, how can you do it," Ann challenged,
derision in her voice. "You wives don't know how much fun
lovemaking can be, and until you do, women like me will always
be able to take your men. You'll pretend we don't exist because
you know that to protest too much may bring scandal or a unexpected trip to the country for you." She reached for the book.
Alexandria stopped her.

"Do you perform these acts with your present protector?"

"That and more," Ann quickly answered. "He has a mouse
for a wife who has no idea how to please a man with his huge
sexual appetite. We could go at it all night if he didn't have to
go home."

Alexandria had an answer to one question: Thorne could
make love to her after leaving this woman. "Don't you feel any
guilt?"

"For what? If she can't please her husband, it's not my fault.
Besides, if I didn't, someone else would. Believe me, they're

not always as good-looking and young as he is. Besides, he is very generous. He's paying for this house." Ann smiled smugly. "I haven't paid for too many things since my first man, at thirteen."

"Aren't your services another form of payment?"

"One that I like," Ann shot back.

Nodding, Alexandria made a notation on her paper, then opened the book. Her fingers trembled as she turned the pages and looked at the pictures of men and women copulating in various positions, some seemingly impossible to twist one's body into.

"Go on, look. Maybe tonight you'll surprise that husband of yours."

Without glancing up, Alexandria asked, "Is this book how you lure men to your bed?"

"Partly, and there's the fact that I never say no." She laughed. "And I do have nimble fingers and an agile tongue. Let me tell you about this one gentleman—"

Willing herself not to reach up and pull every strand of hair out of the woman's head, Alexandria listened for the next thirty minutes to stories about Ann's love life. By the time she stepped into her hansom cab, she was trembling with fury. "Mouse of a wife who didn't know how to please her husband? I'll show both of them you don't have to be immoral to be seductive and please a husband."

The carriage halted and the door opened. Paying the driver, she turned to see Thorne, tight-lipped, standing in the doorway. Without a word, he took her arm and led her into his study.

"I assume you have an explanation for worrying me with your absence?"

"You missed me?"

"What the hell does that mean? I went to check on you this morning and you were gone. No one had seen you, why wouldn't I be worried?"

"I'm going to my room." She turned toward the door.

He caught her by the arm.

"Take your hand from me," she almost hissed.

He looked into her eyes, then released her. He had never seen her look as if she couldn't decide if she wanted to scratch his eyes out or to get as far away from him as possible. "Alex, are you feeling all right?"

"I'm going to my room," she repeated, this time making good her escape.

Thorne watched her go and had no idea what had just happened. He'd expected that once she'd arrived he'd show her that she was to obey him in all things, that he was in charge of the household. Instead, she had shown him that he controlled nothing, least of all his wife. Walking into the hall, he watched her slowly mount the stairs, each step controlled, as if to do otherwise she would shatter.

Obviously she was upset by something, and obviously she wasn't going to tell him about it until she was ready. Remembering the early days of their marriage, when she had left before dawn to ride her problems away, he imagined he should be happy she hadn't just ridden off.

He'd just have to wait until lunch to see her.

Lunch arrived, but not Alexandria. To his questions of where she was, he was informed by Judith that Alexandria was in her room having some last minute alterations on the gown she was wearing to the party that night. He picked at his broiled beef, his gaze straying to the empty seat in front of him.

How had he become so accustomed to her in such a short time? He thought his irritation with Ann was due to annoyance at his situation. He now realized it was also due to being away from his wife. He found he liked having Alexandria near him.

"Judith, excuse me. I think I'll go upstairs and see if they are finished." Rising, he went upstairs and knocked on his wife's door. "Alex?"

Nelda, the maid, cracked the door. "Your lordship. Lady Grayson asked me to tell you that she's tired—" the elderly woman briefly looked behind her as if seeking reassurance before continuing, "and doesn't wish to be disturbed."

Thorne's expression remained unchanged, but his eyes darkened. "Is the dressmaker here?"

"She's working in one of the bedrooms down the hall."

"Then I suggest you follow your mistress's orders and leave," Thorne said, pushing open the door.

The maid's mouth opened in surprise at his turnabout, then she quickly bobbed her head. "Yes, your lordship."

Closing the door after him, Thorne continued to the dressing table. Alexandria, her unbound hair flowing down her back, sat on a stool. This time he had no problem discerning the message in her eyes. If possible, she'd send him straight to hell. His gaze captured hers in the mirror.

"Alex, if something was bothering you, you know you could talk to me about it, don't you?"

"And if something was bothering you, you know you could talk to me about it, don't you?"

He plowed four fingers through his hair. "Are you sure you're feeling all right? Perhaps you should stay at home tonight."

"Would you stay with me?"

"I can't."

She glanced away. "Please send Nelda back in on your way out." Rising, she went to the wardrobe.

"I shouldn't have to go out too much longer," Thorne said. She didn't turn. "Did you hear me?"

"I heard you. Please send Nelda to me."

Thorne left and asked a passing servant to send the maid to his wife. Something was wrong. It was in her strained voice, the tenseness of her body. His wife was in trouble and he had to play court to a selfish bitch like Ann to keep Alexandria out of danger. He had to find the killer, and quickly.

"Lord Stonewell, good evening. Allie will be down shortly," Judith said, as she entered the drawing room.

Lord Stonewell lifted her gloved hand and kissed it. "May I

say you look lovely in that white gown? Your dance card will be filled quickly."

Judith's face lost all traces of color. "I-I don't dance."

"So Thorne mentioned." Taking a small jewel-encrusted box from his pocket, he opened it. Strands of Brahms's *Lullaby* drifted outward. Slowly he put one hand on her small waist and took her hand. "Will you do me the honor of dancing with me?"

To keep from crying, she bit her lower lip. "I can't."

A bronzed finger and thumb lifted her chin. "You can. I won't let you deny either of us what I have dreamed of for so long."

"Dreamed?"

"When a man knows only war and death, the one thing he wants to be near more than anything is something pure and innocent," Lord Stonewell said, his eyes dark and intense. "Or is that your reason for not wanting to dance? I was a soldier and caused the death of others."

"No," she rushed to say. "It's me. M-my leg," she confessed, wanting nothing more than to lie down and never get up.

"Your leg does not make you less than another woman. It makes you more. Not many men, nor women, would have gone through what you have and remained so giving and caring," he said softly.

"You give me too much credit. I'm a coward." Her voice trembled.

"You give yourself too little credit," he said. "Only a fool doesn't admit to being afraid of something sometimes."

"The music stopped," she whispered.

"Did it," he questioned softly, then took the first steps to the waltz. His movements were slow, his hold secure.

One-two-three, one-two-three . . .

Awe lit Judith's face. "I'm dancing. I'm dancing."

Stonewell laughed, but it sounded deep and rusty, as if he'd trouble getting the sound out. He stopped and stared deeply into her eyes. "The elegant steel of a rapier is shaped and forged in fire just as you were shaped in pain. You both have endurance, beauty, and strength. No matter what, always remember that."

"I will and thank you." She stepped back. "I think I'll go see what is keeping Allie." Opening the door, Judith started toward the stairs, all her words about Prince Charming running back through her head.

Lord Stonewell was better than Prince Charming, but why would he want a cripple when he could have any woman he desired? He deserved someone he could be proud of. To hope for anything else was foolish. Blinking away the tears in her eyes, she berated herself. Why hadn't she remembered that fairy tales are for children?

Halfway up the stairs, she looked up and came to an abrupt halt. Her mouth formed a silent "Oh." Alexandria stood at the top of the stairs wearing a dress that in no way resembled the one Judith designed. Provocative was the only way to describe the frothy creation of gold taffeta and tulle. If Thorne had been displeased about the other bodice, he would be in a rage at the low décolletage. Two strategically placed stones drew one's attention before you realized others were scattered throughout the dazzling gown.

"How do you like the changes in my gown, Judith?"

"Thorne isn't going to like it," she said, without hesitation.

Head high, Alexandria continued down the stairs. "We both know he won't see my gown, so his opinion is worthless." Alexandria smiled. Her turquoise eyes matched the brilliance and color of the stones in her gown. "Shall we go? I have a feeling this is going to be a memorable night at the Cromwells'."

Something was wrong and he was going to find out what it was.

Getting out of the carriage at the Cromwells', Thorne felt an impatience at odds with his usual control. Yet somehow he had a feeling he had missed something in talking with Alexandria that afternoon and it was going to cost him dearly. An hour was all he had been able to take of Ann's overtures.

He had told her he was leaving and if she wanted him to take her home to get her wrap. She had laughed and he had walked out without looking back. On the way to the Cromwells' he had gone by the Duke of Singleton's house and informed him that he wasn't putting up with Ann any longer. Thorne had left his old friend sputtering about how much they needed Ann. Thorne had told him specifically and bluntly what they should do.

Handing his top hat and cane to the waiting footman, Thorne entered the main ballroom. Colors in every hue were reflected in the gilt mirrors that lined the white room. Nowhere did he see gold. Moving around the perimeter of the room, he searched the walls for Alexandria and Judith. Not seeing them or Lord Stonewell, he was unprepared for the surge of fear that swept through him. He was about to turn away when the dance ended and couples started off the floor.

His eyes widened. The color wasn't gold, but white. The woman had black hair, not tawny. Judith's face glowed as she and Lord Stonewell made their way toward him. Nearing, Thorne saw perspiration beaded on her face. He wanted to hug her. Instead, he took the hand she offered and squeezed.

"Does this mean I'll have to find another dance partner?" he said.

Judith smiled. "There'll always be room on my dance card for you."

"Why would you want to dance with your boorish brother when you could be dancing with me?" Lord Stonewell asked, one corner of his mouth lifted in amusement.

"Lady Judith, you promised the next dance to me," said a fresh-faced young man with brown hair.

Judith caught both Thorne and Lord Stonewell glaring at the man. "Of course." She placed her hand on his extended arm.

Thorne watched them walk away with a mixture of joy and trepidation. "Will she be all right?"

"She'd better be. I had a talk with each man on her dance

card. By the way, since I had to eliminate one or two undesirables on her card and that was our third dance, I explained my attentiveness by saying we were distant cousins. I hold Lady Judith's reputation as highly as you do."

Thorne nodded his satisfaction. "Thanks. I owe you an apology. Now, if you will just point me in the direction of my wife, I'll—" The request was no longer necessary. Alexandria stood not more than twenty feet in front of him, looking like a sinful angel.

Her hair was an artful display of jumbled curls that gave the appearance she had just crawled from a man's bed. With each movement of her body the multilayered skirt lifted and fluttered, drawing your gaze; it was as if one expected the entire thing to flare up. If that wasn't enough, he could see her . . . my God!

"Those two dark spots can't be her nipples."

"Turquoise stone," Stonewell said. Thorne whipped his head around, unawares until then that he had spoken aloud. "If you'll look again, you'll see other stones."

Thorne looked around and straight into Alexandria's eyes. Surprise registered on her face, then she was swept into the arms of her dance partner. The gown glowed like prisms beneath the gas chandeliers.

"Once the men saw Lady Judith dancing, they gathered around Lady Grayson like hungry wolves. I thought for a moment I might have to leave the floor and stand guard," Stonewell said.

"How long has this been going on?" Thorne asked between clenched teeth, his gaze on his wife.

Stonewell looked startled at the rage in Thorne's voice. "This is the first night Lady Grayson hasn't stayed by Lady Judith's side. No one missed how devoted she is to your sister, and your lady has the backing of the Duchess of Singleton who is here, and several other ladies. I understand from Judith that more than one wants a similar gown."

Alexandria twirled within ten feet of Thorne. Her neck arched and a bubble of laughter floated from her lips. Her partner almost drooled. Thorne started forward. Stonewell's hand on Thorne's arm, stopped him.

"Take your hand from me," Thorne said without turning.

"If I do, you're going to flatten Viscount Pearson. It's bad enough he has a father who is going to run through his entire fortune before he inherits, without his having a broken nose. It might put a damper on his getting a wealthy wife one day. Your lady is simply having a good time. She has done nothing to cause the slightest talk. If you flatten Pearson, that will change. Do you want that?" Lord Stonewell's fingers uncurled.

The laughter sounded again and it was like a prod to Thorne's heart. Damn it, he shouldn't be jealous if his wife shared her laughter with another man, but he was. Today she had shared only her anger with him. He'd be damned if he was going to let it continue. "Please collect Judith and meet us in the foyer. I think my wife has had enough fun for one evening."

Without giving Lord Stonewell a chance to answer, Thorne moved onto the dance floor. His movements were lithe and predatory. Dancers moved out of his way. Seeing him, Viscount Pearson faltered. Alexandria's chin lifted.

"Good evening, Pearson. I wonder if I might have my wife?"

"Of-of course," the ruddy-faced man said, and stepped back.

Ignoring Thorne, Alexandria turned to the younger man. "Thank you, I hope in the future we might finish our dance."

Pearson's chest pushed out. "It will be my pleasure."

Thorne had the strongest urge to punch the preening man in the nose and turn Alexandria over his knee. Instead, aware of the ears twitching and eyes watching, he said, "So nice of you to understand, Pearson. Something has come up at home that demands our immediate attention."

Then, to annoy Alexandria, he added, "I would count it a pleasure if in my absence you'd look after my wife. Women are fragile, so it is left to us to care for them."

"You may let your mind rest easy," Pearson said.

Nodding, Thorne led a bristling Alexandria from the dance floor, his arm possessively draped around her waist. He might as well have had his arm around an iron poker for the hardness he felt. Bidding their hostess goodnight, they met Judith and Lord Stonewell outside. Telling his friend goodnight, Thorne escorted the women home. Apparently sensing the tension between her brother and sister-in-law, Judith excused herself and went to her room.

His hand clamped around Alexandria's elbow, Thorne entered her bedroom, dismissed her maid, then told her to tell his valet he wouldn't be needed either. With a quick look between master and mistress, Nelda scuttled from the room.

"Alex, I want an answer, and I want it now. Your behavior tonight was inexcusable."

She shrugged out of his hold and tossed back, "So was yours."

Frowning, he came to stand before her. "What are you talking about?"

"Are you having an affair with Ann Masters?"

Twenty-two

"Answer me. Did you bed that whore Ann Masters?"

"You shouldn't use such language."

"Did you?"

"Alex, you're becoming hysterical."

"I told you once I wouldn't be a cuckolded wife."

"There is no such thing as a cuckolded wife."

"So you won't deny it," she said, her voice brittle and thin.

"I didn't say I wasn't denying it."

"Then what *are* you saying? Explain why you have been with her for the past five nights."

"Who says I was?"

Alexandria wanted to hit him, but afraid she might not stop, she curled her hands into tight fists instead. "You were seen at the Addisons' house two nights ago with her. She wore a red gown. You wore a scowl."

"Observant, wasn't he," Thorne said, aiming for boredom and hoping to defuse his wife's anger. "I was taking care of matters that have nothing to do with an illicit relationship."

"You hypocrite," Alexandria shouted. "All your talk of fidelity was nothing but lies and I was stupid enough to believe them. Did you and Ann have a good laugh about what a simpleton you married while you looked at that obscene book of hers?"

His body tensed. "What did you say?"

She had gone too far to back down. "I went to your paramour's house and talked with her."

"God, Alex. How could you have been so irresponsible? If you were seen, your reputation is irrevocably ruined."

"You can bed the wench for all to gossip about, but I can't set foot in her house," she sneered sarcastically.

He grasped her arms. "Did anyone recognize you?"

"Don't worry, I wouldn't want anyone to see me at your mistress's house any more than you do. I'm already degraded enough. Your mistress thought I was a newspaper reporter." She pushed his hands away. "You won't have to hear about your wife, I'll just have to hear about my faithless husband."

Thorne relaxed somewhat. "I told you my seeing Ann has nothing to do with us."

"If I were seen with a man in a similar situation, what would you do?"

"Kill both of you."

The absoluteness in his voice caused her to gasp. "Killing you would be too quick. I'd shoot you where your so-called honor is kept," she snapped. "Now, get out of my sight."

Thorne didn't move. "If this marriage is to work, you are going to have to have complete trust in me."

"Why were you with her if it wasn't for the reasons she said?" Silence reigned. "Say something."

"You have to trust me. I have never lied to you."

"You were with that woman!"

"If memory serves, your father took the same attitude when we were found together. You berated me less than a week ago for jumping to the same conclusions. Think about it, Alex, before you find yourself in the same trap." He walked from the room.

Alexandria plopped down on the nearest chair. She had two choices: pack or fight. Except for Thorne, she had never run from anything in her life. Whatever the Masters woman could do, Alexandria could do better.

"You won't get him without a fight."

* * *

The overcast skies matched Thorne's foul mood. Sitting down to breakfast, he snapped his white linen napkin. The sound made him think of breaking bone and he pictured *The Shadow*. Yet however pleasant the prospect, it would solve nothing. But putting an end to Ann's little game would.

With a would-be killer stalking him, he needed Alexandria's complete trust. There might come a time when doing as he said could mean the difference between her living and her dying. Distancing himself from her no longer seemed the best way to protect her. Restoring her faith in him was.

He trusted Alexandria, but she was too impulsive. Emotions, not a steady head, ruled her actions. Her visit to Ann proved that. His scowl deepened. Knowing Ann, she had enjoyed shocking Alexandria. No wonder she had acted so strangely. He didn't like knowing she was upset, but for the moment, there was nothing he could do.

She'd just have to trust him. This morning at breakfast she would see he did not act guilty, and by tonight they would be in bed, making love. His body heated. He took a sip of tea.

The door opened and Thorne glanced up. Tea spewed over the tablecloth. He blinked. The vision of his wife wearing a revealing negligee did not go away. This time there were no stones. The two rosy points jutting forward were her nipples.

His gaze lowered and his body tightened in spite of himself. If he looked hard, and he did, he could see a shadowy triangle between her—his head whipped up and he saw the elegant curve of his wife's back and shapely buttocks. Going to the side table, she poured herself a cup of tea, then prepared herself a plate.

Trembling with rage, he stood. "You will go upstairs and change immediately."

She sat, a seductive smile on her face. "Don't you like my attire, Thorne? Your paramour assured me this is what you liked."

"I thought I had taught you once that in an open war, you will lose." Abruptly he turned her to face him, then placed his hands on the arms of her chair. "If you insist on acting like a whore, I'll treat you like one."

Alexandria looked at him through a sweep of lashes. "Does that mean you'll start treating Ann Masters as your wife, or do you plan to have two mistresses?"

Behind them, the door opened and Judith stuck her head inside the room. Thorne straightened and stepped in front of Alexandria. Out of the corner of his eye he saw her scoot lower into the chair. "What is it, Judith?"

"Excuse me, Thorne. I know Allie asked not to be disturbed, but I wanted to remind her that Lord Stonewell will be here shortly to take us for a carriage ride."

"She will be there directly."

"All right, and I'm sorry." The door swung shut.

Thorne turned to Alexandria. Heat stained her cheeks. Apparently she wasn't as calm about her attire as she wanted him to believe. "You can go upstairs and change or pull that off and prepare to service me. We don't have much time, but I'm sure I will rise to the occasion so to speak."

In spite of herself, her gaze lowered. An unmistakable bulge pressed against his pants. Her gaze snapped upward. "You wouldn't dare!"

"I told you about baiting the lion when the cage door is open. One way or the other, you're going to learn not to defy me and expect to win." His hand palmed her breast.

Shoving his hand away, she leaped from the chair. Her chest heaving, she studied his expressionless face for a long moment. "And you're going to learn that some reports of victory are premature." Head in the air, she swept from the room with regal aloofness.

Frowning at her words, Thorne followed in time to see Alexandria, wrapped in a heavy cloak, running up the stairs. Nelda, although slower, was behind her. In spite of everything, he smiled. His meddling, stubborn, beautiful wife had just tried to seduce him back from a non-existent mistress.

She hadn't cried or pled, she had used the same weapons her

opponent had, and from the tightening of his loins, hers were a thousand times more provocative. She was a woman a man could tussle in bed, and one who in the harsh light of day would stand by his side with her fists doubled. Or with a raised umbrella, he added.

Turning, he went to finish his breakfast, his appetite suddenly on the upswing. He piled his plate high with eggs, ham, and buttered scones. Tonight was soon enough to let Alex know she had won. Yes, tonight would solve their disagreements.

"Please, I need to ride."

Lord Stonewell looked at Alexandria's beseeching face and his hands tightened on the reins. He should have expected this, after seeing her with the horse, instead of in the carriage with Judith. Unsuspecting fool that he was, he believed her story that the horse needed exercise and permitted the sidesaddle to be changed to a regular saddle for him to do the "exercising." Now, on his grandmother's estate outside London, Lady Grayson wanted to ride astride.

"Lady Grayson, you know I'd do anything for you, but do not ask me to do this."

"Can't you understand? I need to think, and the only way I can do it properly is to ride." Her hand lifted in helplessness. "I tried other ways, but I keep making the wrong decision."

"Let her have the horse, Lord Stonewell," Judith said.

Stonewell's gaze connected with Judith's. She had to know he could not deny her the first thing she had ever asked of him. "You are not playing fair."

"Women have to do something to win." She grasped Alexandria's hands. "If riding will help, do it. There is no one to see that Lord Stonewell and I are unchaperoned and you know he will keep me safe." She took the reins from Stonewell's hands and placed them in Alexandria's. "Please give her a hand up."

"All right," Stonewell said. Cupping his hands for Alexandria, he lifted her into the saddle, then frowned on seeing the

man's breeches beneath the habit encasing her legs. His hand
fisted in the horse's shiny mane. "A storm is approaching and
I won't let Lady Judith be caught in an open carriage. Start
back immediately if the sky becomes more threatening. If you
miss us, the estate is a mile and a half up this road."

"Take care of Judith. I-I can take care of myself." Her voice
wobbled. Jerking on the reins, she wheeled the animal and took
off toward a clump of evergreens and disappeared, the blue velvet riding skirt flapping in the wind.

Judith touched Stonewell's hand. "She'll be all right, won't
she?"

Without thought his arm curved protectively around her
shoulder. He didn't know if she was talking about Lady
Grayson's emotional well-being or her physical well-being. He
gave the only answer he could: "She'll be fine."

Out of sight, Alexandria dismounted and rid herself of her
hat and riding skirt. She wanted nothing to impede her or negate
her control of her mount. In the saddle again, she tore through
an open grove. The demanding ride required all her skill. Setting
a breakneck pace, she jumped fallen logs, ducked overhead
branches. Leaning lower in the saddle, she urged her mount on.
Wind, cool and heavy with rain, whipped across her face and
pulled the pins from her hair and dried the tears she refused to
admit she shed.

She did not love him; she did not. Leaning lower over the
horse's neck, she jumped a fence, thought of Thorne and the
fox hunt, and fought the sudden stinging in her throat. She did
not love Thorne. She would not.

A rumble of thunder caused her to glance up. Unwanted came
Thorne's memory and the first kiss they had shared. Shaking
her head, she pulled the horse to a halt, admitting she could not
run from Thorne.

His presence was there, constantly baiting her, intriguing her,
making her want him. But it was all a lie. He had broken their

bargain. She turned toward the carriage. She would not admit he had broken her heart.

Fifteen minutes later Alexandria rode up to the carriage where Lord Stonewell and Lady Judith sat and announced without preamble, "I am leaving Thorne."

Lady Judith cried out. Lord Stonewell cursed and scrambled out of the carriage.

"Lord Stonewell, if you would please take me to the train station, I want to go home."

He took the horse's bridle. "Your home is with Lord Grayson."

"He has broken our bargain and I refuse to stay. If you refuse to take me, I shall go by myself," Alexandria said.

Lord Stonewell pointed out the obvious. "Lady Grayson, you can't go riding through London wearing men's breeches. It would create a scandal."

"As I never plan to return to London, it doesn't matter."

Feeling the tug on his bridle, he tried again. "Then think of the scandal for Lady Judith. I can't take her back home unchaperoned."

"You won't have to," Lady Judith said. "I'm going with Alexandria." Lord Stonewell shot Judith a thunderous look, which she ignored. "As for her breeches, I'm sure we can find her skirt."

"Neither of you is going anywhere," he told Judith, recalling that earlier he had been sorely tempted to kiss her; now he wanted to tie a gag over her delectable mouth. "In case you have forgotten, there is a storm brewing. We'll be lucky if we don't get drenched by the time we reach shelter. Lady Grayson, please get down so I can find your missing clothes."

The horse backed away. "Not until I have your word you won't send Thorne word I am leaving him."

"Lady—"

"Your word or we're leaving," Judith interrupted.

"The man she is leaving is your brother," Lord Stonewell said tightly.

"Who has obviously done something to upset Allie," Lady Judith said, looking at him as if somehow by being a man he should be included in their umbrage.

"You have my word," he finally gritted out.

Alexandria dismounted and handed him the reins. "I shall stay only long enough for the storm to pass."

"We shall stay," Lady Judith corrected, clasping Alexandria's hand as they sat in the carriage.

"Drive on," Lord Stonewell ordered gruffly, and rode in the same direction Alexandria had first taken. Despite what either woman said, they were not going anyplace. Judith wasn't leaving him just when she'd started trusting him. He knew Thorne would follow Alexandria through hell if she tried to leave him.

Spying a patch of blue, Lord Stonewell dismounted and picked up Alexandria's discarded riding skirt and hat. She was a determined woman who matched Thorne's fiery temperament. For himself, he liked a more compliant female. Recalling Judith's outspokenness moments earlier, he smiled. He was always open to new things.

His smile faltered. He might like new things, but his grandmother was a stickler for propriety. One look at Alexandria's dishevelment and his grandmother would be outraged. The breeches might send her into a decline. Lost in thought, he didn't move until a drop of rain hit him in the face.

Vaulting into the saddle, he rode toward the estate. There was no help for it now. Alexandria was on her own. It served her right for putting him in such an awkward position. How was he going to alert Thorne without breaking his word?

The answer to Lord Stonewell's dilemma came in the form of his diminutive grandmother, Dowager Stonewell, his father's mother. Despite her seventy-two years, her brown eyes were still shrewd and discerning as she greeted her unexpected visitors in the drawing room.

During introductions and explanations, she missed nothing. Not her favorite grandson's obvious unease, nor the protectiveness of the impeccably groomed black-haired woman for the unsmiling woman with hair like an unruly lion's mane. The woman also had the audacity to appear in public without petticoats beneath her habit.

"Lady Grayson, I assume you have an explanation for appearing this way."

"Leaving one's husband tends to make a woman forget about her attire," Alexandria said, her voice thin. "If I have offended you, I'm sorry. I'll wait in the stable until the storm has passed."

Dowager Stonewell's parchment colored skin paled. She pressed a rose-scented handkerchief to the lace at her throat. "Leaving your husband?"

"He broke our bargain," Alexandria said, clamping her eyes shut.

Lady Judith rushed to put her arms around her. "We won't disturb you further."

"Grandmother, if they go, I go," Lord Stonewell threatened.

"Who said anything about anyone going?" the older woman said. "Make yourself useful and ring for the maid to show your guests to a room to freshen up, then come back here. I wish a word with you."

Knowing it was an order and not a request, Lord Stonewell did as he'd been asked. As expected, his grandmother wanted to know what had transpired and how he was involved. It didn't take her long to discover his interest was more involved than simply to help out a friend.

"So you see, Grandmother, I can't tell Thorne to come get his wife or I will break my word."

Walking to her writing desk, she lifted a pen and began to write. "I made no such promise."

"The name of the agent is Count Pierre Fortenot."

The Duke of Singleton looked at Thorne sitting casually across from his desk in a red leather wing chair and shook his head. "Fortenot is a wealthy and influential man. It will cause quite an upheaval to have him disappear. Are you sure Ann told the truth?"

"She told the truth." Ann had been too frightened by her kidnapping for anything else. After being lured to a jeweler, Thorne had taken her to one of the worst sections of the city. He didn't like to think of what happened next, but it had gotten him results. "However, she wants no part in any further operations."

The duke nodded and wisely refrained from asking further questions. "We owe you a debt of gratitude."

"Someone owes me more than that." Thorne turned to look at the man standing in the far corner of the room. "We both know that if it hadn't suited your purpose to agree to Ann's scheme, you could have gotten the information yourself."

"I wondered how long it would take you to reach that conclusion. I guess worrying about a woman makes a man think more slowly," the man said derisively. "Ann needed to be taught not to bargain with people's lives and I decided you were the best one to teach her that."

The word "bargain" sealed Thorne's purpose. He rose and slipped off his jacket. "You need to learn not to play with people's lives."

"Gentlemen, please," the duke said, rising from his desk, and glanced from one man to the other. "Surely this is not necessary. We have what we needed."

"Not quite. Not until *The Shadow* learns a lesson."

"You have never beat me before."

"I have never had enough reason."

"If you break anything in here, Henrietta will have your heads," the duke said. "I must—"

Thorne's left foot shot out. *The Shadow* deflected the blow, spun, then lashed out with his foot. Thorne dodged and sent a slashing blow to *The Shadow's* neck. *The Shadow* caught his hand and twisted. With his free arm, Thorne elbowed the other man and sent him crashing over an end table. Neither paid any attention to the frantic banging on the door or to the woman who rushed into the room.

The Shadow rolled to his feet and kicked. This time it was Thorne who went down and just as quickly came up.

"Lord Grayson, you have an urgent message from Lord Stonewell," the Duchess of Singleton said, her voice raised to be heard over the two men falling over a lamp table.

Thorne felt the air leave his lungs and knew it had nothing to do with being on the bottom as they fell to the floor. Fighting the rising panic within, Thorne shoved *The Shadow* aside and rushed to the duchess. "What did you say?"

"Your servants came by looking for you earlier, but I told them you weren't here." She frowned at the man Thorne had fought with. "I didn't know Lord Radcliffe was here either."

"Duchess, what was the message about?" Thorne asked impatiently.

"I don't know. The footman left when he was told you weren't here."

Without a word, Thorne ran from the room, his heart pounding in his chest. Something was wrong with Alex. He felt it. If anything happened to her because of her impulsiveness, he was going to . . . Alex, please be safe. Just be safe.

Lord Grayson,

Come immediately and collect your wife before she makes good her threat to leave you. I do not wish my name or that of my grandson's to be associated with the scandal that will surely follow.

Dowager Stonewell

Thorne crushed the note in his fist, his face furious. He was going to kill her for scaring the life out of him. She certainly wasn't leaving him.

"Is her ladyship all right?" Benson asked.

Thorne glanced around at the butler, Alexandria's maid, his

valet, and an assortment of other servants. All of them wore expressions filled with concern. All apparently sensed that the urgent message had something to do with Alexandria.

Why else would a sane man drive a team of prized horses at breakneck pace through the treacherous streets during a thunderstorm, race into his house, snatch a note from his butler's hand, then proceed to read said note while dripping water all over his Aubusson rug?

Who else but Alexandria could turn his life into one long crisis? "Her ladyship and my sister have been detained by the storm. Lord Stonewell did not wish me to worry. However, I think I shall join them."

Benson slapped his hands together. "Peter, go to the stable and tell them to prepare his lordship's coach. Nelda, pack her ladyship a bag. Nan, do the same for Lady Judith. Corbin—"

"I know how to take care of his lordship," Corbin sniffed. He turned to Thorne. "Your bath and some fresh clothes will be waiting upstairs."

"Anything else, your lordship?" Benson asked.

"No. Thank you, Benson."

"Very good, sir. I shall go see that everything is carried out." He turned to go, then said, "We were all concerned. We are all very fond of her ladyship."

"I shall take her your regards," Thorne said, and watched the servant disappear.

"I wonder if your butler would like a job change."

Thorne turned to the man standing behind him in the foyer. "I don't think he would like the way you handle things any better than I do."

The Shadow looked at Thorne strangely. "You really care for her, don't you?"

"She's my wife."

"Wife or not, it has been my observation in the past that you have never fought *for* a woman, nor *over* one. You have done both for her. Why?"

"She is my responsibility." Thorne answered the only way he

knew how. "Now, if you will excuse me, I have a journey to make." He started for the stairs.

"There were two notes, Grayson. Instinct tells me all is not so simple as you'd like us to believe."

Thorne spoke without turning. "I thought you already knew. Nothing is simple with Alexandria."

Something warm and soft grazed her cheek, then downward to the curve of her neck. Alexandria twisted her head on the pillow, allowing the warmth to continue downward. In a dreamy haze, Alexandria murmured, "Thorne . . ."

"Nice to know you haven't forgotten me."

Alexandria's eyes snapped open. Thorne's face filled her vision. He was in bed with her. Pushing against his chest with all her might, she scrambled from the bed.

"Get out of my room and put some clothes on."

"It's rather difficult to make love to your wife clothed, my sweet."

Alexandria swallowed and cursed her weakness for being affected by his nakedness. Lying in her bed, his hand propped under his head, he looked tempting and dangerous. Heat centered in her stomach and her body yearned for the rascal. "I won't be your wife once the divorce is final."

His indulgent expression hardened. He rolled from the bed. "Not while there is breath left in my body."

The fierceness of his words made Alexandria's heart beat faster until she thought of another possible reason. "Afraid of the scandal? You should have considered that before you . . . don't you come any closer."

"I'm going to come a lot closer and you're going to enjoy every second." He kept walking.

Alexandria turned as if to flee. The moment his hand touched her arm, she spun, throwing up her left hand to deflect his hand, and kicked with all the force of her anger.

Her first motion caught him by surprise. He anticipated the

kick, but he was still thankful the voluminous nightgown slowed it enough for him to catch the foot aimed for his groin.

"Turn my foot loose."

"Not if I want us to have children."

"There will be no children. I am divorcing you, and nothing is going to change my mind."

"Another challenge, my dear. This one I gladly accept." Lifting her foot, he sent her backward, her arms flapping like the sails of a demented windmill to regain her balance. He caught her just as she completely lost her balance.

"Take your hands off me," she ordered.

"Certainly." Without warning, he pitched her into the bed. Surprise and indignation widened her eyes. By the time she caught her breath, his powerful body had settled over hers. "I think I'll take the top this time."

She cursed. Twisting and turning, she fought to be free. He pinned her hands beside her face and anchored the lower part of her body with his leg. Feeling his manhood against her naked thigh, she stilled.

"I wondered when you would notice."

"Did you confuse me with your mistress?"

"I didn't get drenched and ride through a thunderstorm to listen to your hysterics."

"I didn't ask you to come. Lord Stonewell is as unprincipled as you are. Get off me. I won't let you come to me after being with that woman."

"I told you, she has nothing to do with us."

"Liar. I saw you with my own eyes standing beside the slut. You were angry because men were watching her in that disgraceful dress," she cried. "I thought you were in trouble, so I followed you to help. I was a fool, but you won't make me a bigger one."

Fierce anger swept through him at the danger she'd put herself in. "I have told you the truth. I'm done with talking."

His mouth took hers in a punishing kiss. He was using his body to defeat her, making her admit once and for all he was the master, not she. His hand touched the dewy wetness between her thighs and he knew he had won. Sure of his victory, he positioned himself over her and looked into her eyes. They were glazed with desire, but something else was also there.

"If you want me to beg you to stop, I will." Tears glistened in her eyes.

Her words shattered his anger as nothing else could have. How had he brought this proud woman to beg? "Look at my face, Alex, and tell me if it is the same expression you saw that night." She shut her eyes. "If you want the truth, you have to be brave enough to hunt for it."

Slowly she opened her eyes. In the flickering candlelight she saw the handsome face that had made her heart ache with pain and longing. She lifted her gaze to his eyes, glittering with suppressed desire, and saw a possessiveness and a determination to keep what was his at any cost.

He released her hands. "I won't force you. Either you trust me or you don't."

In those telling words Thorne admitted his vulnerability. He needed her unconditional trust as much as she needed his reassurance. In her mind's eye she saw his anger, but none of the possessive hunger in his face. Her lashes swept downward. What if she was wrong?

She felt his body lift from her. Her lids snapped upward. He sat on the side of the bed, his shoulders rigid, his fists clamped. "I won't bother you again."

The ragged hoarseness in his voice caused her heart to cry out in pain. "Don't go," she cried, throwing her arms around his waist. For better or worse, she loved Thorne. "Don't go."

Hands that trembled pulled her to him and his lips found hers.

In the past he had always loved her with his body; he hadn't known until he'd almost lost her that he had loved with a part of him that was dangerously near his soul. He no longer cared.

Later, he pulled her into his arms. She snuggled closer, then he heard them: muffled noises: She was crying.

"Alex."

Shaking her head, she resisted his attempts to lift her chin so he could see her face. "I'm just tired."

Stroking her arm, he stared up at the canopy of the bed. She hadn't believed him, but she let him make love to her. She had shown her vulnerability to a man she didn't completely trust. No one had ever given him so much.

"Ann Masters had information vital to the security of England. She refused to give it to anyone except me. I had strict orders not to tell anyone."

The muffled sounds stopped. Alexandria rose up on her elbow, unconcerned that her breasts were uncovered. "Why are you telling me now?"

"Because it's not worth one of your tears. And damn it, I can't stand the thought of you looking at me the way you did earlier," he confessed.

"Perhaps you had better tell me everything," she said, lying on his chest.

Thorne lifted an eyebrow. "That's what I like about you, Alex. You give in so gracefully."

A short while later Alexandria knew everything except who his contacts were. She smiled with relish when he told her of kidnapping Ann and getting the information from her when he realized the secrecy of the mission was endangering their marriage. For that bit of information Alexandria gave him a kiss. He kissed her back and it was a long time before he released her.

Late the next afternoon Thorne and Alexandria left their bedroom. The rain had finally ceased and the sun shone. Descending the staircase, his arms possessively around her, they found Judith, Richard, and Dowager Stonewell in the drawing room.

"I see you two have reconciled," the matronly woman said, after greetings were finished.

Alexandria smiled. "Yes, and I understand I have you to thank."

"We both owe you a debt of gratitude," Thorne said. "I'm sure my sister shares our gratefulness for your hospitality."

"The countess has been very gracious," Judith agreed, her voice stilted.

"If you call having a maid follow you every step, she has," Stonewell said. "I thought you had more trust in me, Grandmother."

Dowager Stonewell looked surprised. "I do. Lady Judith asked for the servant. Since you are both unattached, I thought it a wise decision."

Richard's brown eyes centered on Judith. "I see. I didn't know my presence was so unwanted." He stood. "I'll take the open carriage back to town."

The door closed with a decided snap after him. Judith bit her lip to keep from crying out that she hadn't meant to hurt him. Didn't he understand that he was becoming too important to her? That she was starting to believe in fairy tales again?

She looked around and caught three pair of eyes intently staring at her. Not wanting to see the pity she was sure was in their gaze, she went to their host. "Thank you again. Goodbye."

Blue-veined hands pressed against soft white ones. "Something tells me that I will see you again."

Judith spoke around the tightness in her throat. "I don't think so." Head high, she walked from the room.

Twenty-three

Lying in her husband's arms two nights later, Alexandria felt a mixture of guilt and sympathy for her sister-in-law. "Judith is unhappy."

"I know, and it's my fault again. If I hadn't asked Stonewell to escort you two, none of this would have happened."

Frowning, Alexandria sat up, sending her hair spilling down her naked back and over her shoulder, "You're wrong. There was something between them already. I saw the way they looked at each other."

"You imagined things." Thorne stroked the curve of her back. "They've been friends since he came home with me six years ago while he was my second-in-command."

"Sometimes friends become more than that," Alexandria said softly.

Gentle fingers brushed her hair aside, then returned to brush across a dusky nipple. "I know," Thorne said, his voice gently teasing.

Laughing, Alexandria batted his hand away. "You won't get by me this time. I missed supper and I'm famished."

"So am I," Thorne said, his head descending toward Alexandria's breast.

"Oh, no, you don't." Alexandria scrambled from the bed and away from temptation. Picking up his black silk robe from the floor where Thorne had tossed it earlier, she pulled it on. "I'm not going to satisfy your hunger until mine is satisfied."

Completely disregarding his nakedness, Thorne got out of

bed and began rolling up the sleeves of his robe. "Since mine is going to take considerably longer, I guess I have no choice."

"I'll be back before you notice." She lit another candle and turned to leave.

"Why don't you ring?"

She paused with her hand on the doorknob. "I'm not waking up anyone at midnight to feed us. I can prepare something."

"You're a coward, Alex." He laughed. "You know that if you ring, the servants will know why we're up and why we're hungry."

"The thought had crossed my mind."

Downstairs, in the kitchen, she found meat and bread, then began to look for a tray. The door leading to the servants' quarters opened and she swung around. Benson, holding a meat cleaver, was as startled as she.

"Sorry, your ladyship. I heard the noise and came to investigate." He placed the cleaver on the table.

"I . . . that is, we . . . were hungry," Alexandria explained. Feeling heat climb up her neck, she berated herself for not being quieter.

"Let me help you." Gathering silverware and plates, the butler placed them on the tray, then picked up a bowl of strawberries. She started to object until the butler informed her, "Strawberries are one of his lordship's favorites." From another cabinet he produced a bottle of Madeira. He picked up the tray.

"No, thank you, Benson." Alexandria held out her hands for the tray. "I can manage."

He didn't budge. "Your ladyship, I think it might prove rather awkward for you to try to climb the stairs."

Glancing down at Thorne's robe dragging the floor and falling over her hands, she blushed again. "You're observant, as usual." She left the kitchen. However, at the head of the stairs, she turned for the tray. "Thank you, Benson, and goodnight."

This time he complied. "Rest assured, your ladyship, in the future I will see the kitchen is stocked for such forages." He went down the stairs.

Smiling, Alexandria continued to Thorne's room. Putting the tray on the floor, she opened the door, picked up the tray, then pushed the door closed with her hip. "I was caught."

"Who?"

"Benson," she confessed, handing Thorne the tray. "But he acted as if there was nothing unusual about me searching for food at midnight. He even told me that in the future, he would see the kitchen was well stocked." She climbed into the bed.

"I think after I carried you home that night, with Wolf refusing to leave your side, nothing surprises him anymore." Thorne popped a lush red strawberry into his mouth.

"I miss Wolf and Father."

"I can't leave now, but I promise to take you for a visit soon," Thorne said, pouring her a glass of wine.

"Does that mean you don't think I'm capable of going by myself?"

He set the bottle aside. "That means I don't want to be without you for one day."

Warmth curled through her. "You just saved yourself from getting wine dumped on your head. Now, eat your strawberries. Benson sent them especially for you."

He held up one for her. "Want to share?"

"Not unless you want me to break out in a rash and get splotchy." She picked up a piece of bread.

"You're allergic to strawberries?"

"Yes. Father said it's my punishment, because when I was five, I took a huge bowl from the kitchen without permission and stuffed myself with them."

Thorne shook his head and ate one strawberry, then another. "I might have known you were always headstrong."

Alexandria punched him playfully in the stomach. "I tend to see it as asserting my individuality."

"Just so you remember that asserting your individuality can get you into trouble, and I won't have that." All playfulness left his voice.

"The way you never let me out of sight anymore, there isn't much chance of that."

Frowning, Thorne put down the strawberry, then splayed his hand over his stomach. "Any objections?"

Alexandria gave a long-suffering sigh. "Well, I do miss the opera, and you must remember, I—" She halted abruptly as Thorne lay back, his eyes tightly shut. "Thorne, what's the matter?"

"Don't know. Stomach hurts."

Her heart thumping in her chest, Alexandria scrambled out of bed and set the tray on the floor. Pulling the cover over Thorne, she tried to keep the panic out of her voice. "Maybe you're allergic to them, too."

His eyes focused on her, then shut as he drew his knees up to his chest. His face twisted in pain and something else. "P-poison."

"What?" Her face blanched. She shook his shoulders. He didn't say anything else. Perspiration beaded his face. She jerked on the bell pull again and again. Praying, she fought to keep the tears at bay. She didn't know why he thought the strawberries were poisoned, but she wasn't going to risk his life by not listening to him.

"Come in," she yelled, as someone knocked frantically on the door. She only glanced up to see a startled Corbin in his dressing gown. "He's been poisoned. Get a doctor immediately." The man ran from the room.

Alexandria turned back to Thorne. "You're going to be all right." Stroking his face, she kissed his forehead. "Everything is going to be fine. I sent for the doctor."

"Your ladyship, the footman has gone for the doctor," said a voice she recognized as Benson's.

She nodded, not taking her eyes from Thorne. He was moaning, his teeth clenched. "He was fine, then he just—" Her voice broke.

A tentative hand touched her shoulder. "Corbin and I will

stay with Lord Grayson. Perhaps you should get dressed before the doctor arrives. Nelda is waiting to help you, " Benson said.

"No." Alexandria clamped her hand tighter around Thorne's. "I'm not leaving him."

"Your lady—"

"I'm not leaving him!" she yelled.

Corbin, who had returned, and Benson exchanged looks. Benson went to the connecting bedroom.

Alexandria bent over Thorne and spoke softly to him. "You're going to be fine, Thorne. Don't worry. I'm not leaving you."

Pulling his hand from hers, he circled his stomach with his arms and drew his knees to his chest.

"Lady Grayson, Nelda is here to help you dress. Corbin and I will wait outside until she calls."

Tears rolling down her cheek, Alexandria stood by helplessly as Thorne withered in pain on the bed. "Can't you understand—"

"I understand that his lordship will be very upset with me if you receive visitors in your present attire," Benson said, his voice slightly unsteady. "You don't want to upset him once he is well on his way to recovery, do you?"

"Benson, he's got to be all right," Alexandria whispered, reaching out to take Thorne's hand, unsure if his sudden stillness meant he was getting better or getting worse.

"We'll wait outside." After one last look at Thorne, Benson led a dazed Corbin from the room.

Nelda pulled the already slipping robe from Alexandria's shoulders as soon as the door closed. Helping her into chemise and drawers, the maid held a dress for her to step into, then began to button the gown. A knock came at the door.

"It's the doctor, Lady Grayson." Benson called.

"Please send him in," Alexandria said, her voice frantic.

A portly man with gray hair and sideburns walked into the room carrying a black bag just as the maid finished buttoning the dress. "Lady Grayson. I'm Dr. Hathaway. What's this about poisoning?"

"I'm not sure that's what it is. Thorne said the word 'poison' just . . . just after he began having stomach pains," Alexandria said, and brushed another tear from her eye. "Please help him."

"I intend to. Lord Grayson is an important man." Dr. Hathaway opened his bag. "If you will leave, I can complete my exam."

"Why does everyone want me to leave?" She grabbed Thorne's hand. "I'm not going anywhere, and you're wasting time."

"I agree with Lady Grayson," Benson said.

"So do I," Corbin agreed.

The doctor turned to see the butler and the valet a few feet behind him. "All right, but you'll have to stand aside and tell me everything he ate."

"He ate only the strawberries." Reluctantly, Alexandria released Thorne's hand and stepped back.

The doctor took Thorne's pulse and lifted his eyelid. "Hmmm. Then why aren't you ill?"

"I didn't eat any. I'm allergic to them."

He straightened and looked at her a long time. "Who brought you the food?"

Alexandria wanted to scream at the man to help Thorne instead of asking stupid questions. "I went to the kitchen myself. Now, help him!" she ordered.

Clenching his teeth, the doctor rummaged in his bag and took out a little brown bottle. "If the poison hasn't gotten into his system, we need to get it out of his stomach." He looked at her. "He's going to be very sick. You should leave. It isn't going to be a sight for—"

"Damn it, save my husband and quit acting like a pompous fool."

Dr. Hathaway flushed, his lips pursed again. Lifting Thorne's head, the doctor attempted to get Thorne to drink from the bottle. He resisted. "He has to take the medicine."

Alexandria snatched the bottle from the doctor. "Thorne, you have to drink." She held it to his lips. "Please, darling. If you do, I promise to be the most obedient wife in all of England."

Thorne's lips parted. "That's it. A little more. You're going to be fine. I promise you," she said.

Almost as soon as he finished the bottle, he gagged. Alarmed, Alexandria whirled toward the doctor. "What did you do?"

"The medicine is working. If you're going to become hysterical, perhaps you should leave," Dr. Hathaway said condescendingly.

Thorne's body jerked. All attention centered on him.

"Get the chamberpot," the doctor ordered.

Alexandria forgot about the odious doctor. She ached for Thorne as he fought the twin demons in his stomach. After what seemed an eternity, he lay back. Perspiration bathed his body.

Dr. Hathaway checked him again. "Now we wait."

"Is there nothing else you can do?" Alexandria asked.

"All we can do is wait. Perhaps if I knew the name of the poison? Do *you* have any idea?" he asked curtly.

"No, I don't," she answered.

"Are you sure?" the doctor persisted.

"What are you implying?" Alexandria asked, her voice and her temper rising.

"You didn't eat the only food that apparently caused Lord Grayson's illness. I am notifying the authorities," the doctor said, snapping his bag shut.

"Thank you for coming. If you'll send a bill, your fee will be paid in the morning."

"I'm not leaving—"

"Leave of your own accord or I will have you thrown out," she said, her voice soft, but no less threatening. "Benson, show him the door."

"Gladly, Lady Grayson."

Dr. Hathaway looked from the open door to his patient. His accusing gaze came to rest on Alexandria. "I'm leaving, but I advise you to take care of Lord Grayson." The door closed behind him.

Trembling, she turned back to Thorne, who lay still. "You'll be fine, my darling."

"That he will," Corbin said, his voice suspiciously thick. "I'll go prepare some water to sponge his face. Will you be all right?"

"You don't believe him, do you?" She glanced up at Corbin.

"No one on the staff will believe the man. Obviously, the doctor is senile. I'll be back soon."

Alexandria picked up Thorne's hand and held it to her cheek. Could someone really have tried to poison them? And did it have anything to do with his intelligence work? Was Ann that vengeful? Questions swirled in her head. One thing she knew for sure, she would not leave Thorne's side until he was conscious and able to defend himself.

The police constable arrived thirty minutes after the doctor had left. The sergeant, a wiry man with a long mustache and cold, wandering eyes, looked at the strawberries on the tray as if expecting them to jump up and attack him.

"So, the butler left you at the top of the stairs?"

"I've told you that twice. Can't this wait until morning?" Alexandria asked, her gaze going back to Thorne. She refused to leave Thorne, and the constable refused to leave until his questions were answered.

"Strange, the only food poisoned is the food you're allergic to," he said thoughtfully, his eyes never leaving her.

"No one knows it's the strawberries. Why don't you eat one and stop bothering me?" she said, her irritation and fear finally catching up with her.

His beady eyes widened and he snapped to attention. "Are you threatening me?"

Alexandria momentarily closed her eyes and prayed for enough patience to put up with another fool. "No, I'm telling you to go away so I can take care of my husband."

"The doctor feels you might—"

"I don't want to hear that man's idiotic assumptions. He's angry because I told him to stop acting like a pompous fool. I can't say you're acting any better. I've answered your questions. Leave."

"I think we should go downstairs and talk."

"I'm not leaving this room."

"It's an official request," the officer said, drawing himself up to his full five feet, eight inches.

"Official? Are you arresting me?" she asked with disbelief.

The policeman glanced at the sleeping Thorne before answering. "Until things are clearer, I plan to protect his lordship."

Alexandria's eyes flashed. She advanced on the man and he backed up a step. "I am tired of this stupidity. My husband is fighting for his life, and you want to take me away from him. Well, I refuse to go quietly. You'll have to drag me kicking and screaming from this house, and I assure you, when he wakes up, he is not going to be happy with you for taking me or daring to touch me. Neither is my father, Squire Carstairs, who happens to be very influential. Now, get out of my sight."

The man gulped. "I-I'm staying. I won't neglect my duty."

"Then sit in that chair and be quiet," she ordered, pointing to a chair near the fireplace. Dismissing the man, she went back to the bed and took Thorne's hand. "Thorne, please wake up."

Benson cleared his throat. "Perhaps you should send for Lady Margaret at Lady Elleby's." Surprise lifted Alexandria's gaze. "She told me her plans, in case you happen to leave unexpectedly."

Alexandria didn't blame Lady Margaret for taking the precautions because she had almost been right. Until now, Alexandria hadn't thought of anyone else's pain, but her own. However, to send for Lady Margaret meant Thorne might not recover. She turned back to Thorne. "We needn't worry her unnecessarily."

"My lady, if you are with Lord Grayson, who will be with Lady Judith?" Corbin asked quietly.

"I told you not to disturb Judith," Alexandria said.

"We didn't, but she will know as soon as she awakens," Benson reasoned. "Both ladies would want to be here. Wouldn't you?"

Alexandria's eyes shut. Without thought she leaned against Benson's thin frame. "Do what you think is best. I can't think." Tears flowed down her cheek. "I tried so hard not to love him, and now all I can think of is that he might never know."

The butler awkwardly patted her shoulder. "Lord Grayson knows. I've never seen the master happier."

She glanced up at him, her beseeching eyes glittered with tears. "Do you think so?"

"I do."

"He's right," Corbin agreed. "Never seen his lordship happier than the last few days." He produced a handkerchief. "Now, you dry those tears. Can't have you worrying his lordship when he awakens."

"Thank you," she sniffed. "I wouldn't want to worry his lordship."

Through the night Thorne altered between breathing so shallowly that Alexandria kept her hand on his pulse to assure herself he was alive, and crying out in delirium for her. On those occasions when he cried out, the police constable would rush to the bed. His large ears almost twitched, as if he expected Thorne to say his wife had poisoned him. Returning to his seat, he'd always look at the dish of strawberries that now sat by his chair.

Moving quietly around the room, Corbin extinguished the candles and opened the heavy draperies. Bright sunlight shone inside.

"It's not right for the day to be so pretty," Alexandria murmured, then felt ashamed. She couldn't give up. Picking up a cloth, she began to sponge Thorne's face.

He moaned and turned his head toward the cloth.

"Thorne! Corbin, he moved," she yelled, and dipped the cloth in the water to bath his face again and again.

Heavy black lashes fluttered, then finally won the battle to remain lifted. "Alex?"

His voice sounded rough, but to Alexandria it was the sweetest sound she had ever heard. "Yes, darling. You were sick."

"Thirsty." His eyes closed.

Pouring a glass of water, she and Corbin helped Thorne to sit and drink. Water ran down the side of his mouth and trickled onto his chest. He lay back against the pillow. "I feel . . . like a herd of horses . . . ran over me."

"Lord Grayson, you claimed you were poisoned. I have reasons to believe your wife did it," the constable snapped, a few feet away.

Alexandria whirled in exasperation. "Be quiet or leave. You're upsetting my husband."

"I'm not leaving until you go with me for questioning."

"I told you her ladyship didn't poison Lord Grayson."

"I'd rather hear it from Lord Grayson," the constable said, refusing to budge.

Thorne looked from Alexandria, in a disheveled state, with fear and worry in her eyes that she made no attempt to hide, to Corbin, bristling with anger, to the righteous indignation of the policeman. "Alex, come here. Corbin, bring me my gun."

Both Alexandria and Corbin moved simultaneously. Neither showed the slightest surprise at the request.

The policeman, however, looked worried. "Lord Grayson, there is no need to take the law into your own hands. I'll arrest your wife and take her to jail myself."

Thorne took the pistol and laid it on top of the counterpane. "Constable, if you dare attempt to take my wife anywhere or charge her with anything, I'll have your badge."

"But . . . but . . ." he sputtered. "You said the strawberries were poisoned."

"If they were, my wife didn't do it. Now, please leave my house before in my delirium I shoot this gun by mistake."

"Lord Grayson, Lady Grayson is obviously an attractive and wealthy woman, but—"

Thorne lifted the gun.

Spinning on his heels, the policeman went to pick up the bowl of strawberries. "Leave that."

Disapproval heavy in his thin face, the man set the bowl down. "If she does you in, you'll only have yourself to blame."

"If I shoot you, you'll only have yourself to blame."

The door banged shut.

"Corbin, no one is to come into this house unless I give the order. Have all food purchased the day of my illness destroyed. Send for Lord Radcliffe."

"Right away, your lordship." Smiling, Corbin stopped at the door. "Might I say, it is nice to have you well?"

Thorne looked at Alexandria. "Do you have anything to say?"

She fell into his arms crying. "You are giving orders as if nothing happened. I was so frightened I couldn't think. I didn't know what to do. Then that stupid doctor thought I poisoned you because I didn't eat the strawberries, then the police—"

His mouth settled over hers. Reluctantly, he lifted his head. "I'm glad you're allergic to strawberries."

She shivered, her arms tightened. "Then you think someone tried to kill us."

The thought that someone wanted to harm Alexandria chilled him. "I think someone wanted me out of the way and didn't mind who else was harmed. I think it's about time you visited your father."

Rising, she glared at him. "I'm not going anyplace."

"Alex, it's too dangerous for you to be here."

"I'm not going. You can't make me go alone, and if you take me, I'll just come back." she said fiercely.

"Alex."

"No." Tears ran down her cheek. "I was so scared. Don't send me away. Please."

Thorne fiercely draw her to him. "I won't send you away." I can't, he thought. God, he hoped he was doing the right thing.

* * *

"I guess that proves you were right about the berries," Lord Radcliffe said, staring at the dead canary beside the strawberry.

In a secluded spot in the garden, Thorne pushed from his knees, his insides still tightening at what might have happened to Alexandria if she hadn't been allergic to the fruit. "The killer is no longer concerned with my death looking like an accident. He must be getting desperate. I wish I knew why he was after me."

"It might be a woman. The other sides have female agents as well." Radcliffe slowly rose.

"I told Alex I think it is related to my contact with the government. But the more I think about it, the more I'm convinced it has nothing to do with my government ties." Frustrated, Thorne shoved his fingers through his hair. "I've made some enemies, but none I know of who would coldly plan my murder."

"Do you plan to send your wife away?"

"She won't go."

Radcliffe nodded. "I imagine she wouldn't. Your lady has spunk."

"Glad you finally noticed." Thorne glanced back at the birdcage. "I'll have someone take care of this later. We had better get back to the ladies."

Radcliffe grunted. "For a moment I had doubts they were going to let you out of their sight. I'm not sure your ladies believed your story that someone must have accidentally mixed up the containers of rat poison and sugar."

"I know. That's why I've already asked Aunt Margaret to take Judith home with her this afternoon. At least I won't have to worry about them." He frowned. "It's still difficult to believe Aunt Margaret was only a few hours away."

Rounding the corner, they saw a footman hurrying toward them. "Your lordship, come quick."

"What is it? Is it my wife?" Thorne demanded, dread rushing through him.

"No. Your mother is here with the police. Benson is holding

the door, but he said to tell you to hurry. Lady Grayson sent Corbin for your gun."

Thorne ran. He heard the raised angry voices the moment he entered the house. Benson and another footman attempted to hold the door. Lady Margaret and Judith stood together nearby. As expected, Alexandria was behind Benson.

"What is going on here?"

On hearing his voice, everyone turned. The people outside, seeing their chance, pushed inside. Utter chaos broke out. Thorne snatched the gun from Corbin and fired once into the air. Women shrieked; several of the servants ducked for cover. Bits of plaster fell from the ceiling.

Alexandria smiled. "I see you and I have like minds."

"Benson, close the door. I'm certain we've given the neighbors enough to talk about." He handed the gun to Corbin. "Not another word until everyone is in my study." He reached out and Alexandria placed her hand in his.

Inside the study, he sat Alexandria behind his desk, noting that Radcliffe seated Judith and Lady Margaret on a small couch, then stepped behind them.

"Constable," Thorne said, "I thought we finished this morning."

The man shoved his way past another policeman, Dowager Grayson, and Stephen Jiles. "After talking with your mother, I thought I might return. She said you and your wife did not get along."

"His wife has made a spectacle of herself on several occasions. She is capable of such a foul act," Dowager Grayson shouted, pointing a pudgy finger at Alexandria. "She attacked me."

Alexandria surged from her seat. "I may do so again if you continue to defame me."

The dowager stepped back into the protective embrace of Jiles. "You see how evil she is."

"The only evil person I see here is you," Thorne said, his gaze chilling. "If I didn't want to get this mess cleared up, you

and that person with you would not have set foot in my house."
He ignored her gasp and Jiles's angry green eyes. "If the constable is stupid enough to believe your lies, then I shall talk with his superior as to his capabilities or the obvious lack of them. Because if he is an example of the law enforcement officers London has, then it's no wonder the streets are unsafe."

The man's eyes widened, his mouth gaped. "Lord Gray—"

"As a member of Prince Albert's council, I must concur with Lord Grayson." Lord Radcliffe stepped forward. "While his mother is naturally concerned, her accusations against Lady Grayson are unfounded and unwarranted. I would suggest, Constable, you see that the lady and her escort are taken home."

Untangling himself from the dowager, Jiles pushed forward. "Perhaps this gentleman is correct. A mother sometimes overacts when those she loves are threatened."

"You know the way out," Thorne said.

Jiles struggled with his anger. "Your mother is concerned not only about you, but also about her daughter. Perhaps it is best that Lady Judith go home with her mother until this entire episode is settled."

Dowager Grayson appeared as surprised by the turn of events as anyone. At a hard look from Jiles, she reluctantly said, "Perhaps that would be best."

Judith's face drained of color. She stood and took a step backward. "I—I don't want to go with you."

"You don't have to," Thorne said.

"Considering the danger she is in, and since Dowager Grayson is her legal guardian, you have nothing to say about it," Jiles snapped.

"I've had about enough of you." Thorne started toward Jiles, who raised his cane. In a flash of speed, Thorne blocked the blow with his forearm, then sent the man through the air with a kick. He landed in a heap against the far wall. The dowager rushed to his side.

"Stephen. Stephen." The woman whirled on her son. "You

thoughtless fool. You're not fit for anything. I wish she had succeeded in killing you."

An impatient knock sounded on the door. No one noticed or moved. All eyes were on the dowager.

A hush fell across the room. The policemen appeared shocked by the vehemence in the woman's voice. Lord Radcliffe found a seascape to study over the mantel of the fireplace. Lady Margaret turned away from her sister and took her trembling niece in her arms. Alexandria touched Thorne's arm. It was as rigid as steel. Her heart went out to him. Of all the things he had to contend with, now there was his vengeful mother.

The door opened and Lord Stonewell filled the doorway. His gaze scanned the room, finally coming to rest on Judith. He crossed to her. "I came as soon as I heard," he said, his gaze on Judith's pale face.

The dowager's lips curled. "So the cripple—"

"Shut up!" Thorne yelled, advancing on the cowering woman. "Take yourself from my house, and if you ever set foot here again, you'll wish you hadn't."

Alexandria opened the study door. A footman and Benson were waiting. "Please help this woman and man out of our home." She gazed at the policemen. "I trust you can remember your way out."

The policeman, who had said nothing, quickly left. A subdued constable followed. The footman tried to pick up a dazed Jiles.

"I was on my way out. I'll help," Radcliffe offered.

Alexandria closed the door. "Thorne, you really must show me how you do that."

"Stonewell, what brings you here?"

"This," Lord Stonewell answered, and handed Thorne a newspaper.

Thorne read the headline printed in bold black letters. Alexandria looked on. Her gasp was lost in his muttered curse.

"What . . . what does it say?" Judith asked softly.

"That the police suspect me of poisoning Thorne," Alexandria mumbled.

"The police are fools." Thorne crumpled the newspaper. "Stonewell, please escort Judith and Aunt Margaret to her townhouse. Alex, get your parasol and hat."

"Where are we going?"

"To show London what I think of these lies." He flung the newspaper into the fireplace.

Twenty-four

"Are you sure you want to go?" Alexandria asked, sitting next to Thorne in the closed carriage.

Thorne took her hand. "I should be asking you that."

Alexandria shrugged a bare shoulder. "The past three days haven't been so bad. The worst part wasn't what people thought of me; I've never cared one way or the other. It was knowing that I could be looking directly at the person responsible for trying to kill you and I wouldn't know."

"Don't think about it, Alex." He turned her to him. "All I want you to think about is how much you mean to me. I want you to know I'm not going to let anything happen to either of us."

She palmed his cheek and managed a smile. "Of course you're not." She didn't doubt he would give his life for her, yet with each passing day she wondered if his possessiveness stemmed from love for her or because she would carry his heir. Love wasn't a part of their bargain, but she couldn't help wishing for it anyway.

He pressed warm lips against her palm. "Even your father has finally come around. He was as angry with the stupidity of the police and the newspapers as I was. Not once before he left did he mention taking a horsewhip to me."

"I wish Wolf could have come with him."

"Would you feel safer if he were here?"

"No," she answered, without hesitation. She loved Wolf, but

being away from him didn't make her feel as if she were missing half her soul. "I feel safe with you."

"Thank you." The coach pulled to a halt. "We won't stay long." Stepping down, Thorne assisted Alexandria.

The Duke and Duchess of Singleton met them in the entrance of the guest-filled drawing room. "Good evening, Lord Grayson, Lady Grayson," the duchess greeted them. "I'm glad you could come."

Alexandria steeled herself against the sudden quietness and the fluttering of fans she knew women were whispering behind. "As always, I'm delighted to be here."

Though barely moving her lips, the duchess whispered, "You are going to do fine."

Trying to smile despite the stiff muscles in her face, Alexandria crossed the room on Thorne's arm to speak with Lady Margaret and Judith. As always since Thorne's illness, Lord Stonewell stood protectively by Judith's side.

"Courage, Alexandria," Lady Margaret said.

Alexandria's smile brightened. "Thank you. You don't know how much it helps, knowing you and Judith believe in me."

Judith clasped Alexandria's free hand. "You are family and we love you. Your quick thinking and courage saved Thorne's life. I can't thank you enough for that or for helping me regain my own courage," she finished, throwing a quick glance over her shoulder at Lord Stonewell.

"Your courage is different, but as great as Lady Grayson's," Lord Stonewell said, his steady blue eyes fixed fondly on Judith. She blushed prettily and held his gaze.

Alexandria watched the two with growing happiness. It appeared as if her sister-in-law had finally found her Prince Charming. Alexandria glanced up at Thorne, who smiled down at her. He was becoming her strength; he was already her Prince Charming. She hoped with everything within her that theirs would be a happy ending.

"Dinner is served, your grace," announced the butler.

"Let's hope strawberries aren't on the menu," Lord Kendricks said aloud.

Alexandria felt the gaze of everyone in the room. Only the fact that Thorne's arm tightened around her kept her from fleeing.

"Kendricks, you owe my wife an apology."

The blond man laughed. "It was only a joke."

"In bad taste," the duchess said, and stepped beside Alexandria. The duke joined his wife.

People near Kendricks began to move away. He glanced around in surprise. The arrogant expression on his handsome face changed to one of doubt.

Thorne walked to Kendricks, then began taking off his glove. "You have three seconds to apologize."

"Dueling is il—"

"Two seconds."

Kendricks eyes widened in alarm. He glanced around the room as if seeking assistance and found none. "I . . . I apologize? I meant no disrespect."

"Do you accept that, my lady?" Thorne asked.

She looked at Kendricks's beseeching face before she spoke. It was time he learned that women were not to be used for his own fiendish pleasure. "An apology is worthless from someone who is dishonorable. However, if I have misjudged you, you could show your sincerity by leaving so I do not continue to be reminded of your unpleasantness."

His monocle popped from his eye. He didn't appear to notice.

"Well said, my dear," Thorne said. "Kendricks, I'm sure the duchess will understand if you have another engagement."

His mouth gaped. "B-But—"

"Of course, I will," the duchess interrupted. "Now let's go to dinner. Thorne, come here and give me your arm; my husband will seat your wife." She nodded at the butler. "Please show Lord Kendricks the way out."

Totally humiliated, his shoulders bent, Kendricks left. The guests proceeded to dinner, led by the duke and Alexandria.

Taking her seat, she smiled at her husband, who was seating the duchess. She shouldn't have worried. As long as Thorne was with her she was safe.

"Thorne, I'm going to be sick." With those words Alexandria leaped from the bed the next morning and grabbed the chamberpot.

Fear twisted Thorne's gut and made his hand tremble as he knelt beside Alexandria and pulled her hair away from her flushed face. "Did you eat or drink anything after we came back from the party?"

Eyes wide with growing realization and dread lifted and searched his before the urgency of her stomach sent her head back over the pot. Finished, she leaned weakly against Thorne. Her entire body quivered.

Picking her up, he lay her in bed, jerked the bell pull, then began sponging her face. "I'm sending for the doctor."

"But . . . but my stomach isn't cramping."

"Just indulge your husband, for once," he told her, trying to sound reassuring and painfully aware that his voice trembled.

A discreet knock sounded at the door. "Come in."

Opening the door, Corbin took one step into the room. He saw Thorne's nakedness and the valet's gaze immediately went to Alexandria in bed.

"Send for the doctor and tell him to hurry," Thorne ordered.

The door closed and Thorne turned back to Alexandria. "You're going to be fine."

"I know. I feel better already." She cocked her head to one side. "Aren't you going to get dressed?"

Thorne glanced down at his nakedness. He hadn't thought of anything except Alexandria. "I think we both should get something on."

A knock sounded again. "Corbin, are you alone?"

"Benson is with me, my lord. A footman has gone for the doctor," came the answer through the door.

Thorne pulled the cover up to Alexandria's chin. "Come in."

Both men entered the room. Corbin picked up the dressing gown he had laid out the night before on a chair and Benson positioned himself by the connecting bedchamber door. After helping Thorne into the robe, the valet nodded. Benson opened the connecting door and the maid appeared holding a nightgown.

"We'll wait outside for the doctor," Benson said, his voice suspiciously thick.

"I hope it's not the same quack," Alexandria said, trying to hide her own worry.

"Rest assured, Lady Grayson. This is a new physician." He and Corbin left.

"I'll take that, Nelda. Thank you," Thorne said.

Her eyes glittering with tears, the maid curtsied and left. His hand fisted on the gown. They all meant well, but they all acted like Alexandria was dying. She was going to be fine; she had to be.

"Thorne, don't you think I should put that on?"

He looked at her with eyes that burned. His throat felt tight and achy. "Nothing is going to happen to you." The words were a solemn vow he hoped he could keep.

The gown had barely settled over her head before a knock came again and Benson's voice said, "The doctor."

"Come in," Thorne called, his hand squeezing Alexandria's.

A sandy-haired man in his early thirties with kind eyes entered. "I'm Dr. Sanderson, Lord Grayson." Going to the bedside he picked up Alexandria's wrist. "Would you care to wait outside?"

"No." The answer came from both Thorne and Alexandria.

The young doctor's brow puckered into a frown as he looked from patient to husband. After a moment, he nodded, pulled back the covers, and opened his bag. "Perhaps you should tell me why you sent for me with such urgency."

Watching Alexandria with worried eyes, Thorne related her illness and his poisoning of the previous week. If the doctor

was shocked by what he heard or realized this was the infamous
couple from the newspaper, his face showed no sign. He simply
continued his examination, asking questions as he proceeded.

Ten minutes later, he replaced his stethoscope and pulled the
covers up. His frown was gone. "Congratulations. Your wife is
going to have a baby."

Thorne blinked. "A what?"

"A baby," Alexandria whispered, her gaze and her hand going
to her stomach.

Looking dazed, Thorne sagged on the bed.

The doctor grinned. "I can see you're not going to be much
good during delivery." He picked up his bag. "Try weak tea
and biscuits in the morning before rising, and don't get out of
bed so abruptly."

"Thank you, Doctor."

"You're welcome. I wish all my cases had such happy endings." He walked to the door. "May I tell the people waiting
outside that Lady Grayson is all right? I suspect you want to
tell them the good news yourself."

"Yes, thank you."

Nodding, the doctor left.

Alexandria looked at Thorne's tense face and uneasiness
swept through her. "You don't want the baby?"

"Don't want it? How could I not want our baby? I was just
surprised, that's all." He stood. "I'll tell the staff and have Nelda
bring you some tea."

"Aren't you going to stay?" Bewilderment laced her voice.

"You need to rest."

Alexandria watched in dismay as Thorne strode from the
room. He had acted as if he couldn't stand the sight of her.
Cheering noises erupted from the hallway. She placed her hand
on her stomach. "Why did you scare him? I thought that was
why he married me."

Two hours later Alexandria was just as puzzled when her
bedroom door opened and Thorne preceded two footmen car-

rying her large trunks. She had seen him only once since he'd
left and then only briefly.

"I've sent word to your father of the situation, and I think
it's best you visit him until things are cleared up."

"Is that how you see my carrying your child—as a situation?"
she asked, her voice raspy thin.

His body tensed. "This morning I realized that for all my
talk of protecting you, I was helpless. I didn't like the feeling."

She touched his rigid arm. "Sometimes you can be too
strong, Thorne."

"What does that mean?" he asked abruptly.

"You see weakness in yourself where there is none. I am fine
and our baby is fine."

"I plan for you both to remain so. Nelda will be in here
shortly to help you get dressed. We're leaving in three hours."

"I'm not going." She pressed back in the bed. "You can't
make me."

His face settled into determination. "We both know I can.
Nothing is going to happen to my child." The door closed.

Alexandria curled up into a ball. She had her answer. He
cared only about the baby. Its mother was secondary. She had
fulfilled the bargain. What she wanted no longer mattered. She
was being banished to the country with all the other superfluous
wives. Only she wouldn't even be at her own home. She would
have to suffer the indignity of being returned to her father's
home like an unwanted parcel.

All through getting dressed she tried to tell herself it didn't
matter that he didn't love her; his love for the baby was enough.
The aching emptiness in her heart told her she'd lied. She
wanted Thorne to love her, needed his love with a growing
urgency that occupied all her thoughts.

Thorne knew he was being unreasonable and hasty. It did not
matter. Not for the first time his control had lapsed and there
was nothing he could do to regain it until Alexandria was safe.

Looking out the train window, he tried to forget the terror that had stricken him on seeing her sick. He had thought he would never be so frightened as when they had the boating accident. He was wrong. He had never felt that kind of paralyzing fear, not even during the thickest and bloodiest moments of battle.

Turning, he saw Alexandria reclining on a love seat in his private coach, her face pale, her eyes closed. But she was safe. She hadn't spoken to him since they'd boarded the train. Why couldn't she understand he could not, would not, go through such terror again?

She moaned. Instantly he was by her side. "Can I get you something?"

"Yes. You can get me off this train."

He wiped her face. "The train is the fastest way to get you home."

Her lids lifted. "I forgot how eager you are to get rid of me."

"Alex, I'm doing what I feel is best. Try to understand that."

Her eyes closed and she turned away. Putting the cloth away, Thorne picked her up. He wasn't surprised by her initial struggles. "I'm going to hold you, so stop fighting and try to get some rest."

"If I was well, you wouldn't get away with this."

"If you were well, there'd be no need." She stiffened in his arms. It was a long time before he heard the even sounds of her breathing and he knew she was asleep.

"Welcome home, Allie." The squire beamed down at Alexandria lying in her bed in her old room. "I can't believe you're going to make me a grandfather."

She didn't return his smile. "Thank you, Father."

At the squire's questioning look, Thorne spoke up. "The train ride was rather unsettling."

"I'll have Mrs. Swanson prepare you a light supper," Tillie said from the foot of the bed.

"I don't want anything. If you don't mind, I'd rather rest."
She looked at Thorne. "Goodbye." She turned away.

"Thorne, I'd like to see you," the squire said. It wasn't a
request. The moment they were in the hall he asked, "What the
hell is wrong with her? She wasn't this despondent when people
thought she was a murderer."

"She didn't want to come." Thorne shoved his fingers
through his hair. "I can't make her understand I'd go crazy if I
had to go through something like this morning again. Here,
with you, I know she's safe and I can find out who tried to kill
me."

"Did you tell her?"

Both men whirled to see Tillie. She lifted her chin. "I love
her, too. Lord Grayson, it seems to me you have some explaining to do. Has she eaten today?"

"Very little."

"I'll get her a tray. Carrying a baby is hard enough without
thinking the father doesn't want you." She walked away.

"The next time I see my daughter, I want to see some life in
her eyes, or I may save the man who's after you the trouble,"
the squire said, and walked away.

Thorne opened Alexandria's bedroom door and stepped inside. She was curled up on her side, her back to him. She must
know he wanted her. Neither of them could hide his desire from
the other. At the moment, however, what he felt wasn't desire,
but a need to protect and cherish.

"See she eats every bite." Tillie handed him the tray, then
pulled the door shut.

Alexandria spoke without turning. "Whoever it is, please
leave."

"It's your husband, and I'm not going anyplace until you
eat."

"Don't worry, I won't let anything happen to our baby."

"I know that. I'm concerned about the mother."

She looked over her shoulder. "You don't have to pretend."

"I see we do need to talk." He sat the tray down and began undressing. "And I need to hold you."

"You do?"

He climbed into bed and pulled her into his arms. "I do. Why do you think this morning was any less frightening to me than it was for you when I was ill?"

"You brought me home," she said accusingly.

"Because I need to know you're safe. Unlike at Grayson Hall, you know all the people here and no one is going to get near you without arousing suspicion."

She gazed into his troubled eyes and relaxed against him. "I acted like a spoiled child."

He kissed her forehead. "After what you've been through, I should have explained things to you. I just wanted to get you to safety as quickly as possible."

"Now that we're both safe, can't you stay?"

"We're not safe as long as that maniac is free. I'm returning to London in the morning, and this time, I'm going to find out who it is."

"I'm afraid, Thorne," she whispered, fighting tears.

"I'm not going to take any chances, Alex. I have too much to live for."

Thorne left early the next morning. Not even Wolf's presence could lift Alexandria from her depression. He had to be all right.

"It's nice to have you back, Miss—Lady Grayson," Mary said, setting the tea by the bedside table.

"Thank you."

"It's been exciting here with them finding out John Duckett kilt Lord Curtiss and Lord Hempstead."

"What?"

"Didn't your father tell you? Duckett's wife told the police yesterday after he didn't come home from working at the mill. He killed them because they testified against his father and he was hanged. John put heavy doses of laudanum in their wine. They went to sleep and never woke up."

Alexandria frowned. "Why did his wife finally tell?"

"The tavern girl is also missing." Mary handed Alexandria a cup of tea. "Duckett and the girl were carrying on. His wife said if she couldn't have him, no one else could."

Alexandria thoughtfully sipped her tea. A jealous woman. Could Ann, Rachel, or Kendricks have been that jealous? She had to write Thorne with her suspicions. In the meantime, she was going to get out of bed. There was no reason why she couldn't run the Grayson estate. To her relief, her father didn't object.

"On the conditions that Wolf and two men go with you and you stay only a couple of hours a day."

Kissing her father, she set off for the estate with her escort. She received another surprise when the housekeeper told her Lord Grayson had informed the staff that she might come by. Smiling, she settled herself behind Thorne's desk and sent for the estate manager. Wolf found a spot by the fireplace. She could almost imagine things were as before, if not for the loneliness that always seemed to be a part of her.

"Come in," she answered to a heavy knock at the door.

A robust man in tweed pants and a homespun shirt entered, his cap between large hands. "Lady Grayson, I'm Ian Baskim, the estate manager. You sent for me."

"Yes, Mr. Baskim. I have decided to look over the estate records and possibly implement some changes," Alexandria told him brightly.

"His lordship didn't say anything to me about any changes," Baskim said, his brown eyes narrowed.

"I'm telling you, Mr. Baskim. I assure you I have my husband's permission to do so."

Twisting the cap in his hand, the man hesitated.

Alexandria was not used to disobedience and she wasn't going to tolerate it. "It was my desire to work together with you in harmony. Since that does not appear to be possible, please have the estate records brought to me at once."

His jaw slackened. "You're turning me out?"

"I intend to see that changes are made on the estate. Since you refuse to cooperate, you are the one turning yourself out."

"I didn't say I refused to help."

Alexandria sighed in exasperation. "When I give an order, I expect it to be carried out, not questioned. Can you take orders from a woman?"

"Yes, your ladyship."

"Good, then bring me the records. I intend to return each day until I have enough knowledge to change some things."

"You aren't staying here?"

"No, Lord Grayson thought I would be more comfortable with my father until his return. Now, the records."

The estate manager turned to the door, his feet dragging as if they carried a hundred pounds of weight.

As the next two days passed, the man's spirit didn't improve. Of all the people at the estate, he was the least jovial.

"I can't take this waiting. Why don't you come straight out and fire me?" Baskim asked.

Alexandria glanced up. "Fire you?"

"I know I let Lord Grayson down, and after what he done for me, too, but I swear I didn't mean no harm. I checked the boat."

A chill ran down her spine. "The boat Lord Grayson and I had the accident in?"

"I swear it was seaworthy. Sure, I was rushing to get to the tavern to see . . . well . . . see someone, but I checked the boat. It shouldn't have sunk." He bowed his head. "I'll never forget the look on his lordship's face. It was as cold as death when he walked out of your room the day of the accident and asked me about the boat."

"Naturally, he was upset, Mr. Baskim. We almost lost our lives due to our carelessness."

He shook his head. "Then why did he ask me if I had checked

the boat? I must have missed something, but I swear I didn't see anything. He's finally decided to punish me by taking my job."

Alexandria's mind whirled with the new information. Someone had tried to kill them then, and Thorne apparently had known all along. The two footmen who had accompanied her in London now made sense. But who?

"Mr. Baskim, I'm going to take a chance that I can trust you because my husband has chosen to do so. I need information and I don't have a great deal of time. Can I trust you to be discreet?" His head bobbed up and down. "I made up the story about the boat sinking to protect Lord Grayson from unfair accusations. Do you think you and he could both have made a mistake in checking the boat?"

"No." Baskim shook his head. "He hadn't sailed in a long time, but I taught him 'bout boats when he was a small boy."

"Then obviously someone tampered with the boat. I want you to tell me exactly who you spoke with after my husband told you to check out the boat."

"As I said, I hurried to the tavern afterward. Betsy was angry because I was late. I explained that I had to work."

Alexandria sat forward in her seat. "Did you mention the boat?"

He opened his mouth, then snapped it shut and slumped against the chair. "Oh, God, what have I done?"

"What is it?" Alexandria asked, coming to stand over the shaken man.

He didn't appear to be able to look up from his clasped hands in his lap. "She was angry and threatening not to leave with me after work. I wanted to impress her, so I bragged that Lord Grayson only trusted me to check out the boat he planned to take his new wife out in. She still acted kind of huffy and this gentleman offered to buy me a drink, saying he had several ships." Baskim's graying head dropped lower. "He said he missed the water and wanted to see something larger than a creek. Since Betsy was acting uppity, I brought him back here."

"If he wanted to come back later, no one would suspect anything, since he had been seen with you earlier," she murmured softly.

Baskim finally lifted his head. "When Lord Grayson asked me if I checked the boat, I never thought about the gentleman."

"What did he look like?"

"Right handsome, with light hair and green eyes."

Alexandria's heart beat faster. She knew two men who disliked Thorne who fit that description. But which one? "Could you recognize the man if you saw him again?"

"Yes," he said with certainty, his face hard.

"Good. I want you to take the first train to London."

Loneliness sat upon Thorne like an invisible weight, pressing him down, making it difficult for him to get through the day. He didn't want to go to bed; the loneliness was worse there. Instead, he turned down the wick of the oil lamp on his desk and sat in the moonlit room.

He missed Alexandria. He missed her teasing smile, her softness, the quick rush of desire he felt whenever she was near him. Even the wanting was preferable to the aching void her leaving left. He could no longer deny she was important to him. He'd fought against it and lost on the morning he'd thought she'd been poisoned.

She had kept her end of the bargain and more. She had stood beside him with a fierceness that astounded him. Once she committed herself to something, she did so wholly. There was as much goodness in her heart as there was beauty in her face and winsome body . . . a body that would soon grow with their child.

A child who would never have to cry because it was unwanted or stand tight-lipped after being slapped. She'd give her heart to their child. He allowed himself to wonder what it would be like to be loved completely, with nothing held back.

For once, he was unable to hold back the rush of longing that

that image brought. Then, just as quickly, he pushed it away. He swore never to be vulnerable again. Yet the temptation was a lure wrapped in silken skin and honeyed laughter, with eyes of shimmering turquoise that turned dark blue when passion overtook her.

The door cracked open. With a rustle of silk, a shadowy figure moved across the room. A woman, and she was going to the safe hidden behind a picture on the far side of the room. He reached for his gun on his desk and turned up the lamp.

The gun clicked the instant the flickering flame steadied and illuminated the room. With a gasp, the dowager countess turned. Her face looked eerie, frightened in the light. Laying the gun aside, Thorne crossed to her. "So you've added stealing to your list of crimes."

"I wouldn't have to steal if you'd take care of me as a son should," Marianne hissed, her composure regained.

"How did you get in?"

She stepped back, her hand tightening on the reticule.

His gaze followed. He held out his hand. "One way or the other, you're not leaving until I have the key."

Jerking the reticule open, she took out an elongated key and flung it toward him. He caught it. He should have remembered that she'd often let her "friends" in though the back door. "The locks will be changed by tomorrow." He turned away.

"I need money," she said, the desperation in her voice stopping Thorne.

"Ask Jiles."

Marianne's face hardened into anger. "I can't. He left me two days after you hit him. It's your fault."

"You should thank me."

She looked incredulous. "Thank you for sending away a man who might have loved me."

"You don't know what love is," Thorne said.

"Neither of us does. I'm your mother, yet you look down your nose at me as if I were vermin that caught to your boot. I am what I am and I don't know any other way to be. My parents indulged me shamefully. I thought everyone would, until I married your father and he didn't know how to meet my needs any more than I did his."

"So you sought other men's beds," Thorne said contemptuously.

"It's so easy for you to condemn. I wanted to be loved; I needed that attention. Your father was bookish and he bored me to tears; he didn't try to understand me."

"Did the men after him understand you any better?"

"No. Not then, and not now. Only now I have to seek men out. Don't turn away from me." She briefly caught his arm. "You are no better than I am. Why is it acceptable for men to pay for companionship? You have had plenty of mistresses. I can't stand to be by myself." For a moment she looked wild, desperate. "I fear growing old and alone."

"That was your choice," Thorne said through clenched teeth.

"My choice. You stand there and say that when you took the last chance I had," Marianne cried. "You took Judith, the only person who always gave without question. You turned her into a cripple who needed love, and I didn't know how to give it."

"So you turned your back on her."

"Yes, and she continued to take. Do you know the reason I finally agreed to send her to you? Men were starting to look at her and not at me."

Thorne advanced on her. "If you let one of them near her—"

"Even I haven't stooped that low."

He turned away. "I think you'd better leave."

"Not without money."

He whirled around, astounded at her gall.

"I'm living at a boardinghouse, and the rent is due tomorrow."

"Pawn the ruby necklace you're so proud of."

"It's already gone."

"My God. How could you have let yourself come to this?"

She looked every day of her fifty-two years and then some. "I didn't want to be alone."

"You're alone now, and soon you'll be on the streets, being used like . . ."

This was the woman who had given him life, and he felt nothing, not hatred, not pity. She had thrown away everything looking for someone to love her when she already had them. Going to his desk, he took out some pound notes and handed them to her. He didn't expect thanks and she didn't offer any.

She stuffed the money into her reticule. "I'd have gotten on my knees for the money and hated your guts."

"Now you can simply hate my guts. Tomorrow afternoon, see my solicitor. He'll set up suitable accommodations for you. I won't have Judith shamed with stories about her mother." He walked to the door. "I'll show you out."

"Afraid I'll steal something on the way out?"

He said nothing, but simply waited. She left the room. At the front door, he unlocked it and stood aside.

Marianne looked out at the fog-shrouded streets and pulled her cloak closer to her body. "I don't want to stay in London. Do you think those accommodations could be found in Paris?"

"Yes."

Still she hesitated. "That man who went to Judith . . . is he in love with her?"

"Alexandria thinks so."

Marianne looked at Thorne with desolate eyes. "I wonder what it feels like to be loved." She went down the steps and disappeared into the fog.

Stepping inside, Thorne closed the doors, knowing she had chosen her own path, yet the knot in his gut didn't lessen, nor did the burning in his eyes. He didn't know if the misery he felt was for Marianne or for himself. He knew only that whether he wanted to admit it or not, they had something in common. He also wondered what it would be like to be loved by Alexandria and was suddenly afraid he might never know.

Twenty-five

He had overlooked something.

Pacing the length of his study the next morning, Thorne went over the three attempts on his life. If he hadn't had another close call with poison while on a mission five years ago, he might not have recognized in time what was happening to him. Yet something continued to bother him about the attempts.

A trained assassin would have made sure the intended target ate the fruit and would not have left it to chance. Yet the strawberries had been poisoned and left for anyone to eat. Benson reported that the berries were picked that morning in the conservatory.

Whoever had tried to poison Thorne had to have a good knowledge of the staff and access to the kitchen. There had been no new servant in the past three years. But there had to be someone . . .

Bracing his hands on his desk, he glanced down and saw the elongated key. His body tautened. Picking it up, he twisted the cold metal between finger and thumb.

The dowager countess would have such knowledge. Even as the thought formed in his mind, he rejected the idea. Marianne was capable of a great many things, but he didn't think murder was one of them. But if anything happened to him and Alexandria, his mother would become Judith's guardian again.

Pocketing the key, he crossed to the door. He needed to have another talk with his mother.

* * *

Alexandria's mind raced with possibilities as the carriage took her to Grayson Hall. The estate manager had left yesterday on the train to London and at this moment he could be talking to Thorne. He would know how best to find the man and everything would be all right.

Refusing to believe otherwise, she glanced out at the passing countryside and wondered when Wolf would catch up with them. In another two miles they would turn onto the estate. Although they tried not to show it, some of the servants were still afraid of him. It was best if they arrived togeth—

The coach halted abruptly and with it Alexandria's thought. She threw out her hands to keep from plummeting to the floor. Righting herself, she pushed her hat off her face. That wasn't like Ethan at all. Usually the coachman drove so slowly she teased him that she could outrun his carriage.

Sticking her head out the window, she saw another coach blocking the road. Just as she was about to ask the coachman to help, gunshots rang out. The door she was reaching for jerked open and a burly man, his face covered with a dirty, shaggy beard, stood with a pistol aimed at her stomach.

"Get out."

Alexandria pressed back against the carriage seat and placed a protective hand over her stomach. "I'm not going anyplace with you."

The man's hairy face twisted in anger. "I got orders not to do ye in now, but not about givin' ye a lick or two."

Alexandria looked at the cold brown eyes and left the carriage. She had to keep her baby safe. She hadn't gone three steps before she saw the driver and two footmen sprawled face-down on the ground. Fear and anger shot through her. "You bastard."

She started toward them, but a grimy hand on her arm stopped her.

"Ye' better worry 'bout helpin' yerself," the man said roughly. "Now git in that coach."

"I'll triple whatever price they're paying you to do this. You must know my husband and my father are very wealthy," she said, stalling for time.

The man sneered. "He told us ye'd say that an' give us a rope 'round our necks for payment."

"What 'he'? Who sent you?" she demanded, despite her quaking voice.

"Git in that coach!"

If she did as he asked, she'd seal her death warrant. There had to be something she could do. She looked at the thin-faced man driving the carriage and back to the man with the gun. If she could disarm him, she might have a chance. She had practiced Thorne's fighting technique over and over. Slowly, she clutched her dress and moved her foot back, her eyes on the gun.

The click of the gun snapped her head upward. She stared into pitiless brown eyes. "Move, or I'll knock ye' out and dump ye' inside."

She believed him. He'd give no more thought to shooting a woman than he would to squashing a bug. The man who'd sent him was probably just as unfeeling. She went to the carriage and got in.

She gripped the seat as the horses bolted forward, hating her helplessness as much as she hated the boards nailed over the windows. Whoever wanted her was making sure no one saw her. But did they intend to use her to lure Thorne to them or simply to kill her? Her hand clutched her stomach. She didn't know if she wanted him to come or not. She wanted to live, wanted her child to live, but she wanted Thorne safe.

She lost track of time as the coach jostled and careened over the dirt road, then slowed and stopped. The door opened and the man with the gun motioned her out.

In front of her was a cabin, aged and sagging. The driver barely managed to unstick the warped door. A broad hand in

ie small of her back propelled her inside the filthy room.
Beams of sunlight filtered though the many cracks in the roof.
She glanced around hoping to see the man who had ordered her
idnapping and instead saw a three-legged table, a cot with a
ilthy bed covering, and a straight chair.

No one had lived here for a long time, and no one could live
iere in the condition it was in. She realized with alarming clarity
hat she wasn't going to leave the cabin alive.

"Sit down."

Her gaze swung to the man who always carried the gun. His
:yes remained as predatory as a hawk's and as merciless. This
ime she didn't argue. The isolation of the cabin, the unblinking
tare of the man with the gun, chilled her as nothing else could.
Sitting in the wooden chair, she pulled her cloak around her.
Her only hope was Thorne, and he was miles away.

"I'm sure Lady Grayson is fine," Radcliffe said, his feet
oraced as the carriage raced to Grayson Hall.

Thorne heard, but he didn't answer. Radcliffe had repeated
:he words in various ways since they'd left London by train that
morning. He said the same thing when they arrived at the
squire's house and found Alexandria gone. But they knew the
man they were dealing with wasn't always rational . . . that
made him unpredictable.

Thorne's hands clenched and unclenched in helplessness. He
needed to see she was safe. She wouldn't even know the bastard
meant to harm her until it was too late. Thorne's chest hurt.
Damn, his entire body ached. He couldn't lose her.

"We're slowing down. I wonder why," Radcliffe said, looking
out the window.

"Lord Grayson, it's your carriage," the coachman yelled, pulling the horses to a halt.

His heart thundering in his chest, Thorne jumped out of the
carriage and ran. He didn't stop until he'd looked inside the
empty carriage. Swinging around, he saw Lord Radcliffe and

the coachman moving to the three men on the ground. From the hard look on Radcliffe's face, Thorne knew all three were dead.

"That bastard has Alexandria," Thorne said, his voice ragged with rage.

Radcliffe straightened from crouching over the last man. "Do you plan to let him keep her?"

The words were spoken with such detached calmness that Thorne's anger was momentarily directed at Radcliffe.

The coachman saw Thorne's face and stumbled back. Radcliffe took a step closer. "The man I know wouldn't stand there looking as if he's suddenly found himself in hell, he'd do his damnedest to send the men responsible there."

Thorne unclenched his fists and swiftly walked to the horses on Alexandria's coach and began to unharness one. "Go on to the estate and send out a search party, then send someone to contact the squire to do the same."

"Where are you going?" Radcliffe asked, as Thorne swung onto the horse's back.

"To trade places with the men holding Alex," Thorne said, and rode off.

"Good evening, Lady Grayson."

Alexandria jerked around at the sound of a man's cultured voice. Shock, then anger, swept through her. Stephen Jiles stood in the door with a gun in his hand. "Is Thorne's mother having you do this?"

"This is my idea," he said, and motioned the two men out of the room. They quickly left.

Moistening her lips, Alexandria rose. If the other men were gone, at least she'd have a chance. "Why would you want to harm me or Thorne?"

"Money. With you and Grayson out of the way, Marianne would have guardianship of Judith. It wouldn't have been difficult to get her to marry me, and then I would control it all."

His face harshened. "Unlike my first wife, I might have let her live if she'd stayed out of my way."

Alexandria swallowed the bile clawing at the back of her throat. "You killed your first wife."

"I'd like to think I sent her to her reward faster so I could receive mine. Served the fat sow right for holding the purse strings so tight," he said calmly. "I chose Marianne after careful consideration, only to have your husband prove intractable. Then he married and I had to deal with the possibility of an heir." He shrugged. "The only sensible thing was for both of you to die. I didn't count on you being allergic to strawberries."

"Thorne will find out," Alexandria told him.

"No, he won't. In fact, his sending you to the country helped me. I thought after you both escaped the poisoning, I might not get another chance. I even left Marianne and was looking for another lonely woman. Luckily, I still had your house watched."

"You won't get away with this."

"Who is going to stop me? You will be dead, the victim of a robbery, and your husband, in his sorrow, will kill himself, with a little help from me. I shall rush to Marianne's side and console her in her time of need. I have no doubt she will take me back. You see, I'm very good at what I do." He raised the gun.

"I shall enjoy telling your husband how you died just before I kill him. He should not have stricken me. Goodbye, Lady Grayson."

"No," Alexandria screamed, and launched herself forward the same instant the window behind Jiles crashed inward.

Shoving Alexandria away with one hand, Jiles whirled toward the noise with the gun in his other hand. With the weapon lowered, his eyes widened as a wolf skidded to a halt several feet away.

The animal whirled, and with fangs bared, leaped for Jiles's throat. Staggering back, Jiles lifted the gun.

A shot exploded.

Alexandria cried out again, expecting Wolf to fall. Instead,

she saw a rapidly widening red spot on Jiles's chest, then Wol
hit Jiles in the chest, his powerful jaws clamping shut on hi
throat. She turned away from the sickening sound of his wind
pipe being crushed.

"Alex." Thorne rushed inside, a smoking gun in his hand.

With a cry of gladness, Alexandria rushed into his arms. He
held her so tight that her ribs ached, and she tried to hug him
just as tight. "I knew you'd come."

"I see I can't let you out of my sight," Thorne said, his voice
unsteady.

Suddenly she pulled away. "What about the two men?"

His face harshened for a moment. "I already took care o
them." He looked over her shoulder at Jiles lying dead on the
floor and Wolf standing over the body. Thorne had traded places
with the men and sent them to hell. "Let's go home."

Later that night Alexandria lay in bed beside Thorne. The
constable, her father, and Lord Radcliffe were all gone. Earlier,
in his study, Thorne had explained that he'd become suspicious
of Jiles and had been on his way to talk to Marianne when the
estate manager had arrived. Thorne took the man with him. He
identified Jiles from a photograph in Marianne's flat.

Afterward they'd talked to Jiles's first wife's sister, who'd told
of her suspicions that he'd murdered her sister. He had a vicious
temper. Remembering the bruises on Marianne's face, and unable to locate Jiles, Thorne had started for Grayson Hall and
had left Stonewell with Lady Margaret and Judith.

"I can't believe how close I came to losing you," Thorne said,
pulling Alexandria closer, his lips trying and failing to find hers.

"I can't," she said, and pushed out of his arms.

Thorne was instantly alert. "Are you sick?"

"No. I just can't keep pretending any longer," she said, her
voice whispery thin.

Thorne thought his chest might burst, his heart was thumping
so hard. "You've been pretending?"

"Yes, I've been pretending I didn't love you," she said, searching his face for some sign of happiness. "Today I realized how foolish that was. I could have died and you never would have known how much I love you."

It was what he had wanted to hear, but he was suddenly afraid. "It's the excitement of this afternoon. Why don't you go to sleep?"

She resisted the tug on her arm and sat up. "I love you, Thorne. I knew the night you came to Lord Stonewell's grandmother's estate. What I want to know is, do you love me?"

"What difference does it make?" he asked, looking almost desperate.

"A great deal. I want a real marriage. Not a bargain . . . but if that is all there is to be, I am carrying your heir and there is no longer any need for you to come to my bed."

Irritation swept across his face. "What difference does it make if I say I love you. I could lie to you and you still wouldn't know the difference."

"I trust you not to." She took a deep breath and asked, "Do you love me?"

"You're obviously distraught from this afternoon." He blew out the candle. "Goodnight." He felt her moving away from him in mind and body. He didn't want that. When he had thought about her loving him with nothing held back, he honestly hadn't thought how he'd feel about making the same commitment.

Marianne's words about his not knowing how to love came back. He shut his eyes against a wave of emptiness and rolled on his side to keep from reaching for Alex. He wanted her love more than he wanted his next breath, but he didn't know if he was able to give her the same thing she asked of him. Could he be that vulnerable?

The next morning Alexandria asked the same question.

Three days later she was still asking. On the fourth morning she went down to breakfast to find Thorne gone. Tears streamed down her cheeks. She had lost him. But she needed the words.

She needed to know they shared more than passion, that she was more than a possession, more than the mother of his heir.

By late afternoon she was tired of the sympathetic looks from the staff and sought solace in the garden. Wolf lay at her feet. Strange, she hadn't seen him since the day at the cabin, and yet once Thorne had left, Wolf had reappeared.

"Did he tell you to keep me company? He should be here. Why don't you go home to Mrs. Wolf?" Leaning over, she looped her arms around the animal's neck. "I love him so much. Why is it so hard for him to say the words?"

A sheaf of paper floated down a few feet away, followed by another, then another. She glanced up. The sky was filled with white paper. Catching a sheet, she read:

I love you.— *Thorne*

Looking up through the tree branches, she saw the fast-moving air balloon passing over the house. Holding the paper to her chest, she ran through the house to the front expecting Thorne to land. Wolf ran with her, playing and nipping at the papers. Letters continued to fall from the balloon, but it didn't land.

Grinning broadly, she waved and yelled, "I love you!"

Servants who had come out to see what was going on smiled as they read the papers.

Carrying as many sheets as possible, she ran back into the house and up the stairs. Thorne would be home as soon as whoever he was with landed the craft. It must have taken him days to write all the notes. It was romantic and frivolous and she couldn't have thought of anything that would have pleased her more. The papers were going to be all over the countryside and everyone would know he loved her.

He loved her and he didn't care who knew.

Opening the door to her bedroom, she came to a complete standstill. Thorne, with a devastating smile on his face, lay in the middle of her bed, a sheet draped over the lower half of his body. From the waist up he didn't have any clothes on, and knowing Thorne, he didn't have any on below the waist, either. "I'll be right back."

Going into the hall, she looked for a servant and for once, didn't find one. Hurrying down the stairs, she learned why: the front door was open and the servants, including some of the people from the stable, were picking up Thorne's notes.

"Lady Grayson will want these for a scrapbook," Benson directed, as he stooped to pick up a sheet of paper.

"Isn't this romantic?" Mary said, taking a wide berth around Wolf, who lay on a pile of papers.

Benson straightened. "You are not to discuss the lord and lady."

"That's right," Corbin said, his hands full of paper.

"I wasn't discussing them, I was pointing out how romantic this is. Just like a fairy tale I once heard about," Mary defended.

Benson and Corbin exchanged looks and said nothing.

A distant howl rent the air. Wolf got to his feet and sent up an answering howl. He looked toward the doorway where Alexandria stood. The gaze of the staff followed.

"Go home to Mrs. Wolf. Thorne is here."

Wolf took off.

"Lord Grayson is home and is tired after his journey," Alexandria said. "Please see that we aren't disturbed."

"Of course, Lady Grayson. A tray will be outside your door within the hour and the kitchen kept ready," Benson replied. "We have to keep you and the future master healthy."

Alexandria thought for a moment about a boy, in the likeness of his father and just as arrogant and strong, and she smiled. "As usual, Benson, you think of everything."

Watching the smiling faces of the staff, she knew they realized what the lord and lady were going to be doing. Alexandria lifted her head and returned their smile. She didn't care if the world knew. Turning, she went back to her bedroom.

Her voice was thick with emotion when she spoke. "I love you. If you can't say the words, I understand."

Rising up, he gently pulled her down into the bed with him.

The shadows and doubt were gone from his eyes. "I understand something, too: I can't deny you the same thing my soul craved from the moment I saw you. I made the bargain to get you, but it is no longer enough. I love you, Alex. I want more than a bargain. I want your love, your independence, your impulsiveness. Will you love me and keep me sane?"

She smiled though her tears. "Yes, because it is the only way I'll stay sane."

Slowly he undressed her. As he exposed each inch of silken skin, he kissed it and said, "I love you. I love you. I love you."

Dear Reader,

The first romance I ever read was *Shanna,* by Kathleen Woodiwiss. Since then, I've always had a special place in my heart and on my bookshelves for historical romances. One of the elements that fascinated and lured me to keep reading these wonderful stories was their heroines, who refused to be viewed as brainless and incapable of making a logical decision simply because society and family viewed women as meek and subservient. Strong-willed, independent, ahead of their time in thought and deed, these women refused to bow down before a society that didn't value them. I loved these characters. In writing *The Bargain,* I wanted a heroine who was as strong, as independent, and as intriguing as the characters I'd loved so much.

When I created Alexandria Carstairs, she started as an homage to all those feisty women, but soon she took on a life of her own. I know I enjoyed her adventures, and I hope you did, too. Writing my first historical was, in its own way, an adventure, as well. It took a lot of research, a lot of immersing myself in another time and place, but it was wonderful when my characters started to become living and breathing entities, who lived in a world I could only imagine. Victorian England was an exciting time, a time when the seeds of the world we live in today were sown. It was quite a shock when I had to surface and come back to the present. *The Bargain* is the first of what I hope will be many excursions into the past—and I hope you'll join me and my characters the next time we go voyaging.

All the best,
Francis Ray

**LOVE STORIES YOU'LL NEVER FORGET . . .
IN ONE FABULOUSLY ROMANTIC NEW LINE**

BALLAD ROMANCES

Each month, four new historical series by both beloved and brand-new authors will begin or continue. These linked stories will introduce proud families, reveal ancient promises, and take us down the path to true love. In Ballad, the romance doesn't end with just one book . . .

COMING IN JULY
EVERYWHERE BOOKS ARE SOLD

The Wishing Well Trilogy:
CATHERINE'S WISH, by Joy Reed.
When a woman looks into the wishing well at Honeywell House, she sees the face of the man she will marry.

Titled Texans:
NOBILITY RANCH, by Cynthia Sterling
The three sons of an English earl come to Texas in the 1880s to find their fortunes . . . and lose their hearts.

Irish Blessing:
REILLY'S LAW, by Elizabeth Keys
For an Irish family of shipbuilders, an ancient gift allows them to "see" their perfect mate.

The Acadians:
EMILIE, by Cherie Claire
The daughters of an Acadian exile struggle for new lives in 18th-century Louisiana.